SET
FOR LIFE

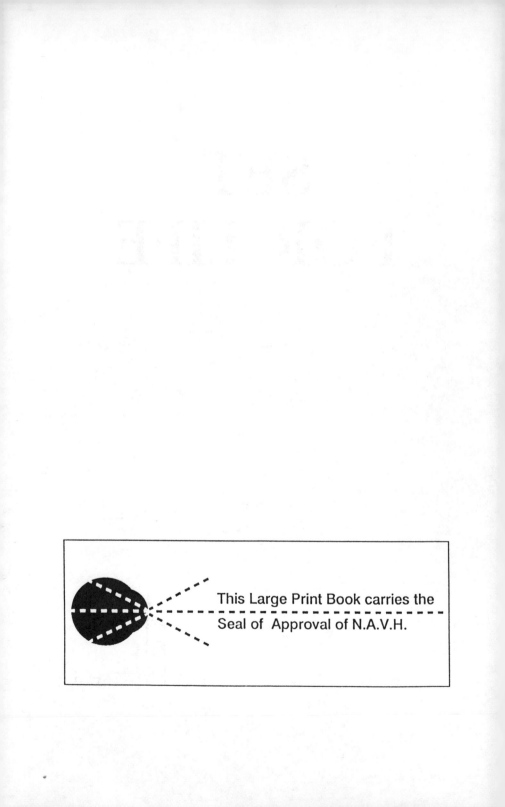

This Large Print Book carries the
Seal of Approval of N.A.V.H.

SET
FOR LIFE

Judith Freeman

Thorndike Press • Thorndike, Maine

Library of Congress Cataloging in Publication Data:

Freeman, Judith, 1946-
  Set for life / Judith Freeman.
    p. cm.
  ISBN 1-56054-357-4 (alk. paper : lg. print)
  1. Large type books. I. Title.
  [PS3556.R3915S48   1992]   91-46599
  813'.54—dc20   CIP

Excerpts from *To Urania,* copyright © 1988 by Joseph
Brodsky. Reprinted with permission of Farrar, Straus &
Giroux, Inc.

Thorndike Press Large Print edition published in 1992
by arrangement with W. W. Norton & Company, Inc.

Cover design by James B. Murray.

The tree indicium is a trademark of Thorndike Press.

This book is printed on acid-free, high opacity paper. ∞

For my son,
Todd

The author wishes to thank the Ucross Foundation of Wyoming for support during the writing of this novel, and Dana Wetzel of Coeur d'Alene, Idaho, for supplying valuable research assistance.

All the events and persons depicted in this novel are purely fictional. However, the rise of a strong white supremacist movement in northern Idaho during the 1980s was real. The people of the city of Coeur d'Alene and Kootenai County fought back, providing assistance to victims of harassment, developing laws against neo-Nazi violence, becoming the prototype for a successful grass roots response to racism. For their efforts, the city, and the task force, were recognized by the United States Holocaust Memorial Council in 1988 and received the Raoul Wallenberg Award in 1987.

JUDITH FREEMAN
Los Angeles, 1991

"Oh what a lonely person
is the aged man who, sunk in
himself, stands full of sap
like an old tree in autumn:
He has become deep; he has dug
a deep place for his heart, and
its beat comes from afar off as
from the center of a mountain."

—RAINER MARIA RILKE
The Collected Letters

PART ONE

SPRING

1

Phil Doucet awoke in the darkened room, jolted by sudden pains and the feeling he could no longer breathe. A great watery weight pressed down on him, as heavy as the sea. He sat up in bed and clutched his chest. His heart pounded urgently. He began panting, gasping for air. He grabbed at the sheets, arched his back, and held on. A knot like a bubble of gas moving under his breastbone, expanded in his ribs. With a jolt, the bubble broke in a sudden burst of pain. A sigh eased out of his mouth, and he began trembling. All he could think was, It's passed . . . I'm still alive.

After a while he got up and struck a match in front of the clock. Five-thirty. The mornings were still cold, although spring had finally arrived, ending the long fierce winter that had imprisoned him. He made his way downstairs very slowly, clutching the railing, and started a fire. When it grew lighter, he called the doctor. Following a short conversation, he hung up the phone and put the kettle on.

When he had eaten his breakfast, he dressed

carefully, putting on his good clothes for the trip over the mountain. He sat down and rested before putting on his shoes. His ankles were badly swollen, and so were his feet. The effort it took to get his shoes on left him feeling shaky. For many nights now he had slept badly, propped up in bed on half a dozen pillows. His tailbone was sore from the weight of sitting up, night after night, waiting for the sleep that rarely came. Taking down his old straw hat from a peg near the door, he left the house and walked down the path to where he'd left the car parked under the willow tree. He felt the wind twist the brim of his hat, and caught it before it flew off his head. His breath came short. All the water in the sea, he thought, and not a drop to drink.

The highway took him south to Ovid, across Ovid Creek, and into Paris. Driving slowly through the tiny town, past the tabernacle and the soda fountain and the lumberyard, he cautiously picked up speed again when he left the city limits.

He continued down the road in his old Buick, a huge green car moving slowly and purposefully through the landscape. He peered out from under the straw hat to gaze at the hills, their heights drawn with a brimming light. His eyes were as calm as the cloudless sky. He felt a little dreamy at the wheel of his car, which he had been forbidden to drive for so long. Dreamy and rather happy, after a fashion. He was out in the world. He was still alive. He was going to see his grandson. And most important, he was driving himself.

St. Charles and Fish Haven went by, little towns all boarded up, awaiting summer's arrival. A farmer, so old he needed a cane to walk, hobbled unsteadily through a muddy corral, dragging a red plastic sled loaded with hay toward his waiting cows. Soon, he thought, there would be no one left in this valley but the old people, clinging to their dying farms. Enrollment in the high school had dropped drastically in the last four years. Where did all the children go? They drained away, disappearing as completely as the spring runoff, flowing into distant, more vigorous rivers.

Snow still lay against the fences in places. There were pools of still water in the greening fields. He passed broken houses, pioneer-built, wood sagging and rotten, and new houses, cheap and poorly constructed — vacation homes boarded up against the elements — and then there were no houses for a while, just the lake and the purple mountains that were reflected on its surface. He was surrounded by an unending quiet.

The lake eddied on the surface, a tiny chop shimmering as if the water were dancing in place rather than moving in any particular direction. It appeared clean and beautiful today, a brilliant aquamarine, like a pristine glacial lake. At Garden City he turned and began the steep climb up the face of the mountain, the Buick straining over a series of switchbacks leading past lots for sale and cabin sites, hasty little developments connected by dirt roads that looked like scars on treeless slopes. Hardened snow covered the open hillsides and north-facing tree branches. He felt the chill on his ankles where the wind came through a vent and blew up his pants legs. He turned on the heater in the car, and the acrid smell of warm dust filled his nostrils. The higher he climbed, the more it seemed he moved backward into the season that had just passed. The snow grew deeper, the air cooler. Tall thickets of pines lined the road and blocked out the sun, lending the air around him a blue winter darkness. At the summit, the fields of snow were glazed with an icy sheen. He broke out of the trees into the brilliant sunlight. The glare burned his eyes. He was back in the arms of winter.

★ ★ ★

The doctor had said to him, "You're better off in the hospital, Phil. You know that. I realize you don't want to come back in, but you must. We need you here where we can watch you."

Watch me die, he thought.

For three months he had been at the top of a list of people awaiting a new heart. It didn't matter where he was on the list. A donor hadn't turned up. When the doctor said, "Come back in, Phil," he had hung up the phone and sat for a long time in the kitchen thinking about it. He was afraid of dying in a hospital. That was the truth of it. The phone had rung while he sat there thinking, but he didn't try to answer it. He'd been pretty sure it was one of his daughters calling. The sound of the ringing in the empty room, the noise erupting over and over, had made him feel as if he'd become a ghostly presence in his own house, already long departed.

In the lower part of the canyon, the scrub oak was leafing out a lighter color of green against the serviceberry and hawthorn. The river, swollen with melting snow, tumbled alongside the road with a furious and beautiful force. At the bottom of the canyon he dropped into the narrows and followed the river past farms and orchards until he came to the dirt drive that led to his daughter's house. A new sign had been tacked up near the old one: Joyce's Sew 'n Save. Her newest business venture. Now there were three signs at the end of the driveway: Beery's Orchard, Ark Animal Care, and Joyce's Sew 'n Save. They couldn't make ends meet in the fruit business. She and her husband had half a dozen things going. Making cakes for special occasions, catering parties. Repairing chain saws. Dog sitting and tree trimming. Now it was sewing clothes.

The dogs in the kennel barked wildly in greeting as he walked up the drive. His daughter Joyce stood at the kitchen counter, working on a cake as he entered. She looked up briefly, then gazed out the window and said, "That's your car out there."

"I reckon it is," he said.

"You drove yourself over here? You know you're not supposed to be driving!"

"I know."

"Why are you driving when you were told — "

"I wanted to."

"But what if you have an accident?"

"I won't," he said. "I haven't yet."

"You should have called me. I would have

come to get you."

"What's that you're making?" he asked, changing the subject.

"Oh, I'm just finishing up this cake."

The cake was built around a Barbie doll, which poked up in the center. From the way she spread icing around the doll in swirling tiers of pink frosting, he supposed that the icing was meant to look like a skirt. Actually, the doll seemed suspended in pink quicksand and looked as if she were fighting going under. Her arms were raised in the air.

"What's it for?"

"What?"

"What's the occasion?"

"It's Jane Thurman's daughter's birthday." She glanced up at the clock on the wall. "Jane's going to be here in about two minutes and I'm not done."

His daughter looked harried. She hadn't yet done her hair. Curlers covered her scalp. Her slippers were broken down at the heels, and she wore an old bathrobe over a thin nightgown with a ragged edge of lace at her throat. This was his daughter in a poor state. He rarely saw her this way. She was one of those women who went to great lengths to make themselves over each day, adding more layers of cosmetics each year in an attempt to achieve youthful results, wearing brighter clothes with each passing birthday. Now she stood exposed in the harsh morning light streaming through the kitchen window, and the circles of darkness under her eyes, her dry and wrinkled skin, gave away her age and caused him to feel older as well.

"Maybe you ought to think about putting some clothes on that doll," Phil said. Its upper half, the part that wasn't swamped in pink frosting, was bare. The swells of plastic breasts, so hard and unreal, disturbed him.

"Oh, I've got a little jacket I already made for her, but I didn't want to put it on until last so I wouldn't get frosting all over it." She stopped what she was doing and reached behind her and picked up a tiny gold jacket.

"See?" she said. "Isn't that cute?"

"It looks okay. Where's Luke?"

"He's helping Dan out in the orchard."

"I'm going into the hospital again this afternoon," he said, keeping his voice level, as if he were still discussing something as inconsequential as a cake. "I talked to the doctor this morning."

"Oh, Dad." She looked up at him. Her mouth drooped.

"Nothing's really changed that much," he

said. "I just don't feel so good, you know. I'm having more trouble breathing. I can't seem to get any sleep." He sighed, tipped his hat back, and rubbed his forehead.

"What time do you want to go? Dan and I will drive you down there."

"That's not necessary."

"You can't drive yourself — "

"Leora will take me."

"Leora? Oh. Your waitress friend," she said. He didn't like the way she put it. *Your waitress friend.* He wanted to say, *That's exactly what she is, just a friend. Don't try and make anything more out of it.*

But the doorbell rang just then. Jane Thurman, a small, dark woman in a jogging outfit, had come for her cake. Phil slipped out the back door while Joyce explained to her it would only take a minute to finish things up. Just as he was leaving, he heard Jane say, "How gorgeous!" He was glad to have an excuse to cut off the visit with Joyce. Ever since he'd found out about the letter she'd forged from President Reagan he'd felt cross with her. What he really felt was something close to disgust, that his daughter could do something so morally skewed. Strange how a man's children could end up so different from himself. What had he done to deserve a Republican for a daughter?

21

★ ★ ★

He looked down the rows of cherry trees, searching for his grandson. The orchard was budding. A whole new season was beginning. He couldn't see Luke anywhere. Green light suffused the orchard. A tan litter of last year's leaves lay on the ground, and three robins, pecking through the leaves, stopped and looked at him, raising their breasts so the rust-colored feathers flashed brilliantly. Then they were gone, lifting plump bodies on thin wings.

He couldn't walk into the orchard.

He went as far as the first row of trees and sat down on a log.

A while later, he heard the thrum of the tractor motor and slowly stood up. He shaded his eyes with one hand and peered down the rows of trees, where, in the bottle-green light, he saw his grandson at the wheel of the tractor, rumbling toward him. He waved.

"Hi, Grandpa," Luke said when he was beside him.

"Turn off that motor so I can talk to you."

Luke shut the tractor down and climbed from the seat. He wore a T-shirt that said "Double-dating in Idaho" and showed two men in a truck with their arms around their dogs. He sat down on the log next to him.

"The company got the bid on the new county building," Phil said. He'd sold his carpentry business to two fellows from Soda Springs, but he wanted the boy to know he had a job waiting for him this summer, if he wanted it.

"Yeah?" Luke looked down between his feet. He didn't seem very excited. Neither spoke for a moment. A washboard pattern of clouds had moved in, and the light changed, dropping a little.

"I don't think I can work any construction this summer," Luke said.

"Why not?"

"There's an exchange program at school. I applied. I think I've got a good chance of getting chosen. I'd go to Mexico for two months — if it happens. I don't know whether I'll be accepted for sure, but if I am, I want to go. I wouldn't be here for the job."

Phil felt a little disappointed. Two summers Luke had worked alongside him, learning the carpentry trade. Not that he imagined he'd be in any shape himself to work with him this summer. He knew he wouldn't. Mexico. They'd always talked about the possibility of making a trip there together one day. Of course, he wanted Luke to go. He only wished . . .

"Where in Mexico would you go?"

23

"The Yucatán."

"When do you find out if you're accepted?"

"The first part of May."

"What would you do down there?"

"Live with a family. Visit the ruins. The pyramids. I've been reading about them. The Mayans. How they were buried with all these things."

Phil thought of a woman he'd met recently at the Ranchhand, a truck stop outside of town. She worked for a mortician on the Navajo reservation. She told him all sorts of things, how the Navajos wanted their belongings buried with them. A new set of pots and pans. Solar watches. A pack of Salems and a book of matches. Tape players with country music playing as the coffin was lowered. A favorite horse, shot and interred with the deceased. Apparently all of these requests were met, an idea that pleased him. Somehow it made more sense to form a bridge between worlds with a beloved object than the dead words of a preacher. What would he ask to be buried with if he could make the request? Maybe one thing. A photograph of his wife, May, in the dress covered with little violets.

"You won't be disappointed if I don't take the job this summer?"

"Listen," Phil said, "I was only thinking

of the money you could earn. Money's nothing next to the chance to go to Mexico." One of their favorite shared pastimes — aside from fishing for browns in Current Creek — had been studying the atlas, reading about foreign lands, discussing distant cultures and the ways in which other people lived, bonded by a fascination with the infinite variety in the world.

"Well," Luke said, "that's the thing. I have to make some money for the trip somehow. I know Mom and Dad can't help me. I wouldn't want them to think they should."

"Don't worry," Phil said. "We'll find the money."

Luke smiled. "Thanks. You know I'd pay you back."

"Now I have to be going," Phil said. He stood up, but found that his head was suddenly swimming and the luminous green glow in the orchard had become mottled with watery black spots. Pain, like slivers of ice pricking his heart, filled his chest, and again his breath came short.

He didn't know how it happened, but Luke had him in his arms, bearing his weight. He pressed against him and clasped his shirt. This was what he'd wanted, after all, what he'd longed for, the chance to hold the boy next to his heart.

"Grandpa? Are you okay?"

He couldn't answer. He needed to stay very still. He rested his head on the boy's shoulder, smelled the sour odor of sweat, felt the strong muscles across his back, then slowly he pulled away.

"I'm going back into the hospital this afternoon."

Luke studied him, his eyes keen and steady. "I'll come tomorrow," he said. "After school."

Phil patted his grandson's shoulder. "Yes," he said. "I'd like that. Bring the cribbage board."

"Grandpa . . . ?"

"Yes?"

"Do you want me to go with you now?"

"No, son."

"Why?"

"Because I want to be alone." He smiled at Luke. "You know how that feels. I just wanted to see you again."

"Yes, I know." The boy looked frightened now.

"I'm going to leave now, son." He began backing away. "I'll see you in the hospital."

"And when you get out, too."

Phil stopped and swallowed hard. "I like your optimism," he said.

"You want me to drive you over there?"

"No, son," he said.

"You're sure?"

"Very sure."

He circled around the side of the house, avoiding the kitchen window. Jane Thurman's car was still in the driveway. He imagined the horrible plastic doll rising up out of the frosting. What a mess. What was wrong with a simple chocolate cake, some candles, maybe the words "Happy Birthday"? People wanted things these days he couldn't understand.

He drove toward town. Gulls were wheeling in the sky above the plowed fields like pieces of blown paper. He parked in the handicapped space in front of the convalescent home and walked slowly to the door, stopping twice to rest on the hand railing.

Ralph was watching the TV anchored to the wall opposite his bed. He moved his eyes in Phil's direction when he saw him come through the door. It was about the only thing he could move. His eyes, his mouth, his head just a little.

"Haaalllooo," Ralph said.

Phil patted his chest gently. "I'm going into the hospital this afternoon. I wanted to see you before I went." He stared down at his old friend, who was also his relation by marriage. Joyce had married Ralph's son, Dan, and it was for Ralph she had forged the letter from Reagan, filling it with bogus words of praise for "a lifelong servant of the Republican Party" who had "suffered terrible misfortune." She had gotten the official-looking stationery from her friend Marlene Davis, who worked for the Republican National Committee, then written the letter and had Marlene post it from Washington. Reagan was Ralph's hero. When he received the letter, he'd cried. He showed it to everyone who visited him. Word passed quickly through the convalescent home that Ralph Beery had received some kind of commendation from the President. The first time Phil saw the letter he knew it was a forgery. President Reagan's signature bore a suspicious resemblance to his daughter's handwriting. But no one else seemed to notice. When he confronted Joyce, she admitted forging the letter but made him promise not to tell anyone. She seemed rather proud of the letter, as if it were simply another clever creation, like a tiny doll's jacket or a fancy cake. "I didn't think it would hurt to do something for an old man who doesn't have anything else in his life," she said. Phil had not agreed, but he kept quiet.

Phil took off his hat and sat down on a chair next to Ralph's bed. Nothing ever changed here. Eight years ago Ralph had suffered a stroke that left him paralyzed from the neck down. Nobody had expected him to live more than a year or two. But he had lived. It was almost unthinkable that a body could be immobilized for so long and go on functioning. Now it seemed he might outlive Phil.

"Going into the hospital, huh?" Ralph said, when Phil had given him the news. His words garbled into a language that took practice to understand. He blinked, and kept his mouth open, lips tight across his teeth. His head had become skull-like, so large compared to the rest of him. His body was covered by a sheet, and his stomach formed a big hump under the bedclothes.

"You'll be all right," Ralph said. "You're too ornery to die." He laughed, his dry lips spread wide, but little sound came out. *Hahaha,* all breath.

Phil looked up at the TV. A game show. They were spinning the wheel. This was the content of Ralph's days. He would be spared this, at any rate.

The nurse came to bathe Ralph. As she lifted the sheet and began washing him, Ralph said something, and Phil leaned forward, trying to catch his words.

"Socks?" Phil asked. "You want me to

get you some socks?"

"Red socks."

"Red socks? You want the red socks?"

"No!" Ralph growled. "In training. The Red Sox. Spring training."

"I don't care much about the Red Sox. I've always been a Dodgers fan."

"Five dollars," Ralph said.

"For what?"

"A bet."

"I can't take your money."

"You won't."

His flesh was just pale weight on a mattress. Neurons firing amid a terrible silence. The nurse lifted his gown. Ralph was diapered, he smelled the odors. She took the damp cloth and smoothed it across Ralph's white chest, rinsed it, and stroked beneath his arms. For eight years, every Monday, he had been visiting his old friend, watching him go through this ritual.

They were close to the same age. Sixty-nine and seventy. But Ralph had had a different kind of life. He'd been manager of a radio station. A socializer. A golfer, member of Kiwanis and the country club. Phil was a carpenter and had never belonged to anything except a union.

When the nurse had finished washing Ralph's body, she took a fresh cloth, soaped it up, and started on his face, stroking his hair, his ears, his neck. All the while Ralph blinked, keeping his mouth open, and a small bad odor issued forth from between his teeth. His eyes were still alert, rather wily, as if glimmering with the crafty secret of survival. Phil thought of military hospitals, where he had known other wounded men and cared for them. On other occasions he had bathed Ralph himself, but there was no energy left for that. The nurse finished with him, and noiselessly disappeared from the room.

Slowly Phil stood up. "I've got to be going."

"Is it going to rain?" Ralph asked. He always did this. Stalled at leaving time. Wanted to keep you with him a little longer.

"No, I don't think so."

"What's the weather like today?"

"It's about the same. A little overcast. But it feels like spring."

Ralph wrinkled up his nose. "Smells like rain."

Of course, he could smell nothing in this room, but the idea that he would pretend he could touched Phil. "Your honker's off," he said, grinning at him.

Ralph said something else, and Phil had to bend low to hear him. Just a whisper. He repeated it.

"Balls," he said.

Phil laughed and moved slowly toward the door, stepping rather uncertainly on his badly swollen feet, which felt numb after sitting.

"They're crapping like hell on TV," Ralph warbled as Phil walked out. He meant, of course, clapping.

He drove back over the mountain, glimpsing his first sight of the lake from the top of the switchbacks. A dappled blue shadow covered the valley, which was moist and giving up mist. A wedge of light, faintly edged with color as a rainbow would be, hung over the lake. It lasted as long as it took him to reach Ovid, and then it disappeared.

The first thing he did when he got home was to pour himself a glass of forbidden scotch and take it out on the porch. The sun had come out in force and was shining over the lake, but the sky was still clouded above the mountains, and the sun wasn't doing much good there. Smoke curled from the refinery over the hills, holding its shape until it rose to where it met the sky and blended in. There were two chairs out on the porch, his and May's. At times he'd missed her so much it seemed pointless to go on without her. Maybe now he wouldn't. But two years he'd been alone and survived days that held a terrifying emptiness. The crows came, Trouble and More Trouble, and he went inside to get some bread. Trouble took the piece he offered and ate it sitting on the railing. More Trouble shied from his hand and flew off cawing, his beak empty. He looked north and saw a pair of blue cranes crossing the sky, their necks extended and undulating gracefully. He poured himself another scotch, enjoying the heady glow it imparted to the afternoon.

The air grew very still. Even the weeping willows were motionless. Glory to the naked birches, weeping willow, spears of crocus. What a shame to leave such beauty. He sighed in sorrow, and resignation.

As the light began to wane, he rose from his chair with some effort and went inside to call Leora. He cleaned out the fridge, throwing away a few leftovers, wiped the shelves down, and set a new box of baking soda inside. He was quite certain the baking soda would outlast him. He turned off the gas heater, extinguishing even the pilot light. Then he climbed the stairs and lay down on his bed, lifting his eyes toward a patch of sky he could see outside his window.

Leora arrived at five-thirty, coming straight from the cafe. He locked the front door and took a look around before getting into her car, saying goodbye to the house he'd built himself so many years ago. Bowing his head slightly, he thanked his Maker for such a pleasing home for so many good years.

By seven o'clock he was lying in a private room in the University Hospital, a heart-strengthening drug flowing into his veins. A green oxygen tube snaked beneath his nose, held in place by a strip of tape running across his upper lip. It felt as if he'd grown a sudden mustache, or let milk dry there.

A young nurse came in and took his wrist; he let it go limp in her warm hands. She had a small, dark mole on her cheek, almost hidden by her hair. He looked at the way the material of her dress pulled slightly around her hips. He smelled her womanly smells — perfume, warm odors. She stood so close, her arms raised, working now to adjust the IV flow. He felt a heat emanating from her. Something inside him stirred. The thought of dying made him hungry for life.

"Okay, Mr. Doucet. You're comfortable?"

He nodded.

"You should feel those pills pretty soon."

He did. The world seemed contained in a gentle hiss of oxygen flowing through a tube, and the lovely sleep he'd wanted for many days began to enfold him, first his limbs, then his back, neck, and finally his face.

You heard all sorts of voices, but oh what a sense of well-being.

What killed you out there, he thought, in the world where people were still moving, bending to tasks, unbending from the day, wasn't the lack of anything but the *abundance* of something: Time in its purest form. And none of it, none of it was his.

2

Bear Lake. The twenty-ninth of March.
Going south, Louise came to Ovid, Ovid
Creek, then Paris. The road skirted marshes
and fields where cows plodded through mud
up to their knees. Just beyond Paris, at a
turnout for a historical marker, she pulled
the car over to the side of the road and
parked under a cottonwood tree. She shut
off the engine. The broken hull of an overturned boat was lying in the sand near the
edge of the lake. Droves of black gnats circled
above it, drawn by the carcass of a huge
carp rotting on the sand. She stretched, arch-
ing her back, and let her eyes close. She
wanted to sleep — wanted desperately to
sleep. She'd been driving since midnight,
eight hours in her parents' stolen car. She
felt heavy and dull with fatigue.

She dozed. Birds called from a tangled
thicket of brush beside the road. When she
opened her eyes, it was to the sight of
branches, flitting wrens, and a little abandoned house, made of chinked log, glimpsed
through the trees. Very briefly, she imagined
settling into the little abandoned cabin, squat-

ting for a few days, but she quickly discarded the idea. She had no blankets, no bedding, nothing with which to make herself comfortable. And what if she was discovered there? They would soon be looking for her.

She could read the words on the historical marker next to the car: "The Oregon Trail: The first covered wagons came into the Rocky Mountains in 1830. Well-marked wagon ruts and stories of Indians and settlers indicate the first wagon migration to Oregon followed the southwesterly shores of Bear Lake where you are presently standing. . . ." She looked away, too bored to finish reading the words on the plaque. History didn't interest her. But she could see, on a promontory jutting out into the water, three horses, and horses did interest her. One horse was white, one black, and the other spotted like a dalmatian. They grazed peacefully. Beyond them, she saw the little gray roofs of a town. Again, she grew drowsy. Sleep overtook her and she drifted into that half-conscious state where things are heard in multiple voices. She dreamed she was in her old bed, the one she had slept in as a child, falling in the middle of the night from the mattress to the floor. Her body jerked against the car seat as she landed in her dream fall.

A car passed on the road, and she came

awake quickly, feeling nervous, and watched it disappear around a bend. When it was gone, she relaxed again and lapsed into half-sleep, and then deep sleep, and didn't awaken for what seemed like a long time.

When she came to and checked her watch she found only twenty minutes had passed. It seemed to her that hours had gone by. The sleep revived her enough to continue. She pulled out onto the two-lane road and drove slowly toward Garden City. She'd been certain she'd find a motel in one of these towns that had looked so promising on the map, but everything was closed. Garden City was the last possibility. After Garden City, the road ran through long barren stretches where there were no towns, crossing into Wyoming.

When she reached Garden City it didn't take her long to realize that everything was closed here, too. The place had an empty feeling, as if its inhabitants had fled some disaster. All the houses appeared deserted. The businesses were boarded up and the street was empty of cars. One after another she passed the "closed" signs and realized with a sinking heart that she'd have to go on. Cruising slowly down the street, she understood that she had arrived at the wrong time of the year. These were all little resort towns, dependent upon the arrival of summer for business. She wished she'd picked a different route. Who would have known that everything would be dead? No motels. No place to stay. No gas stations open. And she was so tired. She felt hungry, too, and a little sick. She laid a hand on the small lump of her stomach and sighed.

She pulled over to the side of the road and studied her map for a while, then put it away, and backed recklessly into a muddy lane and turned the car around. There was nothing to do but head back the way she'd come. Casper was another four hundred miles. There was a women's clinic in Casper her friend Beth had told her about. Four hundred miles was still a long way. She'd never make it in her condition. But if she could rest, if she could only have a night's sleep. Retracing her path through the empty little towns of Fish Haven, Ovid, and Paris, she drove thirty-five miles back the way she'd come, fighting heavy drowsiness.

She checked into the Michelle Motel in Montpelier at two in the afternoon. The clerk, an older man with some kind of surgical implant in his neck — a little metal opening surrounded by gauze, which reduced his voice to a whisper — asked her how old she was. She lied and said, "Eighteen." He gave her the key to her room and told her it would entitle her to a discounted meal at a local restaurant. "Which restaurant?" she asked, thinking of the little money she had.

"The Ranchhand Cafe," he told her. "Take that key out there and show them and they'll give you ten percent off the price of your meal."

She thanked him and went to the room, which was dark and cool. She undressed quickly and crawled between the sheets. It killed her to pay sixteen dollars for a room — seventeen, with tax. But once she'd taken off her clothes and was nestled down in the pillows, she forgot about the money.

She awoke feeling hungry. Remembering what the clerk had told her about the discounted meal, she dressed and headed out for the truck stop just outside town.

It was a windy evening, the fading light low and cloudy with dust. The wind whipped her dress around her legs as she got out of the car in the parking lot. All around her were open fields and farms dotted with cattle. She smelled manure on the wind. She grabbed for her skirt and held it crossing the asphalt. By the time she reached the front door, she was anxious to get inside.

There were phones in every booth. That's the first thing she noticed. The place was full of truckers and farmers, ranchers and their wives, people who looked windblown and beaten, both relieved and tired, as if they'd finally found some long-sought oasis. The truckers had taken seats at the booths, while the ranchers and the women sat on stools along the counter, alone, or clustered in twos and threes.

She took the only available booth, near a window, and threw her bag on the seat next to her. Frowning slightly, she opened her purse and counted her money. She wondered if she had enough for a meal and the gas it would take to get to Casper. It was impossible to imagine what she would do when she ran out of money. She sighed and looked out the window, watching a trucker pull his big rig into the parking lot. He climbed down from the cab and stood for a moment, looking up at the sky while he tucked in his shirttail. He was slim and slightly bowlegged and wore cowboy boots.

The truckers had parked their rigs end to end, blocking her view of the highway. An American flag whipped fiercely in the wind high above the trucks, and billows of dust scudded across the parking lot, swirling between the rigs. What a cold, harsh place this was, she thought. Even the trees were twisted by the wind and grew at an angle.

The waitress came and asked if she knew what she wanted to order. She said, "Hamburger, fries, and a beer."

The waitress stopped writing and looked at her.

"I'll have to see your ID."

"Forget the beer," she said.

The waitress shrugged, then turned and walked away. Her shoes made little squeaking sounds against the linoleum, like yelps from newborn pups.

She stared at the phone sitting at the end of her booth, wondering who she might call. She had an urge to talk to someone, to tell someone what she'd done, but when she imagined who that might be, her mind drew a blank. She thought of calling her mother. Hello, Mom, she would say. This is Louise. I'm calling you from a phone at a booth in a truck stop.

She couldn't foresee a conversation beyond that point that wouldn't involve her mother's anger and fear spilling out. Poor Hilda. Married to him. The savior of his race. *"Don't mouth off to me!"* he had yelled at her the night before. He'd raised his hand to slap her but her mother had stepped between them and taken the blow — a hard, flat-handed slap which sent her glasses flying across the room and left her with a bloody nose. The blood was surprisingly bright, a festive red against her mother's ashen face.

She thought of them, her mother, her step-father. It seemed to her there were only two kinds of people in the world — bullies and their victims, the Teds and the Hildas. When they fought, which they often did, she stayed in her room and listened through the heat vent to the abuse they hurled at each other.

She used to think it wouldn't have been so bad if there'd been someone else, a sister, a brother, someone she might have talked to, someone to whom she might have said, listen to them. She might have had someone to confide in then, but as it was, she was an only child. What rotten luck. She had absorbed all their hatred alone, and it had warped her, sent her early on into the sullen reaches of her own brooding, created an angry, closeted self. She wondered now, looking out over the barren fields in the sinking light, if she might not have waited too long to make her escape. So much time had been spent shielding herself from emotion. What capacity for feeling remained?

He had come home drunk the night before, wearing his paramilitary attire, reeking of scotch and cigars and something less identifiable — a smell of lighter fluid? Kerosene? Gun powder? His uniform resembled that of an appliance repairman — dark-blue waist-length jacket, matching pants, shirt, and tie. What distinguished his uniform from that of a Sears repairman was the patch on his shoulder, showing a sword, a crown, and a swastika.

Everything had been quiet in the basement room until he entered, sometime after ten. She sat at the kitchen table finishing her homework. Her mother stood at the cutting board, carefully slicing the prickly skin off a pineapple. (If anybody had asked her *why* her mother was cutting up a pineapple at ten at night, she would have explained her efficiency. How she was constantly *preparing* — working, suffering. Slaving, really. Everything a chore, a labor, a duty. Duty to her husband, the swaggering drunk at her side. Breakfast would be pineapple, ready-cut.)

"We paid a visit to the evolutionist," he said, removing his jacket, chuckling. Beneath his jacket, he wore a shoulder holster and a gun. His girth strained against the thick straps. She looked up from her books at her stepfather, narrowing her eyes as she gazed at him. The "evolutionist" was Mr. Porter, her biology teacher, a quiet man whose wife had just had her first baby. What had they done to him?

As if reading her mind, her stepfather turned and said, "We left a little message for that nigger-loving ape."

She glanced in her mother's direction. She showed no reaction. She simply looked tired. Her mother wore a faded housedress with short sleeves exposing her plump arms. Each time she brought the knife down against the pineapple, it hit the cutting board, and the flesh on her upper arms quivered and swung loose like the skin on a cow's neck.

He moved to her mother's side, and with an easy familiarity, patted her buttocks, then grabbed her ample flesh, bunching up her dress and raising the hemline. He exposed the tattered edge of a gray slip at the back of her mother's knees, while bringing his face to her neck.

Her mother turned away from him. "What have you done to your clothes?" she said. "You smell."

"I spilled a little lighter fluid."

Another cross, Louise thought. They had burned another cross.

He turned toward her. "I want you out of that fairy's class," he said.

She looked up at him. He had grown fatter,

and uglier, over the years. His jowls were heavy now. She remembered him when he'd first dated her mother, how thin he'd been. Now his face was plump, and so florid it looked perpetually bruised. A quarter-sized spot of shiny crimson skin remained on his left cheek, near the corner of his eye, where a large brown growth had been removed last year.

"I told you," she said, "I can't transfer. I tried. It's already the middle of the second semester. I have to finish the class or I'll get an F in science."

"Get an F then!" he yelled. "But don't go back to that class!"

"Ted," her mother said. "She has school. She can't just cut class — "

"Take the fucking F, who cares! I'd rather you flunked! Goddamned evolutionists! Trying to tell you that you and your children evolved from an ape. I'm not going to have you exposed to *that* bullshit!" He made a big sweeping gesture with his arm and teetered off balance. Grabbing for the counter, he knocked the plate of pineapple to the floor.

"Damned it, Ted," Hilda muttered.

"Ah, sorry," he said, stepping back and stretching his neck out jerkily. He made no move to clean up the mess on the floor.

Instead, her mother bent down and began picking up the pieces of pale yellow pineapple, studded with dark thorny spines.

"White people must know who they are," he said, looking down at his wife's back. "They must know who they are, where they came from, and why they are here. I tell you, we didn't come from apes. Aryan man is the son of God."

God. If there is a God, she thought. And what kind of God would have *him* for a son?

"Anybody who says we came from apes is our enemy. Our enemies," he said, stabbing the air with his finger, "will regret having become our enemy!"

His words were slurred. He laughed. "Right now, I would say the evolutionist has gotten the message."

She imagined Mr. Porter, bespectacled, hair thinning, at home on a Wednesday night. Ten o'clock. Perhaps watching the news with his wife. Sitting, unsuspecting in his living room, or maybe rocking his newborn baby, a swaddled and sweet-smelling bundle in his arms. Then looking up, seeing the light. The flickering light, odd at this hour, odd at any hour, just beyond his windows. Standing up, lurching forward, going to his front door and throwing it open to see —

47

A bright flaming cross burning uncontrollably among his fitzers and pyracantha. A cross of fire raging above his winter-white lawn.

How they must, at this very moment, now fear for themselves, and for their little newborn child.

Disgusted, she stood up abruptly and went out the back door. Harsh cold and the smell of dank cement greeted her in the stairwell. The apartment was in the basement of a duplex. Upstairs, light shone in the Wilder's curtained windows. She climbed the stairs and came out into the moonlit night. Purple patches of shadow and pale white light. Frozen grass, bare trees. I should have grabbed a coat, she thought. She looked up at the moon with its cold light and eerie face. Her stepfather's truck was parked under a big tree, *Ted's TV Repair* painted on the door, stippled in moonlight. Next to it, her mother's mustard-colored Pinto. A dog barked in the neighborhood. Otherwise, quiet. After-bedtime quiet. Standing out in the dead night, she could believe herself the only one still up and awake. Several thoughts came to her, one following the other in rapid succession. How had it happened? What could she do? What was the way out of here? *Casper,* maybe. What would he do if he found out what had happened before she could do something about it?

Looking at the Pinto, it had come to her so clearly: *she could leave.*

She *had* to leave. And why not that night?

She returned to the stairwell and stood at the door, listening for a moment before she went in.

"Oh, for Christ's sake — "

". . . drunk, drinking, always drunk — "

"My life. I told you."

"Lying, drunk, burning crosses, I didn't ask for this — "

She pushed open the door and stepped into the kitchen and without looking at them, started for her room, but he stopped her, grabbing her arm.

"You're not to go back to that class and I don't care what happens, I don't care how many F's you get, I don't — "

"I'll do what I want. You can't tell me what to do." She pulled away from him and stepped back. He raised his hand. She saw it coming, his hand, as he said, "Don't mouth off to me!" And then her mother was in front of her, taking the blow, glasses hurtling, and clattering on the floor. The first bright blood appeared on her upper lip, puddling in the little cleft where her lips met. The

49

corners of her mouth stretched downward, as she began weeping.

Absentmindedly, she tapped her fork against the table and stared out toward the parking lot. Would they be looking for her yet? She had a vision of them waking up this morning, finding her gone, discovering the car missing. She had no trouble imagining her stepfather's brooding fury. The anger with which he would begin to plot her punishment. Once he caught her. When she came back. But she wouldn't go back. Not ever. And he wouldn't catch her. He couldn't, or else it would be all over.

She had a headache. She couldn't remember a time lately when she hadn't had this headache. The strange thing was, her heart ached too, as if these two parts of her body — her heart and her head — were immutably connected.

The phone beckoned to her, a line to the world outside. Her real father had once told her that he could look out from the deck of a ship at night and see the arc of the earth on the watery horizon. The stars, he said, were not only above him but also below. They rested on the curve of the earth, the dark watery sea, they rode the crests of waves. She wished she could talk to her father, but he was dead. She lifted the receiver and listened to the buzzing of the dial tone. He'd been a radio operator during the war. Could call anywhere from the deck of a ship. She couldn't think of anyone to call. She imagined speaking to him. He was never far away; he stood pale behind the thin walls of her being. Dad, she said, the word forming silently in her head: *I got away. Good* he replied through the dead buzzing. *Good girl.*

Nobody washes these phones, she thought as she hung up the receiver. Her hand felt dirty from holding it. She imagined all the calls made on this phone by truckers trying to reach distant wives or girlfriends. Her hand smelled like oil and smoke.

She took the map from her purse and unfolded it on the table. Idaho was pink, shaped like a fireplace with a tall chimney. Wyoming was a big green rectangle. She located Casper. It was more or less in the middle of the state. She put her finger on Casper, and traced her nail along a road, past Rawlins and Rock Springs and Green River, slowly following the freeway, then the black line marking the highway leading to the little corner of Idaho, whose stateline intersected a small blue circle labeled "Bear Lake." That's where she was. It seemed so far from Casper to Bear Lake. She had no idea how much gas it would take to travel that distance. She'd never driven that far, nor had she ever left the state of Idaho — at least not since she'd moved there many years ago as a small child.

The waitress brought her food. She was in the middle of her meal when she realized someone had walked up and was speaking to her. She looked up to see the man she'd noticed earlier getting out of his truck in the parking lot.

"That your red Pete?" he asked.

"What?"

"Is that your red Pete out there?"

"No . . ."

"I thought maybe you were the gal I was talking to earlier. You're not the one. Forget it. She ought to thank me, since I ended up getting the ticket."

"Oh, yeah?" She was thinking, What is he talking about? He thinks I could be a truck driver? Red Pete? He thinks that's my red Peterbilt truck parked out there?

It became clear to her. He'd been on the CB to someone, warned her of a speed trap, and then gotten a ticket himself. He thought he'd been talking to her.

"I could have sworn I'd beat it," he said, "but the cop got me up the road."

"Oh," she said. He loomed over her, a

tall man with a square, handsome face and black hair. She could see the marks of a comb in his hair, as if he'd just wetted and combed it.

"Can I sit down?" he asked.

She looked away from him, staring at the row of feet belonging to the people sitting on the stools at the counter.

"Is it okay? Can I sit down with you for a minute?" he asked again.

"I don't think so," she said.

There were men with deep wrinkles on the backs of their sunburned necks and women with scarfs covering their hair. Worn, tired people who looked beaten down by the lives they led. It made her sad to look at them, and she felt herself getting edgy.

"I've got a long way to go tonight," he said. "I just want a cup of coffee and the chance to sit down for a few minutes, that's all. You haven't got anything to be afraid of. Besides, there aren't any empty booths. How about if I just sit down until one comes up?"

She shrugged, and he slid across the seat opposite her. She looked into his face. He was glass-eyed, like the stuffed deer head hanging on the wall. Glass-eyed and grinning. Messed up on something, she could see that now. His eyes burned red, like a high school drunk's. But he seemed happy, and there was something soft and pleasant in his smile.

"Go on and finish your meal," he said. "Don't let me stop you. Do you live here or are you just passing through?"

"Passing through," she said.

"What's your name?"

"Louise." She stared down at his hands, clasped on the table in front of him. His nails were pink and neatly trimmed. He looked too clean and tidy to be a truck driver. He might have been a country and western singer. His shirt was unbuttoned halfway down his chest. She could see there was no hair there, only a smooth, almost feminine whiteness to his skin.

"Louise? That's my mother's name! How about that. I won't have any trouble remembering your name."

"It's not a name you hear too much," she said, keeping her voice flat.

"I like it."

"You don't think it's too old-fashioned maybe?" She narrowed her eyes as she gazed at him.

He looked at her very directly, and shook his head. "No, not at all. I'm Wendall."

He signaled the waitress and ordered a cup of coffee and a piece of pie. Then he leaned across the table, spreading his palms against the surface, as if he were going to push himself to his feet. Instead, with his arms looking awkward, elbows pointed out that way, he began talking about driving. Portland to Pocatello. Straight through. Survived it, he said, by listening to Chet Baker, and the CB.

"You hear all kinds of things on the CB," he said. "It's like a soap opera sometimes. I listen, all the way across the country. Just keep the thing on, listening."

"Oh yeah?" She intentionally tried to sound bored. It wasn't hard to do.

"I just heard these guys making a drug deal." He shook his head, and then went on to tell her the details of a conversation he'd overheard, how he knew the guys were talking about drugs even though they kept mentioning the word "pencils."

He talked on and on, rocking against the seat, shaking his head now and then. (Was he always this talkative, she wondered, or was it because he was hopped up on something?) The way he spoke made her think he liked the freedom of the road. He was describing a trip he'd made the week before, which took him through Las Vegas where he'd won a hundred and twenty dollars, when out of the corner of her eye, she saw a highway patrol car come down the highway and slow down in front of the truck stop. Her heart began thumping with fear. Was he looking for her? Would the cop notice the Pinto in the parking lot? Had officers all over the state received a bulletin — *missing person, stolen car?* Or was it too soon to worry? She had to dump the car as soon as she could. She had to get out of Idaho. Maybe she shouldn't go back to the motel, except to get her things, and head for Casper tonight. The patrol car made a U-turn in the parking lot, heading down the highway again. She breathed out slightly in relief.

"Of course, now that I see you up close," he was saying, "I realize you couldn't have been the woman I was talking to on the CB earlier."

"Why couldn't I?" she asked.

"Well, for one thing you don't look old enough to be driving a rig, and for another, you've got a skirt on. I haven't ever seen a woman truck driver yet that wore a skirt. I just saw you from across the room, saw that red Pete out there, and put two and two together, but I kind of added it up wrong."

She ate a French fry and tasted its mushy coldness, tallowy and unpleasant.

"How old are you?" he asked.

"Old enough," she said.

She took another bite of her hamburger, which has also grown cold. It was hard to finish her meal in front of him. Every movement felt like a conscious gesture. He seemed perfectly relaxed.

"You have pretty eyes, you know that?" he said.

Part of her wished he would go away. But another part of her felt flattered. At least he was someone to talk to. She simply didn't know what to say to him or how to react to his compliment, so she sat there, staring out the window, letting the silence build up.

He ran his fingers through his hair and sighed. "I've got to go all the way to Casper tonight." He paused, then asked, "Where are you headed?"

"I'm going to Casper, too," she said. She smiled at him, suddenly becoming softer and nicer, because already she had begun to think. Something had come to her without her even expecting it, a subtle, promising sign, and in the split second it took her to decide to receive it, to welcome the unlikely messenger, she felt the subtle flow of her life reverse, and knew the meaning of the word "deliverance."

3

The light came through the treetops and made a pattern of shadow on the cement in front of him. Luke squatted near the bare raspberry canes and looked out over the valley in the late-afternoon stillness. He could see orchards, barns, and a road cutting into the fields. The brook nearby dropped, burbling through a narrow channel, its banks lined with brambles. The dogs panted near his elbow. The heat of their breath and the way it stirred over his skin made him think it was the only moving thing in the landscape. It seemed he had been waiting a long time for his mother to return.

He had come away from the hospital the day before feeling very low after seeing his grandfather, whom he cared for deeply, lying tethered to tubes, a sight as cruel as that of a dog confined to a patch of dying earth by a short chain.

Life hardly seemed worth living if you had to live that way, cooped up in a body that no longer worked, shut away in a sterile hospital where the sheets were so stiff they suggested a state of premature rigor mortis.

They had him all tucked in tight with those sheets, and the first thing he'd done was to walk around the hospital bed, pulling the sheets free so his grandfather could move his legs and arms and sit up for a game of cribbage. During the visit the distinct feeling had come over him that his grandfather would never leave the hospital, a thought that must have occurred to his grandfather, too, considering the request he made.

He had put it simply: "I'm not going to give up the ghost in this hospital bed, son. Dying here just isn't a good idea. I'm afraid I wouldn't even know what was happening, and besides, I don't even have a view. I know I can count on you. If I get bad, I don't want them to be able to prolong things too much. I want you to take me out of here if that happens. I've put my wishes in writing." He had handed him an envelope. "They call it an 'advance directive,' or 'living will' . . . if you can imagine that. That's just a copy I've given you. The doctor has the original. Don't mention this to your mother yet. She likes to think I'll be around forever. But I know I can count on you. When the time comes, take me home."

His grandfather was the only person he knew over the age of twenty who didn't automatically assume there was inherent superiority in the position of being an adult. Luke didn't want him to die, pure and simple, because he loved him so deeply. How could he not love the man who had taught him many of the most important things he knew? How to tie a fly and make a perfect cast. How to think something through until you knew your own mind. He never told him "Do this" or "Do that": he would say, "Try this." He seemed to understand that the really important discoveries were the ones you made on your own. He had taught him the names of birds and plants during fishing expeditions, when they tramped the banks of Current Creek. He had made it clear there were rules in the world. No shooting birds on the ground, no lies to cover up a failure, no undersize fish, no going back on your word. Luke was not prepared to watch him peter out at the end of green tubing in a horrible place that smelled like Lysol and sickness. So it was a good thing his grandfather had asked him to help, although it made his throat constrict in a knot of pain to think about it.

He heard the sound of the car coming up the lane, the tires crunching the gravel. His mother had finally arrived home. The car door opened and slammed shut. He stood up and walked down to the edge of the patio and stepped into sight.

"Luke!" his mother said, startled by the way he had suddenly appeared from behind the house. "Good heavens." She held one hand to her throat. "You startled me."

"Sorry, Mom. I was just waiting for the car."

"I thought you went out with your dad."

He shook his head. "No."

The dogs rushed her and raked her crotch with their muzzles. "Don't," she said. "Tell these dogs . . . I . . ." She started to say something else, and then she stopped and bent over the dogs and halfheartedly greeted them. Her dress climbed up the backs of her legs, and he saw the ropy blue web of articulated veins. "Hi," she said. "How are the baby dogs?"

"I thought I might go for a ride," he said.

She didn't respond immediately.

"All right, Mom? Okay if I take the car for a while?"

"I guess," she mumbled, already heading for the front door. She clutched her purse to her chest and shuffled like an old woman.

He left the dogs at home instead of taking them with him as he usually did, in order to make room in the car for Rebecca and

Melanie, who were waiting for him at Rebecca's house.

Rebecca was his girlfriend. She lived out of town, near the sugar beet factory and the stockyards, in an old farmhouse surrounded by junked automobiles that her father, a disabled veteran, never seemed to get around to fixing. It was hard to tell which smelled worse, the stockyards or the sugar beet factory, but together they filled the air with an overpowering stench that made him want to hold his breath. As he pulled up in front of her house, two old dogs, tied up to a water pipe, stood up and began barking. He honked. Rebecca came out the front door almost instantly, followed by Melanie, her best friend. They hurried down the front steps, rushing toward the car.

"What took so long?" Rebecca asked, sliding across the front seat. Melanie climbed in next to her and slammed the door.

"Mom," he said. "She just got home."

They drove back to the highway and headed west on a road that curved around the end of the lake, riding through country that was dry and barren and rolling. They crested hills and dropped down into gullies where golden light illuminated sagebrush and skunkweed growing up to the shoulder of the road. They drove out to where low hills separated the shallow desert valleys and pools of stagnant water gathered in the bottom of ravines, attracting swarms of insects, drawn by the scum on the sluices, which gave off a smell like hard-boiled eggs spoiled by the sun. The swamps infused the cool air with a mossy sharpness, wet and acrid, that mingled with the smell of sage.

"Would you look at that?" Rebecca had edged forward on the seat and was staring at herself in the rearview mirror. "A damned pimple." She touched a plump little mark on her chin.

"Don't do that," Melanie said.

The car picked up speed and sailed past boulder-sized tumbleweeds. The sun was starting to set, and a chill settled in the car. Rebecca asked him to roll up his window. Nobody spoke. Instead they listened to music, a pounding, surging noise from four speakers.

He passed the marker at the turnoff for the chemical plant and took the dirt road branching from the highway. At a point beyond the plant, he turned south on a rutted road, moving farther and farther into the empty salt-pan country, dotted here and there with stands of tall cottonwoods.

It was midweek, Wednesday, three weeks after Easter, and it felt like dead time to him. Light flooded the landscape evenly.

Nothing moved or escaped the commanding silence of the late afternoon. He thought of his grandfather and the living will, a document so simple and final it seemed unreal to him.

"Where are we headed?" Melanie asked.

"I don't know," he said. "Maybe we'll go up to Kemmerer and get something to eat."

He looked out the window, watching for some sign of movement. A few cows stood perfectly still on a hillside, catching the last warmth of the sun.

"Kemmerer?" Rebecca said. "I can't be gone that long. My dad said an hour. I have to be back by six."

"Why don't we go back to town?" Melanie said. "We can get something to eat at The Raspberry Shack."

He didn't answer. He was thinking, If his grandfather wanted to leave the hospital, he knew now what that would mean. He imagined his grandfather at home. He could see him upstairs, lying in his old, four-poster bed, the life slowly ebbing out of him. He saw himself sitting next to the bed, watching and waiting. Was that how it would be?

"You're awfully quiet today," Rebecca said. She laid her hand on his thigh. He looked down at her plump fingers and the bright pink polish on her nails. The polish had flaked off in places, reminding him of his mother's chipped dishes. She jiggled his leg.

"What's going on?" she asked. "What are you thinking about?"

"Nothing much," he said. He shrugged, turned briefly, and forced a smile. He couldn't say, I'm thinking of my grandfather and death, wondering if I'll have the courage to be there for him, right to the very end. A small knot of pain gathered in his throat.

Melanie took a brush out of her purse and began brushing her hair. "I'll tell you," she said. "I am so sick of geometry."

"Luckily there's only three months of school left," Rebecca said.

"I wish it was going to be over tomorrow," Melanie sighed. "I don't think I'm going to make it."

He listened to the girls, who continued to discuss school, but he wasn't really interested in their talk. He focused on a hawk circling in the distance, pursued by a smaller bird that dipped and fluttered over the hawk, as if attacking it. The car bumped over the dirt road and hit a deep rut, jostling them. Rebecca bounced against his shoulder.

"Hey," she said, "slow down."

"Sorry," he said, and eased off the gas.

"When you said we were going for a ride I didn't think you meant this," Melanie said, turning to look up at him. Her brush had fallen out of her hand, and she was feeling around on the floor, looking for it. She found it and straightened up, flipping her loose, long hair away from her face. "Where are you taking us? To see the sagebrush?"

He didn't really know where he was headed. He only wanted to be driving. He felt good behind the wheel of a car, as if movement itself was a form of freedom, a way of escaping the tedium of ordinary life. He especially liked side roads that took him into the country where there was a pristine feeling to the landscape and a quietness. A person could notice things in such a place. The way light fell on bushes and trees. The darting flight of birds. But it didn't feel good to him today. It might have been all right if he'd been alone, but with the girls there, sending him the message they were bored, he began to feel distracted himself, unable to enjoy the ride.

"We can go back to town if you want," he said.

"Yeah," Melanie said. "Let's check it out. There's got to be a lot more happening there than there is out here."

"Okay," he said. He pulled to the side of

the road, backed up in the loose dirt, and made a U-turn.

In the fields near the chemical plant, a farmer was feeding his cattle. He stood in the back of his truck and threw bales of hay to the ground. Some of the bales broke up as they hit the earth, and the cows lowered their heads over the hay quickly. Before he could even climb down and get his knife out to cut the twine, the animals tore into the hay, turning the bales with their teeth, loosening the feed from its ties. They were impatient today. He was late with the feeding.

The farmer heard a car off in the distance, coming down the two-lane road. What struck him was the sound of the engine. It was the high-pitched whine of a car moving fast, kicking into overdrive. He looked to his left but couldn't see anything. Then he looked to his right. The setting sun forced him to squint. When his eyes adjusted, he saw the car, speeding down the road. Damned kids, he thought. He was sure it was teenagers, going that fast. They liked this stretch of road because of the bumps. The road dipped down into gullies and rose up again. At high speeds, you could get quite a ride. The roller coaster road, they called it.

The sight of anything moving that fast in

the otherwise perfectly still landscape caused him to keep his eye on the car. He saw how it came up over a rise and seemed to leave the ground for a second or two before landing. It was a little, older car, a sedan. He began thinking about his own car, how much he'd like to trade it in, get a newer model, or even one of those Japanese compacts that got such good mileage, when the car flew past him and he caught a glimpse of the three figures inside. Kids, just as he'd thought, out for a joy ride. Still moving at high speed, the car dropped down into a gully and disappeared from sight.

He turned away, bending over a bale of hay, and slipped his knife beneath the twine, when a sudden, terrifying noise exploded behind him — a brutal, shattering sound, so loud and frightening it caused him to drop his knife and spin around. The cows scattered around him, running off in different directions, bits of hay still hanging from their mouths. He saw the car, careening away from the cottonwood tree, dust rising around it, and knew instantly what had happened.

My God! he thought. Oh my God.

Throwing himself forward, he clambered behind the wheel of the truck. But the truck wouldn't start. Over and over he tried to bring it to life. He cursed his old equipment.

He swore at the poverty of his life, at the old battery and the bad timing that it would choose this moment to give out on him. Then he abandoned the truck and began running toward the car and the cottonwood tree, a lone figure loping across broken fields, his heart fluttering with fear.

He reached the car out of breath. He didn't hesitate, but ran to the wreckage and peered inside, afraid of what he might see. The doors stood open. Glass lay shattered on the seat, and a purse with its contents strewn around. It took him a moment to realize that what he was searching for wasn't there. No one was inside. The car was eerily empty. He began searching the area next to the road, moving rapidly from one spot to another. He walked back along the path of the car, parting the long weeds next to the ditch with his knees. He saw where the car had gone off the road, crashed through willows and a barbed wire fence, before hitting the tree and bouncing into the ditch. Moving through the brush, he startled a killdeer, which in turn frightened him with its cries.

Then he found them, two girls, lying in a clump of bush-grass, a few feet apart, and bleeding from wounds so extensive they horrified him.

He knelt at the first body. There was no

pulse beneath the flesh at her throat, and none at her wrist, either.

He turned the second girl over. Her face was largely obscured by blood. No pulse there, either. He turned away from the bodies and held his head for a few moments.

God help me, he wanted to cry. He felt like retching. He wanted to scream for help. He felt like calling out for his wife. He needed someone, anyone, to be there with him, to help him. He grew so frightened he couldn't think.

In the stillness surrounding him he heard a moan coming from some weeds growing at the bottom of an embankment. He scrambled down the loose dirt and stood perfectly still. Insects chirruped. A meadowlark called. He listened harder. Geese honked in the distant fields. An airplane droned overhead . . . and then he heard the moaning noise again. He walked in the direction of a stand of willows and came upon the body of a boy, crumpled in the ditch. The water parted around him, as if for an island. He was turned faceup, seemingly unconscious, but showing no evident injuries.

The farmer bent over him, and suddenly the boy opened his eyes and looked at him. He uttered one word. The farmer couldn't make it out.

"Son?" he said. "Son?"

The boy didn't answer. His eyes rolled back, the lids shut. Could he move him out of the water? Should he even try to? He put a hand under the boy's neck to raise his head, and as he did so, he had the odd sensation of touching something unnaturally soft, like the center of a watermelon. The water turned instantly red. He laid the boy's head down again in the shallow ditch, afraid to touch him.

The boy was alive. He had to let someone know. Yet he hesitated to leave the boy's side. Shouldn't he try to stop the blood flowing from his head? What could he do?

He stood up and looked around him. Somebody should be coming. Where was the traffic from the chemical plant? He walked up the road a little way and checked the horizon.

How am I going to get help? he wondered. Where did help come from at these times? He turned to see a car coming down the road, straight toward him, and he began waving his arms frantically, motioning for the car to pull over. It stopped not far away from him, and a man and a woman got out.

"What happened?" the woman said.

"Oh my God," the man cried, eyeing the mangled car not far away. Its front end had been pushed back to the windshield. "Has there been an accident . . . ?"

Help has arrived, the farmer thought, bidden by me. That's how it comes. It just does. It simply arrives.

Everything happened quickly after that.

Nobody was told how bad it was, not in the beginning, certainly not the boy's parents, who got a call at six-thirty in the evening. Joyce Beery had just put her robe on, planning to spend a quiet night at home, and was wondering if it was a good time to call her sister, Helen, up in Moscow when the phone rang.

Her husband, Dan, was outside letting the water in. According to the schedule agreed upon by all the members of the water district, he got his turn at irrigation water between four in the afternoon and midnight every Wednesday. If he missed his turn, he had to wait another week before he could draw from the ditch. He pulled out the sluice gate, shoved it down again at a right angle, and watched the stream change course in the ditch. The black water boiled up against the plank and then began flooding out onto the lawn. Water swirled around his rubber boots, and he stepped back, moving out of the way. Above him, the first stars were beginning to emerge between ragged pale clouds in a still-blue sky. He took his time at the gate, dawdling over his last chore of the day, caught up in a reverie of pleasant feeling.

He was interrupted by his wife calling out to him from the kitchen window. At first he couldn't make out what she was saying, because a truck passed on the highway and drowned out her voice. He picked up his shovel and crossed the lawn, calling out, "What?"

And then he understood her: there'd been an accident out on the road near the chemical plant. Luke and some girls had been taken to the hospital. "Hurry!" she cried. "Get the truck!"

It all sounded unnatural to him because of the strange high pitch to her voice and because he didn't quite believe what he was hearing.

In an instant she had reached the front yard and he'd changed out of his irrigating boots and they were in the truck, backing out of the driveway. He forgot completely about the water, flooding out over the lawn, and by the time he remembered it, many hours later, it had risen to several inches, spilled through a basement window, and flooded the rumpus room, ruining the carpeting.

Things had taken their course.

The girls were dead on arrival at the hospital. The boy, who had suffered massive head injuries, was pronounced brain-dead by early morning. But before that, before the parents had even arrived, a team of doctors had made a quick analysis and called the University Hospital cardiac transplant team to inform them of a potential donor. They had a heart. An accident victim. The brain had ceased functioning but the heart was fine. It was better than fine. It appeared to be in perfect condition. A beautiful heart.

Nobody yet understood the chain of events about to be set into motion.

The local papers the next day headlined the accident, but it was only the beginning, and over the next few days, as the details accumulated, the story grew into one of national interest. Nothing like this had ever happened before. The heart of a brain-dead sixteen-year-old had been successfully transplanted into his ailing grandfather's chest.

4

In the still of the moonless night, she could feel his heart beating against her hand, which lay palm up on his chest, the fingers curling inward like the legs of a dead spider. The blue light from a neon sign shone down on the cab of the truck. A faint reflection of their faces appeared on the window.

"So how long can you drive at a stretch?" she asked.

"It depends," he said.

"On what?"

He turned toward her and grinned. "On how good my drugs are."

"Oh," she said, and yawned.

"Do you want something?"

"Like what?"

"You know," he said, and slid his hand over her thigh.

"No," she said. "No thanks."

He rolled away from her. "Well, I'm going to catch a little sleep then."

She turned her face toward the window and breathed deeply, grateful for the moist freshness of the air seeping in around the glass. She had no idea where she was, except somewhere in Wyoming, parked at a twenty-four-hour truck stop, lying on a mattress in a cubicle behind the seat. She knew the name of the man lying next to her was Wendall, although she did not remember his last name, or whether he had ever even offered it. She'd left her parents' Pinto parked in the lot of the Ranchhand Cafe in Montpelier. When it was finally discovered, she knew, she would be listed as a runaway. There were things she wished she'd remembered to bring. Like her binoculars. If she had her binoculars now, she could be looking at the Milky Way, which spilled across the sky in a river of light.

They didn't reach Casper until late the next afternoon. He took her to his apartment in a building on the outskirts of town. The apartments were surfaced with flesh-colored stucco, which had cracked and fallen in patches on the bare ground next to the walls. A steep, narrow stairway led to his apartment on the second floor. The stairs were covered with strips of black adhesive that curled at the edges.

Inside, there was a couch, a set of barbells, and a bookcase. The bookcase held old copies of *Penthouse* and *Playboy* and several bowling trophies. In the next room she found an unmade bed. The kitchen was cluttered with unwashed dishes and cereal boxes and fruit turning rotten in a wooden bowl. Ashtrays full of butts were everywhere. The walls had yellowed around the heat vent.

He stripped to his shorts and strolled from room to room, walking through the kitchen, the living room, the bedroom. She sat on a chair and stared at the view outside the window, telephone lines scalloping into infinity above the rooftops of other apartments. A dog had been left chained to a trailer in a field of golden weeds. She tried to avoid looking at Wendall, at the obvious bulge he displayed. She felt he was presenting himself for her, strutting back and forth, confident he was something worth looking at, which in a way he was, only she felt shy, and uncertain of herself.

"The rent's cheap," he said on one of his passes through the living room. "That's not why I live here. I could afford more. I make good money. But I needed a place to park the rig when I'm not on the road. There's the empty lot next door." He flipped the TV on. "Watch the news," he said. "I'll take a shower. Then we can get something to eat."

The television sat on overturned milk crates. A bent hanger rose from the top of it. The picture was black-and-white, charged with dancing points of light. She listened to the easy banter of the newscasters and marveled at the stupidity of the world. The Reagans were in Santa Barbara horseback riding. The consumer price index was down. The governor had asked for an investigation into the state's pension fund. Wolves were making a comeback in the Bitterroot Mountains, but ranchers had been shooting them. The last item was a human-interest story: an ailing Montpelier, Idaho, man had just received the heart of his sixteen-year-old grandson, who had died in an auto mishap.

Mishap. She wanted to laugh at the word. The world was full of mishaps, wasn't it? Bad luck, misfortune, wrong turns. The twisted path of the unforeseen. She wondered if she might describe her own condition as a mishap. It certainly was bad luck.

Something constricted in her throat. She stared at the overflowing ashtray on the coffee table and the large dark stain on the carpet near her foot. In the strange room, sitting alone for the first time in many hours, her predicament became clear to her. She had really gotten away. No one knew where she was. They would find the car in the parking lot. What then? Wouldn't she be impossible to find? Who would think of Casper? Who would imagine this building, this room, as a hiding place? Her suitcase sat on the carpet, pea-green plastic, puny when she considered how everything she owned was inside. She had crept out of the house just after midnight, afraid to take more than she could carry in one trip to the car, climbed into the Pinto, heart pounding, released the brake, rolled out of the driveway, navigated the darkened streets, stopped for gas at the 24-hour station before the on-ramp, and then driven the interstate through countryside she could not see, and had never seen, until dawn broke over Pocatello, revealing black chunks of rock, stacked like blocks alongside the road. At McCammon she'd headed east on a two-lane road, driving into the rising sun. All this seemed to her to have happened weeks — not hours — ago. *I am gone now. I belong nowhere. I have no one. I am here, in a stranger's rooms, with bowling trophies and a TV on an overturned box in front of me.* She imagined her stepfather driving through the city, the countryside, making calls, looking for her. She imagined *him* — Larry — pulling her down against the carpeted floor in the back of his van. And she imagined a watery presence inside of her, not human, not life yet, but part her, part him, nestled in her womb.

She listened carefully to make sure the

shower was still running, and then she picked up the phone and dialed information. When she had the operator on the line she asked for the number of the Women's Free Clinic. She wrote it down on a piece of paper and stuffed it into her small purse.

He emerged from the bathroom wearing only a towel, tucked tightly around his waist. His wet hair was combed neatly into slick planks, like thick bird wings sweeping up from his ears.

He came and sat down next to her on the couch. "Are you hungry?" he asked, stroking her arm.

"A little." She felt nothing except a sort of hiccuping pain at the center of her chest and at a point midway between her eyes. He lifted her hand and kissed the palm. Her mind went blank. She wanted to hunch over and protect herself, curve her arms around her aching chest, where her heart seemed to shake in its fragile sac, bursting forward against her ribs and receding again with a shudder. She knew she was on the verge of crying. It had something to do with the way he'd kissed her hand.

"Are you all right?" he asked.

"Why?"

"You look upset."

"I'm just tired."

"Hey . . . are you in some kind of trouble?"

"I don't know what makes you say that." She lowered her head, trying to hide her face from him. A tear squeezed out of the corner of her eye and fell onto her arm in a little plink of wetness.

"You haven't really told me anything about yourself."

"Like what?" she said.

"Like where you're from. Like why you're alone. I don't know. . . ."

"I told you I hitchhiked down from northern Idaho." She pressed her lips together. She wasn't going to say any more. He continued holding her hand. The fridge made a terrible noise in the background.

"Well," he said finally, "I'll get dressed and we'll go get something to eat."

Two days later he left on a long-distance haul to the East Coast. He wouldn't give her the keys to his pickup, because he said his insurance wouldn't cover her, but he did leave her the key to the apartment and also some money for food.

That evening, after he'd gone, she sat on the little balcony jutting out from the living room, and watched the light fade over the fields. There was a rusted grill next to her, filled with sodden charcoal ash and cigarette butts. A rubber mat was draped over the railing. She was aware of the things surrounding her, but most of all she was aware of herself, and the emptiness — empty rooms behind her, empty fields beyond the railing. A loose and uncertain evening stretched before her, hours that were hers to fill up. The excitement she felt, and the sense of strangeness, were almost indistinguishable. To the small notebook, lying open on her lap, she confided these words:

People have left me, and now I've left them. I didn't think it would be so easy. I knew there would be something else. Somebody to help me when the time came. Now if only tomorrow goes well.

She walked into town the next morning. She didn't mind walking. The two-lane road led past ranches and fields patterned with a soft, pale cobweb of dew. She stopped to pet a piebald horse, fed it a handful of emerald grass, and pressed her face briefly against its cheek. Farther on, she saw a red hawk sitting on a fence post and slowed her pace, hoping to pass without disturbing it. But as she drew closer it lifted its wings, barred with bands of red and gray, and took to the air, passing just overhead and gazing down at her.

There were signs of spring everywhere, although she could see, now and then, the grimy crescents of hardened snow lying in shadows in the barrow pit. There was little traffic on the road, but once in a while a car passed and broke the stillness of the morning. Meadowlarks called from open fields, a sound so lovely it lifted her heart. Once she startled a killdeer, and it made a noise that sounded like *chee chee chee* and scurried up an embankment, dragging its wing and feigning injury in order to draw her away from its nest. Nature had an order, she thought, which included a devotion to offspring that she'd never experienced in the human world.

The sun lit the landscape evenly, shining down on sage and sprouting grass, falling brightly on tender shoots of furred mug-wort and the tiny spears of lupine. She felt hopeful. The emotion produced inside her a little burr of happiness, something she hadn't felt for a long time. The radiance of the dappled morning buoyed her spirits. She was free. She had forty dollars in her pocket. And she had a place to stay.

By the time she reached town she was perspiring and could feel tiny blisters beginning to form where her shoes had rubbed against her heels. She stopped for a moment in front of the clinic to rest and compose herself then climbed the steps, pushed open a door, and entered a room lined with couches where a half a dozen women were waiting.

She gave the receptionist her name and took a seat. The walls were lined with a fabric resembling burlap. The room seemed much too warm. Her head began to throb. When her name was called, she was led to a small room and left waiting. Later a heavy-set woman came in and talked to her. Louise explained why she was there, how she had heard about the clinic. She mentioned that she had no money. And then she waited.

The woman took so long to respond Louise began biting her lower lip, feeling quite suddenly nervous. Finally the woman spoke up. "How old are you?" she asked. Before Louise could answer, the woman added, "You're not eighteen yet, are you?"

It seemed too late to lie. "Do I have to be?"

The woman nodded. "I'm afraid so. Unless you have parental consent. Do you think your parents would consent to the procedure?"

A wild, fluttering feeling started in her stomach and slowly began to rise, threatening to cut off her breath. "Nobody said that . . . nobody told me . . ."

"If you need someone to help you talk to your parents, we have trained volunteers who could help you — "

"No! I . . . I couldn't ever talk to my parents about this." She stood up abruptly and turned away from the woman. Her eyes focused on a container in the corner labeled "Infectious Waste." She saw in an instant her mother's glasses flying across the room, shattering against the wall, and she remembered her stunned look, not a look of pain so much as surprise.

She spun around and faced the woman. "Please," she said. "Please help me. How could anyone find out? If you don't . . . I don't know what I'll do."

The woman stood up and took hold of her hand. "It's not the end of the world," she said softly. "I know it seems that way now. But there are other options for you. Other ways we can help you. You have many more choices than you think, Louise. But tell me about your parents. Do they know yet? What's your relationship with them like?"

She stood very still, breathing in a shallow way, as if to conserve her feeble hold on her feelings.

"You don't want to try and talk with your parents?"

She shook her head.

"Have you actually been tested to make certain you're pregnant? That's the first thing you should do. We can do that here for you today and have the results for you tomorrow. Let's go ahead and do that, all right?"

Louise, mute, nodded.

The woman went to a cupboard and took down a specimen cup made of plastic with a cardboard lid that fit tightly like an ice cream carton's.

"We'll need a urine specimen, Louise. There's a bathroom down the hall. Write your name on the label and the date and just leave it in the little window outside the bathroom. Come back here to this room and I'll have one of our counselors come in and talk with you, okay?"

Louise stared at her, then nodded. "Sure," she said, imbuing the word with as much disgust as she could. As soon as the woman left the room, Louise went to a mirror. She stared at herself. It was possible to look at your face a million times, she thought, and still be surprised by what you saw. She opened the door, walked quietly down the hall, strode quickly past the reception desk, and was gone.

She ran. She had the sensation she wasn't moving at all, that she was on a treadmill, flying down a stationary sidewalk with the trees and houses keeping pace with her. She kept her eyes on a corner and a Big Stinker gas station sign, a revolving skunk, which seemed to grow no closer. She should not have told them her name at the clinic. Her heart bucked and flopped like a bird struggling against a captor. She had tried to tell him once, the man responsible for her condition, how she felt everything in her heart. Every joy. Every sadness. "I mean literally," she said. "Everything?" he asked, as if he didn't believe her.

His name was Larry and he imported nuts from around the world. He drove a van that said "Nuts to You" on the side. He had a plump wife with an overbite and two small children, one of whom was partially deaf and wore a tiny hearing aid the color of bubble gum. She'd met him one day in her stepfather's TV repair shop, where she worked sometimes after school. A "Nuts to You" assortment sat on the counter in a display box. Her stepfather got a percentage of everything he sold. The day Larry came to the shop he was wearing a tooled-leather belt with a buckle that said "World's Greatest Nuts." He hauled in a box and set it on the floor, straightened up, and grinned at her. Then he leaned over the counter and studied her face for a moment. "Do you know the secret of success?" he asked in a low and confidential tone. He looked like the sort of man who might know that kind of secret.

"No, I don't," she said.

"Personal magnetism," he said, and smiled so wide she could see the curve of his tongue at the back of his mouth.

She didn't know whether to laugh or believe him.

"Where's Ted? Are you his daughter?"

"*Step*daughter," she said pointedly.

"Oh, *step*daughter," he said, mimicking her.

"He's making a house call."

"A *house call?*"

"Checking on somebody's TV. If they're too big, the customer doesn't bring them in, he goes out to fix them."

"Just what the world needs, huh? Bigger TVs." He took a pistachio from his pocket and cracked it open, taking out a nut the color of pond slime. "Want one?" he asked, and before she could answer, he slipped it between her lips and pushed it into her mouth with his finger.

"They're good for you," he said. "Do you know what pistachios give you?"

"No." She thought he was going to say Vitamin A or B or C. But he didn't say anything like that at all.

He said, "Grandeur."

She began laughing. "Grandeur?"

"No kidding. That's what you get from pistachios. Now almonds . . . they give you an entirely different thing."

"I bet," she said.

"You don't want to hear, I won't tell you."

"Okay. What do you get from almonds?"

"Poignance," he said. "A lot of poignance."

"I'm sure," she said. Close up, he looked as if he came from a foreign country. He had black eyes, an oddly shaped nose, and skin darker than usual in her town.

"I'd tell you what you get from walnuts, but I think you're a little young."

She rolled her eyes. "Right."

"How old are you?"

"Almost seventeen."

"That means barely sixteen, doesn't it?"

She looked away, pulling her hair back with her hand into a makeshift ponytail. "Quit giving me a hard time," she said, smiling.

He had grown serious then. "Tell me something," he said. "Your stepfather. He's part of that group up in Hayden Lake, isn't he?"

She could feel the way her face dropped, as if little sinkers had been added to her cheeks. "What group?" she said coolly.

"You know the group. What do they call themselves? The White Democratic Front? Isn't that it?" He waited for her to answer, and she felt those dark eyes, as liquid as oil, trained on her.

"I don't know," she mumbled, although she did know, and it wasn't the White Democratic Front, but the Aryan People's Party.

"But you know what guys I mean? The ones who've been burning crosses on lawns lately? The guys who put the swastika on Sid Fishbein's restaurant? The same guys who've been harassing that Dutch woman whose children are part black? I heard your stepfather is in with those people. That's the name I heard. Ted Blanchard."

She took her hands away from her hair and let it fall down on her shoulders, sitting up straighter. "If you want to know something about my stepfather, why don't you wait until he gets back and ask him?"

"I would, except he might get suspicious." He reached inside his pocket and took out another pistachio. This time it was a red one, the color of Merthiolate. He cracked it and popped the nut into his mouth, not taking his eyes off her. His tongue curled around the nut and drew it deep into his mouth. He chewed it slowly, and when he was finished, he said, "If he got too suspicious, he might not keep selling my nuts, right?"

He leaned over the counter until his face was a few inches from her. She could smell his breath, an odor that was earthy, like wet soil and pine cones. "You don't believe in that stuff, do you?" he asked.

Without flinching, she said, "I don't believe in anything."

He straightened up. "I like you," he said. "I think I'll come back again."

The next week he had driven her to Smelterville and bought her dinner in a fancy restaurant called the Jolly Rabbit. Throughout the meal, he rubbed her thigh under the table, releasing in her a dazzling shower of feeling. He wanted to talk more about the Aryans. He seemed quite preoccupied by the subject, as if it were very disturbing to him. She opened up a little, just a little, to him, and it felt good to release some of the fear and disgust she had kept inside for so long. After dinner, they made love in his "Nuts to You" van, parked on a dirt road in the mountains, beneath pines that seemed to talk in the wind.

After that night, it had been a different town each week. Cocolalla, Talache, Chilco, dinners in little cafes in places where he

didn't do nut business and there'd be no
chance of anyone recognizing them. No one
had ever taken her so seriously or shown
more sympathy for the crazy pattern of her
life. They chose nights when his wife visited
her parents in Opportunity and he could
make the excuse of late deliveries.

No more than two months had passed when
she missed her first period. When she told
him, he said he didn't understand it. Every
time he had used protection. It wasn't true,
he hadn't. She reminded him of the one
time they had taken a chance, when he didn't
have anything with him. An ugliness had
crept in when he implied there might be
someone else. There had been arguments and
bitter feelings. "I can see my life unraveling
here," he had said one night, the last night
she had seen him. The next thing she knew,
he had gone to California, taking his wife
and two children.

She reached the Big Stinker station out of
breath, and darted into an alley that smelled
of old garbage. She sat down between two
buildings and leaned against a brick wall,
thinking of him in California, a place she
imagined as sunny and crowded. It began
raining, a soft, spring-sweet rain, which fell
on her with warmth. Much later, she began

the long walk back to the apartment, and arrived wet and weary, in a somber mood.

Over the next few days she came to know the soiled hem of Casper, the weedy lots and tract houses, the pocked roads lined with chain-link fencing where she walked each day. In the apartment, she felt an unbearable loneliness, and even when it rained she took to the road and walked. Once she called her mother and listened to her reedy little voice say, "Hello . . . ? Hello . . . ? Hell-ooo?" and then hung up without speaking. Wendall phoned a few times from distant places — Detroit, Cincinnati, Pittsburgh — and she tried to sound cheerful and happy to hear from him.

In the mornings, she began to feel nauseated, a sickness so dispiriting it engulfed her in depression. Food became a matter of indifference. When she had to eat, she took a spoonful of peanut butter from the jar or ate a few crackers. She began to hear things in the night, stirrings in the cupboards, scratching in the bedroom walls. The claustrophobic atmosphere of the apartment, with its yellowed walls and tattered *Playboy*s, increased her anxiety, and she continued walking, even when she knew she'd have to stop somewhere alongside the road and, threading her fingers in chain-link, hang on while the sickness came up. She found herself hurtled each day through a cycle of feelings. The full weight of loneliness descended on her, a new feeling, as if she were lost without hope of rescue.

By the end of the week, she no longer left the apartment. She grew afraid of going outside. Now she spent the days moving from the couch to the bathroom, experiencing nothing except the dreamy motion of her feet stepping lightly on the soiled rug and the never-ending voice of the TV.

5

Joyce Beery leaned over the bed and looked into her father's eyes. She wore a paper mask over her nose and mouth and a plastic cap over her hair, and a long white gown cloaked her body from her neck to her ankles. Even her feet were covered with paper slippers, which fit loosely over her shoes.

"Dad?" she said. "Can you hear me?"

Her father stared at her. His pupils appeared dull and unfocused. She waited. Each breath she took swirled back against her own face.

"Do you know where you are, Dad?" She almost added, "Do you remember what's happened?" but caught herself.

"I'm here. Helen's here, too. And Dan. They're all waiting just outside in another room."

He gazed straight ahead, giving no indication he heard her.

"I love you, Dad. We all love you and we're here with you. Everything is going to be okay. You're doing beautifully. You're going to be fine."

He had so many tubes going in and coming

out of him, tubes emptying a watery fluid from his chest, tubes carrying nourishment into his arms, tubes sending oxygen up his nose. His skin looked bluish-gray. The doctors had said there wasn't any reason he couldn't speak if he chose to, but he looked so ill, so weak, that she doubted he would. She couldn't imagine him having the strength to force a word up out of his throat. Surely it would drop back down in a failed effort. How could he speak? He seemed barely there in front of her, a feeble specter whose real self had been removed to some distant place.

She lifted his hand and leaned closer to him. The breath coming from between his parted lips smelled of medication, and his lips had a dull sheen. He seemed dry and hot to her. His hand had a rubbery and lifeless feel. She squeezed it gently and thought she felt the slightest pressure from his fingers in return.

She noticed something. His lips trembled. "Dad?"

His eyes began to well up with tears.

"Oh, Dad," she whispered, and put her head down on the edge of the bed. Her shoulders began to shake with her own uncontrollable grief. In the silence of the room, her hiccuping sobs sounded inordinately loud, caught in the web of the mask. She felt the starched sheets against her forehead, which jerked against the bed. A powerful, searing ache prevented her from moving. A low cry broke out of her mouth, and then another, like the plaintive cries of a child, and she brought her hand to the mask and pressed it hard against her mouth to try to check the noise. She felt a presence behind her, and then a hand on her shoulder.

"Mrs. Beery . . . ?" The nurse's voice was soft and hushed. Joyce raised her head slightly and looked at her father. His eyes had closed. He appeared ashen, as still as a corpse.

"Come on, dear," the nurse said. "He's doing fine."

Slowly she sat up straight and looked at the nurse. She too wore a mask, and only her eyes were visible, eyes that, separated from the other features of her face, appeared emotionless.

"It looks like he's gone under again," the nurse said. "He'll drift in and out of consciousness for a while until the anesthetic completely wears off. Did he speak to you at all?"

Joyce shook her head. Her eyes were killing her from so much crying. All she wanted to do was close them for a while, to sink into obliterating sleep.

In the small room adjoining her father's, she removed the gown and mask, took off the slippers and plastic cap, and peeled the rubber gloves from her hands and the coverings from her shoes. She felt so weary she wondered briefly whether she might not lie down on the small bed in the room and nap for a while. Instead, she dried her eyes, put on fresh lipstick, and went to find her husband.

She could see him through the doorway long before she reached the waiting room. Walking down the hallway, she reminded herself she must be strong. He was having a much worse time than she was. She needed to help him. Helen and her son, Philly, were sitting next to Dan. Helen stared off into space. Philly was eating potato chips and looking at a comic book. Dan sat hunched over, staring at the floor between his feet, his old cowboy hat draped loosely in his hands. He stood up when she walked into the room. She went to him and put her arms around him and held him briefly. Then she turned to her sister, who took her hand.

"How is he?" she asked.

"He's okay. His eyes were open for a while."

"Did he say anything?"

She shook her head. "No, but he squeezed

my hand a little."

"Don't you want to rest? Why don't you go home for a while? We all need a rest."

"I don't know . . ."

"But you haven't slept at all for two days. You should go on home."

Philly tugged at his mother's arm. "Are we going home, too?" he asked.

"No, Philly." She cupped his face in her hand briefly, then turned again to her sister. "There's nothing you can do here anyway. Philly and I will stay here. If there's any change, we'll let you know."

"I would like to go home for a while," Joyce said. "Okay, Dan? I think we should."

"I reckon," he mumbled.

She took his arm. "Come on, honey. We'll be back later, Helen."

Just as they were about to step into the elevator, Dr. Bowen arrived. He spoke to them for a few moments in a low voice. Then he patted Joyce's shoulder and smiled.

"Thank you," she murmured to Dr. Bowen.

Outside the hospital the reporters waited near the exit. Their faces had become familiar to her.

"Mrs. Beery . . . Mr. Beery . . . excuse me, but have you seen your father? Is he conscious?" The woman who spoke was short and earnest and wore thick black-rimmed glasses.

"We don't want to say anything more right now," Joyce said. "Dr. Bowen will have a statement later."

"Have you seen your father this afternoon? Does he know what's happened?"

"Yes, I've seen him, and he's doing fine."

"Can you give us any more information on his condition?"

"No. We'd like to be left in peace now."

They talked very little during the drive home, riding quietly past the small towns and fields sodden with spring run-off. They pulled into the driveway and parked under the willow tree. Everything was familiar here, and yet at the same time the place seemed strange, as if in their absence their house had undergone a subtle transformation. Someone had mowed the lawn and restacked the firewood. In just a few short days the first tulips and crocuses had bloomed.

Once inside Joyce made a point of avoiding Luke's room. In the kitchen, covered dishes were lined up on the counter. She found more food in the refrigerator. The neighbors had been dropping by with baked goods and casseroles. She discovered she had an appetite and lifted the tinfoil on one bowl, then another. She heaped a plate with food — potato salad, Jell-O, chicken — but Dan wouldn't take anything. He went to the basement. Later, when she went down herself, she found him cutting the wet carpet away from the baseboards.

"Dan, can't you leave that until later? Honey, why don't you come up and eat something?"

"No," he said. "I have to finish here. It's a mess. Everything's ruined."

She turned and climbed the stairs, feeling a deep weariness.

She was exhausted but couldn't sleep, and instead of napping, lay on her bed and stared up at the water stains on the ceiling.

For some reason, she thought of her mother. How would she have dealt with this? The strange and tragic events of the last forty-eight hours. If only her mother was here to help her. To be there for her father.

When she pictured her mother, she saw her in a red wig, made of such stiff synthetic fibers that it never moved, not even in the stiffest wind.

When she was alive there had been times when Joyce had felt deeply embarrassed by her mother, who held strange notions about religion and health. For some reason she remembered the time she came home from school and found her mother in a state of glee, as though something wonderful had just happened.

She was laughing at herself, she said. She'd just made a discovery. She was feeling a little sick — not really sick but just so-so. She had felt bad for days, and then she sat down and concentrated on it and she heard a small still voice say, "May, what you need is some cayenne pepper." She could still see her mother standing at the kitchen sink, dumping red powder into a glass of water and stirring the bright motes into a frenzy.

The telephone rang, but it stopped abruptly and she knew Dan had answered it. Outside the window, plump green buds appeared as grublike growths on auburn twigs and branches. A good year was predicted for fruit. Light snows, a good early freeze, and now the warm weather.

It struck her that Luke wouldn't be here this summer when the fruit would be ripening and the small stand out on the road would be set up. He would no longer run the stand, greeting people with his easy, affable manner, nor would he ever work alongside his father again. No longer would he come in from the orchard smelling of smoke from burning ditches. She wouldn't see his face again. *He was gone*. She stared at the trees and felt her grief very deeply. Her heart seemed to crack in two, searing with a pain that shot through her being. She brought her hands to her face and covered her mouth. A powdery residue clung to her fingers from the sterile hospital gloves. She pictured him. She saw him now as she would forever see him, lying in that hospital bed, dead.

Brain-dead.

She remembered how the doctors had first uttered those words, "brain-dead," as if there were many ways to be dead and not really be hopelessly so. For a few moments, she had believed that it was just another medical complication they were discussing, like a broken neck or smashed kidneys, as if Luke had suffered terrible internal damage but somehow might still survive. And then it had become clear.

The doctors said there was no hope. Luke was gone. His brain no longer functioned. His life was being supported by artificial methods. A while later, a particularly earnest-looking younger doctor had approached her and Dan and said he wished to speak to them about something, although he understood it was a very difficult time to have to do so. He told them about the transplant team and a man who had been admitted to the University Hospital who needed a new heart, and who had been waiting for one for some time. His life hinged on finding a donor. Tests had been run. It looked as though Luke's heart would be a compatible match. As the young doctor spoke to them, Dr. Frederick Bowen, a weary-looking man with dark shadows beneath his eyes, stepped into the room. Everything then became instantly clear. She recognized Dr. Bowen and uttered a small cry. He was her father's doctor.

"My father?" she had said. "It's my father."

"What?" Dr. Bowen said. He looked confused.

"You're talking about my father," she said. "Phil Doucet."

Dr. Bowen had stared at her, unable to comprehend what she was saying.

At first, the doctors were incredulous, as if they'd heard her wrong. Such a coincidence seemed quite impossible. Dr. Bowen had shaken his head. "I had no idea," he said. "I was completely unaware of this."

She had been overwhelmed. Everything seemed unreal. She had broken down and begun crying. What could she do? She could grasp neither the idea of death nor the transplant. She had repeated, "I don't know, I don't know," over and over. "I don't see how we can do this." She had kept looking at Dan, who appeared stunned and unable to speak. The doctors had tried to talk to her, but she hadn't heard them. At one point Dan had left the room. She had gone to Luke's side and wept over him, touching his bandaged head. She had peered into the face of her boy and thought, Not all of him will die.

Dr. Bowen himself had driven them to the University Hospital to talk with her father. By the time they arrived it was four in the morning and still dark outside. Her father had been awakened and was sitting up in bed. No one had said anything to him yet. He saw her and looked startled. "Why are you here?" he asked. "It's the middle of the night."

She had cried so hard she could only give him the news a small piece at a time. First the accident. Then the news that Luke had been killed. They'd just left his side, she said. He was gone.

Her father had wept uncontrollably, and she wept with him. Then, holding her father's hand tightly, she had explained what the doctors were going to do. Luke's heart was in perfect condition. They were going to transplant it into his chest. It had to be, she said. It was what Luke would have wanted.

He shook his head. "No," he said. "I can't, I can't do that."

She had pleaded, pointed out to him that it was God's will. It was right. It was what had to happen. It was the only way. "Please," she whispered. "Please, Dad. Then it won't all be for nothing."

She had seen her father relent; she had seen it in his eyes.

Her son's heart had been removed at exactly five-thirty in the morning and placed in a sterile plastic bag containing a saline solution. It had then been put into an iced cooler and had been flown, by helicopter, to the University Hospital.

She had saved something of her son and at the same time saved her father. In the solitude of her bedroom, the words took on a powerful religiosity. O my father! My son! The Father and the Son. Surely the Holy Ghost was only a whisper away, hovering, advising, forming a holy trinity. She herself could have been the suffering, sacrificing Mary.

From where she lay on the bed she could see the highway. Two horses came into view, loose and cantering down the pavement. Moments later, two riders appeared. The loose horses were herded into a lane and pushed up against a fence. Cornered, the horses tried to bolt past the riders, who began waving their arms and yelling. But the horses managed to break away and began running down the highway, their tails lifted high in the air.

She heard the front door open and then, a few minutes later, shut. Dan appeared in the doorway. He leaned against the frame and looked down at her on the bed. His thinning hair looked stained, a yellowish smudge against his scalp.

"Who was that?" she asked.

"Bill Elkins, wanting to know if there was anything he could do."

"What time is it?"

"Almost six."

"We should go back to the hospital."

"Joyce," he said wearily, "I don't think I can. I need time alone."

"Come over here. Lie down for a while."

He didn't move. There was a little indentation around his forehead. It was rare for him to be without a hat, and he looked rather odd, his skin bleached from the eyebrows up.

"I'm having a very hard time," he said

in a whisper, his words almost inaudible. He made a fist and pressed it between his eyes, squinting.

She propped herself up on her elbows and said, "Talk to me, Dan."

"I don't know," he said.

"Dan? You're exhausted — "

"No," he said. "No. Don't."

"No what? I'm only trying to help."

"There isn't any help," he said.

"That's not true, honey. God will help us through this."

He went limp, as if someone had delivered a blow to his shoulders. "No," he said. "I don't think so."

"Honey, you worry me with that look. Come here."

He couldn't go to her. He uttered something in a weak voice.

"What?" she said.

"Luke's gone."

"Oh Dan . . ."

"Our son is dead."

He turned and fled the house. Before she could say another word, he was out the back door, striding beneath the cherry trees, walking between rows of bark so purple it looked like dried blood. He walked toward the foothills, where a path wound through the oak brush and led up the canyon. A long slender straight river of dull white cloud rolled across the evening sky, stretching from the mountains to the western horizon. He climbed through boulders. He didn't stop until he came to the stream where water ran clear as glass, a strong, unfailing stream, trembling at the surface. There he sat among the stones, the dried moss clinging to their lovely speckled surface, and cried for all he had lost.

6

Louise opened her door and looked down at mud, oily puddles of water deep in car tracks. She hung her head and tried to breathe deeply, sitting very still, her feet braced on the lip of the door. She didn't feel like moving. The drive up the winding road had made her carsick. She lay back, stretching across the seat of the pickup, and looked up at the sky through the windshield. The fleecy clouds created a rippled wash of whiteness against the deep blue. She concentrated on breathing slowly, inhaling the fresh mountain air blowing across her face.

"Louise?" he called. She heard Wendall walking toward the pickup. His feet made a sound like a dog crunching bones. She opened her eyes to see his face, upside down, gazing at her.

"What are you doing? Are you okay?"

"I'm just a little carsick," she said. She swallowed hard and laid her hand on her stomach. He brushed the hair back from her forehead.

"Why don't you get out? It might help to walk around."

"In a minute."

He leaned down and kissed her, and then went around to the back of the truck. She heard him get a beer out of the cooler and pop it open. "Do you want one of these?" he called.

"Not right now." She rolled over and buried her face against the seat, resting her back against the steering wheel, and let her legs hang out the door. Her shoes felt heavy. He reached over her and took down a rifle from the rack just above her head. Lifting her eyes, she looked out at the ground littered with empty shells — bright red and yellow shotgun casings and little brass .22s lying near his feet. He picked up a sack and walked off toward a ravine, the butt of the rifle resting against his hip. The barrel pointed skyward, like a pole without a flag.

She closed her eyes. The sun came through the window and warmed her back. Earlier it had rained, leaving the air in the hills smelling of sage and wild onion. Everything felt better now that he was back, although she knew he would leave again in a few days, this time for California. Already she had decided to ask if she could go with him. In the peaceful quiet surrounding her, she thought about California and imagined standing on a beach looking out at the ocean.

The first shot startled her. It rang out sharply, a hollow yet crisp explosion that echoed around the canyon, abruptly shattering the absolute stillness of the afternoon. The familiar sound of a rifle instantly transported her to another time.

Another shot rang out, and another. What was he shooting? She raised her head and looked out through the sagebrush, where she could see a row of cans lined up near the ravine. With the next shot, one of the cans disappeared, leaving a little empty space where it had stood. She stared at the row of cans, waiting. He missed with the next shot, and the next one. She rolled over on her back. One out of three. She could do better than that. The shots continued to ring out, each one splitting the silence with a sharp crack that reverberated in the hills. She closed her eyes and lifted her hands to her face, remembering.

Her stepfather had taught her to shoot. She had no choice. Every child needed to know how to use a gun. On Saturdays he took her to a place in the hills near the Fourth of July Pass and set up human targets, black paper silhouettes of a man's head and shoulders marked off by white concentric circles. Sometimes Hilda came along and sat in the car and knitted or worked on armbands, hand-sewing little red swastikas onto white circles. The group met at the shooting site and brought their children. Each week it turned into a competition. Who was the best shot? Whose children were the best shots? Each Saturday, a festive little gathering, with kids and wives, beer and chicken, and .357 magnums, mini-14s, .38s, .30-30s, .30-06s, 20-gauges, AK-47s, and Uzis. Everything to make the sound of a little war waged in barren ravines and against hillsides covered with shattered trees. They were preparing for the revolution, the uprising, the time when they drove *them* out. For a long time she thought "niggers and Jews" was one word, like jujubes or bugaboos. The first gun he bought her came from Sears, a .22 rifle with a clip that held ten bullets. At first it was fun. Shooting up cans and bottles and the paper targets. Just a game. What kid wouldn't like it? Watching things explode. But later the guns had gotten bigger and everything became more serious. Everyone, even the kids, had to act out paramilitary exercises. The men dressed in camouflage and boots, holsters and knives and cartridge belts strapped to their bodies. The talk grew meaner and it wasn't a game anymore, it was craziness. Youth groups. Classes in survival. Terrifying days of endless explosions, brutal talk, and swaggering men barking orders. Everything was shot up, even the trees, branches blown away, their fragmented stumps left jagged. Trunks shattered, bursting with splinters. At the end of the day, nothing was left of the black figures except the tufted shreds of paper men. When they drove away, shards of glass covered the ground, glinting in the sun like a mosaic of precious jewels.

"Louise?" he shouted.

She sat up, startled by the voice calling her back to the present.

"What?"

"Bring me the other rifle, would you? And the box of shells in the glove compartment."

She found the box, took down the rifle — a Browning .30-30 — and strolled over to where he stood in the shade of a juniper tree.

"Do you want to set those cans up for me again?"

She wandered over to the ravine. Her pants felt tight around her waist. Nausea began to overtake her. She undid the top button of her Levi's before bending over to pick up the first can. In the bottom of the ravine she could see the layers of glass and debris. She heard his voice: *Every child that an Aryan mother brings into the world is a battle waged for the existence of her people. The Aryan must be ready to battle the united hybrid mongrel races of the earth. Every child shall bear arms.* Her stomach began to rise.

"Don't shoot yet!" she managed to yell and scrambled down into the ravine, vomiting on layers of glass, crouching low to hide herself from him.

When the sickness passed, she stood up and looked around her, searching for cans still whole enough to stand upright. She found half a dozen, as well as a bowling pin that she picked up at the last minute before climbing up the far side of the ravine. Struggling for footing on the muddy slope, she began to arrange the objects in a little clearing.

"Hey!" he called. "What are you doing?"

"What do you think? I'm setting up cans."

"Hell," he yelled. "That's too far away."

She ignored him and finished propping up the cans against the hillside. She had to dig a little platform with the toe of her shoe to get the bowling pin to stand up. When she'd finished, she walked back to where he was standing. He shook his head at her.

"That stuff is so far away I can hardly see it from here."

"It shouldn't be that hard," she said. "You've got a scope."

"I'll tell you what. I'll let *you* go first then." He thrust the rifle toward her.

"No, I don't want to shoot." Her mouth tasted bitter, like aluminum and smoke.

"Hey, if it's so easy, I want to see you pick those things off. Wait a minute. Here. Let me load it for you." He sat down on a rock and began pushing bullets into the magazine of the rifle.

She said, "I really don't want to shoot. You go ahead."

He stopped what he was doing and looked up at her. A lock of hair flopped down over one eye, and he jerked his head so it swung to one side. "What's the matter?" he said. "Haven't you ever been around guns before?"

"That's not it."

"You're not afraid of them, are you? There's nothing to be afraid of. A gun's only as dangerous as the man holding it. I don't look too dangerous, do I?" He grinned up at her, and she saw both the good and bad in his face, the amusement and the challenge.

"No, you don't look too bad," she said, letting her mouth twist into a little smile.

"Well, I didn't think so," he said, "but I'm glad to hear you say it. I'd like to think you maybe like me."

"I'm going to get a beer," she said, thinking that if she left for a moment he would forget about asking her to shoot. But when she returned, he was still standing there, waiting for her, and he held the gun out as she approached.

"Your turn."

"Don't you want a sip of this?"

"You're trying to get out of shooting, aren't you? I can teach you all you need to know in a minute or two." He took the beer from her and tipped it back. She watched his Adam's apple bob up and down as he swallowed. Why don't women have big Adam's apples? she wondered. It must have something to do with needing a bigger voice box to make a deeper, more manly sound.

"Wendall?" she said abruptly. "Can I ask you something?"

"If you can't, honey, I don't know who can," he said good-naturedly. She liked his easiness, his always seeming happy.

"Can I go with you on your next trip? I'd really like to see the ocean. I've always wanted to go to California."

"That's a tough one, honey," he said. "The company's got a tough policy. No riders. It has to do with insurance. I don't know what it is. But I've seen guys get raked over the coals just for picking up a hitchhiker. I took

117

a chance giving you a ride the first time. Taking you on a long haul — I don't think I can do it."

"Nobody would have to find out."

He shook his head. "You're putting me in a tough spot. I just wish you wouldn't ask. I'll only be gone a few days."

"I hate being all alone," she said. She decided to try another tack. "What I'm telling you is, I miss you. I really want to be with you. We could have some fun in California."

He put his arm around her and drew her close. The rifle rested briefly against her hip. "We can have some fun right here," he said.

"I'll make you a deal," she said. "If I can hit every one of those cans I set up over on that hillside, can I go to California with you?"

He began laughing. She laughed too, in part because she knew she had him. She knew something he didn't, which was this: it was a piece of cake to pick off those cans.

"Okay, honey," he said, straightening up. "You've got a deal. But you have to hit everything, and you can't waste one shot."

He handed her the rifle and sat down on the rock, leaning back slightly and crossing his legs. He had a large grin on his face, as if he could burst out laughing again at any moment. As she raised the rifle to check whether the safety was on, he threw his arms up in front of his face and said, "Whoa," pretending to be afraid, even though she stood sideways to him and had taken care to point the barrel down.

She glanced briefly at him, not smiling, because something had caught in her throat the minute she took the rifle. Bitter memories. She looked away, facing the hillside, and for a moment stared down at the rifle in her hands. She thought, Pick the biggest thing first, the bowling pin, and test the sights. She spread her feet, bending her knees slightly, and slowly brought the rifle to her shoulder, looking down through the scope.

Her view of the world was abruptly reduced and at the same time magnified. Rocks revealed their flecks of color, twigs their rippled bark. The furred ruff of mugwort filled her vision with a dusky green. Each thing became sharply individuated, different, particular, unlike any other thing, as if she were looking *inside* nature. She brought the form of the bowling pin into focus, a thing that seemed animate, a shapely white figure, standing at attention. She pulled the butt of the gun firmly into her shoulder, steadied her mind, took a single slow breath, and held it while she squeezed the trigger smoothly. The bowling pin jumped and tumbled, and when it came to rest she saw the bright new splintered wood revealed in the place where she'd hit it. Then came the cans — six of them — each one hit squarely. They hopped like rabbits. She heard him say, "Jesus H. Christ, you did it!" but she paid no attention to him. The other voice had returned. *Perfection is the union between men and women who are fair, with comely eyes. . . . The Aryan People's Party has truly a single point, the child. . . . Aryan youth's aim is to be dedicated to the service of the Race. . . .* She didn't want to stop now, she wanted to start over again, beginning with the bowling pin, then the cans, shooting them over and over until they danced for her, but she was out of bullets, and when she squeezed the trigger, she heard nothing but the feeble click of the trigger.

She lowered the gun and stared at the ground for a moment. A sigh broke out of her, a breathy little hiccup sour with the taste of beer and sickness. She turned around very slowly and smiled at him.

"Jesus Christ," he said again, shaking his head and laughing. "You set me up! You tricked me! Where did you learn to shoot like that?"

"Girl Scouts," she said flatly, and set the gun down against a rock. She took the beer from him. Her knees felt weak and trembly.

"Seriously . . . who taught you to shoot like that?"

"My stepfather." There was a coldness to her voice.

"He must have been a hell of a shot."

"Oh, yeah. A hell of a shot."

"Fathers don't usually bother teaching their daughters to — "

"He wasn't my father," she snapped. "He was my stepfather."

"Sounds like you didn't like him much."

She said nothing.

"What happened to your father?"

"Dead," she said. "A heart attack."

He let a few seconds pass and then said, "Where *are* you from? I just want to know."

"The Milky Way."

For a brief moment he thought this might really be a place. Milky Way, Idaho, or Montana. Then he realized what she was doing. Putting him on again.

He could almost believe she did come from space. She was vaporously thin and white. At her temples, on the inside of her arms, and around her ears, the blue webbing of veins showed through her skin. Her hair was the color of corn silk, but coarse and dry. He wanted her to like him, but he wasn't sure she did. The one thing he couldn't stand was the thought of caring for someone who would not, or could not, return that caring. That had happened to him too often. And one thing he'd begun to realize was that he did care for her, quite a lot. It seemed his days of being alone, of coming home from the road to an empty apartment, might be over. He hoped this was true.

"Do you want to know what part of the Milky Way I come from?" she asked, tipping her head back and squinting down at him. "It's the part where it strings out and gets kind of thin. You can only see it through binoculars. At first, when you look at the sky at night, you only see a few stars, just the brightest ones, even if you have binoculars. But then you keep looking, your eyes adjust, and pretty soon they're everywhere, stars lurking in the darkness, faint little pinpoints of light, and even fainter ones. I come from a very faint star, one of the littlest measles of light."

"That's the kind of thing you do," he said, shaking his head. "I ask you a straight question and pretty soon we're talking about measles of light. How am I supposed to make heads or tails out of what you say?"

"Oh, lighten up," she said, patting him on the cheek. "You're getting too serious."

"It's hard to know what to think of you."

"What you've got to try and do with me," she said, "is guess the part you don't know."

"I can see that," he said. He felt uneasy, as if he'd picked up a stray animal that allowed you to get close, and then ducked away when you reached out to pet it.

She let him hold her back in the apartment, making love with her eyes closed. It gave her a pleasant feeling, like swimming in deep green water. A weightless, floating sensation. Not the intense shower of feeling she'd experienced with Larry, but something less threatening, and more comforting.

When he left the room to take a shower, she drew the covers over her and lay quietly, still within herself. She began thinking, remembering the strangeness of another room. Coeur d'Alene, where her mother had taken her after the divorce, was very different from Phoenix, the place where she was born. She had moved from summer to winter in one day. In Coeur d'Alene, the basement apartment never seemed warm enough. She awoke to cold and went to bed between cold sheets.

She once asked her mother, "Why do we have to live where it's so cold?"

Her stepfather had jumped in with the answer: "Because the cold climate up here keeps out all that darky riffraff you find in

California and the South. Right now there are only seventeen niggers in this county, and by the time we're finished, there won't be any."

Her room had been freezing. In the mornings, the high windows in the little bedroom, which opened onto earthen pits surrounded by shrubs, leaked a pale gray light into the room, a light so feeble it often seemed night had not yet passed into day. She would lie shivering in her bed, awaiting clearer proof that it was time to get up, which came when her mother opened the door to tell her they were leaving for the shop. She dressed herself for school in socks with holes at the heels, in unironed blouses, and in skirts worn for weeks without washing. She kept believing her father would come for her, come up from Phoenix, just arrive one day and say, "Kitten, you're coming to live with me."

But instead another day arrived, a date she wanted to forget, a date she could never forget. April 20. Hitler's birthday. There was some horrible shame in knowing that her father had died on Hitler's birthday. The call came in the middle of a party. When the phone rang, her mother picked it up, standing beneath a banner that hung in the archway separating the small kitchen from the living room. Couples were crowded into the apartment, and there was noisy music. Her mother had turned her back to the room, huddling against the wall, and shouted, "What? What's that? Who is this?" Later, when everyone had gone, she took her into the bedroom, held her in her lap, and pressed her face against her chest. "Louise," she said, "this is terrible. Your father has died. He had a heart attack this morning." She couldn't breathe, or feel anything, except the crushing pressure of her mother's chest against her face, and the pounding of her own heart.

He heard her vomiting, and pulled back the shower curtain to see her pale form, naked and crouched, clinging to the toilet. He turned off the shower and said, "Louise? Hey, honey? You're sick again?"

It had happened earlier this morning, and yesterday, too. She began coughing, and he stared at her back, where the knobs of her spine protruded like knuckles on a fist. Her shoulders rolled and shuddered in dry heaves, and he knew she couldn't bring anything more up. A few moments passed, and she sat back on her heels and drew the back of her hand across her mouth.

He reached for a towel and began drying himself. "Hell, honey," he said, "that's the third time you've thrown up. What's wrong?"

"I don't know. I can't keep anything down."

She began shivering. He saw how her skin had turned to gooseflesh.

"I'm cold," she said.

He wrapped the towel around his waist and took his bathrobe down from the hook on the door. Bending over her, he wrapped the robe around her shoulders and helped her to her feet. "Come on," he said gently. "You'd better get back in bed."

He covered her with extra blankets and went to make some tea. Green tea. That's what his mother had given him as a child whenever he had a stomachache. Green tea and soda crackers. As he waited for the water in the kettle to boil, he searched through the cupboards, wondering what he had that might serve as a substitute for the crackers. He found part of a loaf of bread and toasted two pieces, spreading them with butter. A good feeling passed through him as he worked in the kitchen. He knew it had to do with caring for someone, and with being needed. When he returned to the bedroom, carrying an aluminum pan he'd used for a tray, he found her lying on her stomach, her face buried in the pillows. The sun had set and the room was cast in a cold blue light. He turned on a lamp, which instantly emitted a yellowness that seemed to warm the room.

"Come on," he said. "Sit up and try some of this."

"I can't," she moaned. "I'm too cold to move."

"I'll get you something warm to put on." He went to his closet, moving hangers along the rack, searching for the thick flannel shirt he knew was there somewhere.

"Wendall," she said, her voice partially muffled by the pillows, "I'm pregnant."

He stopped, his arms frozen in place on the hangers. "What?" he said. He thought perhaps he'd heard her wrong, that she might have said something else, like "I'm stagnant," or "fragrant," although even as he thought this he saw the ridiculousness of it. He knew he hand't misunderstood her. Everything fell into place. He heard her stirring in the bed and didn't turn around, but rather lifted one hand and grasped the metal rod on which his clothes were hanging, tightening his fist around it slowly, feeling its weakness under the weight of his hand. The rack bowed as if ready to come crashing down.

"I'm sorry," she said. "There's no point in pretending."

He turned slowly and faced her, catching a quick glimpse of her face before he looked away. "Jesus," he said. "Why didn't you tell me?"

"I am telling you . . . now."

He turned his back on her and faced the closet, staring at his orange hunting vest, his blue jacket, the assortment of shirts strung out on hangers. He began moving the hangers again, this time more roughly, and the room was filled with the sound of wire scraping along the metal rack.

"Listen," she said. "Just listen to me."

"Yeah, yeah, I'm listening." He tried to make enough noise with the hangers so that whatever she might say would have to compete with his frenzied activity. He expected her to speak up immediately, to give him some lengthy explanation that would amount to a sort of apology for having deceived him, but instead there was only the sound of the hangers flying against the rack. What had she said to him just last night? "I'm so happy you're back, I'm so glad to see you, I've never missed anybody as much as I've missed you these last few days." Bullshit! he thought. Goddam bullshit! Where did she get off, telling him those things? Taking his money, staying in his apartment, letting him think she cared, and all the while . . .

"Wendall," she said, "come here." Her voice was full of cooing, like the burred

128

throatiness of doves.

His weight sagged against his bones as if somebody had just put a hundred-pound sack of cement on his back and told him to carry it to Laramie. The effort it took to turn around and face her again was considerable.

"Whose is it?" he said.

"Whose is what?"

He walked to the window, where he could see the first stars appearing in the sky. A jet passed far overhead, its twinkling movement standing out against the stationary stars. The towel felt wet and clammy against his hips. He had taken a chance and felt the loss of security that came with it, knowing that until the chance paid off or the failure became clear he would exist in a realm of vulnerability. But he hadn't expected this. Now it seemed the failure was clear. He just didn't like being tricked.

"I know how it must sound," she said. "You must think — "

"I don't think anything," he said. "I *feel*. And do you know how I feel? Like a fool."

"How do you think I feel?"

He looked over his shoulder at her. She had propped herself up against the pillows, and appeared miserable. Her face was desperately sad, and he saw how her whole body convulsed with spasms of shivers.

"Jesus," he said. "Put some clothes on. You look like you're freezing." When she made no effort to move, instead shaking harder because she had begun to cry and was trying to suppress her sobs by turning even more rigid, he couldn't help feeling he should do something. He went to the foot of the bed and picked up the robe and tucked it up under her chin, covering her small breasts, which had turned as hard and dark as two little chokecherries. Seeing those breasts, so tiny really, like a child's, made him feel sorry for her.

He sat down on the edge of the bed and blew out a sigh, filling his cheeks with air and letting them deflate slowly.

"Okay," he said. "It's just the shock of it, that's all. What the hell am I supposed to think? What do you want me to do?"

She stared ahead in stony silence, then shook her head, as if dodging a fly, a movement that seemed to break her from a trance. "Help me," she said calmly. She sighed. "I don't want . . . I can't . . ." She bit her lower lip, and sighed again. "Take me to California with you and lend me some money so I can get things taken care of."

She lifted her pale eyes and stared at him. There wasn't a thing in those eyes, he thought, except sadness.

"Do you even like me?" he asked abruptly.

"Of course," she said, as if genuinely shocked by his question.

"Why are you asking me to help you? Why don't you go to whoever it was who made you pregnant and ask him for help?"

"Because he's gone," she said flatly, "and because he never cared enough in the first place."

He leaned over and let his hands fall between his knees and stared at the floor. He could see white flecks of popcorn stuck in the rug, left over from some earlier solitary night spent in this room. So this is what it came to. Nobody ever got all of what he wanted, only a little piece of it, compromised, altered almost beyond recognition. He felt her hand creep out of the covers and slide over his knee. It rested there, a warm, irresistible touch, beckoning and light. Almost without understanding why, he lifted his hand and covered hers. She moved over and threw back the covers. He let the towel drop from his waist and climbed between the sheets, lying next to her. She held on to his neck with a fierceness he hadn't felt since high school wrestling days. He felt the moist breath on his neck, how it came in spurts of hiccuping sobs, and he gathered her tighter against him. It wasn't much later when he felt her arms go slack and realized she'd finally gone to sleep. He lay quietly in the small room, staring at the saucepan sitting on the aluminum tray, thinking how the tea was cold, seeing how the toast had dried up, the crusts beginning to curl upward, like the edges of an old shoe.

7

"What time is it?" Phil asked. His eyes had opened suddenly.

"Four o'clock," Helen answered. She closed the book of poems she'd been reading, feeling the spell had been broken. The poetry had mesmerized her, carried her far from the hospital room and the smell of medication hanging heavy on the air. She had been reading a poem by Joseph Brodsky. The beauty of the words had descended on her like a blessing that only she was receiving amid the much greater suffering and chaos of the hospital. Setting the book aside, she shifted forward on her chair, once more a heavy woman trapped in a cumbersome body.

"The doctor should come by soon," he said. He was propped up in bed. Light coming from the window behind him made his wispy hair look like filaments in a light bulb.

"I've been lying here thinking," he said.

"I thought you were sleeping."

"No, just thinking."

"What about?"

"There's something I wish I knew."

"What's that?"

"Oh, just something."

"Are you going to tell me?"

"It's nothing. What I mean is, I don't think I'll ever know the answer."

"The answer to what?"

He didn't speak.

"Will you please tell me?"

"Why were those kids speeding? That's what I'd like to know. One of those newspaper articles that your sister brought me said they were going seventy miles an hour."

"I don't know, Dad." She was very aware that this was what people were saying. It hadn't been a random accident. Luke had been going much too fast.

"What would make kids do that?" he asked. "I can't understand it."

"Who knows what happened out there? I don't think there's much point in thinking about it."

"I'd like to know why kids would do something so crazy."

"Oh, you know kids. They never think about what they're doing, that they could get killed."

He said, "Luke wasn't that way. He wasn't a foolish boy."

"No, he wasn't," she said. She had noticed how her father went through phases each day. Mostly he was silent. Then he would become talkative, and want to discuss something or other. The discussions usually involved Luke, and ended in brooding silence, as it did now. He picked up a folded newspaper and began studying it intently.

"What's that you're reading?" she asked.

"Oh, I'm trying to do this crossword."

"I didn't know you did crosswords."

"I don't. I've never done one before in my life. What else is there to do?"

She picked up her knitting, and her mind settled into the rhythmic clacking of needles. She was faintly aware of the Muzak being piped into the room. The music you heard in dentist offices and at the end of a telephone when the gas company put you on hold. She heard dogs barking outside. The barking grew louder and began to grate on her nerves. She got up and stood at the window to see if she could tell where it was coming from. A dog had been left in a car. Its barking seemed to float out over the valley in a series of annoying yaps. The sun had disappeared behind clouds, and everything lay in shadow.

She noticed her father had dozed off, so she went to his bed and took the pen out of his hands so it wouldn't get ink all over the sheets. As she put the crossword on the bedside table, she looked at it. "Eased" was the only word he'd filled in. The clue was "disburdened." She leaned over him and very carefully removed his glasses, noticing the red indentations on his nose, and how his skin was so beautifully smooth, now such a lovely color of pink.

She took the elevator to the first floor and walked outside. The hospital was nestled up against the foot of the snow-capped mountains. The snow looked clean next to the blue, blue sky. People were still skiing up in those mountains. Below her the city extended way across the valley, stretching to the shores of the lake. A breeze came down out of the mountains, carrying an icy edge.

She sat down on a bench in a little patio area between two large hospital buildings. She could smell something like school lunch, and noticed a vent in the side of a nearby building and thought, That must be the hospital kitchen. Instantly she felt hungry, even though it hadn't been that long since she'd eaten. She was trying to diet, a perpetual struggle.

Inside her purse she found her cigarettes and a bundle of newspaper clippings. She lit a cigarette and took out the clippings. "Transplant Eases Pain for Family," said one headline. She shook her head. It seemed to her the family had no secrets left, no privacy.

Reporters had descended on the story with alarming aggressiveness. All they wanted was a good quote, the latest development. But how to communicate the tragedy? How to put it into words? All the reports seemed trivial and superficial. Luke's death and her father's subsequent ordeal had been totally raked over, exposed to readers turned voyeurs. New stories kept appearing with headlines that caught the eye: "Three Teens Killed in Auto Accident." "Idaho Man Better After Receiving Grandson's Heart." Helen sighed. The good part was that it was coming to an end. Her father would be going home soon. His recovery meant an end of the story as far as major papers were concerned, although she knew his ordeal would not be over once he left the hospital. Local reporters still managed to wring copy out of the situation. Today's headline was "Heart Patient Shows Progress."

She finished her cigarette and put the clippings back into her purse. The wind stirred her short hair. The lake in the distance looked like a sheet of tin. She was thinking of a sentence from one of the newspaper clippings: "It was by chance that the boy's heart size and blood type matched his grandfather's."

Chance.

There was an element of mysteriousness

in what had happened. She searched her brain for a word that would describe what she felt, and though she knew such a word existed, she couldn't find it. It was the unnameable. Life could change so quickly. Things happened without warning. Synchronicity was perhaps the only law governing the universe. It suited her as a math teacher to think this way.

But her father seemed so wounded. Physically he was doing beautifully, but spiritually he seemed to be suffering terribly from a mixture of guilt and pain. She didn't know what to do for him. It upset her to see him suffering so. A report in today's paper said her father was fine but "still grieving over his grandson's death." That didn't begin to describe what she saw on her father's face, day after day. It went beyond acute sorrow.

She wished she could say to him, This is one of those miracles, Dad. Something very improbable that you didn't ask for. It has this terrible side because Luke's dead. But there is this other part, your life. The *coincidence*. Rarely do life and death interconnect people so obviously or fit parts of families together so literally. But there you have it, it happened, as only it could in modern times, where we salvage organs, put our names on lists, and wait for a swift clean death to deliver a heart, eyes, kidneys, bits of healthy and precious tissue.

When she returned to her father's room, he was standing by the window, lifting his arms slowly over his head and lowering them, like a pilgrim paying obeisance to Mecca. The physical therapist, a young black girl with a quiet, unhurried manner about her, stood next to him, counting slowly. "Eight . . . nine . . . ten.

"That's good," she said. "Now let's try stretching your arms out to the side. Ready? You feel okay?"

Her father nodded, but Helen couldn't help noticing the beads of perspiration on his forehead, and how he hesitated before starting the next set of exercises, as if gathering up all his strength. It must hurt like hell, she thought. She could almost feel a painful pull across her own chest muscles as she watched him move his arms out to the side and slowly retract them. She imagined the new heart stitched in his chest, shrouded in bodily darkness. Luke's heart. The doctor had told her a remarkable thing: the heart had begun beating on its own the moment it had been sutured in place. There had been no need for any electrical stimulation, as there often was. Luke's heart had sprung to life without assistance, even though it had lain for hours in icy suspension. It was almost unfathomable that a detached organ should have such urgent, willful power. Like something out of science fiction. She could not help feeling that in her father's case, that willful heart carried with it the shadow of another being.

When her father had finished with his exercises, the therapist left the room and he returned to bed, seemingly exhausted by his efforts. He closed his eyes and she resumed her knitting.

Time passed so slowly here. Hospitals were the strangest places. Emotions ran so high. You could see it in the faces of people everywhere, in the hallways and the elevators, the looks of strain and concern, the muted glimpses of grief and heightened feeling. You saw it in the way people reached for each other's hands as an elevator descended, the way they looked at the floor as if trying to work through some particularly complicated emotion. You saw red eyes, and heard faint sighs and whispered snatches of doctors' reports. Groans and cries filtered out from behind closed doors, leaving you to imagine the suffering inside. It was all about death and illness, the failures of the flesh. Of course, there was the bright side, the healings and reconstructions. Still, two weeks here had left her feeling edgy and sad, and she was not sorry that this was her last day. Tonight she would be going home to Moscow.

Her father was awake and sitting up when Dr. Bowen arrived. He swept into the room, followed by two younger doctors, his manner that of a man who has many pressing appointments to keep.

"Well, how are you today, Phil?" he asked. "How are you doing? You look fine."

"Well, I feel better than I did a few days ago. The bloat has passed. For a while there, I couldn't, you know . . ."

"That's good. Each day you'll feel better. The physical therapy is going all right? Not too much pain?"

"Uh-uh," Phil said. He smoothed his hair back and fidgeted with the button that raised the bed until he was sitting up a little higher.

"Let me just listen." Dr. Bowen leaned over Phil and slid his stethoscope just inside his pajamas. He listened intently, his brows furrowed. The other doctors stood behind him, equally intent looks on their faces, as if they too were listening to something.

"Excellent," Dr. Bowen said, straightening up. "You're in very good shape considering what you've been through. Really. I don't know how it could be any better. You continue to show absolutely no signs of rejection, and of course now that possibility is quite unlikely."

"That's good," her father said quietly, looking down at his hands.

"When you have health, you have it all, don't you?"

Phil nodded without much enthusiasm.

"I would say you'll be able to do most things in a few months' time. You should be back to a pretty normal routine."

"Can I go back to work?"

"Not that, no, not for a while."

Phil looked disappointed.

"Listen, Phil. You're going to need a few months of rest. You're not going to be doing much. Just getting your strength back. By fall, you should feel quite normal."

"When will he be able to leave the hospital?" Helen asked.

"I should think by the end of the week." Dr. Bowen turned to Phil. "Have you thought about your living situation when you get out?"

"What do you mean?"

"It might be a good idea for you to stay with one of your daughters for a while. Not that you couldn't manage alone. I'm sure you could. But you might want the support of family."

Her father nodded, but he looked uncomfortable.

"Well, we'll talk more later," Dr. Bowen said, patting Phil's leg before he slipped out the door. As soon as he was gone, Phil picked up the paper with the crossword and held it up in front of his face. She could see him frowning — scowling, really — as if very troubled by something. She moved to his bedside and looked over his shoulder at the puzzle.

"I like crosswords," she said. "They always remind me of the pitfalls of looking at a thing in just one way."

"Well, here," he said, thrusting the paper toward her. "You do this."

"No, you go ahead. You're doing fine." She felt an unpleasant patronizing aspect to her words as she said this, and regretted the comment instantly, since she could see he'd made no further progress. "Eased" was still the only word he'd filled in. She felt a surge of love for him as she looked at the word. She'd always felt this kind of love for her father, even when she was a little girl. She trusted him because he was fair and kind. She had always felt his goodness, which amounted to a sort of naiveté, an openness that led to blind trust and faith in the world. He was so gentle, and it was as if this gentleness now worked against him because it made him more vulnerable to his terrible sorrow and guilt.

"What's the capital of the Maldives?" her father asked abruptly, jarring her out of her train of thought.

"What are the Maldives?"

"They must be islands, don't you think?" he asked. He held up the crossword. "Four letters . . . the capital of the Maldives."

"I've never heard of them."

"Aren't they near Africa?"

"Africa?"

"Yes. I believe I remember, now. I think they're off the coast of Africa. Do me a favor. When you get back to the house, look it up in the dictionary. The one on the shelf above your mother's desk."

Two years her mother had been dead. He still talked about her desk, her drawers, her closet.

"I don't think it would be in the dictionary," she said. "Don't you have an atlas?" Of course, she knew he did. Several of them. Different editions. That was his private passion, geography, and he had passed it on to Luke, who had loved the subject from the time he was small, and could recite, on request, the names of the countries in Africa, the height of the tallest mountain in the

144

world, the largest desert, the longest river. On paper, the world had been as familiar to him as his father's orchard. Pity he never actually saw any of it.

"Look in the back of the dictionary," her father said. "It will be there, in the gazetteer section." As if reading her mind, he added, "Luke would have known about the Maldives. Wouldn't he?"

"Yes," she said softly. "I think he would have given us the answer right away."

A look of pain crossed over her father's face that was almost intolerable to witness. He looked suddenly very, very tired, and she herself felt quite exhausted.

"I think I should go now, Dad."

"Col is coming for you tonight?" he said.

"Yes."

"Well, drive carefully going home, won't you?"

"Would you like to come up to Moscow and stay with us when you get out of here?"

"No, Helen, thank you, but I want to be in my own home. I've already decided. I want to go home."

"I'm sure you'll manage. You'll just have to be careful."

There was something else she wanted to say, but she couldn't think of how to put it exactly. It was about Luke. She knew if she opened her mouth and started to speak she would come out with something. But wasn't it better to leave it unsaid if she couldn't be precise and correct about what she wished to say? And it was impossible to be precise about something that was only a vague intimation of advice, a wish to comfort him somehow one more time, to encourage his optimism and discourage guilt. Crudely put, it was this thought: Don't feel bad about walking around with Luke's heart. It was just chance . . . synchronicity.

Instead, she said something quite simple. "I'm glad you're going to be well and strong again."

"Yes," he said. "Thank you."

She began gathering up her things, winding up the ball of yarn, organizing her magazines and books of poetry in her satchel. On impulse, she took out the book of poems by Joseph Brodsky she had been reading earlier. She wanted to give the book to her father, to offer him something in parting. It gave her pleasure to know her father shared her love of poetry, though they had not always liked the same poets. He preferred Frost and Whitman and Wordsworth, the old-fashioned poets, while she was inclined toward William Carlos Williams, and men like Brodsky, poets who caught the haunting tone of modern life.

She handed the book to him. "Here," she said, "I'll leave this with you. You might like these poems."

"Oh, thank you. And thank you, Helen, for being here with me."

"Goodbye, Dad. I'll call you tonight." She leaned over him, and he formed his lips into a small, moist kiss.

She drove through farm country where vast multitudes of starlings swept round in whirlwinds, narrow black flecks swirling around, then descending upon fields in clouds, like ash being shaken from the sky. God was great, but never greater than in nature. She disliked the word "God," yet found it came to mind more readily than other terms. Still, she wished to reject it, and so she rephrased her thought: Nature was great, but never greater than its infinite parts. That would do, at least for now. Driving up over the pass, she gazed at woods that were dark and dreamy and imagined spirits moving among the branches. She felt liberated after so many days in the hospital, pleased not to be returning there tomorrow, and happy at the thought she would see her husband and son quite soon.

Back at the house, she relaxed on the couch and listened to Mozart. The light in the room was beautiful, golden and soft. Much of the furniture had been made by her father — another of his hobbies — simple pieces, oak tables with clean lines, chairs with straight high backs and wide, functional arms. The house itself was a work of art. Some people could love houses, as she did this one. Others saw houses as real estate, things to be bartered for cash, a roof for the time of rain and sleep. This house had a great comforting presence for her. It was a beautiful place to retreat from the world, and she could understand perfectly well her father's wish to return to it. She was happy to be back in the house where she had grown up. It was lovely to be alone where everything was so familiar.

At dusk she went outside and walked down the narrow path that led through cottonwoods to the lake. Standing on the beach, which was marked by the tracks of geese, she turned and looked back at the house rising in the distance. The house had a stone foundation, a porch held up by solid stone pillars, and two great stone chimneys, all the work of her father. She could see how the smooth stonework reflected the light coming from across the lake. The full force of the sunset lit the stones, causing the two chimneys at the ends of the house to appear like towers from a fairytale, glowing rock edifices with a webbing of wooden rooms stretched between them. Who knew how to work with stone anymore? It was a lost art. The house was so unusual, purely the work of her father, whose buildings were marked by his craftsmanship.

When he'd become so sick, she had wondered who would get this house when he died. How could she and Joyce share it? The thought of selling it to strangers was impossible. But would either of them be able to live here? What would happen to it? Of course, now he wouldn't die. He would go on living in his handsome house, and she felt slightly embarrassed that she had imagined him dead before his time and begun to long for this house for herself.

It might have been her conceit, but Helen had always felt her father favored her a little over her sister, Joyce. She thought this, though there wasn't much proof of it. It could be nothing more than the evidence of the sibling rivalry that existed between them. She was not close to her sister, although she had been when they were young. From childhood they had gone their own ways. Joyce was a deeply religious person, while the best Helen could do was to muster occasional reverence for the animistic world, believing as she did that all life was produced by a spiritual force separate from matter, that natural phenomena and objects — rocks, trees, the wind — were alive and had souls. Joyce would have found this ridiculous: she happily subscribed to the notion of a singular, male God, dwelling in an orderly heaven. Religion was only one of their differences. Deeper schisms existed, which were usually glossed over in favor of the appearance of family harmony. In truth, there was nothing to connect them except the fact they had been born to the same parents. There were many women with whom she felt a sisterly alliance, but Joyce was not one of them. It produced a little sadness in her to realize the natural intimacy they had shared as children that might have allowed her to be more of a comfort to her sister now, was gone.

She thought of other things quite randomly, remembering the legends of the monster in the lake that had enlivened her imagination as a child. The Shoshone said there had been a great beast in the lake, but that it went away after the extinction of the buffalo. Early white settlers had seen the lake monster, too, and reported its head rose from the water, like a serpent; it had ears like bunches of grapes, and it swam much faster than a horse could run on land. Many afternoons as a child she had sat in this spot, studying the surface of the water, waiting for the monster to reveal itself so that she could add her name to the list of lake monster witnesses. Of course, it had never appeared.

She recalled how she had investigated every foot of this lakeshore as a child, hiding in thickets of willows while her name was called over and over by her mother. Her mother. People had found her terribly odd. She had such a strange and insistent brand of spirituality — mystical notions borrowed from Edgar Cayce, fervid spiritualism combined with more traditional Christianity, a predilection for séances, an obsession with health and natural cures. She remembered her own rejection of these things, how she had embraced the orderly world of science and math while still in grade school to counter the sometimes bizarre atmosphere at home. A grade school teacher named Mrs. Wahlquist had been exceptionally kind to her. She had once asked Helen, when she appeared in class one day with cloves of garlic strung around her neck, why her mother had made her wear this. It's for my cold, she had said, blushing. Mrs. Wahlquist had gently asked if she wished to leave the garlic in her desk during school hours, and she had nodded with relief, grateful for such understanding.

She thought of the long rides on crowded school buses with narrow aisles, the cold walks home over snowy roads with the wind driving against her legs. Her memories evoked a feeling of harsh, endless winters, cold so bitter it burned her lungs, and the smell of food when she entered the house. She would go immediately to the kitchen to find the consoling warmth of steaming pots and pans, and cookies in the shapes of animals. Escaping the cruel boys who taunted fat girls, comforting herself with food. Always it was food, beautiful food, that made her feel she was home and safe and loved.

She thought of porcupines.

In scouting class, Mrs. Borden had told them that if they ever got stuck in the wilderness, they could always survive by eating porcupines. They were slow and easy to catch. "Hold the porcupine down with a big stick," Mrs. Borden had said, "and press on the small bone between its eyes. The bone punctures the brain and causes instant death." Scout leaders believed girls capable of this delicate killing, but Helen knew such things were really the natural province of boys, who needed no knowledge of bones between the eyes, only a stick big enough for a club. In high school the boys bragged of going out at night, driving dark mountain roads that led to Kemmerer and Evanston or Soda Springs, traveling as much as 250 miles in one night, all the while watching the road for the sluggish porcupines to show up in the headlights so they could spring from the car and club them to death. The same boys called her fatty pants, thunder thighs, lard ass.

Coming home did this to you, she thought. It reminded you of all sorts of things.

The wind shifted over the lake. The water had changed color in the time she'd been standing there, turning from bottle-green to midnight-blue. That was the thing about this lake. It was forever changing, constantly shifting in color, a condition that had to do with a tiny crustacean living in its depths.

In many ways, her mother had been the most ordinary of women, a devoted mother and wife who was forever inventing games for her children, cutting animals out of plywood and painting them, making puppets for herself and Joyce and then scripting little shows. The same imagination that allowed her to believe she might contact a spirit in a séance could infuse an elaborate make-believe game with her children. She had been grateful to both of her parents for many things, but especially for this: neither of them apparently felt the need to replicate themselves and create children who thought as they did. She had always felt free to go her own way.

Her mother's death had been painful and difficult, a horrible bout with cancer. She remembered the time she came home to help her father care for her mother following her first round of chemotherapy. Her mother had been so weak. She remembered helping her shower one morning. She hadn't actually gotten into the shower with her but stood just outside the stall and ended up getting wet anyway. She supported her mother and rubbed a soapy cloth over her shoulders and back. The beauty and youthfulness of her mother's breasts had surprised her, and she'd never forgotten the way they looked.

Later in the week her mother had seemed stronger, and she'd decided to plan a little picnic for her. She invited Belle and Jack and the Vawdreys, old family friends. From the beginning, her father didn't think the picnic was a good idea. He had tried to tell her that. Her mother wasn't well enough, he kept saying. But she felt the fresh air and a festive little event would lift her mother's spirits.

It turned out her father was right. The picnic hadn't been festive at all. Her mother was anxious, afraid of becoming sick. Belle

and Jack ended up talking about their grown
son, who had recently died of a heart attack.
The Vawdreys had been involved in a car
accident the week before, and though they
themselves were unhurt, they had seen two
people die. All these stories were told slowly,
and they were full of unpleasant details. Everyone seemed stunned or sick or grieving.
Afterward her mother suffered a relapse and
seemed much worse. For a long time, whenever she thought of the picnic, she wondered
how she could ever have had such a bad
idea.

The sun had set, and she realized she was
growing a little stiff with the chill. Slowly,
she started back up the path, still thinking
about her mother. Much later, long after
dark had fallen, she remembered the Mal-
dives. She went to the desk and took down
the dictionary. Then she called her father.
"Were you asleep?" she asked.
"No. Not yet."
"The Maldives are south of the Laccadives
in the Indian Ocean."
"What's that?"
"The Maldives — "
"Oh, right."
"You were asleep, weren't you?"
"No, just dozing."

"Go back to sleep, Dad. I'll call tomorrow."

"All I do is sleep."

She looked out the window and saw headlights coming down the lane. Col and Philly.

"Where did you say the Maldives are?"

"They're islands in the middle of the Indian Ocean. I'm afraid they're not very close to Africa."

"Oh, well. It was just a guess. What's the capital?"

"Male," she said.

"Mail? Like airmail?"

"No. Like male of the species."

"Are Col and Philly there yet?"

She looked at the headlights growing closer. No one came down the long lane unless he was headed for her father's house. "They're just arriving," she said.

"You'll check to see that everything's turned off. The stove, appliances, all the lights . . ."

"Yes, Dad. Don't worry. Your house will still be here when you arrive. And Dad . . . it looks so beautiful. I . . . I just want you to know that."

"Drive safely," he said.

"Good night, Dad."

Col kissed her when he came through the door. His breath smelled of beer and corn chips. Philly, who had been sleeping in the backseat, woke up when she opened the car door. She saw his plump face, peaceful with sleep, and reached down to ruffle his hair.

"Go back to sleep, honey," she said. "We're leaving right now." She would have preferred to spend the night, but Col had a class the next day.

There was no moon as they drove away from the house. A blackness of inky depth, a satiny, foggy darkness, covered the land. The lights of the car were as solitary and insubstantial as candle flames in a gigantic temple. She sat behind the wheel and headed the car down the lane, moving away from her father's darkened house, bumping over rutted earth. Just before she reached the highway, she saw it.

A porcupine waddled out of the cattails.

She hit the brakes to avoid running over him, and for a moment he stood frozen in the headlights. His eyes glittered like fluorescent green marbles. Huge and unmoving, he seemed mysteriously transfixed. His head moved from side to side, as if he were trying to peer beyond the beams. Then slowly he began moving again, his spines rolling on his loose skin; he became an undulating silvery ball, a penumbra of light.

The sight of the porcupine thrilled her.

It was as if she had conjured up the animal by having so recently thought of him. She saw how impossible it was not to believe in something, to subscribe to some kind of spiritual thinking, even if it was simply animistic, or dressed up as scientific principle, like synchronicity, the truest principle in the universe. Was it also perhaps one of the most religious? The porcupine waddled off into the darkness, leaving her with a feeling of having been visited by a small wonder.

8

By the time Wendall and Louise reached Los Angeles, all the windows facing west in the city were lit by the golden sunset. They took a room at the Mayan, a horseshoe-shaped motel near downtown, and left the truck parked on a side street. Each room was a separate little adobe unit with a kitchenette, facing a courtyard where plastic roses had been wired to live bushes. A small patch of lawn, filled with curling tendrils of devil's-weed and crabgrass, separated each of the units. Across the street stood a little white church with a pink neon heart sitting atop its spire. Next to it was a prayer garden where a life-size statue of Christ had been enclosed in a glass-fronted case. His arms extended toward the passing traffic in a gesture of all-embracing love.

Wendall unlocked the door to the room and stood aside for her to enter. She smelled ammonia and stale cigarettes. Immediately he went to the television mounted on the wall and turned it on. Then he folded back the covers on the bed and propped the pillows up into a pile. Without speaking a word to her or glancing in her direction, he disappeared into the bathroom, and she heard the sound of water being run into the tub. He was doing all this for her, she knew. She sat down on the edge of the king-size bed, which took up most of the space in the room.

On the television screen in front of her, an elephant charged down a dusty path, heading straight toward her, growing larger and larger. The huge ears of the elephant flapped like wings as he ran. It seemed like the elephant was going to run right out of the picture. As it came closer, she could see the way its tusks disappeared into its face, enfolded by many layers of wrinkles. They looked like huge toothpicks holding back the corners of its mouth into a perpetual smile. The elephant stopped in front of the camera, moving from side to side, lifting first one front foot off the ground and then the other, curling and uncurling the tip of its trunk. Quite unconsciously, she began swaying slightly too, rocking gently from side to side, while staring up at the single beautiful eye the elephant had turned to the camera.

"What are you doing?" He put his hand on her shoulder, and she stopped swaying.

She brought her fingers, decorated with flaking red polish, to her lips and said,

"Watching the elephant."

"Don't you want to take a bath?"

She nodded, keeping her eyes fixed on the screen, where now people were standing in front of a huge pile of tusks — a mountain of ivory, as the narrator called it. One man was sprinkling kerosene around the base of the pile, shaking the liquid out of a can as if throwing grain to chickens. Another man lit a torch and moved quickly from place to place, touching the flame to the ivory. She didn't see how ivory could possibly burn, something so hard, like stone. But it did. The flames took off, licking up the pile, devouring the beautiful tusks in a swirling inferno.

"Come on, then," he said, and lifted her arms, pulling her sweater over her head.

"The curtains," she said, indicating the window, where the drapes were open. The little neon heart atop the Superet Light Church glowed cheerfully against a pale ocher sky.

While he closed the drapes, she stood up and stepped out of her jeans. In the mirror attached to the small dresser beneath the TV, she saw how her stomach had begun to bow out slightly, making a curve that had the same shape as her rump. She caught him staring at her.

"What you haven't told me," he said, "is how far along you are."

"About three months."

He nodded. His face looked very tired.

"You'd better check on the tub. I'll go out and get us something to eat."

"Wendall?"

"What?" He stood with his hand firmly on the door knob, waiting. She wanted to say "I love you," but it wasn't true, and she knew it wasn't. What she felt was something else, not love but gratitude that someone, anyone, would care for her this way.

"Get some ice cream, please," she said.

He started to leave and then stopped and faced her. "When are you going to . . . ?"

"Tomorrow," she said, understanding what he meant.

"Do you need me to go with you?"

"Oh, no. I'll be fine. I can call a taxi." She tried to sound cheerful and confident, as if she felt less frightened than she did. She made it sound as though she took taxis every day.

The next morning, he left the motel early and drove to Compton to deliver a load of liquid fertilizer. Before he left the room, he put a neatly folded stack of bills in her purse. When she had showered and dressed, she

162

consulted the Yellow Pages and began making phone calls, dialing the number for one clinic after another until she found the cheapest rate. She phoned for a cab and went outside to wait, standing on the sidewalk not far from where a group of people were waiting for a bus.

She had never been in a city before. The first thing she noticed was the strange light, how it flattened everything out. The sky was white, not blue. An acrid, unpleasant odor, like the smell of burning rubber, hung on the air. When she stepped to the curb and looked down the wide street, distant buildings dissolved into a haze of yellowish-gray smog. She was alarmed to see a black man walking up to her.

"Want to buy a watch?" he asked. He held up a gold watch on two fingers. The underside of his fingers were a surprising color of pink.

"No," she stammered. He shrugged and strutted away, his hips moving like a woman's. A little breeze came up, and hot air blew over her face. An old woman with dark skin, her head covered with a shawl, stopped at the gates of the prayer garden across the street, looked up at the figure of Christ, crossed herself, and then turned and walked on. Everyone around her was dark-skinned — black or Mexican. She began to be a little frightened. She felt very out of place.

She retreated to the shade of a small tree growing out of a hole in the sidewalk near the entrance to the motel, grateful to be out of the heat of the sun. But the shade offered little relief. The sun didn't seem to shine down directly. Light came from all directions with an intense brightness. Even the sidewalk seemed to radiate heat and light. She began to worry the taxi wasn't going to show up. At the bus stop, a man touched the arm of the woman he was with and pointed to something. The woman began laughing. Louise stepped forward and saw he was pointing to a billboard that showed a picture of an ordinary shopping cart. Above it were the words "Thou Shalt Not Steal." Someone had scrawled the word "survival" across the billboard in bright red letters.

She stared at the billboard for a long time, unable to comprehend what it meant. Everything seemed alarmingly foreign, as if you had to live here in order to understand anything. Then a homeless person rounded the corner, an old woman dressed in heavy layers of torn and dirty clothes, pushing a cart from which hung numerous plastic bags, and quite suddenly the meaning of the billboard became perfectly clear to her.

The taxi finally came for her at quarter to eleven. The driver was black, with long ropes of matted hair that stuck out from beneath a knitted hat. He sat on a mat made out of wooden beads, which looked very strange and uncomfortable. The taxi itself was a green-and-white station wagon with a hard, flat backseat that seemed enormous to her. Although she had never been in a taxi before, she knew enough to get into the back, not the front, seat.

"Where to?" the driver asked without turning around.

"Vermont," she said, and gave him the address.

"You talkin' down by USC, da Coliseum, dat area."

Whatever he had said, she didn't understand it. In any case, it didn't seem to matter, as he pulled out into the traffic so quickly the tires made a little squealing sound.

They passed a park where a group of men were kicking a black-and-white ball around on the grass. Couples were stretched out on the grass beneath palm trees whose trunks reminded her of the legs of the elephant she'd seen on TV the night before. She wished she could stop in the park where it looked so cool. It was hot in the cab. She rolled down her window and felt a blast of warm, metallic air. The street was clogged with traffic and the cab moved slowly from one traffic signal to the next. The silence in the cab felt awkward. She decided to try talking with the driver.

"What's that thing you're sitting on?" she said. "That thing with all the wooden beads?"

"Dis? Dis is for my back. You don't think my butt gits tired sitting here all day long you think again." His voice had a singsong quality that fascinated her. She wanted him to talk some more, but he didn't, and she couldn't think of anything else to say to him.

She stared out the window, looking at the people moving briskly down the sidewalk, gazing at passing stores. All the buildings were one- or two-story and looked drab. Grafitti were scrawled everywhere, on the sides of buildings, high up on billboards, even on the smooth gray bark of trees lining the sidewalks, words that were totally indecipherable, like a foreign language. What an ugly place this was. Trash had accumulated in gutters and blown up against buildings and fences. Again she was struck by the fact there didn't seem to be any white people on the street. Everyone looked Mexican. Everyone had kids, two or three at least, and the women wore bright colors, their black hair shining like the feathers on crows.

Soon, however, they turned a corner and a few blocks later everything changed. Now everyone looked Oriental and all the signs on the stores were written in squiggly characters. Still farther along the same street, things changed again, and soon they were surrounded by black people, children playing in yards where wash had been draped on the chain-link fencing, and old people sitting silently in overstuffed chairs on shady porches. A group of boys with the sides of their heads shaved so that the hair on top stood up like birthday cake were shoving each other and fooling around in front of a store with thick black bars on the windows. The cab soon pulled into a small parking lot in front of a little L-shaped cluster of stores.

"Dis it?" the driver asked.

Louise quickly scanned the row of stores — a doughnut shop and dry cleaners, a video store and a place that sold tacos. At the very end, next to the cleaners, she saw the Vermont Medical Center, a small storefront with blinds covering the windows. She felt instantly uneasy.

"How do I get a cab to come get me?" she asked, giving the driver the money she owed him.

He handed her a card. "Call dat number."

Once inside the clinic, she found herself in a small, poorly lit waiting room, no bigger than the room at the motel. It felt even smaller because it was crowded with folding chairs, set in rows facing the front. A few people sat spaced out on the chairs. All the faces in the room turned to look at her as she walked in. There was a smell of rubbing alcohol, as well as something much more unpleasant, like spoiled meat. She approached the receptionist and waited in a line, standing behind an elderly black man on crutches.

She could hear a woman arguing at the front of the line. "That *is* covered by Medicaid!" she yelled.

"No," the receptionist said in a voice so controlled it sounded mechanical and dull, "it isn't. It would be covered by Medical, not Medicaid, but you don't have Medical — "

The woman said, "Oh, fuck this!" and grabbed a little boy standing next to her and hoisted him up on her hip. She started for the door and then stopped and yelled back, "Hell's gonna freeze over before you get a dime outta me!"

The old man in front of Louise shook his head, leaning heavily on his crutches, then he looked down at her and in a voice liquid and gentle said, "We all got problems, don't we?" The whites of his eyes were yellow, the color of pale daffodils. "Don't mean we shouldn't be po-lite, though, does it?"

Louise said, "No," and felt some deep inexplicable pleasure in simply having been spoken to so kindly.

She waited a long time for her name to be called, an hour, maybe more, during which time she filled out a form, paid the receptionist the money, and read a tattered copy of *Parenting* magazine. There was no clock and no sense of time in the little clinic, where even the shifting light of day had been blocked out by the blinds over the windows. It was like no place she had ever been. For one thing, she had never before been the only white person in a room.

She recalled something her stepfather used to say to her whenever she had made a mistake or done something wrong, causing his temper to erupt. He would yell at her, "Act like a white person, for godsakes!"

She had never understood what that meant. Exactly what was she supposed to do differently? At the time she had imagined white people were naturally endowed with something that — although she was white — she had missed out on. Some sense of propriety, an innate understanding of what constituted correct behavior. But what this didn't take into account was all the accidents in the world. How could even a white person avoid accidents? For that was when he yelled at her, when a glass of milk slipped from her hand and spilled on the floor, or when she fell, tumbling in the dirt and soiling her clothes. What terrible bullshit he'd unloaded on her.

A small child crawled up on her lap, a little boy with beautiful eyes and skin the color of hot chocolate. She touched his woolly head and smiled at him before his mother called him back to her side. For a long while, she could feel the almost magical sensation of that touch on her palm.

When her name was called, she was led into a hallway, not a room but a hallway, where there was a lot of human traffic going back and forth in front of her. Blood was taken, and a quick medical history. She had already given her age as eighteen, something that she herself almost believed now. The procedure was explained to her. She was told what to expect. Finally, she was taken to a room where she undressed and lay down on a table, fitting her feet into the cold metal stirrups, and covered herself with a thin paper sheet.

She waited, but no one came. She began

to feel very chilled. The bare walls seemed to emanate coldness. The longer she waited, the more anxious she became. Goose bumps emerged on her skin, which looked bluish and sick in the harsh light. Her heart felt brittle, as if frozen in a meat locker. The nausea and the depression that had worn her down for days now caused her to feel weak and dull. She wondered, when it was finally over, would she feel better immediately? Or would it take days to regain her strength and appetite? She hoped they would give her something, some drug to obliterate her surroundings and the anxiety she felt. If they didn't offer, she would ask for something. She wanted to feel nothing. Nothing at all.

The doctor, when he arrived, took her arm and rubbed his large, smooth hand over her skin. He peered into her face and told her his name: Dr. Small. She thought it inappropriate, since he was a large black man, rather potbellied. He had the face of a sad little mole. While he set about making his preparations, wheeling a small machine into position at her feet, a nurse entered the room and gave her a shot. The doctor explained that it was Valium and it would relax her for the procedure, which he said would last only a few minutes. The nurse stayed at her side, and she felt the light touch of her fingers against the crown of her head, as if someone had placed a little cap there.

The world suddenly softened. She felt herself becoming lighter. Everything began to feel better. She was suffused with feelings of warmth toward the doctor and nurse. She smiled at them and said, "I feel fine now," and they smiled back at her and nodded.

A coldness entered her and she heard the sound of a machine starting up, felt a small twinge of pain, and then another, sharper this time. She stared at the ceiling, where she could see a reflection of herself in the metal cone of the overhead lamp. Her face distorted into a gigantic nose and mouth with tiny eyes and ears, and she smiled up at this looming, gross self, so comic in its ugliness.

She thought of Wendall, who was somewhere not so very far away, probably now finished with unloading his cargo of fertilizer, and she wished that she could have more feeling for him than she did. But when she thought of him it was completely without passion or desire. Instead she felt something that made her feel uncomfortable, which was a sense of obligation, as if she had incurred a debt that would sooner or later begin to bother her. Again she felt pain, this time a sharp, gut-clutching pain, and her mouth opened wide with the shock of it, though she made no sound. Great horse-sized teeth gleamed back at her from the metal cone. She tried to remove her mind to some distant place. Though she had vowed not to think of Larry again, she found herself picturing him, sitting behind the wheel of the Nuts to You van, his loose black hair blowing back from his radiant face. *Don't think of this.*

The machine stopped and a quiet descended in the room. The nurse leaned over and smiled sadly into her face. "It's all over," she said.

The doctor touched her leg, cradling her calf in his palm. "Okay?" he said. "Do you feel all right?" His voice came from far, far away, echoing out of a tunnel.

"Yes," she said, and her tongue felt thick.

"You stay here and rest for a few minutes. The nurse will come back in and tell you when you can get dressed. Do you have someone to drive you home?"

"Yes." 382-7000. Green and White Cab Company. For safety, she had memorized the number. They left the room and she closed her eyes.

She is riding through the fields, trotting

past the bay horse standing with his rump to the wind, his tail blowing through his legs along his belly. The horse beneath her thighs is Lady, an old roan, but willing, and the animal she loves most in the world. Black-and-red-winged plant bugs drift on the air, flying between cottonwoods. She passes a deserted farm with a tangled orchard, the broken windows of the house forming black holes. Soon she's among junipers and cedars, climbing into the hills, with the silky tufted buds brushing her legs. On the benchland, now covered with tender shoots of spring grass, she stops to let Lady graze.

The sky is gray and grave, grained with stippling clouds, bales of clouds broken by slanting flutes, like snowdrifts. She sees down the canyon a valley of small farms, patches of yellow and brown and green, a silver thread of a river, and the spumes of steam rising from the refinery at the base of the far hills. Lady grazes, and she lolls in the saddle, her weight thrown to one side, one knee hooked over the horn. Each time the horse jerks up a mouthful of grass in her teeth, the saddle twitches, and the flowing red mane shudders slightly, like a woman tossing her hair. A fat horsefly lands on Lady's withers and she slaps it dead, wiping the remains of the blood-engorged insect off her hand on the edge of the saddle blanket.

They stay up on the bench until the sun goes down and a chill rides her spine. Coming down the canyon, she startles a mule deer — a buck with the furred growth of antlers between his floppy ears, which swing wildly as he bounds through the brush. When she comes to the flat stretch of dirt road, she gathers up the reins, shortening them in her hands. She pushes deeper into the saddle and squeezes her knees against the leather, and says, "Now!" although the horse already knows, knows as she always does, that they will gallop this last stretch home. She touches her heels to Lady's sides, but the horse has already begun to hop, bunching up her hindquarters, leaping forward against the bit, and soon they have settled into the drumming gait of a gallop, flying down the lane between Lombardy poplars, past fence posts rotten with age, the red mane flowing, and she feels the lift and lightness of speed as the horse ripples beneath her and the ride is more beautiful than she could ever tell.

"You can get up now," the nurse said.

She swung her legs over the side of the table and slid down to the floor, as if dismounting from a saddle.

He was lying on the bed when she returned to the motel room, his hands propped behind his head, watching Phil Donahue, who was saying, "that's fine in theory but it's only in theory what does it really feel like to wake up one morning and find . . ."

"Jesus," he said as she walked in. "I'm glad you're back. I was beginning to worry about you. Did . . . did you . . . ?"

She nodded. The drug had not yet worn off, and she felt light crossing the room, as if her real self hovered slightly above her, preceding her as she moved toward the bed.

"Did it hurt?"

"I need to sleep for a while," she said. "I feel so tired." She lay down on top of the covers and closed her eyes. A moment later, she felt him removing her shoes, undoing her Levi's, peeling them down over her feet. He folded half of the bedspread back over her and lay down next to her, stroking her hair. "Thank you," she murmured, and drifted off to the sound of wailing sirens.

She awoke to a darkened room and for a moment could not remember where she was.

She felt alone and disoriented and sat up quickly. "Wendall?"

He switched on the lamp beside the bed.

"I didn't mean to sleep so long."

"You needed it," he said. "Now you're probably hungry, aren't you?"

"I want to see the ocean," she said. "Will you take me to see the ocean?"

"But it's dark already. We'll go tomorrow," he said.

In the morning, she felt much better, almost as if nothing had happened to her. They drove for what seemed like a very long time down a straight wide boulevard lined with tall buildings, and then smaller ones, until it was clear the ocean must not be far away. The air became abruptly fresher and full of mist. Sitting high in the cab of the truck, she spied it long before they reached the coastline, a great bulge of blue water that seemed to rise up to a horizon dotted with the bright clean crests of whitecaps. It wasn't easy finding a place to park the rig. Finally they found a spot at a curb in a residential area a few blocks from the beach. He said they couldn't stay long, because he had a pickup in Pacoima. She said it didn't matter to her how long they stayed. She just wanted to walk down to the water.

She plodded across the sand, her eyes lifted, moving toward the water like a pilgrim heading toward a holy site. There it was, the endless, unbounded Pacific, the ocean on which her father had ridden on a big ship, standing on a deck at night, looking down on the stars hugging the watery horizon. It didn't matter to her that she couldn't see the arc of the earth as she gazed out over the water, though she had rather expected that she might, or that a band of yellowish-brown smog crowned the skyline instead of stars.

When she reached the hard, wet band of sand where the surf rolled in and receded, she knelt down, picked up a handful of pebbles and sand, and smelled it. Taking off her shoes, she moved closer to the water, not minding that the surf wetted the legs of her Levi's, feeling rather exhilarated by the brisk chill of the water. Rubbery ropes of kelp, the color of cat's eyes, with nubbly, fleshy leaves, floated in on slick green watery tongues, edged in brown foam. She saw the way the water rose in a glassy swell, building to a bulging wave that curled over on itself and sent a great comma of water rushing down, spiraling along a pipeline that flattened out by the time it reached the sand, spreading out into a thick spume of froth. For some time, she simply watched the movement of the water. It felt so remarkable, so beautiful, to actually be standing at the edge of the ocean she'd dreamed of seeing for so long that she noticed none of the minor defects — did not even see the sign posted at the water's edge: "Warning: Beach Temporarily Closed to Swimming Due to Contamination." She saw only the arch and swell of the indigo water and the endless bouncing surface of the beautiful sea, which would forever and ever be associated with the man who had once sent messages to distant shores from a boat floating on its surface so very long ago, and who stood with her here now, sentient behind the thin walls of her being.

Wendall came and stood behind her, enfolding her with his arms. She broke free and picked up a shell — black on one side, iridescent on the other.

"Well, honey," he said, "there it is, the ocean. Are you happy now?"

She smiled and gazed down the coastline, where she could see a little peninsula jutting out into the water, a faint ridge of blue land. Maybe that was Mexico.

"Which way is Mexico?"

He pointed left, down the beach. "That way," he said. "Why?"

"I'd like to go to Mexico. I wonder what

it would be like?"

"Dirty," he said, "and poor."

"Wouldn't you like to go to Mexico?"

"I think I'd rather be in Pocatello." He took hold of her hand. She looked paler than ever, with blue circles under her eyes. "Had enough?" he asked.

"No," she said. "I don't think I could ever get enough of this." She tipped her head back and took a long inhalation of sea air, beautifully tart and fishy.

"Come on, he said. "We've got a long ways to go."

She picked up her shoes and let herself be led across the deep sandy expanse lying between the water and the brown fluted cliffs, feeling even then the way the sea surged and receded behind her like a lover breathing on her back.

PART TWO

AUTUMN

1

Phil sat at his kitchen table, looking out the window to the west where clots of clouds had gathered over the mountains. A letter lay on the table in front of him. Other papers were scattered around, a bank statement, bills, the new Spiegel catalogue. He looked down at the letter, an invitation to visit his cousin in Florida. He had no intention of accepting the invitation and had, this morning, been trying to write a reply, but without success. As usual, he was daydreaming, staring at a stand of maples behind the garage, noticing their brilliant change of color.

The clock on the wall said ten. He figured it was a good time to call. The breakfast crowd would have thinned out. He took a deep breath, picked up the phone, and dialed Millie's Cafe. She answered in a pleasant voice.

"Hello, Leora?" he said.

For a moment, there was silence. "It's you," she said.

"I was wondering if you'd like to go on a picnic tomorrow?"

"A picnic?"

"I thought we might drive up toward Lava Hot Springs and head up one of the canyons. The leaves should be beautiful up there." If she said no, he'd take his shotgun and go out alone. Dove season had opened last weekend, although he'd heard from Lars, his dentist friend, that the hunting was pretty poor. He didn't really care much about the hunting, whether it was good or bad. He just wanted to get out. It had been so long since he'd left the place, if you didn't count the furtive trips to Stinson's Market on Monday mornings when it was sure to be dead in town.

"It sounds nice, a picnic, but I'm supposed to work tomorrow. Maybe I could trade days with someone."

"I'll take care of the food," he said.

"Let me talk to Mary. Hang up. I'll call you right back."

He hung up the phone and waited. The petaled heads of daisies trembled in the wind in the garden outside. Of all the flowers, they had lasted the longest, the ordinary daisies. The asters were spent, the roses gone, the hollyhocks and sunflowers dried to brown sticks. It was hard to believe a whole new season had arrived. For months, he had been alone, protected from intruders by the acres of farmland that bordered his property. He thought of a line from the book of poems Helen had given him: *In winter it darkens the moment lunch is over, it's hard then to tell starving men from sated.* Was he the starving man or the sated?

The phone rang out in the quiet room.

"Mary will work for me tomorrow," she said.

"Good. I'm glad you can go."

"I thought perhaps you'd gone to Moscow. Somebody said they thought you'd gone up there to stay with your daughter."

"No, I haven't been anywhere."

"I've called, but I never get an answer. I was certain you'd — "

"I've been busy outside," he said. "I often don't hear the phone."

"It's been so long."

"Yes, I know."

"Don't you want me to bring something for the picnic?"

"No, I'll take care of it. I have something in mind."

"How about a pie? I could at least make a pie."

"All right. You make a pie."

"Do you want me to drive?"

"No, I'll come by for you about noon."

"Is it all right for you to drive now?"

"It's fine," he said. "I'll see you tomorrow."

He sat for a while after he'd hung up the phone. Then he went downstairs and got his 12-gauge, stuffing his pockets with shells.

The thing about doves, he thought to himself, plodding through the wheat fields at sunset, is they were hardly worth the effort. He could feel the warmth of their tiny bodies lying against his kidneys, nestled in the pouch at the back of his hunting jacket. Eight of them. By the time he had cleaned them, he'd have sixteen little half-breasts, no bigger than plums, and that was if he hadn't ruined any meat with shot. Still, he couldn't help feeling pleased, as he brushed through the stubbled fields, that he'd managed to get as many as he had. It had been a long time since he'd hunted doves, in exactly this place. . . .

Luke, eleven years old, carrying the new .410, trudges beside him, tired after hours in the fields. It's clear he's bored and wants to quit. They haven't seen a single dove. Lars says, "Come on, boy, you've got to work for doves, they don't fall out of the sky for you, you know," and Luke shakes his head. He stops near an old shed and some abandoned corrals and says, "Go ahead, I'm tired, I'll stay here with Beanie."

The dog is still a pup, no more than six months old. She may turn into a hunter later, but for now she's useless to them — in fact, worse than useless, she's a nuisance, ranging too far, banging through fields way ahead of them. Phil doesn't mind leaving them behind to rest beside the shed, and Lars seems downright relieved they can get down to some serious dove hunting without the boy and the uncontrollable pup.

He and Lars head for the wheat fields and tromp around for over an hour. In the distance, he can hear the sound of gunshots, and he thinks it must be Luke, wasting shells. Although they get a few shots off, they return empty-handed to the place where they've left the boy and the dog. As they walk up to him, they can see Luke is smiling, and he begins shouting to them, pointing to the ground beside him. It sounds like he's saying, "I got twenty!" And then they see the pile of doves at his feet. Twenty of them, twice the limit.

"Jesus Christ," Lars says, "where did those come from?"

"They fell outta the sky," the boy says, grinning at him.

"Like hell," Lars said. "They look shot to me. Who shot them?"

"I did," Luke says, beaming at him. "I shot every one of them."

They have to divide up the birds between them to carry them back to the car so they won't get fined if they see a game warden. All the way home in the truck Lars is muttering how he can't understand it. How in the hell had Luke hit all those doves, a boy of eleven, just starting to hunt? Doves were about the smallest thing you could think of shooting, and they flew fast, much faster than pheasant or grouse.

"Skunked," Lars says. "We get skunked with our 12-gauges and he gets twenty birds with a .410. That kid's either a hell of a shot or he knows something we don't," Lars says as he drops them at the house. Luke laughs, and can hardly contain his look of pride. "Next time," Lars calls to him as he drives away, "I stick with you instead of your grandpa!"

It isn't until later, when they are feasting on the doves, which May has cooked in a sauce of red wine and rosemary, that Luke tells him how he did it. Their shots in the wheat fields had sent the doves into the open, where they had flown to some telephone wires near the shed and landed. He had sat on the ground and picked them off the wires, sometimes hitting two with one shot. Doves kept flying out of the wheat fields and landing on the wires, and he kept shooting them until no more doves came. Beanie had fetched the fallen doves and brought them to him.

Though Phil is amused to discover the truth, he feels compelled to tell the boy, right then and there, that it's the last time he wants him to kill a bird that way. If he's going to be a hunter, he has to understand the rules of the sport. No shooting birds on the ground, and no shooting sitting birds. "You have to take them on the wing," he tells him. "It's the only way." He never tells Lars the story of how Luke got the doves. It amuses him too much to think of Lars' face as he drove away, and he wants him to go on believing his grandson is an exceptional shot.

He cut into the birds, dislodging the plump breasts with his knife, rinsing them under the running water in the kitchen sink. This was the difficult part. It took away from the excitement of hunting and the anticipated pleasure of eating a bird to know you had to clean it, becoming more familiar with the insides of the creatures than you really cared to in order to retrieve the little bit of breast they offered up. Yet this was part of it, though he felt rusty and clumsy with the knife. He inserted his fingers into the small cavity and drew out organs, including a tiny crimson knob he knew to be the heart. He held it briefly between his thumb and fore-finger, studying it, then dropped it into the sink. When he had finished cleaning the birds, he had thirteen little pieces of purple meat laid out on the wax paper beside the sink. One and a half breasts had been ruined, shredded with shot.

He floured the breasts and sauteed them with garlic, onion, and fresh rosemary, then added wine and left them to simmer on top of the stove while he made potato salad, using new potatoes gathered from the garden. The kitchen was soon filled with a wonderful smell. While he worked, he sipped from a tumbler of scotch and listened to the radio, a classical station from Boise whose announcer had a soothing, crooning voice. He didn't know the names of composers but he knew what he liked and didn't like. The piece he listened to moved him deeply, music created by a single instrument that produced the most hauntingly beautiful sound, pathetic and noble. The music played on him, pulling his emotions to the surface. "That was Janos Starker," the announcer said at the end of the piece, "playing Bach's Suite No. 1 in G for the unaccompanied cello."

It's possible, he thought, for some people to make something very beautiful out of the unaccompanied, although it didn't seem to work that way with life, where humans needed company. He was glad he'd decided on the picnic, after days of brooding about it. He wanted to talk to her.

In the basement, way back in the cellar, he found the picnic basket, so long unused the dust was thick on the wicker and small dried potato bugs rolled around inside. He sat down on a bench beneath the single bulb dangling from the ceiling and cleaned the basket with a damp rag. The stone walls gave off a chill. The room smelled moist and weedy, like a mountain stream. Bottles of fruit sat on shelves, golden peaches, ruby cherries, pale pears, their colors muted beneath a layer of dust. There was sawdust on the floor, left over from his last carpentry project, a butcher-block table never finished. In the corner, forming a little pyramid, stood some of Luke's things — a pair of skis and some poles he'd stored there, his old .22 rifle, and a fishing rod he'd outgrown.

The sight of these things disturbed him.

He was troubled by a sensation that something of Luke existed within him, some part that hadn't been dislodged from the boy's heart. He sat very still, surrounded by the dankness in the shadowy basement, and felt it, his new heart beating strong. He knew this heart occupied him as if a place had been carved out for it that would never again be wholly integrated with the rest of him. The center of his being was borrowed, and at certain times, like just now, it radiated slightly with a feeling of separateness.

Upstairs, he packed the picnic basket with plates and napkins, silverware and a tablecloth, and placed the food in containers in the fridge. Before putting the dove away, he tasted it, sacrificing one tiny breast, which had a succulent, woodsy taste that pleased him. When everything was ready, he turned out the light in the kitchen and climbed the stairs to his bedroom.

As he undressed, he caught sight of himself in the mirror next to the chest of drawers. He had grown thinner. He saw a younger version of himself, a lean man with a somewhat haunted look about his eyes.

In general he disliked facing himself in a mirror. He had observed that if he looked too long his vision grew dark and his image began to dissolve. He feared he himself might disappear. Still, his surprise at the change in his body often caused him to stand and stare at his reflection — just for a few moments — mesmerized by the sight of his new self.

He looked at himself, a man whose clean jaw, long face, and sharp Adam's apple were his most prominent features. His eyes nestled in his face like small black marbles. His oblong head, a shade browner than the rest of him, was thatched with thick, graying hair. The bloated, white-faced man with painfully swollen limbs had disappeared. Loss of weight had restored a boyish quality to his face, augmented by the months of recuperation spent in the sun — sitting or toiling gently in his garden. Once again he looked like a man whose life had been spent working outdoors.

What the doctor had said had proved true: each day, he *had* felt better. It was astonishing to him how good he felt. Even the sadness lifted, now and then, as it had today out dove hunting. A man couldn't argue with his fate. He had to accept what was given, what was taken. He no longer needed a doctor to tell him what he already knew. His body was having a renaissance. He felt young tonight, happy to be alive.

He turned from the mirror and pulled back the covers on his big wooden bed. Edmund Paul, his father-in-law, had carved this bed. What a generous man Edmund Paul had been. A gaunt, tall man, stooped at the shoulders, wheezy in later years with a chronic cough. He could picture Edmund's face — an English face, ruddy and friendly. Edmund had been a carpenter, a master carver, and a stonemason. It was because of Edmund Paul, who had taken him on as an apprentice not long after he married May, that Phil had learned the carpentry trade.

He left the small light burning on the bedside table, not yet ready to succumb to the dark. Memories began turning up in his mind, somewhat translucent, but persistent and vaguely perceptible, like tiny spines of cactus embedded in a finger. His whole life felt near to him, as if it had not been lived and cast away, year by year, but lay stored in this room, all his experiences synchronously present. He felt torn between regret and contentment. He could not endure both feelings at once. This was the state of his life. Regret was hard to endure, but it remained clear-cut and concrete. Contentment bred guilt: life had been restored to him, but at what cost?

He didn't want to think of that cost. Instead, he let his mind go where it wanted, and he drifted back, allowing other memories to take hold of him.

2

Doucet. He knew it was a French name, Cajun or Creole, attached to him long ago by people now dead. His past had disappeared, faded from him years ago, and he'd never made any effort to recover it.

He had grown up in the Ozarks, which in dreams he recalled clearly as a land forever green. His parents were very strict; they had high moral standards. He wasn't allowed to swear, or drink liquor or even coffee, nor was he expected to date until he was at least twenty-one.

His parents taught him to treat a girl as he would his sister and to find a good woman like his mother to marry. His father and mother were not churchgoers, but they read the Bible in their home, their children gathered around them in the evening, as well as the poetry of Wordsworth and Longfellow.

They always had to make their own recreation in what time there was left after long days at the sawmill. They were good ball players, all the boys. His pa taught him to never lose at anything. Consequently, as a child he always felt himself a winner.

He was near the last of fourteen children, most of whom were married or on their own when their pa died, just before he turned eighteen. He joined the Civilian Conservation Corps, working for the Park Service building trails and roads and bridges. The CCC paid thirty dollars a month, twenty-five of which was sent home.

After a while, the Arkansas boys in the CCC were sent west, where help was needed in the forests of Oregon. None of the boys had ever been on a train before. They were loaded on army troop trains one rainy afternoon. The flat plains of Texas amazed him, he could never have imagined anything that barren and free of greenery and life. The sky was enormous in Texas. The train rolled on day and night, through New Mexico and Arizona and Utah. It cut north and caught the corner of Idaho, where things began to turn green again, and finally, after three days of travel, they crossed into Oregon, where they transferred to trucks. He was taken to the Suislaw National Forest near Eugene, and thus began a period which brought about the biggest change in his life.

The barracks were cold, he hadn't enough clothes, and he wondered if he would ever be warm again. But he was with Arkansas boys who were always good about sharing, and within a few days he had an extra sweater and thick socks that kept his feet warm. Spring came and after a while he found he didn't need the extra clothes anymore. It grew so hot they worked shirtless, sweating beneath the brutal sun.

From the beginning of that first day on the train he knew his life would be different, but he could never have predicted all the changes that would come with moving out into the world. He had never known there were so many different kinds of human beings, especially girls. From the other boys who came from California and the big Eastern cities where things were so different he learned about girls and what they did. He never suspected that the boys might be bragging or simply not telling the truth. He knew these were the kinds of girls his parents had warned him about, and he determined to avoid them. Still, it was something he always thought about, having a girl, and sometimes at night, alone in the barracks, he would imagine what his ideal girl would be like. He always saw someone like his mother only younger.

He discovered the problem was that the good girls would look the other way whenever the army truck brought them to town; they didn't want the Arkansas boys in the uniforms. No matter how polite he was, they shunned him completely.

As the summer wore on they were moved to Camp Rainier National Park in the state of Washington and then to Anacortes on Puget Sound.

He saw the ocean for the first time and caught a steelhead salmon, a fish so beautiful he wished he hadn't ever taken it. The ocean terrified him. Walking along its shore, he stayed back from the surf; he saw how the waves varied and how unpredictable was the force propelling them. No one wave was like the next, and occasionally a breaker rose higher than ever and unexpectedly lashed out, sending a tongue of foam rushing onto the sand. What was to keep such a wave from rushing toward him and catching him in its curl? He'd never learned to swim, and the water frightened him.

In Anacortes the girls shunned him too, except the kind his pa had warned him about, but other boys went off with them and later talked about what they'd done. He never doubted that what they said was true, although he couldn't understand how it was they felt so good afterward, let alone talk so freely about it.

He turned nineteen, then twenty, and shortly after learned that his mother had died. There was no longer anyone to send money to, so he saved it and built himself a little nest egg.

He grew tired of chopping trees, cutting roads, and terracing hillsides, and after two years of living in tents with boisterous men, he began to think of other things. With the death of his mother he felt aimlessly cast upon the world. He'd always imagined he'd return home and be near his mother again, but now he didn't feel the pull of any one place. He felt rootless, and ready for change. One night lying in his bunk close enough to the water to hear the crashing of the endless waves he decided to leave the camp. With the little money he had saved, he struck out for the city.

For a while he lived in a boardinghouse in Seattle, thinking he would find a job, but there weren't any jobs, and soon he ran out of money and slept in a park with other destitute men, who called themselves hobos. He'd learned a lot by then, how some men when they're out of work or luck let themselves go and lose all self-respect and how others seem to increase in humanity, acquiring some extra insight into the possibilities of kindness.

After a while he found a job picking apples. When the apples played out, a fellow got him work cutting logs near the Canadian border. He lived in a lumber camp, which reminded him of his youth back in the Ozarks, where his father had been a foreman at a sawmill. But the man who hired him said he couldn't get paid for his lumber and thus shorted his men their wages. Later he found out the man had lied and sold his lumber for a good price, simply cheating his workers out of their pay. Months of backbreaking labor went unrewarded, and once again he found himself penniless. He would have starved that winter if it hadn't been for some generous neighbors who gave him a shack to live in and shared their food.

He was receiving an education in how men conducted themselves in the world. What was it about human nature that seemed to divide men into two camps — those who shared and worked for the good of all and those whose labors were directed only at increasing their own profits, whatever the cost to their neighbors? During the difficult winter he thought long and hard about this question.

He decided that how you grew up dictated what sort of fellow you'd become. Give me the child until he's seven and I'll give you the man, his ma used to say. There were many greedy people, and he could see how the system that surrounded him might encourage a man to think mainly of himself. He met so many people who like himself were rootless and on the move far from the place of their birth. People had lost their ties to home and what had made them what they were. It seemed to him a man could become forgetful and lapse into an extreme self-interest in such a state of detachment. He felt the loss of something, and knew it was community. He didn't belong anywhere anymore.

When spring came he was offered a ride to California and decided to take it, but he only got as far as Oregon, where he stopped to visit with friends from the CCC days. They talked him into staying throughout the summer, saying he could help out on their farm. People were kind like that, they made you feel you were doing them a favor when actually they were helping you out. Fall came, and winter, and still he was there, enjoying their hospitality. But people were talking about war, and he figured it was only a matter of time until it broke out and he got called up.

One night a man came to the farmhouse where he was staying and invited everyone to a Christmas party at a church. He named a religion Phil had never heard of. The party was being given by the Latter-day Saints, a church in Hillsboro, twenty miles away. He sized the man up and decided he detected in him qualities he liked. He was a cheerful, friendly fellow. But he hesitated to accept the invitation because he wasn't comfortable in crowds — he never knew what to say to strangers. Still, the man was insistent. "We're going to decorate a tree," he said. "It'll be fun. You'll feel like it's really Christmas." He also mentioned there would be girls there. "Lots of girls."

He wanted to reply, What use do I have of girls? The good ones won't have anything to do with me and I don't want the other kind.

The stranger, as if reading his mind, explained that the girls who would be at the party weren't like any other girls: they were missionaries, sent to Oregon to spread the true gospel of Jesus Christ, kind, good girls, full of warmth and high spirits. In the end he gave in and allowed himself to be included in the party that set off for the church.

They drove to Hillsboro and parked in front of a small church made out of plain red brick. They were among the first to arrive, and there were only a few people inside, busy putting up decorations for the party.

He was given a job. His task was to stand on the highest rung of a ladder and decorate the top branches of the Christmas tree. He was slinging icicles over the verdant boughs of a magnificent Douglas fir when two women came in and he heard them introduced as lady missionaries. One of the women came to the foot of the ladder and stood looking up at him. Shy, he had difficulty meeting her eyes. But he was curious to see what she looked like, so he finally glanced down to see a tall, thin, red-haired woman smiling up at him in such a nice way it startled him. He couldn't believe that anyone would smile at him like that, a smile so open and unafraid that his own fears were chased away. She said her name was May. Not until later did he come to understand why he had softened toward girls that night when before he'd been so bitter against them. It was destiny for him and May to meet in such a way. It was the beginning of love.

Although he was never tempted to join her religion, he did anything he could to be near her and felt his deep affection was returned. She was transferred often, and he didn't get to see a great deal of her, but he kept track of her movements, understanding it would be some time before her mission was completed. Then he could ask her to marry him, something he knew he would do as soon as he could.

But the war came first, and he was drafted into the army, serving in the medical corps. He spent two years overseas and survived to come home — only at that point home wasn't any definite place; it was America, the forty-eight states he'd fought for. He made his way to Oregon as soon as he could after his discharge and learned that May had returned to her home in Idaho.

It was spring before he located her.

He found her working in her father's beet fields, hoeing weeds between the long rows of tender shoots. The farm was located in a high valley, dominated by a wide azure lake — a valley as beautiful as any he'd ever seen. Older, and even thinner, May wore an apron over her faded dress, and her heavy shoes were clotted with soil. She lifted her head from her work and watched him stride toward her, her eyes narrowing until she recognized him, and then they grew wide. She greeted him plainly, with the same openness she had the first time she'd seen him, a beautiful smile spreading across her face. "I've been waiting for you," she said.

Their actual courtship lasted only a few hours. After they were married, they took a trip back to Oregon. Their honeymoon was a Greyhound bus ride to Hillsboro.

They returned to Idaho to settle among her people on the rim of Bear Lake — a lake so big that when he first stood on Edmund Paul's property and looked along the water's surface, it reminded him of the ocean, only it lacked the ocean's menacing waves.

Her relatives accepted him readily, but when he first met them he felt overwhelmed by their kisses. He wasn't used to that. His own family hadn't been demonstrative; although he knew his ma had loved him, he could only remember her kissing him once, and that was when he left home. May's family was different. They showed their affection. They loved music. And had private jokes, contained in cryptic phrases like, *I canna helpit he broka da chain,* words delivered in a mock Italian dialect. Even when the meanings of these jokes were explained to him, he still remained outside their pale. Yet the hearty life of the Paul family drew him in, especially at meal times. May, and her mother Martha, were both good cooks, and after his years of subsisting on meager rations, their bountiful meals were inseparable from the idea of love itself.

Something he had not realized until he married her was that May was nearly ten years older than he. It seemed, in some ways, that without his even being aware of it he had found the perfect substitute for the mother he had loved so dearly.

In many ways May was a queer woman, five-foot-ten, with a rangy, big-boned frame on which there seemed to be too little flesh to adequately cover the angles of her body. Her hair, even at thirty, was thinning and dyed the color of carrots. In certain ways, she grew more peculiar as time wore on, and yet his love had only deepened. One day she had become a vegetarian. She simply stopped eating meat, on the grounds she couldn't abide the way animals were treated and so callously prepared for slaughter. Shortly thereafter she took up the practice of spiritualism. The first time he found her conducting a séance sitting at the kitchen table with two women, he felt a deep embarrassment. Later, he came to accept her strange ways.

He also came to see they would never leave the valley. His roving days were over. He was drawn to a vocation he had never considered before and took it up with the fervor of one who has discovered a calling. With patience and kindness, Edmund Paul, May's father, taught him carpentry and how to work with stone. He became his apprentice, and later, partner. When Edmund Paul died, he left Phil his business. He also left him land — beautiful land — the farm first settled by Edmund's Cornish parents, William Paul and Elizabeth Goyne, in 1867. By the time Phil's own children were born, he had built a house on the land, fashioning everything, from the great stone fireplaces, to much of the simple wooden furniture, himself.

Instead of proving to be a passing interest, May's preoccupation with spiritualism and natural healing had deepened. She studied the science (as she liked to call it) of iridology and learned to read the irises of her friend's eyes, diagnosing kidney ailments, guessing the locations of old breaks in bones, and previous illnesses, much to the amazement of her listeners, who usually confirmed that what she said was true. She became expert at massaging feet, learning the pressure points that corresponded with internal organs. She could cure colds by manipulating a person's toes. People came to her, as if to a sorceress, to have their health improved.

She had a ready laugh, and she rarely ever got angry. They had been married seven years when the first of their two children was born. May's hair fell out during her pregnancy, and she bought the first of many wigs to cover her baldness. It never did grow back. With her thick glasses, her wig, and uncommonly tall frame, she often presented a strange figure to the world. But vanity never seemed to touch her being.

What he loved her for was her kindness to him and her generous happy soul. No person who came in contact with her was untouched by this kindness, which sprang from some deep, unwavering source.

Sometimes he would come home from work and find May seated on the floor in front of the fireplace with the girls nearby and they'd be molding clay or painting wooden animals she'd cut out of plywood with her jig saw and it seemed to him that she was essentially as childlike and innocent as the children. In all May did she was so sincere and uncomplicated that even the activities that at first seemed queer to him soon appeared natural and heartfelt, simply extensions of her loving soul. She devoted herself to her children not to make them into what she envisioned but to bring out their own particular natures, whatever they might be. The result was that each girl was different from the other, and he hardly saw himself or May in either one. Helen was studious and intellectually adventurous and early on declared her interest in science. Joyce was drawn to religion and in time revealed a romantic and sentimental side.

One day — and it seemed as though it happened quite suddenly — he and May found themselves alone. Joyce married Dan Beery, a local boy whose family owned an orchard. Helen went off to school in Colorado and much later, at the age of thirty-six, married an astronomer. In some strange way, it was what he'd been waiting for, to be alone again with May. Although the years of child-rearing had seemed happy at the time, he felt a different kind of contentment now they were alone again. He realized how much of his love he reserved for his wife, and he was pleased to indulge it so fully.

There were years of bliss. They didn't lack anything, least of all love.

Two grandchildren were born, one to Joyce, one to Helen. Luke arrived first, and what surprised him, as the boy grew older, was how deep his feelings for him ran. Luke seemed to be the issue of his own heart. He became his shadow. He took him camping and fishing, taught him card games and carpentry. He was an intelligent, wise boy. But what affected him most deeply was how Luke seemed to have inherited his grandmother's kindness.

Helen's child was an entirely different story. It was true he was younger, harder to relate to, but still he had very little natural

210

feeling for the boy, who through an ironic twist of fate had been given his own name. Little Philly was a whiner, and though he tried to show him affection, he found it a difficult task. Then something happened that made everything else, including his unequal affection for his grandsons, seem irrelevant. May fell ill.

Her cancer was diagnosed in October, and she died the following August.

About those months in between . . .

He couldn't explain to anyone how in those months their love had deepened and become so pure in its consummation, so utterly, and perfectly, sweet.

He didn't bury her in a cemetery, as the family had expected, but respected her private wish to be cremated, and turned her ashes into the garden behind the house where they had spent their life. There, over the course of the next summer, he worked peacefully, tending annuals and perennials, coaxing his crops of vegetables to harvest, until his own heart began to fail him the following winter, leading him to believe it was only a matter of time before he, too, rested among the roots in the clotted soil. During the terrible days of his illness, it seemed he was halfway there, already churning in suffocating darkness as he lay sleepless, struggling for breath throughout the long nights.

Now, everything had changed.

A lean man, breathing easily, lay in the quiet of a well-lighted room, a young man's heart beating in his breast, the heart of a boy he had loved deeply. In what kind of world did such things happen?

He was a man reborn, if not in the spirit, in the flesh.

The flesh of his flesh.

3

The day broke clear, although the sky was filled with big, raggedy clouds by the time he arrived at Leora's. She was ready, waiting for him outside, sitting on the steps of her porch.

She lived in a small wooden house on a street near the old library. He had never been inside her house, but from the outside it appeared well-kept and neat, an older house with blue trim and a big pine on either side of the front walk.

She spotted him and stood up and waved. She wore a flowered dress and carried a tweed jacket in one hand and a pie in the other. In many ways, the dress was the same shape as the uniform she wore in Millie's Cafe, and the way she walked toward him, hunched slightly over, striding quickly down the walk in her thick-soled shoes, caused him to think of how she moved so energetically among tables, serving customers in the restaurant. Her hair was braided and wound into a nest on top of her head. From a distance, it looked as if she wore a tidy gray cap. As she grew closer, he could see her eyebrows furrow and then relax as she smiled up at him. "Oh, don't you look well?" she said. "You've lost weight. You look twenty years younger!"

His heart raced a little. Just the way she said this and looked at him made him aware of the foreignness he felt at the center of his chest. He turned quickly and opened the car door for her and said, "Ready?"

They drove north, through the little towns of Bennington and Soda Springs, and soon began climbing through stands of aspens and pines. At the summit, a dirt road branched off and wound back into the mountains, crossing cattle guards and little dry streambeds. He had to steer the old Buick through deep ruts in places where the road had been damaged by erosion, and the car bounced wildly on its worn shocks.

"Oh, dear," Leora said, "you don't think perhaps this road is a little too rough?"

"Oh, no, we're fine as long as we keep up our momentum," he said and felt the oil pan drag over a hump in the road just at that moment. He didn't want to tell her that he was beginning to wonder himself whether they should turn back, but there was no place to turn around and he was afraid of slowing down for fear the old car wouldn't be able to begin climbing again.

In a way, he liked the aspect of adventure he felt as he tried to pick the best path through the rocks and ruts. He only hoped they didn't get stuck. That would be a mess, and he'd end up looking foolish, as men so often did when they presumed to know so much more than women.

They passed a turnoff for a church camp and then another for a Boy Scout lodge. The golden leaves on stands of aspens shimmied in the wind, set against a sky as blue as a boat tarp. The Buick growled as it churned up the road in low gear. When they came to a meadow that looked very peaceful to him, he pulled the car off the road into a little stony clearing and said, "How does this look?"

Even from the road he could hear a stream, the beautiful sound of running water. There was shade, too, and an expanse of grass, beneath some pines.

"This looks wonderful," Leora said. "Maybe we should find a place near the stream." She pointed to the shady area beneath the pines, the exact spot he would have chosen.

They spread the blanket over the grass and sat facing a sunny hillside. As she knelt down and smoothed out the blanket, he noticed how limber she was. A handsome woman, strong and youthful. She had once told him she was sixty-eight, but watching her move now, he thought she appeared much younger. Time had a way of telescoping, and at that moment he imagined they were both much younger than they really were. Again, he had the sensation that all the important events in his life could have happened earlier that day, so vivid were they to him.

"Would you like a glass of lemonade?" he asked.

"Yes, I would, thank you," she murmured.

His hands trembled slightly as he poured the liquid from the jar. He was filled with a strange combination of feelings — joy, anxiety, the particularly unexpected desire to be with someone again, yet the slight fear of it. Smiling, she took the lemonade from him, leaned back on the blanket, and sighed.

"This is wonderful. I haven't done anything like this in ages."

He sat down beside her and began unpacking the picnic basket, placing containers of food on the checked tablecloth. The tannic odor of pines filled the air. A little wind blew out of the woods behind them, carrying the moist fresh scent of running water. He uncovered the potato salad and the little dish of dove breasts, which laid in their burgundy sauce like tiny succulent plums.

"What's that?" she asked, gazing over his shoulder.

"Dove," he said. "I shot them yesterday."

"Dove?" She frowned slightly, and he felt a little disappointed in this reaction.

"You don't have to eat it," he said, "if it doesn't appeal to you."

"No, that's not it at all. I'm just . . . touched, that you've gone to so much trouble. It's quite a treat to have dove. Leland used to hunt them once in a while, but that was many years ago, when we were first married."

Leland had been her husband, who died from cirrhosis of the liver. She rarely talked about him, and he was surprised she brought his name up now. Phil remembered him only as a sad figure, a bad alcoholic disabled in the war, often seen weaving down the street after an afternoon spent at the VFW bar.

"Have you been all right?" Leora asked. "I've worried about you. The last time I saw you, just after you got out of the hospital, and you asked me not to come again for a while because you didn't feel strong enough to have visitors . . . well, I have to admit my feelings were a little hurt. I thought perhaps it was just me you didn't want to see."

"No, that wasn't the case at all." He found it difficult to explain his feelings, to justify excluding people from his life the way he had. It hadn't been easy being alone, but it was the only way he could begin to come to terms with what had happened. She waited for him to say something more, and finally he spoke.

"I keep thinking of something," he said.

"What's that?"

"What I remember is that doctor standing at the end of my bed in the hospital, just as I was about to be released, and saying to me, 'You're set for life, Phil.' Did he think I'd feel like going out and starting all over again, after what had happened?"

"It would be different, I'm sure, if you'd received someone else's heart, if you hadn't known that person and been so close to him. That's the difficult part, isn't it?"

He nodded. "I suppose I could have walked out feeling good. Now I feel, well . . ." Words failed him, and he could only furrow his brow, trying to conjure up a sentence that might somehow describe his confusion, how his pleasure at being alive and feeling so vigorous was always tempered by the uneradicable sense of loss.

"Go ahead," she urged. "Tell me."

"I do feel good," he said. "That's the problem, and the wonderful part. I really believed I was going to die. I could feel death coming for me. Now, I'm not only alive, I feel better than I have in many years, as if in fact I *do* have a new life. Each morning I wake up feeling good, and I'm grateful for that. But I never stop thinking about him, I mean Luke. He should be alive, not me. He had his whole life before him. I'm an old man. What can I do with my life now?"

"But you can't feel responsible for his death. It was an accident, and no one can prevent accidents or even account for them."

He turned away from her and laid out napkins and plates, trying to establish some order. He cut cheese into slices and put them on a little tray with some bread, and stirred the potato salad, trying to avoid looking at her.

"Why have you shut yourself off the way you have?" She didn't want to tell him, because Joyce had asked her not to, but his daughter had come to the restaurant one day to talk to her, full of concern for her father, who she said was becoming a hermit. Joyce said he even refused to see his daughters, allowing them to visit only a few times over the summer. He'd become stubborn and difficult about it, insisting he needed to be alone, that he didn't feel up to company. It was nearly impossible to persuade him to leave his house. She felt Joyce was asking her to do something, but in her heart she knew she couldn't help him unless he asked her to.

"I felt I needed to be alone," he said. "It's been especially hard with my daughter, Joyce. I know she expects much more from me than I've been able to give. She's hurt because I turn down her invitations, but truthfully, I can't bear the thought of visiting that house. And having her visit is almost as bad. She's become more religious and she wants to talk about God and miracles, which is well and good, but she has a conviction about these things I don't. She tries to make it all simple, the result of some grand scheme, God's will. She talks about the gift of life. But what about death? The death of those teenagers?"

"I can see the workings of some high power," Leora said.

"I haven't known quite what to do with myself. I daydream. I've been remembering such odd things. I seem to live in the past. Do you remember Nigger Boy?" he asked.

"*What?*"

"Don't you remember that racehorse Harmon Patterson used to own, the one that became so famous?"

"Harmon Patterson? The mayor? Goodness, I haven't thought of him for years."

"That's the kind of thing I end up thinking about. Nigger Boy. He was such a beautiful horse. I saw him run at a few country fairs. He had a way of moving, it's difficult to describe, he was so elegant and gentle. He'd run a race, and then a few minutes later Harmon would put kids up on his back, knowing they'd be perfectly safe. When he died, Harmon missed him so much he paid for that statue to be erected. Don't you remember that statue that used to be across from the bank? Big, life-sized plaster horse with a tail and mane made out of hemp?"

"I remember the statue but I never knew where it came from."

"Old Harmon used to say everybody used Nigger Boy's statue as a weather indicator. If his tail was blowing, a storm was coming. If he was wet in the morning, you knew it had rained overnight. In the sixties, there was a fuss about the name on the plaque and someone changed it from Nigger Boy to Black Boy."

"I can see why," she said. "The other sounds so offensive now, doesn't it, although people talked that way all the time when I was growing up. I suppose we only learn things in fits and starts. We don't see the cruelty and ignorance at the time."

"I lie awake at night and think of the strangest things. Harmon Patterson. Do you remember when he sent the Duke and Duchess of Windsor a telegram and offered them a free trip through Yellowstone Park? He announced it in the newspaper and the whole town was waiting to see if they'd accept. Of course, he never heard from them."

"That I do remember," she said, laughing. "He was such a showman, wasn't he? Always trying to put Montpelier on the map!"

"Now the town's dying," he said. "You look at Main Street and half the stores are empty." He handed her a plate and she helped herself to the food. He tried the dove and felt pleased. The dish seemed to have improved in flavor overnight.

"Mmmm," she said. "This is delicious."

"There doesn't seem to be much opportunity for young people in the valley anymore," he said, continuing his train of thought. "It seems as if we've come to the end of something, a way of life, and I can't imagine what's going to replace it. What do you have if you don't have children to stay around and bring new life into a place?"

"Never having had children myself, I don't know how to answer that question."

"I'm sorry."

"No, it's quite all right. I got over that

222

longing many years ago." She set down her plate and moved closer to him. He felt a slight pull in his groin, a sudden and insistent twinge of desire. At odd moments lately — much odder than this one — he had felt renewed sexual stirrings. It was slightly disconcerting to have such feelings again. A line from a poem came to mind: *Teeth worn out by the tap dance of shivers won't rattle because of fear.* She reached out and touched the hollow in his throat where the scar ended.

"No keloid," she said. "It healed nicely."

Suddenly the stillness around them was broken by the sound of a motor. A pickup truck came into sight, racing along the dirt road, dust flying up from behind it. Phil sat up straight and peered at the truck.

"Why is that guy going so fast?" he said.

"He ought to know better," Leora said. "He's crazy to be driving that way."

They were both surprised by what happened next. The truck plowed to a sudden stop. Before it had quit moving altogether, the door on the passenger side swung open and a girl jumped out. Leora let out a little cry. But the girl managed to jump free of the truck and land on her feet. She took off running, scurried down a little embankment, and sprinted off across the meadow in front of them.

A young man climbed out of the truck and stood gazing after her. Phil was certain the man would take off running too. But instead he shouted after her.

"Louise!" he cried. "Louise!"

The girl didn't stop. She didn't even look behind her, and before long she had reached the thick forest of trees and disappeared from sight.

"Shit," the man said, loud enough for them to hear. He glanced briefly in their direction, then turned away and stood still with his back to them, as if considering what to do. He climbed back in the truck and sat there, waiting.

"What's going on?" Phil said.

"I don't know, but it's very odd. I can't imagine what's happening here." She stared at the man in the truck, who looked like a thinner version of Elvis Presley, the way his hair was swooped up. He started up the truck and began driving away slowly, as if he were in no hurry now.

"He's leaving," Leora said.

"Where do you think the girl has gone?"

"I don't know. He must be coming back for her. He wouldn't leave her up here, miles from anything."

"It doesn't seem right, does it?" he said.

"The way that girl was running? Like she

was scared to death? No, it certainly doesn't."

"Obviously, she wanted to get away from him."

"Maybe it's a lovers' quarrel," Leora said. The quaintness of the phrase struck him as odd. A lovers' quarrel.

"What if . . ." She frowned at him and looked troubled.

"What?"

"What if it's something else?"

"Like what?"

"Something violent," she said. "A kidnapping. An attempted rape."

Phil thought about this. He supposed it was a possibility. But what should he do?

"Do you think I should go try and find her?"

"I don't know."

"It's very strange, at any rate."

"Well, maybe he'll come back soon."

They waited for a while and nothing happened. A distinct low buzzing surrounded them, the sound of insects. At first he was aware only of the deep silence, but gradually the silence filled up with subtle sounds — the insects, a bird calling in the distance, the muffled thrum of a small plane overhead. The feeling of privacy and the mood of the picnic had been interrupted, and he found himself listening to the sounds in the woods around him in a way he hadn't before, when they had thought themselves alone.

"We might as well have some pie," Leora said. "I picked these gooseberries yesterday in my back — "

"Shhh," he said. He heard a noise in the woods behind Leora, a different sort of sound, the snapping of twigs. He looked up to see the girl emerge from a grove of trees. She looked around quickly, and then began walking directly toward them.

"Look," he said to Leora, and nudged her. She turned around. "Oh, my," she said. They sat still, watching the girl approach.

As she came closer, Phil saw that she was a young girl, a teenager, maybe sixteen, very pretty but disheveled, her hair a mass of blond tangles, her clothes wrinkled. She wore a short dress, which revealed legs as skinny and straight as the trunks of young aspens, and almost as white. Her lips had been painted a startling color of red.

"Hi," she said.

"Hello," they said in chorus.

"Did you see him leave?" she asked.

"You mean . . ."

"The guy in the truck."

"Yes, he's gone."

"Which way did he go?"

Phil pointed up the road. "That way."

She pursed her lips. "That means he'll be back."

He hadn't thought of this, but it was true. As he remembered now, the road dead-ended a few miles farther on at a fire lookout tower.

"Could you do me a favor?" she said. "Could you give me a ride back to town?"

"What's happened?" Leora asked.

"Oh, it's nothing, nothing important." She looked away from them, twisting a lock of hair in one hand, pulling it across her neck.

"What about that fellow?" Phil asked. "Won't he wonder what's happened to you?"

"I wouldn't worry about him," she said.

Phil saw now that she had been crying. It was part of what gave her the disheveled look. Her eyes had the pink, sore look that came only after a good hard cry. "Can't you give me a ride?" she asked, putting her hands on her hips. An old-fashioned white handbag, the sort of purse May used to carry, hung from one wrist. "I'm in no hurry. I'm sorry to interrupt your picnic. I'm happy to just wait until you're ready to leave."

"Tell us what's going on," Leora said gently. "You seem so — " Suddenly they heard the sound of the truck again and looked up the road, in the direction of the noise. The truck had not yet come into view.

"Oh, God," the girl said. "Please don't

tell him you've seen me. Please! I've got to get away from him!" She ran quickly toward the trees and disappeared again into the woods.

The truck emerged from around a bend and slowed down. It came to a stop behind the Buick. The young man got out, looked around, and began walking toward them. When he was a few feet away, he called out, "Howdy."

Phil said nothing. He looked into the face of the young man, studying him carefully. He wore jeans and a hunting jacket over a plaid shirt. A two-day beard darkened his jaw.

"Hello," Leora said.

"Nice day for a picnic."

"Yes, it is."

He stood staring at them. "I'm sorry to interrupt you," he said. He shifted his weight from one foot to the other and cleared his throat. "I was wondering . . . well, this is sort of embarrassing, but you probably saw what happened, didn't you?"

"What's that?" Leora said.

"My girlfriend and I had an argument. She jumped out of the truck a few minutes ago and took off. I was just going to leave her and then I got to thinking about it and changed my mind. I've got to find her. I was wondering if you'd seen her."

They hesitated, and glanced quickly at each other. Leora spoke up first. "Noooo," she said slowly, drawing out the word. Phil added a short, clipped little *no,* and shook his head.

In some subtle way, Phil saw the young man's expression change. He still smiled at them, but his eyes grew steelier, more questioning.

"You didn't see her?"

"No," Leora said again.

"I thought you might have seen her jump out of the truck and run off. I mean, it happened right here."

"Oh, yes, well, we did see that."

"She didn't come back after I left?"

"No."

The man continued to stare at them. "Well, like I said, this is a little embarrassing." He turned away from them and gazed across the meadow. "I guess I'll go see if I can find her."

He strode away and disappeared into the trees. They heard him walking, the sound of twigs snapping, and his voice calling her name, "Louise! Louise! Louise!" over and over.

"I hope we're doing the right thing," Leora said in a low voice. "It doesn't feel quite right, lying that way, does it?"

"No, it doesn't."

"She looked wild, didn't she? Like some animal, I can't think what. A young cat!" she said, brightening. "Yes, a feral little cat."

He emerged from the trees and walked back over to where they sat on the blanket. The sky had begun to turn rosy. Blue shadows fell upon the meadow and the pines looked lush with the dark weight of their needles. How terribly odd this all is, Phil thought. I step out into the world and look what happens.

"I can't see her," he said.

Leora shook her head, but said nothing.

"I'm sorry to have bothered you."

"It's no problem."

"We've had some hard times lately," he said, "trying to get settled in a new place. We just moved to Pocatello about a month ago. She doesn't like it there. All we do lately is argue."

It seemed to Phil that perhaps they had made a mistake. Why had they agreed so readily to cover for the girl? Shouldn't he speak up and tell the truth? Just as he was considering doing this, the young man turned and began walking away.

"I guess I'll just go on home," he called back to them. "So long."

" 'Bye," Leora said, rather too softly.

The man stopped and turned around. Phil saw his worried look. "She's probably going to come out when I leave," he said. "Tell her to call me. I'll come and get her, wherever she is." He strode off toward his truck. Phil noticed he stopped at the rear of the Buick and glanced down at the license plate before he climbed inside his pickup. The truck pulled away. Phil looked up and saw the small face of the girl, peeking out from behind the trunk of a big yellow pine.

4

"Is he gone?" she asked.

"Yes," Leora said. "I think it's safe to come out."

Safe, he thought. Safe from what?

The girl stepped unsteadily across the ground. She was wearing heels, not too high, but very pointy. How had she been able to run in those shoes?

"I can't thank you enough for what you did for me." She rolled her eyes and let out a loud sigh.

"Sit down for a moment," Leora said.

The girl sat down at the edge of the blanket, folding her bare legs beneath her. She lifted the hair away from her neck and said, "Whew!"

"Would you like some lemonade?" Leora asked.

"Thanks. This is really nice of you. I mean, I don't normally ask people to lie for me. I'm sorry."

"What's going on, dear?" Leora asked. "Your boyfriend said you just moved to Pocatello."

"I don't want to be with him anymore,

but he won't leave me alone."

"What's the problem?" Phil asked. She hesitated, and her eyes flickered slightly, nothing too noticeable, just a little jerk of the pupils, like the picture on a TV set suddenly jumping, so quickly you're hardly certain it's happened.

"I'm Louise," she said, extending a pale hand. Phil couldn't believe how light her hand was when he took hold of it. It was like touching a cat's paw, and he remembered what Leora had said about her looking like a feral cat.

"I'm Phil," he said, "and this is Leora."

She shook Leora's hand. Leora said, "He said to tell you he'd come and get you, wherever you were. Don't you think you should at least call him later and let him know you're all right? He seemed quite worried."

The girl let her eyelids close halfway and tipped her head back. Her pointy little chin looked defiant as she said, "I don't want him to come get me. I need to get away from him. I can't take any more arguing."

Phil glanced at Leora. He didn't know what to think. He started to say something, but Louise spoke up.

"Listen," she said, "it's too complicated to explain. But don't worry about him. He'll figure things out. He knew it was coming. I just need a ride back to town."

"Which town?" Phil asked, puzzled.

"Any town," she said. "Anywhere there's a phone will be fine."

"Of course we'll give you a ride, won't we, Phil? We're going to Montpelier. We can take you there, unless you'd rather stop in Soda Springs."

"No," she said, "Montpelier would be fine."

"We should get going," Phil said. "It's getting late. The sun's going down."

"I don't want to rush you," Louise said. "Again, I'm really sorry for crashing in on your picnic."

"Oh, it's nothing!" Leora cried, standing up. "Oooo, I'm stiff. Come on, Phil, let's shake this blanket. Take the corners there."

All during the drive down the canyon, Louise talked steadily, asking them questions. Were they married? Did they have families? How long had they lived in this area? Meanwhile, she offered no information on herself. She kept up her chatter until they reached Leora's house.

Leora, who felt she ought to at least try to offer some advice, turned to Louise before getting out of the car and said, "Don't give up on something too quickly, dear. You might regret it. There's no such thing as perfection when it comes to men." Phil thought of Leland as she said this, and felt a sudden sadness.

Louise said, "Nice to meet you. Thanks."

Leora took Phil's hand and squeezed it. She smiled, and then she was gone.

"Now," he said to Louise, turning around to look at her. "Where would you like me to drop you off?"

"Oh, just anywhere in town, please."

He drove to the north end of the city park and stopped the car at the curb beneath trees filled with chattering birds. There was a pay phone across the street, in front of The Raspberry Shack.

"Is this okay?" he asked. "There's a phone just across the way."

The girl looked at him. She made no move to get out of the car. "Yeah, this is fine. Thanks," she said.

"No problem," he replied. "Are you going to be all right? Would you like me to wait until you make your phone call?"

"Look," she said. "I have to ask you something." Somehow he thought he knew what was coming. "I don't have anywhere to go tonight. I know this is a lot to ask, but I don't know what else to do. I was wondering if you could help me out."

Phil cleared his throat nervously. "Do you need some money?" he asked. He was certain she was going to ask for money.

"No, no, that's not it."

"Would you like me to take you to Pocatello?"

"Pocatello?"

"Yes. I could take you home," he said. Somehow, the thought that whoever the young man was, he'd been telling the truth about having moved to Pocatello.

"No," she said. "I really can't go back there. I don't know what to do."

Phil thought for a moment. "Can I take you to a motel?"

She shook her head. "Yeah, sure, but I don't have any money."

So it was money she wanted. "I can give you what you need for a night in a motel, if that's what you'd like."

"It kills me that you would do that." She looked away from him and scratched her head, burying her fingers in the blond tangles. He noticed a tiny dark spot on her chin, the remains of a pimple standing out against the paleness of her skin. She was a waif, a child.

"It isn't going to do any good," she said. "One night in a motel. What then? Where do I go from there? What I really need is just a . . . a place to stay for a few days until I can call my . . . brother. My brother will come and get me. I don't want to end up on the street if he can't come right away. It's too scary. I'm feeling very frightened."

Phil stared at her. The car was still idling. He didn't know whether to turn it off or leave it running.

"I just need a little time to figure out what to do next," she said. "A place to stay."

He was hoping she didn't mean what he thought she did. "You have to go someplace," he said.

"I know. I really don't know what to do." She rubbed her chin, picking at the little pimple.

"Well, I don't really know how I can help you except by giving you a little money for a room — "

"Couldn't you just give me a place to stay? For a night or two anyway? Please? Just until I can make some phone calls. I'll sleep anywhere. On your couch. On the floor. I could even sleep here, in the car."

Somebody, he realized, was standing across the street waving at him. It took him a moment to realize who it was. DeLloyd Losey. He waved back. DeLloyd turned and walked up to the take-out window at The Raspberry Shack. The big revolving neon raspberry rotated above him, casting purple shadows on his bald head. He thought, She wants to *stay* with me? It surprised him so much he couldn't think of what to say.

"I don't think so," he said. The place inside him occupied by his young heart radiated fear, which seemed almost indistinguishable from excitement. He heard a voice, which he recognized as Luke's, saying, *Help her*. It astonished him to hear this voice so clearly.

"You said you lived alone," she said. "Wouldn't you have room? Couldn't you give me a place to stay so I won't end up on the street? I won't be any bother."

He wanted to say no, but he found he couldn't. For reasons he couldn't understand, he felt compelled to help her, to obey the voice radiating — not from his head, but his heart. Already he was imagining where she might sleep. Not in the car. Certainly not. Perhaps Helen's room. Next to his own.

"Please," she said wearily. "You don't know what I've been through. Please help me." Her pleading affected him deeply, but he was even more moved by the sight of her frailness and the stains on the front of her dress, the twigs clinging to her hair and the tremulous tone of her voice.

"Just let me sleep in the car. The backseat would be fine."

"Of course not," he said. "I couldn't have you sleeping in the car." Children were playing with a ball in the park, and in the stillness he heard a mother call to her son to come and get his sweater.

"I suppose you're in a difficult spot," he said, "or you wouldn't be asking for help."

"I am," she said. "I really am."

"What about your parents? Can't you call them?"

"I'm out of touch with my parents."

He realized DeLloyd Losey had turned around and was staring at him. What if he were to come over and begin talking to him in the middle of all this? What would he say? He put the car in reverse and backed away from the curb.

"There's an extra bedroom," he found himself saying. "I suppose you can stay there tonight." Wasn't this the charitable thing to do? How could he not help her?

"No one has stayed in the room for a while. It used to be my daughter's room. I've stored things in there. I'm afraid it's in kind of a mess."

"I won't mind. Thank you," she said. "Thank you very much."

He felt the pale weight of her hand on his shoulder.

The light was very low as he turned from the highway into the lane. The sky above the hills was a smoky pink. One single cloud, brilliantly colored, stood out in the sky, a banshee cloud with screaming mouth and flowing hair. The lake appeared still in the deepening dusk, and where it met the shore, the water reflected the steep purple mountains, treeless except for a few solitary pines scattered near the ridge and in ravines.

When he reached the house, he parked in front of the garage, and hesitated before getting out of the car. She climbed out quickly, stood for a moment gazing up at the house, and then walked briskly up the path, leading the way without waiting for him. He felt a sudden uneasiness, watching the confidence with which she approached his house. He couldn't keep up with her, so quickly was she moving up the path, brushing aside the tendrils of weeping willow.

"Watch your step," he called. "There's a couple of steps there — "

The warning seemed unnecessary. Her feet glided surely over the stone path, anticipating every little dip, every step and irregularity, even though the walkway lay in shadow. He caught up with her on the porch, where she stood gazing out toward the lake.

"You have a nice place," she murmured.

He stepped in front of her, inserting the key in the lock, and opened his house to a stranger.

Later that night, she found herself alone at last.

The room he gave her was on the second floor of the house. It was an odd-shaped room, and the ceiling sloped down at one end, above a big wooden bed. A window looked out over fields and the lake. On a small dressing table stood three photographs in silver frames. In one, a very thin woman in a wig held two small children on her lap. Another showed an overweight girl in a dark coat standing in a snow-covered field, holding up a snowball as if about to throw it at the photographer. In the last picture, the girl was older, and wore a cap and gown. The cap sat on her head to one side, angled to accommodate hair that protruded in a wavy, lopsided manner. The lampshades, bedspread, and walls were all covered in the same floral pattern. Looking around her, she thought it was the prettiest room she had ever seen.

She went to the window and put her fingers against the glass panes, peering out into the darkness. The stars were out, so plentiful they filled the sky. Even the white swath of the Milky Way was visible. The Sisters formed a murky wedge of light, and Orion's belt dotted the darkness in a line of bright stars. Across the lake, she could see the sparse lights of a town, clustered in the blackness of the night.

In one of the drawers in the dresser she found a flannel nightgown. She took off her dress and slipped the nightgown on. It smelled like an old woman, perfumy and musty. The nightgown was much too large and dragged on the floor as she crossed the room. Still, its warmth was comforting. She took her small blue notebook from her purse and looked around for something to write with. In the drawer of the nightstand she found a pen with writing on it that said, "Doucet Carpentry Company — Get My Bid You'll Be Glad You Did."

What did he think of her? At the moment, she didn't really care. She felt exhausted and grateful to be left alone.

She folded back the covers and climbed up into the bed, which seemed higher off the floor than most beds. With its carved headboard and footboard, it felt like a cozy enclosure. She leaned back against the pillows and opened the notebook to the first blank page. She wrote the date, guessing at it, and began a new entry:

I can't believe I'm back in the place where I met Wendall months ago. We passed the truck stop today, and I recognized it. I'm glad to finally be away from him. Nothing's worked out. It's been worse since

The pen had run out of ink. She shook it and tried scribbling at the corner of the page but she only left inkless scratches on the paper. Closing up the diary, she put it back in her purse. But she could not stop thinking about Wendall, or what had happened earlier that day.

The morning had started out fine. Wendall had come home from a long-distance haul around midnight the night before. As always, she was glad to have him home again. They had slept late. Made love before he got up and took a shower. She was still lying in the water bed when he yelled from the kitchen, "Damn it, Louise. Where's the coffee?"

She let it pass without answering. So there wasn't any coffee. He could go out and buy some at the Safeway around the corner.

He came and stood at the foot of the bed, with his hands on his hips, frowning. "Why

is there never any coffee when I get home?"
he asked. "How come there isn't ever anything to eat around here?"

"I'm not a cook," she said.

"I'm not asking you to be a cook, hell
I'd cook myself if there was ever any food
around. I'm just wondering what happens
to the money I leave for food. Where does
it go?"

She didn't look at him.

"This?" he said, reaching down and picking
up something off the floor. "Is this where
the food money goes?"

She looked up to see what he was holding
— her new leather wrist cuff with blunted
metal studs.

"So I bought something for myself."

"A dog collar?"

"A *bracelet*."

"How much for this?"

"Five bucks," she mumbled.

"*Five* bucks?"

"Yeah, five bucks." She threw back the
covers and got up quickly, brushing past
him as she headed for the pile of clothes in
the corner.

"I'm not made of money," he said.

She grabbed the red dress from the top
of the pile and headed for the bathroom.
He caught her by the arm.

"Do you eat anything when I'm gone?" he asked. "Answer me that."

"I'd be dead if I didn't," she said, "as much as you're gone." She pulled away from him and went into the bathroom, slamming the door behind her.

In the shower, she decided things were going all wrong. She didn't want to fight with him. What she would do is suggest they go out, get some lunch, do something after. Go to a movie. Anything but stay home. But by the time she'd showered and dressed, he'd already made other plans, and she could see plainly those plans didn't include her.

"Going rabbit hunting with Jack," he said when she came out of the bathroom. His guns were lying on the bed. He already had his jacket on, and he wore a baseball cap that said "Life's a Bitch."

Looking at him preparing to leave, getting ready to go somewhere without her again, it didn't seem that she could stand it anymore.

"And what am I supposed to do today?" she said, glaring at him.

He glanced at her and looked away. "What you want," he said. "Do what you want."

"Shit," she said, "I can't believe you."

"I can't believe you either. I can't take much more of this. I don't even look forward to coming home anymore."

She began yelling at him. "What do you expect! You're gone for a goddam week and you come home and instead of — "

"You're sucking me dry!" he yelled.

"Shit, if you feel — "

"You're like a leech!"

Suddenly their next door neighbor began pounding on the wall. "Shut up!" he yelled. "Go somewhere else to fight!"

And they had. He picked up his guns and walked out. She followed him to the truck, told him he wasn't going anywhere without her, and climbed into the cab, where the argument continued. It continued all the way to the Waffle Nook, where he left her in the truck, engine idling, while he went inside the restaurant to find Jack in order to tell him he wasn't going rabbit hunting after all. And it continued as they drove out of town, heading for the mountains.

The argument grew louder. New accusations were hurled. She treated him badly, he said, she bitched at him all the time.

Who was it that found fault in whom? she wanted to know, sitting in the Melody Inn parking lot in Chubbuck, watching him open a can of beer. Who didn't give a shit? he asked, slipping pills into his mouth to wash them down with the beer.

"I got needs," she said, out on the highway, passing the lava fields. "I . . . I can't buy anything without you making me feel bad — "

"I give it to you, whatever you want. Who helped you when you needed it down in L.A., huh? I have helped you, you can deny it. And if I give you money now, don't expect me not to wonder where it goes. I don't ask much in return."

"Except wanting me to be something I'm not."

"I let you go the way you want to go."

"Except when I want to go with you."

"You're with me now, stop complaining."

"Like you really sound happy about it."

"No, I'm not happy! What would I be happy about? Coming home to you . . . you don't say anything. All you do is watch TV." He stomped on the gas, driving a little too fast on the two-lane road, headed for Lava Hot Springs. It wasn't the money, he said. No, it wasn't the money itself. He didn't give a shit about the money. It was what he got in return.

"That doesn't mean I'm trying to buy you or make you feel indebted to me. But I wouldn't mind getting something back. Like a home, a meal once in a while. I don't want a slave. But you don't do anything for me. It's a bummer. Coming home to somebody who sits there, looking half-starved and depressed, and I can't ever get a cup of coffee in my own place — "

"Fuck that shit," she said, as he swung the truck up against the curb in front of the Lava Hot Springs Drugstore.

He didn't say anything. He got out of the truck, went into the store, and came back with a pack of cigarettes. He tore the package open, tapped out a cigarette against the steering wheel, stuck it between his lips, and peeled away from the curb.

"I'd like to know why we're even together," he said.

At the stop sign at the end of the street, she tried to jump out of the truck, but he grabbed her hands away from the door handle and told her to stop acting so stupid. She knocked his hat off trying to pull away from him.

"I've had enough! I want you to let me out. I don't want to spend another minute with you!"

"I'm not going to let you out," he said, and sped off up the road, passing the hot springs, where a group of bathers were clustered on the cement steps leading to the water.

"I'm not going to take it anymore," she said.

248

"Yeah, sure," he said, making a sharp turn onto a narrow, rutted road. She didn't have to stay with him, she said. She could take off on her own. She sure as hell didn't want to stay in Pokey, she snorted, using the nickname for Pocatello that made it sound as dead as it felt to her. No, she wouldn't stay in Pokey. Maybe California, she said. She might just go to California.

"Yeah, right," he said.

"Where are we going?" She could see no point in going on, in going anywhere with him. "Just take me back," she said. "I want to go back to town. Stop and turn around."

He drove on, speeding up the dirt road, not speaking to her but letting his careless driving show how mad he was. It was the silence, his not speaking, that got to her, drove her to say more things to him, until he turned and faced her and said he thought he might like it if she found her own place because he had come to the conclusion anybody who was as unhappy as she was wasn't really somebody he honestly wanted to be with. He didn't know what was wrong with her, he said, but something was. She was damaged goods, too damaged for him to fix. She did not ask him to stop the truck then, she began screaming at him to stop it because if he didn't she was going to jump rather than spend another minute with him. The next thing she knew her hand was on the door handle, and she felt the door give, and swinging with it slightly, she straddled open space for a second or two: the air rushed up her dress as the truck skidded to a stop and her feet touched down roughly in the dirt.

She pulled back the covers on the bed and swung her legs over the edge, easing her feet to the floor. She tiptoed to the door and opened it a crack, listening. The hallway was quiet and dark except for the sliver of light that came from beneath Phil's bedroom door. Very quietly, she crept down the hall and used the bathroom. When she returned to the bedroom, she slid between the fresh-smelling sheets, and looked around the room once more before turning out the light.

Lying in the darkness, she gave Wendall a final thought: I didn't call him, and if he thinks I will, he'll be surprised. I'm not going back. She felt firm in her resolve, if also bitter and sad. In very little time, she ceased thinking about anything, and fell into a deep and heavy sleep.

5

Phil poured more batter into the frying pan. "Would you like another pancake?" he asked.

Louise looked up at him from the kitchen table. "Yeah, sure."

Outside he could hear a woodpecker hammering in the dead oak.

"I called my brother this morning," she said.

"Oh?" This news surprised him. He hadn't heard her make a phone call, and he'd been up before she was. To his knowledge, she hadn't used the phone.

"He said he'd come get me, but he can't get away until the weekend. I was wondering if I could stay until then."

"The weekend?" It was only Tuesday. That meant she'd be staying four more days. "Where does your brother live?"

"Blackfoot."

"Maybe you could take a bus up there."

"Well, that's a problem. He's a salesman. He's going to be on the road. He won't be back until the weekend."

"Oh. I see."

"Would it be okay if I stayed until then?"

251

"All right," he said, but the idea made him nervous. He put two more pancakes on her plate.

"Thanks. My mom used to make pancakes once in a while, but they didn't taste like these."

"Where did you say your parents live?"

"I didn't."

"Oh, I thought you mentioned Coeur d'Alene — "

"They're split up. They live in different places."

"Where?"

"I don't know where my mother lives anymore. I think she might be in Spokane."

Phil frowned. How could you not know where your mother lived?

"You don't stay in touch with your mother?"

"No," she said.

"I see." He didn't see at all.

"You seem pretty young to be on your own."

"I'm eighteen. I've just always looked young." She tossed her head and smiled. "How long have you lived in this house? It's really a beautiful place."

"Forty years. I built it myself just after our children were born. I used to be in the carpentry business, but I'm retired now."

"You did everything yourself?"

"Most of it." He thought of May, pounding nails alongside him. "It's old now and it could use a little work, but I never seem to get around to it."

"I really like that bed I slept in last night."

"I made that bed for my daughter Helen."

"You did? I've never slept in a bed like that, with a headboard and everything. It's like a nest. It makes you feel protected. I slept so well last night. I think it was just being away from him."

"Him?"

"Wendall. The guy you met yesterday."

"Why is it so important that you get away from him?"

"Because all we do is fight. If I could just walk away like a normal person I would, but he wouldn't let me. He hung on to me." She stood up quickly and walked to the window. "I don't really want to get into it. I'm sorry I brought it up."

Phil looked down at the new batch of pancakes he'd poured into the pan. They looked like islands slowly mushrooming toward each other. He hoped they wouldn't touch each other and lose their shape, but they did, and the circles melded, forming one gigantic pancake in the bottom of the pan. He turned his head toward her and studied her back. For the first time he realized she didn't have any clothes except the dress she was wearing. And the shoes. They were suede, with tiny sharp heels. She'd gotten them wet running through the woods, and they'd dried hard and curled up at the toes, like a genie's slippers. It struck him that she would wear these shoes and this dress for the next four days unless he could find something else for her. Already he was thinking, What clothes are there here that will fit her?

"I think there are some boxes of clothes downstairs in the basement," he said. "Maybe you'd like to look through them and see if anything might fit you."

She turned and smiled at him. "Thanks. Listen, you sit down and eat. I'll wait on you. I've been sitting there letting you do everything. I ought to be cooking for you." She took his elbow and lightly steered him to a chair at the table. As she reached over him to clear away her dirty plate, he smelled the odor of her unwashed body.

She overcooked the pancakes. They were dry and way too brown, but he ate them anyway and didn't say anything. Then she insisted on doing the dishes, and broke a glass in the process. He could see that she wasn't used to housework. Her attention span was short. Her mind seemed unfocused. She hopped from one subject to the other, and when he spoke to her, he couldn't be certain she was listening.

After breakfast, he took her down to the basement and showed her the boxes of clothes. He left her to sort through them on her own. As a subtle suggestion, he told her he'd put a towel in the bathroom for her if she cared to have a bath. He went outside to check if the mail had come, and puttered awhile in the garden. The day was overcast and cool. He wondered if he shouldn't pick the remaining tomatoes, then decided it wouldn't freeze yet. He'd leave them a few more days.

When he came inside, he found her lying on the couch, reading a magazine. She wore a pair of baggy jeans, cinched in at the waist with a belt, and a shirt he instantly recognized as one that had belonged to May. It was checked, red and green, worn to a faded softness. It gave him a slightly funny feeling to see her shirt on someone else. He could tell she had showered. Her hair was still wet, and there was a bright, fresh glow to her skin.

"Too bad you don't have a television," she said, looking up from her magazine.

"Television," he muttered. Kids couldn't

do without it. He took a bucket from under the sink and went back outside, walking down to the lake to check on the boat. The wind had blown in the night, bringing down all the withered leaves, and he was sure the boat had taken on water. It was just a little aluminum fishing boat with a thirty-five-horsepower motor, tied off to a dock he'd built himself. He kept the boat in good running order, though he rarely used it now. He pulled out the seat pads that doubled as life preservers and set them against the trunk of a cottonwood to dry. A little water lay in the bottom of the boat. As he leaned down and scooped up a pail of water, he felt the muscles pull across his chest. Each time he lifted something, he could feel it in his chest, where a weakness lingered, a sensitivity to strain. He bailed slowly, taking just a little water at a time. Maybe he would take the boat out soon, before it turned cold and he hauled it out and stored it in the shed for winter. He'd call Lars perhaps, and go fishing.

As he thought of this possibility, he realized he couldn't call Lars, not until she left. He didn't want to have to explain to Lars what she was doing at his house. It would sound too strange. In fact, he didn't quite understand himself what she was doing there.

Things had happened so quickly yesterday. Now it seemed he had to endure a whole week of company. He sighed, thinking how right he'd been to shut himself away for months. He regretted ever having ventured out on the picnic. Now he felt reluctant even to return to his own house, knowing there was another person waiting there.

When he came back up to the house, he found her still on the couch, looking at one of May's books, *Reflexology*, by Dr. Maybelle Segal. She had unfolded May's hand-drawn diagrams of feet that had been tucked away in the book and was looking at them, grinning.

"What is *this?*" she asked and began laughing.

He crossed the room quickly and took the book from her, snatching the drawings from her hand as well. It annoyed him to think she had been rummaging through the bookshelves. "These were my wife's personal things. I don't think they'd interest you."

She shrugged. "Sorry. I was just curious."

He tried to tidy up the house, as he did each day, but as he swept around the fireplace, he could feel her watching his every move, and when he glanced at her, she looked away from him, acting a little surly, as if he'd hurt her feelings by taking the book away. It was better to leave her in the house and work outside.

He stood among his raspberries, pruning back old canes. The sky had grown darker, and a few drops of rain fell around him. From the house, the twanging, pounding noise of the radio erupted. She had turned up rock music so loud it seemed to buzz through the speakers, distorting into a fuzzy blare of electronic instruments. Why did young people insist on such loud music? Such terrible music? It drifted out over the garden, a wailing and pounding he found quite intolerable. Even the cows in neighboring fields seemed to hear it. They stopped grazing and lifted their heads, looking in unison in the direction of the house. He was about to go inside and tell her to turn it off when the music ended. Later, he had forgotten about it, and when she strolled outside at sunset and sat down next to him on the porch and began talking about how pretty the light was, he couldn't deny that in certain ways it was nice having some company.

"What does your father do for a living?" he asked while they were eating dinner, a simple meal of tomatoes from the garden, and leftover chicken and rice.

"He's with the Air Force down in California."

"And your mother? Does she work?"

She set her fork down quietly. "I told you, we're not speaking. I don't know anything about her life anymore."

He rubbed his chin. "What about — "

"Could I have some more rice?"

"How many children were there in your family?"

"Just me."

"What about your brother?"

"Oh, yeah, and my brother. That's what I meant. Just me and my brother."

"Is he married?"

"Divorced."

"Where did you grow up?"

"Different places. Phoenix some of the time."

"And where the rest of the time?"

"Uh . . . well, Coeur d'Alene."

"I've always thought that was such an interesting name for a place," he said. "What does it mean? Do you know?"

"Heart of awl. Or awl of the heart. Something like that. I remember a teacher in seventh grade telling us the story of how it got its name. Something about French trappers who thought the Indians drove such a hard bargain when they tried to trade with them it was like they drove an awl through your heart. An awl is a spiked thing," she said.

"I know," he laughed.

"Oh," she said, blushing. "Sure you'd know that. I didn't until she told us. Funny, I don't remember that much from school, but I never forgot that story." She pushed her hair back from her cheek and stared down at her plate. Her face looked very sad.

"What is it?" he asked.

"What?"

"You look troubled."

"It's nothing. Just thinking about that name, that's all."

She changed the subject and began talking about the weather, explaining how she had read an article that said there was a worldwide warming trend because of increasing pollution. Pretty soon, she said, the ice caps at the ends of the earth were going to melt. Then cities on coastlines were going to flood. The earth was going to turn more and more into a desert. People wouldn't be able to live anywhere except in the north. It would be hard to grow food, and there'd be a lot of skin cancer. This was all according to the article she'd read.

He thought it was a terribly bleak picture of things. Of course, he'd heard these kinds of predictions before. Talk of the greenhouse effect was everywhere these days. Who could understand what it all meant? He knew he would be long dead by the time such things happened, if they really did occur. For her, it was quite different, of course. She was at the beginning of her life, and perhaps in forty or fifty years, the terrible things she spoke of would come true. It troubled him to think that young people had to face such disquieting prospects. When he was her age he hadn't worried about the survival of the planet. He'd thought about baseball and girls. Again, he remembered Dr. Bowen's words: You're set for life, Phil. But what about her? What kind of life was she set for?

He cleaned up the kitchen after dinner, busying himself with extra tasks like cleaning the top of the stove and drying every dish and putting it away, while she sat in the rocker in front of the fireplace and stared into the flames. He went to bed at his usual time, nine o'clock, leaving her sitting in the living room, still watching the fire.

The next day he arose early, thinking he would walk over and visit Lars before he left for work, and ask him about fishing the next week. He dressed quietly so as not to disturb her sleeping in the next room.

He put on his work boots and thick socks, and his old, warm jacket — feeling to make sure his gloves were in the pocket. He'd been wrong about the frost. There was rime on the windowpane.

As he opened the bedroom door and looked down the hall, he saw her standing at May's desk in the den. She was looking through the drawers. He cleared his throat, and she looked up quickly.

"Oh, hi! I was looking for something to write with." The nightgown she wore was so big the material piled up on the floor around her. She rubbed the side of her face with her hand and yawned. "I couldn't sleep. I wanted to write in my diary." She held up a small blue notebook.

"I'll get you a pencil if you just ask." He tried not to sound cross but he rather felt that way.

"I didn't want to wake you."

"You couldn't hear me moving around in my room?" As he said this, he remembered how quiet he'd tried to be.

He found a pencil and gave it to her and left the house, after taking his pills. He felt uneasy about her rummaging in May's desk. The sun was rising over the tall peaks to the east. Wavering spokes of crimson lay on the milky blue water with its slight cording of waves. A dozen geese were gathered down on the beach beyond the cottonwoods, and they honked in annoyance as he approached, then lifted off with running starts.

He unlatched the gate to the Magnussens' pasture and strolled past the cows bedded down under an old oak. Lars would be surprised to see him. It felt good to be out in the world again, going to visit an old friend like Lars. Lars was lucky to still have Erika, his German-born wife, given as he was to notorious fooling around with his young dental assistants. Anybody would be lucky to have Erika. Erika worked in the greenhouses north of town. Tall and strong, with eyes that never blinked as she spoke to you, Erika was a prize, a hard worker, graceful, and one of the best cooks in the valley. Many nights he and May had eaten her cooking at a table set with old china and a vase of fresh flowers, listening to her tell stories of a childhood in Hamburg in a beautifully accented voice. Really, Lars, with his boisterous ways and roving eye, didn't deserve Erika. But how could you say who deserved whom in this world?

He came up on the house from behind and found Erika standing in the yard near the barn, scattering feed for her chickens. She straightened up as he approached and watched him with her steady blue eyes, just a hint of a smile around her mouth. She wore jeans and a thick sweater that looked handmade. Her hair was cut short as a man's, and in fact, standing so erect, with her arms enfolding a bowl of feed, she gave off a kind of masculine strength.

"Hello, Erika," he said.

"So, Phil, we see you at last," she said. "You must have known I baked cinnamon rolls this morning, eh?"

He laughed.

"You look very well, Phil, and it's so nice to see you. Come inside. I give you breakfast."

"Just a roll," he said, "and a little coffee. You know I couldn't turn down your cinnamon rolls. Where's Lars?"

"Lars is pursuing his usual foolishness. This morning, I think it is ducks. Or pheasant. I don't know. I used to fear for those poor birds, but he comes home empty-handed so often now that I think they are safe." She laughed, a laugh rich and full of confidence and warmth. "Come. I show you my new project."

He followed her around behind the barn, where new pens had been built, enclosed with chicken wire. Inside the pens were the most beautiful birds he had ever seen.

"Himalayan pheasants," she said. "I'm breeding them now."

The variety of color in the bird's feathers was unlike anything he'd seen before. They had green-and-copper heads, turquoise-and-blue necks, and their bodies were a mixture of gold, orange, and red feathers. Each color had a metallic sheen. There were a number of small chicks in the cage, and these had ordinary coloring, brownish feathers speckled with white.

"They don't begin to develop coloration until they're older," she said. "Then they show their true colors. Like humans, eh?"

He smiled. Erika had a touch with everything. She could make any kind of flower grow, keep her chickens healthy, and figure out a mechanical problem that would stump Lars. Standing close to her, he felt aware of his attraction for this woman. He had always had such deep admiration for her. What it amounted to was a sort of infatuation. Why didn't Lars just run off with one of those little dental assistants he was always being so flirtatious with and leave Erika for him to court? Thinking this, he felt ashamed of himself. How could he wish Erika such pain? And what made him think he was such an irresistible catch himself? What in the world was happening to him to cause him to feel these unexpected tugs of desire lately?

"The cock," she said, "is quite a handsome fellow, isn't he?"

"Yes," he said, feeling a little disconcerted by her comment.

The kitchen smelled yeasty and sweet. A big vase of delphiniums sat in the middle of the table. She brought him good strong coffee and a thick cinnamon roll. The sun came in through the window that looked out toward the creek and a hillside shady beneath spreading oaks. The light fell on her good walnut table, bringing out the beautiful color of wood. In the corner stood a little cherry table he'd made for her and Lars as an anniversary present many years ago. She brought her cup of coffee to the walnut table and sat down across from him.

"Your body has healed, hasn't it, Phil? I can see that. But what about your spirit? Has there been time for that to heal, too?"

"Not yet," he said, shaking his head. Only Erika would think to ask the question so delicately.

"Perhaps," she said, "there is something you can do."

He waited, wondering what she was going to propose. Knowing Erika, it would be worth listening to.

"I was in the cemetery last week, taking flowers to the graves of Lars's mother and father. Of course, I visited May's grave, too, and left her some gladiolas. They were always her favorite, weren't they? Yes. I couldn't help noticing your grandson's grave. They haven't done such a good job with it, Phil. Just a little flat marker, made of cement. You know the kind they make these days. There's no feeling behind it. I was thinking of the beautiful stone you carved for May and the words you put there."

The words, ah yes, those words, which he had thought about for so long before they came to him. *Blessed is the tie that binds.*

"Why don't you make a little headstone, something beautiful, for your grandson? Put your love for him into it. I think it might be a very healing thing for you to do."

He looked down. His nose tingled with the feeling that had arisen in him. He had been so absorbed in his own sadness he hadn't been able to see there was something he could do. Something he should do. He had not even been able to bring himself to visit the cemetery.

"I think you're right, Erika."

"He was such a good boy, such a fine young man. You will think of something to say to him, and put it in stone, and it will last a very long time."

He pressed his lips together, afraid of all the emotion welling up in him, and yet grateful for it, too, because it brought to the surface his deepest feelings, not only his pain but his love. Now he could see a way of expressing this love.

He finished his cinnamon roll, and she walked with him as far as the gate. He wanted to touch her, to hug her, before he left, but he didn't. Erika had never been one for physical greetings or send-offs. She stood erect, watching him, and as he said goodbye to her, he saw so much warmth and true affection in her eyes that he thought it was perhaps better than an awkward embrace. There was enough truth in those eyes for the whole world.

"I will tell Lars you visited. He'll be happy to know you came."

All during the walk home, he thought about the headstone. He would go into town today and get a piece of marble from the Rasmussen brothers and start on it right away. Of course, it would take time for the words to come. But he could begin somewhere, with the boy's name, and let things flow from there. He became so absorbed in thinking about the headstone he forgot about Louise and felt an abrupt change in his feelings when he came up from the fields and saw the figure sitting on his porch.

"Hi," she called as he came up the steps. She was sitting in May's rocker, lightly pushing off the balls of her feet, moving to and fro. She wore an old brown sweater, one he had discarded long ago because it had holes in the elbows. It fit her like a gunny sack and looked about as attractive. Wasn't there anything else in those boxes of clothing she might have chosen, something that might have made her look a little less like an orphan?

"Where have you been? Out for a walk?"

"I went over to visit some neighbors. I think I'll drive into town. I've got a few errands to do."

"Can I come with you?"

"I suppose," he said. He hadn't thought of this, that she might want to go along, and though he didn't exactly like the idea, he couldn't see refusing her.

They drove the Paris-to-Dingle road, taking the back way through marshes and swampy farmland, surrounded by a misty light. They passed orchards that had been abandoned. Each time he saw these twisted old trees, now dead, their branches leafless and bare, reaching toward the sky as if in supplication, he felt saddened. It seemed such a waste to let good fruit trees die.

Once in town, they went their separate ways. She wanted to look at clothes in Mode O'Day. He stopped at the bank and hardware store before walking the two blocks to Rasmussen Brothers Construction Company, where he found Eldon Rasmussen, the youngest of the brothers, sitting behind a desk piled high with papers. "D-d-don't think we have any m-m-marble right now," Eldon said, stuttering the way he always had. The longer you talked to him, the more the stutter disappeared, but in short exchanges, it was pronounced, and rather disconcerting. "I'd t-t-try Anderson's up in S-S-Soda Springs."

It took him an hour to drive with Louise to Soda Springs, where he had to wait almost another hour for old man Anderson to open his shop. There was a little sign on the door saying "Be back at:" and a clock with movable red hands. The hands were set for two o'clock, but Anderson didn't show up until three. To kill time, they'd had an ice cream cone at Farr's and wandered over to the city park to watch some boys play touch football on the grass.

Anderson unlocked the door of his old shop and led him to a back room. He showed him a dozen pieces of marble, each one quite beautiful. But there was one piece that stood out. It was alabaster and had faint veins of pink — not too large, not too small. He wanted to see it in the sunlight, and he and Anderson each took an end and carried the marble outside. He felt the cool weight of the stone in his hands. The moment they stepped outside and the light fell on it, he knew it was right. He paid Anderson in cash, and they wrapped the slab in an old blanket and laid it in the trunk of the Buick, where it fit nicely.

6

"What's the marble for?" she asked. They were driving away from Soda Springs, passing the grain elevators on the outskirts of town. It was dusk, and the elevators were outlined against the skyline.

"Oh . . . uh, a project."

They drove in silence toward Montpelier, listening to music on the radio. As they passed the Ranchhand, she said, "I know that place. I'm hungry. Are you?"

"A little."

"What are we going to do for dinner?" She put her feet up on the dashboard and turned her head to look in the windows of the Ranchhand as they passed it.

"I hadn't thought about it."

"Why don't we eat out?"

"Eat out? Where?"

"I'd like a cheeseburger."

"Well, I suppose we could find one of those."

"Great." Her face lit up. Phil studied her for a moment. She seemed so childish sometimes. Was she really eighteen?

They drove to the Raspberry Shack and

ordered cheeseburgers, eating them while sitting in the car. Phil hadn't eaten a cheeseburger in a long time. It tasted good. Only when he'd finished it and was sitting quietly, sipping his Coke, did he realize how bad it made him feel. It sat on his stomach the wrong way. On the other hand, she had eaten her cheeseburger and was finishing off her second order of French fries, looking content. He noticed she had an appetite, always, and yet she was so thin, she looked almost undernourished.

"Look at that couple over there," she said abruptly.

Phil looked in the direction she pointed, at an older man and a woman sitting in a pickup truck. He didn't recognize them. He thought perhaps she did, and that was why she was pointing them out.

"They haven't said one word to each other the whole time we've been sitting here. They just eat and stare straight ahead. That's a good reason right there not to stay with somebody too long. That's what happens."

"It isn't always true."

"Love can't last once your neck starts sagging."

Phil shook his head. "I don't think a sagging neck has anything to do with it." He felt

273

rather startled by the callousness of her comment.

"Look at them! Have you ever seen two more unhappy-looking people? They've completely run out of things to say. They look dead. It must be boring as hell to live like that. There isn't anything left for them."

They're just resting, Phil thought. They're old, she doesn't understand.

"Did you keep having fun?"

"What?"

"Did you and your wife have fun?"

"Yes," Phil said. Fun? Fun was hardly the word he would have chosen.

"It kills me you say that. I couldn't even make the good feelings last six months with Wendall."

"Maybe you never loved him," he said. "Have you asked yourself that question, whether or not you really loved him?"

"I don't know," she said. "I really don't know."

"That doesn't sound like love to me."

"The thing is, I feel like that part of myself that might know if I was in love is broken. It doesn't work."

This was an astonishing thought to him, that you might not be able to tell when you loved someone. It could only be because she was young, too immature to know her feelings yet.

"Perhaps you need more time to come to know yourself. That comes with age. There'll come a day when you meet someone, and you won't wonder anymore. You'll know that it's love you feel."

She stared at him for some time. "You're very kind," she mumbled, so softly he couldn't be certain at all this is what she'd said.

Driving home, they passed the Mountain View Drive-In at the turnoff for the sand pits. The giant screen was lit up with a moving picture, which was only partly visible from the highway. Phil caught a glimpse of a muscular man in some kind of primeval outfit.

"We should stop," Louise said. "Can we go to the drive-in? Let's not just go back home and sit around. Let's do something. I mean, wouldn't you like to see a movie?"

"But the movie's already started," he said.

"It won't matter. Come on."

"Well . . . I don't know."

"Look! *Conan the Barbarian*! Turn right there. Quick!"

Hastily, he turned into the drive-in, not at all certain this was what he wanted to do. Yet why shouldn't they see a movie? He felt as he used to with May, when they had done something spontaneously.

He recognized the girl selling tickets, Stan Henderson's daughter, a cheery girl with big glasses. "This is our last week before we close for the winter," she told him as he paid for the tickets. She handed him a speaker and a heater. "It's getting cold. You might need the heater." As she gave him his change, she gazed past him, at Louise. "Don't I know you?" she said.

"I don't think so," Louise replied very quickly.

"Hmmm. Your face looks familiar. Where could I have seen you before?"

"I don't know. Come on, Phil. We're missing the movie."

There weren't many cars at the drive-in. They found a place to park near the refreshment stand. He hung the speaker on the front window and put the little heater next to it. As they began watching the movie, he felt happy they'd decided to stop. It seemed a frivolous thing to be doing, but how long had it been since he'd felt anything like frivolity? The movie was even pretty good, sort of a grown boy's adventure story.

At intermission she asked him if he'd like something to eat, and when he said no, she left for the refreshment stand to get something for herself.

Phil watched the people passing by, heading for the rest rooms and snack bar. He recognized a few people, including some kids who were Luke's age. There were a few families, young couples with children. He remembered taking his own girls to the drive-in when they were small. He'd forgotten how nice it could be. At drive-ins you felt part of the night. Cars and nights and movies seemed to go together, and there was something quite magical about it, especially the size of the picture, projected so big against a black sky.

He looked up. Pinpoints of stars dotted the heavens. The night was fresh and carried a sharp feel of winter. Music came from the little speaker attached to the window. He noticed a baby in the station wagon next to him, her tiny hands pressed against the window. A group of teenagers stood in a circle, their shoulders lifted against the cold. He thought he recognized one of them, a girl. Hadn't she been a friend of Luke's? She was short and compact, with a fresh look, braided hair, and freckles. She stood with her hands jammed into the pockets of her jeans, rocking from one foot to the other. She gazed over at him and smiled. He saw her start walking toward him. She crossed in front of the Buick and came up to his window.

"Hi," she said, her breath making a plume on the cold air.

"Hello."

"Aren't you Mr. Doucet?"

"Yes."

"I'm Karen Cook — I was a friend of Luke's. I met you once when I came to visit him. You were building the new library."

"Oh, yes."

"I thought I recognized you. I just wanted to come over and say hello. How are you doing? It's getting cold, isn't it?"

"Yes, it is."

"You sure look good. Do you feel okay?"

"Yes, fine, thanks."

"I really miss Luke. I'm so sorry he's gone. I'm sure you miss him, too."

"Yes," Phil said.

"I just wanted to say that."

The girl had a lovely simplicity. He remembered her now. "Didn't you come to my place with Luke once? You were on your bikes, I believe."

"That's right!" she said. "I'd forgotten that. Now I remember. You have that wonderful house near the lake."

Out of the corner of his eye, he noticed

Louise, rushing toward the car. When she reached the window, she said, "Can you loan me fifty cents? I'm fifty cents short."

While he dug in his pocket, he heard Louise say to Karen, "Man, it's cold."

"You should have a coat on," Karen said.

"You aren't kidding."

"Here you go." Phil handed her a dollar, aware of how shabby she looked. Her arms were folded across her chest, and her elbows stuck out of the holes in the sleeves of the oversized sweater.

"Thanks. I'll be right back."

"Well, I'll see you later," Karen said, backing away. "I just saw you sitting here and wanted to say hello. Take care, Mr. Doucet."

"Thank you. 'Bye."

He remembered that girl. The day she came with Luke they had the dogs with them, and they'd all arrived tired and thirsty from their bike ride. He remembered her very well.

Louise returned with a bag of popcorn and a Coke, which she spilled getting into the car.

"Shit!" she said. He flinched from the word. "That place is a zoo. One person is trying to do everything. I had to wait in line all over again just to pay. Now I've spilled this stuff."

"Here," he said, and tried to hand her some Kleenex from the glove box.

"God, look at my sweater!" She lifted the sweater and flapped it a few times. Ice rolled off the sweater and onto the seat.

"What a mess. Here, hold this stuff, would you?"

"I think there's a towel in the backseat."

She climbed on her knees, turning around, and leaned way over. He noticed the teenagers staring at them. This was embarrassing. It occurred to him how strange it must look for him to be here at a drive-in with Louise. What did those kids think?

"Well, it'll dry okay, I guess," she said, wiping the front of her with the towel. "That guy at the snack bar was such an asshole," she muttered.

"Stop that kind of talk!" He wasn't so much shocked by her language as disturbed by what seemed an unnecessarily angry reaction to an ordinary situation. If you hit your finger with a hammer, he could understand yelling "Shit!" But having to wait in line was no reason to call someone an asshole. "I really don't think you need to talk like that."

She seemed startled. "What? I didn't mean anything. He was an asshole, I'm telling you. You didn't see how he treated me."

"I still don't think you need to act so coarse."

"Coarse? I said I didn't mean anything." She stared at him for a few moments, and then said, in a rather hostile voice, "The movie's started. Would you turn up the speaker, please?"

Phil paid very little attention to the rest of the film. Their brief exchange had left him feeling troubled. How had he gotten himself into this situation? Who was this young woman? She disturbed him. He felt a creeping fear. What if she didn't leave on Saturday? What if no brother turned up to collect her? What would he do? Throw her out? Take her into town and drop her off, force her to leave? What if things didn't work out for her and she turned up on his doorstep again? Expecting something more from him, assuming because he had helped her once he would do so again? The problem with agreeing to help someone was that you couldn't just stop in the middle of things and say, I've changed my mind, I'm sorry, but you'll have to leave.

He felt a sense of being saddled with her. He had helped her because he believed she was somehow in need of help. But now he felt he was the one who needed help. He needed someone to help him decide what to do about her. He reminded himself that her brother was coming, she had said so. Just relax, he thought. It's only a few more days. Still, he felt himself leaning against the door, slightly repelled by her presence in his car and wishing to move away from her. He knew it had something to do with what she had said, not just the words she had used, but the hostility behind them. And yet he couldn't really look at her and feel much more than pity. He was sure his feelings were partly the result of having been so out of touch with other human beings. He simply wasn't used to any kind of strife.

Up on the giant screen, set against the great blackness, the hero and heroine waded through snakes. The stars arranged themselves in familiar patterns, and cars, their headlights throwing cheerful yellow beams into the darkness, progressed steadily down the highway. In the distance, the 7-Up sign atop the truck stop flashed on and off, the number 7 erupting in the night, glowing like a bold symbol of luck. The world, he thought, has become a worse, not a better, place. *The beeping Morse, returning homeward, finds no ham operator's ear*, the poet said.

When the movie ended, Phil replaced the speaker and heater on their little hooks on the pole next to the car, started the engine,

282

and edged out into the line of cars pressing toward the exit. His head ached. He felt tired and chilled. The idea that he would soon be alone in his own bedroom comforted him. That she would be sleeping in the room next door was disquieting. But at least, he thought, I can close the door. I can be alone again for a while.

"You're mad at me, aren't you?" she said during the drive home.

"No," he said, "not exactly."

"You know what the trouble is? Everything is superficial. What you say matters more than what you really think. Nobody wants to know what you really think. Nobody cares who you really are."

He didn't have the slightest idea what she was talking about. They didn't speak again until they were back at the house. He had trouble getting the marble out of the car, and without saying anything, she came and helped him carry it to the cellar. He said good night to her as they came back up to the living room.

"You're going to bed already?"

"Yes. I'm tired." He climbed the stairs quietly, went to his room, and shut the door.

She sat down at the little dressing table and opened her diary. For a while, she sat thinking, tapping the end of her pencil against her teeth, and then she began writing:

There is something about me that disgusts people, though I can't tell what it is. I can see it with him. He likes me about as much as a dog likes a vacuum cleaner. I get that kind of reaction when I come into a room where he is. I see him slide away, like a dog would if a vacuum was coming at him. He'll move to the next room and kind of peer around a corner at me once in a while to see if I'm gone yet. Tonight after I swore in the drive-in he was hugging the door as if he couldn't get far enough away from me. I have to remember not to swear anymore. I have To try and be nicer when I'm around him.

I'm more afraid than I've been since I first left home. I don't know where to go or what to do. Tonight at the drive-in I thought that girl selling tickets must have seen my picture somewhere on a poster. It scared me. Maybe I won't go to town anymore.

What am I going to tell him on Saturday when no brother shows up? There's over two hundred dollars in a drawer in the other room I found this morning when I was looking around after he left. I could take it and buy a bus ticket to someplace, maybe Los Angeles, but I hate to think I am the kind of person who has grown so low she could steal from someone who is being nice to her. Maybe that's what people see in me they don't like. I've changed. Even I'm surprised at what I'll do.

What did he say to me tonight? You need more time to know yourself. I don't believe he's right about a day coming when I'll feel love and know it. Something's wrong with me that's perminent. I knew that when Lady died and I hardly felt anything. I wonder how you fix feelings so they work again.

I wish I didn't have to go anywhere for a while. I like it here. It's very pieceful.

7

On Saturday, the day her brother was to come for her, Phil returned from a trip to the grocery store to find Louise was gone. Where was she? Everything was quiet. The ticking of the clock resounded in the empty rooms. He put the bag of groceries on the kitchen table, walked upstairs, and knocked on the bedroom door, rapping lightly several times.

"Louise?" he said. "Louise?"

No sound came from the other side of the door. Slowly he opened it and looked inside the room. Everything appeared orderly. The bed was made up neatly, the drapes drawn against the light, nothing out of place, no clothes or personal belongings left about to suggest the room had recently been occupied. The room was cold, as if it had been shut off from the rest of the house for many months. An uncanny feeling of desertion, of hollow long-standing emptiness, permeated the little bedroom.

Has she left? he thought. Did her brother come for her while I was gone? Could she possibly have decided to leave without even saying goodbye?

He walked through the upstairs, and looked around again downstairs, then he checked outside, but nowhere did he see her. Strolling to the edge of the garden, he stood still, straining his ears for any sound. He had an impulse to call out her name again but stopped himself from doing so. He turned and scanned the sheds and woodpile, and gazed down toward the beach. Some part of him felt confused and slightly panicked. Why would she leave so abruptly? He'd been gone less than an hour. Surely she could have waited to say goodbye, unless . . .

A very unpleasant thought came to him: She's robbed me and run off. Suddenly, he was certain that this was what had happened. She'd waited until he was gone, taken what she wanted, and left.

The first place he checked was the drawer in May's desk where he kept a little cash. The money was gone. A panicky feeling arose in him. He began looking in other places, different rooms, searching to see if he could detect anything else missing. May's silver was still in place, the guns, the old clock and the small Indian rugs — all things he counted as valuable, though he couldn't imagine Louise wanting them. He couldn't think what else she might have taken, until he remembered his dresser, where he kept a little jewelry in the top drawer — rings and cufflinks and a few things of May's, mostly worthless items, except for a string of yellowed pearls he'd bought for her birthday one year. When he saw the pearls were gone, he felt a burning anger. She'd stolen the pearls. The money was one thing. But the pearls. How could she have taken those?

He went downstairs and sat at the kitchen table. He knew he should unpack the groceries. There were things that needed to go in the refrigerator. But he couldn't move. He felt numb. For a long time he thought about the girl, becoming angrier and more agitated by the moment. He imagined her face, so pale, her hard little mouth painted bright red, thin lips set in a mocking smile, the narrow, pointed nose and eyebrows darkened crudely with pencil, her blond hair a wild tangle of snarls, but mostly he thought of her eyes, where a hostile, wary glint always flashed. How had he ever thought her innocent? How could he have trusted her enough to leave her alone in the house? What did he know about her? He remembered how she had said earlier, "I don't want to go to town. I'll stay here." Of course she wanted to stay. She had been planning to rob him once he was gone.

A deep weariness filled him. He stared

out the window at fields bristling with weeds. Perhaps there's more missing, he thought, and I should get up and take a closer look. But instead he continued staring through the glass, feeling saddened to the point of melancholy. He could only look at the landscape and think, The fields are bright, the trees are swaying, the sky's flat, she's gone, and robbed me. He felt empty inside. A dullness shrouded his heart.

Then he remembered something, something that made him feel quite foolish.

Helen had the pearls.

She had asked for them, and he had given them to her. Months ago. He'd forgotten. And the money? Now it seemed to him he might have used that money for something. But what? It had been so long since he'd actually looked in the drawer. He simply couldn't remember.

He went to the phone and called Helen. "Did you take those pearls of your mother's?" he said when he had her on the line.

"Yes," she said. "You gave them to me quite a while ago. I don't remember exactly when — "

"All right. I just wanted to know. I thought you had them. I couldn't remember."

"What's wrong, Dad? Are you feeling okay?"

"Fine. I just couldn't remember what happened to those pearls. Don't worry, Helen. It's nothing. I'm forgetful, that's all."

He hung up the phone. He felt exhausted, the way he used to feel before the operation. His heart raced; he felt every beat, each small thud. He needed fresh air. He should unpack the groceries. Yet he couldn't bring himself to move. His legs were heavy, as if filled with water again. It's me, he thought. I'm so out of touch, I'm losing my memory, that's what happens. Standing slowly, he moved to the couch and lay down, covering his eyes with his arm, and giving himself up to his weariness, he fell asleep.

Several hours must have passed before he awoke, because the light in the room had changed. He came to feeling disoriented, thinking he was upstairs until he recognized the arm of the couch and remembered where he'd lain down. He rolled over to see Louise sitting in the rocker, watching him. A feeble fire, poorly built, was smoldering in the grate.

"Oh," he said. He felt groggy, as if drugged.

"I came in and you were sleeping. I didn't want to wake you, but you've been sleeping a long time."

He sat up slowly, smoothing back his hair.

"Are you okay?"

"I'm just a little tired." He looked away from her, not really wanting to face her just then. "Where did you go?" he asked.

"I took a walk. I started down a road and it led to other roads and I just kept going. There were these wide ditches with huge white birds standing in the water. I guess I kind of got lost, but I didn't care. It was so beautiful and I kept seeing those birds. Finally I recognized a farm I had passed and found my way back here."

"You must have gone toward the bird refuge," he said. He rose slowly and looked at the clock. It was after five. No wonder he felt disoriented. How had he managed to sleep so long? He went upstairs to use the bathroom. It seemed to him his suspicions earlier had been part of a dream that had come to him in his sleep. Still, he had an uneasy feeling about the money. Quietly, he slipped out of the bathroom and went to May's desk and checked the drawer again. A thick wad of bills sat in the bottom of the drawer. Now he felt completely confused. Was he losing his mind? Feeling addled, he descended the stairs and found her unpacking the groceries.

"Would you like me to fix dinner?" she said.

"That would be all right, I suppose." He

sat down at the table and watched her moving briskly around the kitchen.

"What about your brother? I thought he was coming today."

"I talked to him earlier," she said. "Now he doesn't think he can get away this weekend."

"What?" He was surprised by the sharpness in his voice, but he thought, This is impossible. What is she saying?

"His car's broken," she said, not looking at him. "He's going to try and get it fixed this week."

"But . . . I'm afraid I don't think it's a very good idea for you to stay." He knew what he wanted to say, but he had great difficulty in putting it simply. She *couldn't* stay. It had already been five days, days during which he'd felt his life completely disrupted. How could she presume to impose on him for another week?

Quite abruptly she turned on him and said, "All right. I'll leave tonight if that's what you want."

"But where will you go?"

She shrugged. "I don't know. I can always hitchhike."

"Hitchhike? Hitchhike where?"

"I don't know," she said. "What does it matter where I go?"

"I don't think that would be a good idea. I think it would be much better if I drove you up to your brother's tomorrow."

As he spoke, he remembered his promise to go to Joyce's tomorrow for lunch. It was Dan's birthday. There was no getting out of it. He had promised he'd be there, though he was dreading the visit to the house he'd avoided for so long. I can drive her to Blackfoot after lunch, he thought. It's only a couple of hours. It's a good excuse to cut the visit short.

"We can leave tomorrow afternoon," he said. "You can call your brother and tell him we're coming. That way he'll expect you."

She shut her eyes, and stood very still for what seemed like a long time, as if overcome by sickness. What was wrong with her? He was about to speak when she opened her eyes very slowly and, gazing at him steadily, said, "I don't have a brother."

"You don't *what?*"

"I don't have a brother in Blackfoot."

"I don't understand — "

"I lied," she said, cutting him off. "I'm sorry."

"You . . . lied?"

"I don't have a brother. There's no one who can come get me. I don't have anywhere to go."

Phil shook his head. This was too much. "Why did you even say you had a brother?"

He really wished she wouldn't cry, but that was exactly what she'd begun doing. Her whole face had contorted, twisting into the most horribly pathetic look. "I don't know why I thought it would be better if I said that," she sobbed. "I just don't know what to do." The sobs shook her body. The way her arms dangled loosely at her sides and her shoulders curled forward, she looked slack and defenseless.

Something occurred to him. "Louise," he said, "did you take some money from a drawer upstairs earlier today and then put it back later?"

She began crying harder, and he could tell without her even answering that he'd hit upon the truth.

"Why?" he said softly. "Why did you do that?"

Bubbles of mucus had begun to appear at her nostrils, and her mouth hung open, spittle shining in the corners. He stood up and got some tissue from a box near the phone and handed them to her. She took them mechanically, like a robot, but made no effort to blow her nose or clean the wetness from her face. He had a great urge to wipe her nose for her, as he would for a child, but he was also repulsed by her, filled with a rising anger.

"Blow your nose," he said. "Sit down. I want you to help me understand what's going on."

"No," she said, and brought the Kleenex to her face, pressing it between her hands as she covered her eyes. She said something muffled and he couldn't understand her, although it sounded like "I want to die."

"Sit down," he said again.

"Leave me alone."

"Louise!" he shouted, his patience gone. "What's going on? Why did you lie? Don't you know that's no way to treat somebody who's trying to help you?"

She dropped her hands. "I don't know what to do. You want me to explain, and I can't, I'm sorry, but I just can't."

"You want me to help you and yet you can't even tell me why you would lie to me and steal from me — "

"I didn't steal!" she shouted. "I put the money back."

"But why did you take it in the first place?"

"I thought I could use the money to get away, go somewhere, but the truth is I don't have anywhere to go, and I realized that walking down the road. I realized something . . . else, too."

She bit her lip, her face contorted by sobs, and tried to control her voice, but she was too overcome and could only stand there, her arms now wrapped around her chest. She looked down at the floor. Small hiccuping sounds began coming out of her mouth, and then she lost the meager control she had and erupted in loud crying, convulsive, gasping wails that increased in volume, until it seemed to him she threatened to become hysterical. He stood up quickly and went to her and took hold of her arm.

"Louise," he said, "try to stop crying. I want to help you. I really do. I can see you need help. But I really don't know what to do. Don't you see that you can't just stay here? Surely you have family, someone you can turn to. Your parents. I think you should call your parents."

"I lie, but I don't mean to, I only want . . . I thought I could do it, I thought I could start over if I got away from them. . . ."

"Them? Who are you talking about?"

"You don't know!" she wailed. "You don't understand — "

"Well, help me understand!" he yelled, trembling with the frustration he felt.

"You don't know anything about me! I can't go back to my family. My stepfather's a fucking Nazi!"

"A what?"

"My parents are crazy. I ran away from them. Now you know. I don't have parents. I want to forget them. They're poison. They hate niggers, get it? My stepfather celebrates Hitler's birthday. My mother sews armbands with swastikas on them for all their friends. They sit around singing, and you know what they sing? 'Nigger, nigger, get on that boat, nigger, nigger, row! Nigger, nigger, get out of here, nigger — "

"Stop it!" he yelled. "That's enough." Nazis, he was thinking. *Nazis?* She grew quiet, pressing her hand over her mouth, and closed her eyes. Could this be true? he wondered. My God, could she really have such a family?

"I'm so ashamed," she said. "I'm so sorry I took the money. I knew it wasn't right, and that's why I came back. It felt to me like one of the worst things I'd ever done."

"I don't know what to think," he said. "If what you say is true, it's quite terrible."

She threw herself against him, encircling his neck with her arms, and held him tightly, sobbing into his chest. He was caught off balance and staggered backward against the table, but she held on to him, and pulled him forward, as if they were a dancing couple righting themselves after a small misstep. Phil opened his mouth to speak, but she turned her head at that moment, pressing her face against his collarbone, and a piece of her hair caught in his mouth. It tasted perfumed and bitter. Her body moved against him as she sobbed, and he felt afraid. This wasn't right. She must let go. He could feel her nails biting into the back of his neck. He was overwhelmed by the physical contact, the insistent pressure of her body against his. It stirred a longing in him, hundreds of little neurons firing inside him, electrified by her.

He patted her back, a panicky reflex, and said, "Louise, let go, please." Instead of loosening her grip on him, she pulled against his neck all the harder.

They were both startled by the knock on the door. He froze, and felt her body go tense. "Good Lord," he muttered and pulled away from her. They looked at each other.

"Who's that?" she whispered.

He cleared his throat. "I don't know." The knocking came again, this time louder. She wiped the back of her hand across her mouth, then folded her arms across her stomach.

"I'd better find out who it is," he said.

He opened the door to find Lars standing

on his porch, a worried look on his face.

"Phil?" he said. "Are you all right?"

"Oh, Lars. Uh, yes, fine. You just caught me at a rather, uh, bad time." He could see Lars was trying to peer over his shoulder in order to see into the room. He stepped out on the porch and closed the door behind him.

"You look white as a ghost," Lars said. "I could hear shouting as I came up the lane. Somebody singing something about . . . I don't want to say the words," he said.

"Oh, that. Well, it's difficult to explain now." Lars stood on the porch wearing a big plaid coat, his eyebrows furrowed, gazing in the window of the kitchen. Phil resisted turning around to see if Louise was standing where Lars could see her. His heart thumped in his breast, racing with anxiety.

"You have company," Lars said. It wasn't a question. He must be able to see her.

"Yes," he said, "I do." He considered lying, saying one of May's nieces was here, an unexpected visit, but he simply couldn't bring himself to lie to Lars. Neither could he imagine offering any explanation.

"Maybe I could come by next week. We'll go fishing."

Lars stepped back from him. "All right."

"Next week then," Phil said, closing the door to a crack. "Monday, or maybe Tuesday."

"You're sure you're all right?"

"Fine," Phil said. "Say hello to Erika."

He shut the door. Dear God, what a mess. How much had Lars heard?

As he walked into the kitchen, she looked up from the table where she sat, slumped down in the chair, her hands playing with a piece of string. He avoided meeting her eyes. For a long time neither one of them spoke. He set about making dinner, frying bacon, flouring several pieces of liver.

She broke the silence. "I'm very sorry," she said.

For what? he thought. For what is she sorry?

As if reading his mind, she said, "I'm sorry I lied to you, and I'm sorry I took the money."

"Listen," he said, "I don't know what to think." He shook his head. "I guess I don't know what to do. It's all very strange. What do you expect of me?"

"I don't know," she said. "I really don't know." She got up from the chair sluggishly, took down plates from the cupboard and silverware from the drawer, and began setting the table.

"I'll leave," she said, "whenever you want me to."

He poked at the liver in the pan, and seeing it wasn't cooking fast enough, turned the heat up higher. "And where will you go?"

Briefly, he lifted his eyes from the stove and looked at her. She met his gaze with a steadiness, and for the first time the look of wariness was gone from her eyes. She regarded him calmly and said, "Does it really matter?"

The meal was so awkward Phil hurried through it, finishing his food while hers lay on her plate, almost untouched.

"You should eat," he said. "Aren't you hungry?"

She smiled and looked down at her food. "I hate liver," she said. "I suppose I should lie now, and say something else, something polite. That's the hard part, knowing how much truth to tell. I really am sorry I've caused you all this trouble. If you could, would you let me stay a few more days, just until I can figure out what to do?"

"You don't really have any friends? Any relatives? Someone you might turn to — "

"No," she said. "It's hard to explain, but we — my stepfather and my mother, their whole life revolves around the group they're a part of. We lived pretty much isolated from other people. I went to school, but I always felt so ashamed. I couldn't really have friends. I could never bring somebody home. I had one friend, Beth, but her family is part of the group, so she can't really help me. If anybody knew where I was, they could make me go back to my parents, and that can't happen. It just can't."

"I'm very tired," he said.

"I'll clean up, don't worry. Go ahead and go to bed."

In bed, he lay in the dark, feeling very troubled, and unable to sleep. What was happening to him? He recalled something from long ago. Once, when the television had still been working, he watched a morning news program on which a famous anthropologist was being interviewed. The anthropologist discussed the plight of young people in America, the decline of love, the despair she saw on the faces of children who had been abandoned by parents whose own personal lives took precedence. It was the children who really suffered in these times, she said, and the only solution was for everyone to take a child. The anthropologist had turned to the camera and stared hard into it, so that she seemed to be peering into the very depths of her unseen audience, addressing each person individually. She shook a finger at the camera. Take a child, she said. Take responsibility for that child, whether the child is related to you or not. Now he understood what she meant.

He gazed out the window at the night sky. A pale silver light surrounded a milky moon, creating a halo of gauze.

He awoke in the night to the sound of cries from the next room, a high-pitched and frightening wail. There was banging, and then a thud, like the sound of a body falling. Grabbing his robe, he opened his door and stood in the hallway in front of her room. The door was opened halfway. In the moonlight, he could see her small body, lying on the floor, not moving. The table lamp had tipped over and was also on the floor. Very quickly, he moved to her side and bent over her. She moaned softly.

"Louise?"

"Don't," she said, and threw up her hands, covering her face.

"It's all right, you've just fallen out of bed."

She sat up slowly. He picked up the lamp and set it upright on the table. When he turned it on, it still worked. The light hurt his eyes. She got up and climbed back into bed. She leaned back against the pillows and squinted against the light. Her eyes were puffy, and her mouth a little scar of pink.

"What happened?" she said.

"I don't know. You must have been dreaming. I heard you crying out."

"I was dreaming," she said. "He was . . . Oh, it's terrible." She covered her eyes with her hands.

"Here," he said. "You're shivering." He leaned over and pulled the covers up and sat down on the foot of the bed. He noticed she was staring at his chest. His robe had fallen open, exposing his scar.

"What happened? That scar?"

"I had heart surgery," he said. "Last spring."

"It's so big. What did they do?"

He hesitated, and then said, "I had a heart transplant."

"You mean you have somebody else's heart inside you?"

"Yes."

She frowned, furrowing her eyebrows. "God," she murmured. "I didn't know. You didn't say anything."

"Go back to sleep," he said. "I just heard — "

"You should have told me," she said.

Phil cleared his throat. "It was my grandson," he said, "who died. I was given his heart."

Louise sat up straighter and stared at him. "Oh my God, I heard about you. You're the one."

He closed the robe around his chest. He didn't know why he'd told her. He didn't need to tell her everything. It seemed like a dream. Here he was in his daughter's room, in the middle of the night, telling someone he hardly knew everything. The floor was cold against his feet and he knew he wasn't dreaming, but he had the sensation that nothing was real around him. The pictures of his wife and children looked down at him from the dresser.

"How old was he?" she asked.

"Sixteen."

"My age," she said.

"You told me you were eighteen. Was that a lie, too?"

"Yes," she said. "The last one."

He looked at her. Now it made sense. Of course, she was just Luke's age. There was something about them that was vaguely similar, very vaguely, but nonetheless discernible, a quality of yearning for life that hadn't yet come to them.

"What . . . what does it feel like?" she asked.

"I was so close to him. It's very difficult to lose someone you're so close to. Even more difficult to think you're alive because of that loss."

"I lost my father," she said. "I hardly knew him. I wish I had."

He sat very still, listening to his own breathing. "How old were you when he died?"

"Nine."

He stood up and went to the window. It was the end of the month, a full moon when hard frosts came. The wind blew and shook leaves from their fragile hold on the silvery poplars. In the luridly beautiful light of the full moon he saw leaves fluttering on the ground, falling even at night, scattered into the crooked rows of the garden. Purple moon shadows shining on the pale leaves caused them to appear as tufts of silvery paper, scattering all over his yard. A steep sloping field caught in the moonlight looked as if it were covered with snow. I don't remember ever having seen my garden this way, he thought. His heart opened more than usual to the sight of the slender elms, the weeping willows, the patch of white running down the ridges of the hills.

"If we hadn't lost the people we loved we would probably be different people ourselves, wouldn't we?" she asked.

"You're young," he said. "You don't understand that we're always the same."

"I hope that's not true," she said, "because if I'm never going to change, I don't want to be the person I am."

He turned and looked at her. "I'm going to bed now."

"Good night, Phil." She caught his hand briefly as he passed her, touching it lightly.

He lay in his bed, gazing out at the few stars shining in the sky. Had she been delivered to him for a purpose? Was it his responsibility to help her? Was it that his own moral judgment was being tested? Cold seeped from around the window. It came gliding in on northern winds, sought out the unstuffed cracks, blew across the room in eddying currents, and settled in his bones. He pulled up the warmth of the covers, his eyes closed, shuddering among the small folds of aging skin, and he became the blind sleeper, awaiting dreams.

8

It took him an hour to get over the pass. The road between Paris and Garden City was blocked by a construction project, and he waited twenty minutes. It rained lightly. The lake was dappled with the drops falling on its light chop. When he reached his daughter's house, he parked down by the highway, leaving the car in front of the Ark Animal Care sign.

He walked slowly up the lane. From inside the house he could already hear the noise, the sound of voices and the clatter of dishes. All in all, he really didn't want to be here, where the sense of Luke was so strong. He knew there would be a whole group here today, some cousins on Dan's side, their children, Dan's Uncle Charlie and Aunt Maxine. Ralph would be here too.

He entered the kitchen through the back door. Joyce looked up and saw him come in and waved a spatula in his direction.

"Hi, Dad," she called. Children were swarming around in the kitchen. A huge turkey sat on the counter, and a ham decorated with pineapple and maraschino cherries.

Joyce was whipping up something in a bowl, and the sound of an electric mixer filled the air.

He could see Maxine and Charlie sitting in the living room. They all had just come from church and still wore their Sunday clothes. Maxine yelled, "Phil! Come in here and say hello!"

"You look good," she said as he leaned over to kiss her cheek. She grabbed his hand in a strong grip. "Doesn't he look good, Charlie?" she asked her husband, who sat next to her on the couch.

He shook Charlie's hand. "Tough old bugger, aren't you?" Charlie said in a hoarse voice. He laughed raspily, the noise coming out burred and deep, the result of a lifetime of smoking. His skin was a patchwork of wrinkles and welted flesh. The piney odor of scotch drifted up from him.

"How do you feel, Phil?" Maxine asked.

"I feel fine," he said, settling down in a chair across from them. "Where's Dan?"

"I think he's gone to get Ralph."

"We're just watching the Reagans in Russia," Maxine said, indicating the TV, a big console model that took up most of the space at one end of the small living room. On the screen, the President and his wife were shown in evening dress, standing stiffly next to the

Gorbachevs. An enormous crystal chandelier sparkled above them, but otherwise the room in which they stood appeared strangely bare and cavernous.

"That Raisa Gorbachev has certainly been stinking to Nancy on this trip," Maxine said.

Joyce, who had just walked into the living room, said that was exactly what she thought.

"Talk about being treated rudely," she said.

"We certainly didn't treat her that way when she was over here."

"No, we rolled out the red carpet for her."

"And what happens over there? Nancy is a little late for a trip through a museum and when she shows up, Raisa treats her like she's a dog."

"I think they've been very snotty to her," Joyce said.

What does she have on her head? he wondered. He looked at his daughter. She wore some kind of — it was hard to say what it was. Some kind of cap with plastic disks all over it. The disks were pearly pink, iridescent, and each time she moved her head, the disks shimmied.

"I think it's terrible the way they've treated her," Maxine said. "Did you hear about what happened in the museum when Nancy accidentally touched something she wasn't supposed to and they gave her a reprimand?"

"I think I would have packed up my bags and come right home," Joyce said.

Feeling bored, Phil left the world news pundits and wandered outside. He strolled across the lawn to where the orchard began. A gray light suffused the orchard. It was shadowy back under the trees. Moist air hung heavily about the branches. The rain had been brief and now the humidity lingered after the storm. It did not escape him that this was where he had talked to Luke the day he entered the hospital, in just this spot. He folded his arms across his chest and looked up the rows of the orchard, and he could see the boy coming toward him again, driving the tractor down the wide row beneath the leafy bower. He could easily picture him just as he'd been.

There were things that continued to trouble him when he thought about them. An image he'd seen in the newspaper, a picture of the wrecked car, a policeman taking measurements beside the road. The words "heart removed at 5:30 A.M. and placed in a sterile plastic bag." He remembered all the plans Luke had. Mexico. The trip never made.

He shook his head and murmured, "Luke, oh Luke."

Why were you so careless?

Why? What I want to know is, why?

311

I'd always made it before.

Why take such a chance?

The wind blew through the chime hanging on the eaves of the house, and the leaves rustled around him.

You were young. Your life was just beginning. What about the things we were going to do together? What about Mexico?

What makes you think I'm not there? Or here? Everywhere. . . .

The leaves shook wildly in the gusts of wind, clattering, rustling, and the hairs on Phil's scalp gently lifted. Then the air around him became incredibly still, as if the last of the storm had just then decided to pass. He heard the insects, the birds returning, and he stood very still, listening, and felt again the separateness radiating from his heart.

At that moment, he heard a car in the driveway and looked up to see Dan had arrived. He could see Ralph, stretched out on a gurney in the back of the station wagon, and went to help.

Dan greeted him with a handshake, as he always did, and the usual tight, stern look. He hadn't been well. Vague ailments troubled him, an overall tiredness and aching — strange flulike symptoms he'd taken to several doctors, the last of whom had made a guess about Epstein-Barr syndrome. His paleness had increased since Phil last saw him. He didn't look well. Phil couldn't help thinking it was grief that had destroyed Dan's health. As Dan opened the back of the station wagon, he moved slowly, all stooped over. Phil peered inside at the mummylike figure of Ralph, tucked in with a sheet and strapped down for the ride.

"Let's get him out slowly," Dan said.

The wheels on the gurney had been locked and tied to the seat with cords. Dan loosened the cords, and very carefully they rolled Ralph out, supporting the stretcher between them until the legs extended, one end at a time, and the gurney was finally standing on the ground.

Phil looked down into Ralph's big face. Ralph smiled the only way he could, which meant the corners of his mouth pulled down, toward his chin, instead of curving up.

He bent closer to him, leaning over the gurney. "Nice to see you, Ralph."

"Yeah." Ralph's voice was like a whisper, hoarse and breathy. His hair was peaked, reminding Phil of Dagwood Bumstead, the cartoon character.

"Good to see you, too. You been operated on, huh?"

"Yes."

"Got out of the hospital alive?"

"Yes, I did."

"Had any dates lately?"

"No. Have you?"

"Oh, one or two."

"The nurses must be drawing straws to see who's the lucky one," Phil said, smiling. How could you be paralyzed for eight years and still have so much good humor left in you?

"They all want me," Ralph whispered. "I give them turns."

Dan said, "Come on, Dad, let's get you inside."

Phil heard the words "miracle of modern medicine" just as they came through the door with the gurney and knew what they had been discussing in the kitchen. Maxine, Joyce, and Dan's niece, Judy, were all grouped in front of the stove, and fell quiet when they saw him.

He helped Dan roll Ralph into the living room. They positioned him where he could see the TV. Maxine followed them, the scent of her perfume filling the air, its heavy sweetness making Phil feel a little sickened. Charlie stood up and bent over Ralph to greet him. Kids rushed in and lined up next to the gurney, gawking at Ralph.

"Do you want your drink now?" Dan asked, looking down at his father. "Straight?

Or water today?"

"Straight," Ralph mumbled. One of the few pleasures allowed to Ralph was two scotches, no more than two, each time they brought him home. He looked straight up at the ceiling, blinking slowly. Maxine leaned over him.

"Did you bring it?" she asked. "Did you bring the letter to show us? I told Dan I wanted to see it."

Maxine was shouting. Phil noticed people often shouted at Ralph, as if he couldn't hear very well. They didn't understand. It wasn't that he couldn't hear. He couldn't speak very well. His ears were fine, except for the fact people were constantly yelling into them.

"The letter," Ralph whispered to his son, when he brought him the drink. "Get the letter." Dan folded back the sheet and produced a plaque, which had been placed on Ralph's chest and strapped down for the ride. Then he set the drink in the little metal holder affixed to the gurney near Ralph's face and inserted the flexible straw into his mouth.

When Phil saw the letter, his heart sank.

"Look at this, Charlie!" Maxine cried. "A letter from President Reagan to Ralph."

She began reading the letter aloud. As she

did so, Joyce came into the room and stood at the end of the couch. She had a pleased look on her face.

" 'Dear Ralph Beery, It's come to my attention that you have been a lifelong and devoted servant of the Republican Party in Bear Lake County, a willing and able worker on behalf of the ideals all Americans cherish. . . .' "

Phil wished he could leave the room, but family members stood in every doorway, listening to the bogus letter. He was the only person in the room, besides Joyce, who knew the letter was a fake. She'd even managed to deceive Dan. The knowledge of the forgery made him extremely uncomfortable. Maxine's voice droned on.

" 'Life demands exceptional things from exceptional people. Nancy and I want you to know that we're proud of you. Your courage has not gone unnoticed. . . .' "

Phil looked at his daughter, and their eyes met. She gave him a strange smile, both defiant and satisfied. He looked away from her, staring down at the carpet, which showed signs of a recent vacuuming, while Maxine finished reading the letter.

" 'In all sincerity, President Ronald Reagan.' "

"That *is* lovely," Maxine said. "Very special."

"Quite a letter, Ralph," Charlie added.

Joyce went to Ralph's side and adjusted the straw, which had flipped out of his mouth, placing it back between his lips. "That's better," she said, "isn't it, Dad?" For a moment, Phil thought she was speaking to him, and glanced up quickly. But she had turned away, and was busy propping up the letter against some sheet music on the piano.

I need a drink, he thought, and went to the kitchen, where he found the scotch and helped himself. Noticing the dogs standing out in the kennels, he went out to visit them, taking his drink. It was a mistake. Seeing the dogs cooped up behind the chain-link fence, their pens fouled, littered with their own filth, he could only think of how much Luke had loved them, how he had taken these dogs everywhere with him, and now they appeared so neglected and sad. It broke his heart. He would have to speak to Joyce.

He knelt down at the fence and stared through the wire at the dogs. Beanie looked up at him with moist, dark eyes. Red cowered in the corner of the next pen. The kennels gave off a rank smell. How in God's name could they have done this, so neglected these animals? Beanie pressed herself against the fence. He reached through the chain-link to scratch behind her ears, and felt the hard matted clump of fur, tangled into one big knot.

He spoke to the dogs for a while. He finally managed to get Red to come over to the fence, too. He thought about Louise. What was she doing?

"All right, Dad!" Joyce called. "Come on! We're ready to eat!" He downed the rest of his scotch and reluctantly headed for the house.

There was a great deal of food for lunch, much more than could be eaten. Phil hadn't ever forgotten the winter when he'd survived on turnips and potatoes during the Depression, or his days in logging camps and years of menial work, including a time of unemployment when he had known the kind of hunger that could make a man weak and preoccupy his mind. It upset him to see how much food was wasted. Almost everyone took more than he or she could eat, and at the end of the meal, food was scraped into the wastebasket. Joyce had kept crying to get everyone to eat more. "Take more!" she said. "I don't want leftovers." But everyone complained of being stuffed, and in fact, they looked that way. The whole family was overweight except Dan, who had a haunted look of illness. They sat around the table, lethargic and silent, staring at each other.

One by one, they retired to the living room and settled down again in front of the TV. The remote-control device was in the hands of one of the younger boys, who hopped from one station to another. Phil found that the most horribly confusing atmosphere was being created. He felt assaulted by the noise and images: guns and screeching cars, a preacher in a red tie, football, canned laughter, Red Square, *This Bud's for You!* and an enormous piece of pie, glistening with cherries the size of Christmas ornaments, then more guns, and bowling . . . he couldn't stand it.

"Leave it on one station, why don't you?" he said to the boy.

The child, whose pale hair stood up like gleaned wheat, looked up at him with a blank look.

"Why don't you pick one thing?" he said. "Why don't you watch football?" He wouldn't have minded seeing a little football.

The boy shrugged. "Do you want it?" he said, extending the remote control to him.

"No, I don't want that thing. That wasn't what I meant."

"You can choose something, I don't care."

"Here, let me have it," Charlie said. "I'd like to see a bit more news." He changed channels. Suddenly there they were again. The Reagans. He didn't understand why they disturbed him the way they did. But he felt it had something to do with deceit. They seemed like selfish people, isolated by their power and wealth from any feeling for those who were less advantaged. They pretended to care, all the while filling up the White House with expensive china. Reagan appeared to him to be rather stupid. He stared at the picture of him. The President wore a tuxedo, and was grinning foolishly at the camera.

"One thing Reagan's done is earn us some respect abroad," Maxine said.

"That's because they know they're dealing with somebody who's going to be tough," Charlie added.

"He knows how to ride a horse, too, damned good," Ralph rasped, grinning from his gurney at the image of his hero.

"I'd like to see them extend the presidential term so he could stay in office a little longer," Maxine said. "We need him." She picked her teeth with a toothpick that was gradually turning red with lipstick.

Charlie nodded. "It seems to me," he said, suppressing a burp with the back of his hand, "that this country is in better shape than it's been since Eisenhower. There was all that nonsense in the sixties, and then we elected a boob like Carter. Reagan has given us a new kind of credibility."

A new kind of poverty, you mean, Phil thought. He stared at the TV, feeling more upset by the moment. He wanted to say something, but he knew he couldn't. He'd seen honest men and he'd seen dishonest ones and what he didn't understand was how an honest man, if he was that, could look as dishonest as Reagan did. There was something untrustworthy about him. Everything was so easy, so smooth and polished. He always had the words ready, but they seemed empty. He was sick of it, of the empty words behind the practiced delivery.

The President's wife now filled the television screen. The camera moved in close. Her eyes shifted uneasily from side to side, and then she stared straight ahead. He saw the look someone had once described as that of a startled deer, frozen in headlights. She appeared frightened. But of what? Frightened of making a wrong move, of showing any expression whatsoever except the mask of a fixed smile, frightened of someone touching her, of seeming even momentarily uncomposed, of displaying any spontaneity that might even briefly reveal something she didn't want known. She seemed alert to the potential mistake, the unexpected event. She grinned tightly. She looked hard and thin and brittle with wariness. But didn't she have the same problems everybody did? No. He could only conclude that she didn't. Her problems were different. One problem was, her head was too big for her body.

The picture changed as the news report progressed and the Reagans were shown at the airport, waving feebly from some steps leading to a plane.

"I'm glad to see women wearing hats again," Maxine said. "When the First Lady wears a hat, it makes a big difference for the whole country."

A hat? he thought. It looks like a bedpan, upside down.

"She's got a beautiful sense of style, Nancy, doesn't she?" Joyce said. "Mother never wore hats, did she, Dad?"

"No, she never did. Not that I remember."

"Although I do remember she had the damnedest assortment of wigs," Maxine said, laughing so suddenly that the sound came out like braying. "I always said that only May could get away with some of those hairdos. You just kind of accepted it because, well, she was so different."

Phil felt his face flushing.

Charlie said, "Yeah, I just wish Reagan could run again. I'd sure vote for him."

Phil had had enough. He said, "I wouldn't. I didn't vote for him the first time, or the second, and I sure wouldn't now."

Charlie frowned at him. "What's that?"

"I said, I wouldn't want Reagan again. You talk about him as if there was only one side to the matter."

"Well, there is, as far as I'm concerned," Charlie said.

"I see it a little differently."

"Yeah?" Charlie said, becoming belligerent. "Just how do you see it?"

"What I see is the country is worse off now than before he got elected. The rich are getting richer and the poor are getting poorer, and there's more of them. Look at the homcless — "

"Reagan can't be blamed for that."

"He certainly isn't doing anything about it."

"Well, hell," Charlie said, "you can't expect anybody to turn things around overnight."

Phil laughed. "Well, he hasn't even tried. He's had eight years almost, and everything's gotten worse, the deficit, the number of people in jails — "

"By damn he has tried!" Charlie shouted.

Joyce said, "Come on, Charlie. Cut it out. You too, Dad. It's Dan's birthday."

Charlie said, "This country is in great shape because of Reagan! Stronger than ever!"

"Kids can't even read," Phil said, "and the teachers don't know what to do. And look at the farmers. You've got to say they're in poor shape. They've been sold a bill of goods. He hasn't helped them. He doesn't care about the poor, the homeless, the blacks — "

"If blacks wanted jobs," Maxine said, "they'd have jobs. Goodness, I'm always seeing signs at McDonald's that say 'Help wanted'."

"Maybe they'd like a little better job than that," Phil said dryly.

"This isn't right," Charlie shouted, pounding the coffee table with his fist. "You're trying to blame the President for every little wrong!"

An awkward silence settled in the room. He knew he shouldn't have said anything. Charlie and Maxine were flushed with anger. Ralph lay rigid, his eyebrows slightly furrowed. Joyce and Dan seemed embarrassed by him. The children in the room were still, as if the drama unfolding before them was better than anything that had preceded it on TV.

"Don't you see," Phil said, "we can't go on this way, so many poor people, jails filling up, more homeless, kids dropping out of school, drugs. There are so many problems, and no one, least of all a fellow as out of touch with life as Reagan, is able to confront the truth."

"I beg your pardon," Charlie said, "but you can't say that in front of me. You can't start calling our President a liar."

Joyce stood up suddenly. "Let's forget this whole discussion. You two shouldn't even talk politics. You've got a Republican on one side and a Democrat on the other. That's the problem. I don't want my Sunday dinner ruined!"

Dan said wearily, "Yeah, I'm sick of you guys arguing over something as silly as politics."

"You and Charlie aren't ever going to agree on anything."

"Just what is so wrong, anyway?" Charlie yelled, unwilling to give it up. "We're the richest country in the world!"

"It's like a sickness," Phil said. "We become more used to things the way they are. We sit here and accept misery and suffering in others as long as it doesn't come too close to us. I think we're living in a terrible time. We dominate the world but we don't seem to care much for it."

Charlie shook his finger at him. "You don't

seem to remember the Marshall Plan. Where would the world be without our generosity — "

"Our greed, you mean."

"You know, I've been sitting here listening to you talk all this crap, Phil, and I'm pretty damned mad. I figured you for a smarter man. Here you are talking down our President in front of these kids. If there's one honest man in this country it's Ronald Reagan!" he shouted. The veins on his temples stood out. His face was purple.

"He's a man of the people," Maxine said, her voice becoming unnaturally sweet, as if she were trying to balance out Charlie's anger. "He's a good man. Why, he even took the time to write this letter to Ralph." Her head wobbled slightly as she spoke to Phil. "That's what I mean when I say he's a man of the people." She shook her finger in the direction of the letter on the piano. "A man who writes that kind of letter is a good man. An honest and sincere man."

"Reagan? That letter?" Phil turned and glared at his daughter. "Tell them the truth, Joyce," he said.

"Don't do this, Dad," she said, and left the room.

"All right, she won't tell you, so I will." Something inside urged him to stop, but he couldn't. "Joyce forged that letter," he said. "It's a lie that it came from Reagan, because it didn't. This is what I've been trying to say. Things aren't always as we want to see them. Sometimes people think they're doing you a favor by hiding the truth, but in the long run, it makes things worse. She wrote that letter because she thought it would make Ralph feel good."

There was silence. Then Maxine said, "What do you mean?"

"You ask Joyce." Phil stood up, or tried to, but he lost his balance and fell back against the cushions on the sofa. He wanted to get out of there quickly, but he couldn't even get up off the sofa. Pushing himself forward, he finally stood on his feet. For a brief moment, he caught the look on Ralph's face. He saw the terrible disappointment in his eyes.

"I'm sorry, Ralph," he muttered, and walked out of the room, rushing through the kitchen. Once outside, he hurried toward his car, striding down the lane as fast as he could. In his haste, he stumbled and fell to his knees, landing amid small pebbles that bruised the flesh on his palms. He scrambled to his feet, brushed himself off, and hurried on, afraid that somebody might come after him, somebody who would stop him and make him go back and face his daughter. But no one came after him. He reached his car safely, climbed quickly inside, and headed off in the direction of the pass.

He drove over the mountain, hardly aware of anything around him. The storm had regathered over the lake, and the leaden sky was roped with dark clouds. From the sky bright scrawls of lightning broke out occasionally, glimmering flashes bursting in sudden, snaking light, so quickly gone he wondered whether he'd actually seen them. How does a family go on, he wondered, with so much pain? The unraveling had begun with his wife's death, then Luke's. He knew loss was supposed to bring you closer to people, but it hadn't done that at all. He'd lost the linchpins to his family, and now it wobbled precariously, not bound by forces of natural love and true affection. They were held together by duty, and he could feel the bond weakening.

As he walked from the garage to the house, he looked up at the ominous sky, where dark thunderheads, dense and steely, formed a low lid over the valley. He felt a pain like ice freezing skin to metal, only the feeling was inside him, as if some great cold had swept into his being. Like a man fleeing a pursuing mob, he shut the door quickly behind him and leaned against it, closing his eyes.

Louise bent over her diary, writing in a crabbed hand:

He came in a while ago very upset. I'd made a chocolate cake, which didn't come out too good, thinking to surprise him, but he didn't want any. He wouldn't say what's wrong. I knew something must have happened at his daughter's. At least I didn't think it was me who'd upset him this time.

He went down the basement, looking so white I felt a little afraid for him. I could hear hammering down there. I let him alone for a while, but when he didn't come up at dinnertime I decided to go down and see if he wanted me to fix something. I found him chipping away at that piece of marble we bought the other day, working around the edges with a chisel and hammer so it looked like an animal had been nibbling at it. He just kept working and didn't even look at me. I started to feel like he didn't even know I was in the room with him.

"What's that going to be?" I asked him. When he said, "A tombstone," it gave me such a funny feeling. I thought maybe he was making his own tombstone. "Oh," I said, trying to act like I wasn't surprised, like I'd seen people making tombstones every day of my life. "Who's it for?" He sighed, and took a long time to answer, like he really didn't want to tell me, and I began to feel sorry I'd even asked him. I don't seem to know when to say something and when not to, or what's the right thing and the wrong one. But finally he told me it was for Luke, his grandson.

I could tell he didn't want me there with him, so I came back upstairs, and just sat in front of the fire for a while, thinking about what he told me last night about getting his grandson's heart. How could you live with that?

Later he came upstairs and said, "It's the wrong time to be working on something I need to be putting love into." He still seemed real upset to me, and I asked him again what was wrong. He told me about going to his daughter's and getting into an argument over President Reagan and how his daughter had forged this letter. I really didn't mean to, but I started laughing, but then finally he started laughing, too, just a little.

He said, "The thing about family, Louise, is you can't count on getting paired up with people you would naturally choose to be with under any other circumstances." I said, "You're telling me?"

Right then I had the best feeling. It seemed like we were family just then, him and me. He taught me how to play cribbage. We played four games before he went to bed. Tonight, I go to sleep with a very good feeling.

9

He awoke to a world totally new, a world awesome and forbidding outside his door. He was on his land, the land he'd lived on for many years, but everything had changed. Darkness covered the earth, a polar winter had arrived. The strangest luminous sights flashed in the sky, eerie configurations lit from within like the aurora borealis, and he wasn't certain if the light came from radiation or if it was the old bodies of the heavens, the sun, stars, and moon, going about their business in a new way. He wandered, lost, with Maxine and Charlie and Joyce as companions, hungry-eyed wraiths, silent and watchful. They came to the ocean. Ice caps had melted, sending huge floes bobbing out to sea. The waters of the world rose up, and they witnessed a wall of rushing blue.

They wandered the world, flying above its surface, and saw camps everywhere, in country after country, where children starved, huddled together. Food had grown scarce. Grubs, crickets, roaches, and things pried loose from beneath the earth gave scant, bitter nourishment. Trees stood like ancient sentinels, leafless and barren, in a landscape of sand and dirt. The wind had taken the soil away, exposing the ribs of the earth. The ground lay hard and barren beneath the feet of wanderers.

At night, they huddled around fires. Wooden fences and buildings were fed to the fires, board by board, plank by plank, and still the nights were bitter. The cities were empty. Commerce had ended. In the countryside the bones of animals lay scattered in dry fields. Men had lost the energy necessary for survival, hunting only for the protection of shade in which to lie down, and women no longer bore children. The rains came and burned the skin and they hid in caves, in culverts, beneath the concrete underpasses of the long-abandoned freeways, waiting for it to pass. When the sun emerged again, they covered their heads with cardboard and rags to protect themselves from the merciless rays and moved on. Their faces were marked by red sores, and their eyes were dimmed.

The near-blind led the blind, the old left the young behind, and the young banded together in feral packs. They avoided them, hiding from their ferocity. The young were no longer young anyway, their faces were wizened, pocked, dry. There were no new children, and among the older ones there wandered a pale girl child in red shoes, her long colorless hair clotted with weeds. . . .

Phil awoke from his dream with a horrid, hollow feeling. The house was quiet. Already the sun was high enough to slip through the curtains in a sliver of pale light. He had slept later than usual. He turned his face to the wall and lay very still, the dream weighing on him. His mind replayed the desolate scenes he had wandered through in the night, unfolding with the clarity of a moving picture. The sense of a troubled, disordered world accompanied his dressing. In the bathroom, he peered out the window. The sun was a molten cap crowning the ridge, suffusing a scrim of gray clouds with streaks of pink.

He went outside, took his hoe from the shed, stuffed his clippers in the pocket of his jacket, and walked to the garden. Steadily, with a feeling of singular purpose, he worked among the plants. He kept looking up, studying the sky, the horizon, the surface of the lake, in order to assure himself that the world was still a clean, beautiful, inhabitable place. A little later, she came outside and stood at the end of a row of tomatoes and stretched.

"Good morning," she said.

He looked at her, so sleep-heavy and disheveled.

"Good morning."

"Did you sleep well?"

"No," he said. "As a matter of fact, I had a bad dream."

"What was it?"

He told her about the dream, recounting its details, although as he spoke he could feel how inadequately his words captured the atmosphere of the dream, which eluded ordinary language. He did not tell her that the last image in the dream had been of her, wandering lost through the barren landscape. It seemed too bleak, and he didn't want to admit he'd been dreaming about her.

"Anyway," he concluded, "it was a very strange dream."

"They always are, aren't they?" She wanted to tell him what she thought about dreams, which was that people actually left their bodies at night and visited the places they dreamed about, but she was afraid he would think this too odd. So instead she said, "I bet you had that dream because of what we talked about at dinner the other night. You know, when I was telling you about the article I read?"

"Perhaps," he said, resuming his work.

She bent over a leafy plant. "What's this?"

"Rhubarb."

"And this?"

"Chard."

"They almost look alike, don't they?" She wore the big brown sweater over jeans, and a pair of tennis shoes that looked big on her feet. To whom, he wondered, had those tennis shoes once belonged? May? Joyce? Helen? Which of the women of this house had once worn those shoes?

She handled the rhubarb, stroking the fleshy red stalks. "Beautiful, isn't it?" she murmured. After watching him silently for some time, she said, "Can I help you?"

"You could cut that," he said, indicating the rhubarb. "Cut it down close to the ground. Here." He threw her a little knife, which landed near her feet.

Turning his back on her, he bent over his tomato plants. Every tomato was coming off today, even the green ones, which could ripen on the windowsill. He intended to harvest the lot before the frost took them. The wind picked up and clouds suddenly covered the sun, casting shadows over the furrows. He was reminded of his dream, which he knew would stay with him throughout the day, coloring his waking hours. Quite abruptly, it grew lighter again. A mutable day. His arms, his hands, his coat smelled strongly of tomatoes from brushing through the vines. Leaves fluttered down from the maple tree, drifting past like swarms of butterflies.

She cut all the rhubarb and laid the stalks in a bushel basket with the tomatoes.

"What's this?" she asked, lifting a limp vine.

"Potatoes."

"I don't see any potatoes."

He chuckled. "They're underground. Take that shovel and turn the earth. You'll see them."

"I didn't think they grew like that."

"Well, how did you think they grew?"

"On plants, aboveground, like tomatoes."

"And you an Idaho girl," he said. "Didn't they ever tell you in school that potatoes grow underground?"

"They didn't talk a lot about potatoes in school."

Her big brown sweater made her look slightly like a potato herself, forming a baggy russet sack around her body, from which her thin legs and long neck protruded. Miss Potatohead, he thought, remembering the plastic toy his children had played with.

"If you'd like," he said, "you could go ahead and dig up those potatoes. Take those

337

gloves over there so you don't get splinters from the shovel. Just turn the earth one shovelful at a time and look through the soil. Kind of dig around gently. You don't want to be chopping potatoes in half. Put them in that other basket."

She uncovered several big, earth-clotted potatoes, and held them up, grinning. "Hey, look! I found some!" She squatted down and began digging in the earth with her bare hands, uncovering more potatoes.

"Why don't you use those gloves?"

"I like the way the dirt feels," she said.

"Soil," he said, correcting her, "not dirt. There's a difference."

A smile spread across his face as he turned away from her. Work. That was what she needed. And a sense of where things came from.

The temperature began to drop, but neither of them felt the cold as they worked steadily in the garden. They stayed outdoors until early afternoon, when hunger sent them inside. Phil made a lunch from the vegetables they'd gathered, mashed potatoes and parsnips, fresh sliced tomatoes and green beans with bacon. It was the coldest day yet. His thermometer hanging outside the window said 38 degrees. He built a fire.

While he cooked, Louise sat at the kitchen table, looking through a Spiegel catalogue. He felt a peacefulness surrounding them, a quiet infusing the atmosphere in the house with a feeling of ordinary family life, something he hadn't felt for a long time. Occasionally she commented on some item of clothing she saw in the catalogue. She would like this, or that, she said, pointing to something and holding up the magazine for him to see. She liked red. Red was her favorite color. And she liked black. If she could, she'd wear only red and black. He listened to her quietly, thinking of Luke. He, too, had had very specific likes and dislikes. When he was small, Joyce had dressed him up in little suits and bow ties, and even then Luke had protested having to wear such things. He remembered saying to his daughter, "Let the boy wear what he wants, for heaven's sakes."

When he put the food on the table, she ate ravenously, her appetite stimulated by all the work she had done. Afterward she curled up on the couch in front of the fire, completely absorbed in the clothes in the catalogue.

He did the dishes and went upstairs and sat at May's desk. He opened the book of poems Helen had given him, read a few, stared at the picture of his wife, and began daydreaming. From the second story of the house, he could see across his neighbor's fields. A dying row of hollyhocks shook in the wind, and beyond them, a stand of even taller cornstalks fluttered, their dried leaves waving like festive little streamers. The branches of a pine sectioned off the sky into patches of muted color.

He felt a terrible sadness. The dream, mixed with the horrible events at Joyce's, had left him troubled. The past is always sad, he thought, why shouldn't the future also be that way? It was cruel to have to go on without the people you loved most. May had died in the month the raspberries came on, a month of hot weather. He had fed her raspberries with his fingers, one by one, bringing them fresh from the plants so that they still had the furred warmth of the sun in them.

In the room below, where he'd raised his children and watched them grow, the radio came on, blaring out rock and roll. The noise erupted abruptly, shocking him. It took him back to another time. She's just like them, he thought. How often had he told his own children to turn down the music when he could no longer stand it? Yet he tolerated the noise now, though it contributed to the edgy traffic of emotions inside him. He failed completely to see what he should do about Louise. Weren't there laws against sixteen-year-olds being on their own? Yet if her parents were the sort of people she said they were, who could, in good conscience, want to force her to return to them?

When he could take the music no more, he went downstairs and confronted her. "Please," he shouted, "turn off that radio or at least turn it down! It's too loud for me."

She was dancing in the living room, gyrating in front of the sofa, her legs spread wide apart, thrusting her hips forward and backward while strumming some sort of imaginary guitar at her pelvis. Her head was thrown back and she shook like a person caught in ecstasy. When he saw her in this state, he felt embarrassed. She stopped moving when he spoke to her, but remained slouched backward, her pelvis stuck out, arms dangling loosely at her sides. Slowly, she raised her head and regarded him with a blank look.

"Okay. I didn't know it bothered you."

"It bothers me very much," he said sharply.

"I didn't think it would be so loud upstairs. I thought you were in your room with your door closed." She straightened up with a little flip forward and shut the radio off. They stood opposite each other, tense and wary. She fluffed her hair with both hands, flopped down on the couch, and slouched back against the cushions, a sullen look on her face.

"I can't take it," he said. "If you could only play the music a little lower."

"It's not the same," she said, her mouth set in a frown. Her sullenness angered him.

"I don't know why you act like I've done something so terrible by asking you to turn the music down. After all, this is my house and I'm used to things a certain way — "

"You don't have to remind me it's your house and I don't belong here. Believe me, I know it."

"Why don't you read?" he said, pointing to the shelves of books next to the fireplace. "If you're bored, why don't you try to find a good book?"

"If only you had a television. I don't know how you stand it without one. Maybe you don't want one. You're one of those people who thinks TV stinks and rots the brain."

"It broke," he said, "and I never bothered to have it fixed. Besides, I should think you could survive without television for a while."

"There's nothing wrong with television," she muttered. "You should try it. It might liven up your life."

"You're being rude!" he shouted. "Who are you to tell me what I need to liven up my life? What do you know about my life, anyway?"

She glared at him. "I just think you'd get lonely living all the way out here, all by yourself."

"Sometimes I do. So what? Do you think television is going to make me feel any better?"

"It might," she said. "You don't seem all that happy to me. Maybe you're just making life hard to . . . punish yourself, I don't know."

"What?" Her impudence shocked him. How dare she comment on his life when her own was such a mess?

"Come on, you get it, grandpa." She dropped her head back so he could see her tiny Adam's apple and the underside of her pointy chin. She swallowed, and the little lump slid up and down.

He felt furious with her. He had the feeling she was taunting him, trying to make him angry. But why? Surely she must know he could turn her out at any moment he chose to. Her knees spread carelessly apart. He couldn't see her face at all. Headless, faceless, her small body appeared knob-

kneed and sloppy. She was graceless, unfathomable, and hostile.

"I don't understand you, Louise. I don't
know what's wrong with you. I raised two
daughters and I never felt — "

"Sorry," she said. "There's nothing to do.
I'm in limbo here." Her head snapped forward, and she looked at him. He saw that
thing in her eyes he didn't like, the cunning
lack of innocence, burning again.

"If he were here, what would you do?"
she asked.

"If who were here?"

"Luke," she said. "Your grandson."

"Oh, I don't know." He felt annoyed by
the question. Was she going to keep bringing
him up now as a topic? She shouldn't assume
such familiarity.

"Well, think about it," she said. "What
did you two use to do?"

"Many things," he said tersely.

"Did he come over here a lot? I mean,
were you really close, or was it just one of
those forced family things?"

"I don't know what you're talking about,"
he said, "but I wish you'd drop it."

"If you really cared about each other as
deeply as you say, I think it's very rare. I
mean that you actually liked doing things
together, being with each other. Do you think

he trusted you? Did he tell you the truth?"

"Why are you asking me these questions, Louise?"

She ran her fingers through her hair. "Why? Why not? I'm curious, that's why."

"Why would it matter to you whether I was truly close to my grandson or not?"

She shrugged. "I just wanted to know if you were really close to him. Did he come and visit you?"

"Yes, he did."

"And what did you do?"

"We talked," he snapped. "We played cribbage. We built things together. Occasionally we went hunting or fishing. Now I think I've said about as much as I want to about my grandson. He isn't a subject you need to bring up. If I want to talk about him, I'll bring him up myself."

She stood up and began pacing the room. "I'm sorry. I think I know what's wrong with me," she said. "I'm jealous."

"Jealous?"

She stopped pacing. Her arms were wrapped tightly around her body, and she stared at the floor.

Jealous? He didn't know what to say. It wouldn't have occurred to him she might feel this way. What did she mean, anyway? Jealous of whom?

"Nobody ever did things like that with me," she said. "Not even my dad. He was hardly ever around, of course, except when I was real little."

She wandered over to the mantle and picked up a little figurine of a hunting dog, looked at it closely, and then set it back down.

"I keep thinking there must be people in the world who actually love each other, not because they're supposed to or because they want something. They just, you know, love each other. I guess that's the way you and your grandson felt about each other."

She smiled, a pale, wan smile, directing it at the figurine of the hunting dog. "Nobody ever took me fishing," she said. "I just got to blast the hell out of targets and play soldier." She sighed. "Oh, nevermind."

He did not understand what she was saying, but he felt a tenderness toward her just then. He cleared his throat. "It's cold today, I know," he began, "but I've wanted to take the boat out for some time. Maybe we could do that this afternoon. If you feel like it. We might take the fishing poles and see if we could catch something." For a moment, she didn't answer, and he thought, She doesn't want to go fishing. Of course she doesn't. Fishing wouldn't interest her. But then she lifted her chin and smiled at him.

"Yeah," she said. "I'd like that."

"I like to troll," he said, heading the boat into the wind. His hand was on the throttle, twisting it halfway open. The air was cold, and yet exhilarating. The boat plowed through the water, its bow smacking the waves.

"I don't like to still-fish the way some people do," he went on, happy to be talking about something he loved. "I don't mind fly-fishing a stream, but if I'm out on a lake, I want to be moving a little."

She huddled beside him on the seat, wrapped up in his big wool coat. Her hands were tucked between her knees, clad in old leather gloves. He reached over and pulled the collar up around her ears. The wind blew her hair back from her face and made it look smaller. She wore no makeup today, and her cheeks appeared naturally pink.

As the boat chugged farther from the dock, he said, "To still-fish you've got to have pop gear. I never use pop gear. I don't want all those cowbells hanging on my line. If you're going to still-fish you can use cheese or night crawlers. Me, I don't mess with worms, and cheese falls off the hook."

"So what do we fish with?" she said.

"I'll show you in a minute."

"We don't seem to be going very fast. Is this as fast as this boat goes?"

"It's plenty fast enough. Storms come up quickly on this lake. You wouldn't want to be out here with anything less than a thirty-five-horsepower motor."

"Is that what we have?"

He nodded. "You get a storm coming up on you, you want to have enough power to get back to shore fast. A day like today could go either way." He lifted his face and looked up at the sky. Dark clouds, black at the edges, were rolling in over the mountains. He caught a whiff of ozone on the air. "It could rain on us," he said. "We'd better get our lines out."

He showed her how to work the engine and steer the boat, and she took over at the throttle while he prepared the fishing rods. He put a large fly on her line. On his own he tied a spinner. "We'll just have to try a few different things and see what those fish are going for today. You can't argue with the fish. Whatever they want, you'd better give 'em."

He stood up and cast her line out. The gear on the end of it dropped into the water with a little plunk. "Here now," he said. "You take this."

He cut the engine so they were just moving at a crawl across the surface of the water, and cast his own line out. She held the pole awkwardly, dipping the tip too low. He wedged his pole under the seat and put his arms around her, taking hold of the pole to show her how to keep her line from dragging, how to lock and unlock the reel, and how to let a little line out or take it in.

"What do I do if I get one?" she asked. Her face was inches from his own. He felt her warm breath on his cheek as she turned toward him to ask this question.

"If you feel a tug," he said, "you jerk up that pole and set the hook in the fish's mouth, and then you just start reeling him in steadily, and hope that he's a great big fat rainbow."

So much good came from simple things, he thought, settling back in his seat and picking up his own pole again. There wasn't anything more satisfying than the simple act of fishing, even on a cold day like today. Maybe days like this were the best because you felt the mutable forces in nature so keenly, the strength and ebb of the wind and the speed of the clouds, the changing light and water. On still, warm days you got none of that. He reached inside his jacket and took out the little flask of whiskey. It went down warm, the heat sliding through the center of him. As he started to put it away, she said, "Can I have some of that?"

"I don't know," he said. "No use getting you started on bad habits." He remembered using the same words with Luke. Of course, he'd given in to him, once he'd turned fifteen, and let him have the occasional tug.

"Come on," she said, socking his arm lightly.

"Go light," he said, handing her the flask.

He headed the boat east, moving out into deeper water, where the lake was a little choppier. Mud ducks floated not far away. On the distant shore, he could see smoke rising from the chimney at Lars and Erika's place. A feeling of great happiness engulfed him. It pleased him to be with her, moving across the water slowly in the little boat. He felt acutely alive, and at peace.

An hour later, when the sun had set behind the mountain, a bitterness began to ride in on the wind, and he felt the cold deep in his bones. He reached out and rubbed her back through the thick coat. "Cold?" he asked.

"A little."

As much as he'd hoped she'd catch a fish, it didn't look like they were biting. He'd changed flies twice and tried three different kinds of spinners, without luck. Maybe it was time to go in. He hefted the flask, which had been on the seat between them. Feeling its weight, he knew it was almost empty.

"Ready to quit?" he asked, downing the last bit of whiskey.

"If you are," she said, forcing a smile. He could see she was cold, and yet she hadn't uttered a complaint. Not like Luke. He'd let you know the minute it got too cold for him. Maybe she didn't feel she could complain.

"Pull in your line," he said. "We'll start back."

The fish hit her line as she was reeling it in. That's the way it often happened. They struck at a fast-moving spinner.

"Ooohhh!" she yelled. "I got something!"

"Pull it up," he cried, cutting the throttle. He could see it was a rainbow, and it was fighting, the way rainbows did, wiggling up out of the water and falling back down again. She struggled with the reel, her fingers clumsy in the big gloves.

"Don't lose it," he cried. "Keep the tip of your pole up."

He had a great urge to take the pole from her, but he fought it, knowing it was much more important to let her try to bring the fish in on her own, even if it meant losing it. He got the net ready and moved to the edge of the boat, all the while saying to

351

her, "You're doing fine, that's it, he's coming closer!"

"Oohh!" she kept yelling. *"Ooohhh!"*

The rainbow bucked in the water, dragging the line from side to side, jumping high and slapping down again with a splash. He caught sight of her face, wide-eyed with excitement, and he felt thrilled himself as she drew the fish up alongside the boat. He dipped the net under it, chasing it around for a few moments before he had it, and hefted it up out of the water. It was a beautiful trout. Twenty-two, twenty-four inches, maybe three and a half pounds.

He held the fish up in front of her. "Well, my girl," he said, "you got yourself a trout most fishermen on this lake would give their eyeteeth for."

She began laughing, and reached out to bring the net closer so she could look at the fish. It had stopped fighting momentarily and lay curled in the bottom of the netting, its silver scales glinting with pale color. A sentient thing, captive, its gills puffed with breath, one eye gazing at them. "Poor fish," she said, but her eyes were sparkling.

"Poor fish is going to make us a dinner!" Taking it in his hands, he wrested the hook from its jaw. Its body was cold and hard. It squirmed in his hand as he picked up the wooden club and thwacked the trout sharply on the head.

"Ow!" she said.

He heard the sound of a motor and looked up to see a boat speeding across the surface of the lake toward them. He recognized the boat, and could make out Lars standing at the helm. It was too late to get away.

"Oh, hell," he said.

"Hellooo!" Lars called, cutting the boat's engine and drifting toward them. The wake from Lars's boat caught up with him and sent their own boat to rocking.

"What you got there? Don't tell me you actually caught a fish, Phil!"

"Louise caught it," he said. He nodded toward her. "Louise, this is Lars."

Lars touched the brim of his cap. "I saw you out here through the binoculars. Erika says come back for dinner."

Phil shook his head. "We've got our fish here to cook — "

"Bring it back to the house and cook it. It looks big enough to give us all a taste anyway. Besides, it'll go with what Erika fixed. She's got sauerbraten and red cabbage. We'll have a feast!"

"Sauerbraten and fish? That doesn't sound like a very good combination."

"That's the trouble with you, Phil," he

called. "You don't know a good combination when it's staring you in the face." He looked at Louise and grinned. "Come on. I'll see you back at the dock."

Oh, well, what the hell, Phil thought, watching him speed away. "I guess we've got an invitation to dinner," he said.

Louise shrugged. "Sounds okay to me."

The thing about good friends, Phil thought, pushing the last forkful of sauerbraten and cabbage into his mouth, is how the consistency of their affection can absorb even sudden, inconsistent elements with aplomb. Lars and Erika had accepted the presence of Louise with matter-of-factness, asking only one question when they'd first arrived at the house. Where was Louise from? Erika had asked after being introduced to her.

Louise had said, "Northern Idaho," and added, quite sensibly he thought, "I was hitchhiking back home, and Phil gave me a ride and a place to stay for a night or two. It's so pretty around here I wanted to stay a little longer."

Even to Phil this explanation sounded perfectly logical, and he had at once relaxed, thinking things are only as strange as you make them seem.

"Well, Erika," he said, pushing his plate

away from him. "As usual, a fine meal."

"I think it was Louise's fish that added just what we needed to this dinner," Erika said, lifting her eyes to look at Louise and smiling at her.

"That's the first fish I ever caught," Louise said. "And boy, did it taste good."

"There's a rule about fish," Lars said. "The ones you catch yourself always taste better than those somebody else catches. Of course, I haven't caught a fish for so long, I'd hardly know!" He laughed heartily.

"In Hamburg, after the war," Erika said, "I went to work in a fish-canning factory. Every day, I stood at tables with other girls and gutted fish. Cod. Big, slimy fish, stinky like you wouldn't believe. Eight hours of gutting fish — "

"Jesus, Erika," Lars said, "do you have to tell this story just after we eat?"

"Oh, Lars," she said, poking him in his ample middle, "you're so delicate. Look at that big delicate stomach! At night," she said, going on with her story, "when I came home from the factory, I smelled so much of fish it wouldn't go away, not even with a bath. Then an old woman at the factory told me to put lemon on my skin and hair to take the smell away. But who could get lemons in Hamburg after the war? So instead

I used vinegar. I didn't smell like fish anymore. I smelled like pickled fish!"

Louise was listening to her intently. "You . . . you were in Germany during the war?"

"Yes," Erika said, and her eyes grew a little wider, and her voice a little breathier. "I was young, perhaps just your age. My father was the postman in town. From the very beginning, he supported Hitler. So did my mother. They became very good Nazis, as did all my relatives, though they tried to deny that later. When war came, everyone had to help, even the teenagers. I was given three choices. I could go to work in a munitions factory, I could man searchlights at the border, or I could become a tram driver. I chose to drive the trams in Hamburg, which was a mistake, because we were badly bombed and the tram drivers were the last ones to go into the shelters and the first to come out. I saw so much death and destruction, which all these years later, I haven't forgotten."

"How did you come here?" Louise asked.

"I just left," Erika said. "After the war, I worked and saved my money from the factory, and in 1950 I bought a ticket to come to New York on a boat, without knowing anyone in this country. Not a soul. I only knew I had to leave all the memories and begin over somewhere else. I didn't like New York, so I came to California, where I met Lars one day on a bus in San Diego. After we were married, he brought me here, to the place where he was born. And here we are still."

"Did you ever see your parents again?"

"No," Erika said. "They were lost to me forever. I could never forget how they had loved Hitler."

"I hate Hitler," Louise said, "and I hate Nazis." Her words slurred a little. They had drunk wine with dinner, and Phil realized the wine, combined with the whiskey he'd let her have on the boat, had probably made her tipsy. He shouldn't have let her drink so much. He should take her home.

Erika regarded Louise with a very serious look. "I'm surprised," she said, "that someone so young, like yourself, would say what you just did. History is so quickly forgotten. Evil becomes abstract, even an evil like Hitler, which was so concrete and real. No one thinks it could ever happen again, especially not in this country. But I know better. I know how it creeps up, a little bit at a — "

"Oh, listen," Louise said, shaking her head, "it could happen here, it's already happening — "

Phil stood up abruptly. "I hate to interrupt,

but I just noticed how late it is. I think we should go."

"Stay for a brandy," Lars said.

"You two have your brandy," Erika said. "Maybe Louise will help me clean up in the kitchen."

As he sat before the fire with Lars, sipping a brandy and listening to him talk about his plans for a new duck blind, Phil could hear the murmur of voices in the kitchen, though he couldn't make out what was being said. He wondered what they were discussing in there. It hadn't occurred to him that Louise and Erika might have anything in common. But thinking of the conversation at the dinner table, he saw how they did. It was still difficult for him to believe her parents were Nazis. In America, how was this possible? He must ask her more about it.

"The ducks just don't use that pond near the old blind much anymore," Lars was saying, "so I figured if we built a new one, we should put it up by the pumping plant. I've been watching that area and it looks to me — "

"Lars," Erika said, coming into the room, "I want to send some eggs with Louise and Phil. Would you go out to the henhouse for me and bring me a dozen, if you can find that many?"

Lars rose slowly. "These damned chickens," he said, grumbling in a good-natured way. "They're more trouble than they're worth. But Erika says we can't have store-bought eggs because of the hormones they feed commercial chickens. I tell her I don't mind a whore-moan. It's when they don't moan I feel bad." Phil looked away from Lars, filled with distaste for his joke. He saw how Erika's eyes filmed over with hurt.

"Lars is big talk," she said, "but you know what they say: big talk, little — oh well, never mind."

"I want to see the chickens," Louise said, putting on her coat and gloves. "I'll go out with you, Lars."

When they'd left, he went into the kitchen with Erika and accepted the package of left-over sauerbraten she gave him.

"She's a nice girl, Phil," she said suddenly, "but she's very troubled, isn't she?"

He didn't know quite what to say.

"She tells me her parents are Nazis, and that she has run away from them. Is this true?"

"That's what she says."

"I worry that she may be in more trouble than you think," Erika said. "Be careful, Phil. Surely someone is looking for her. Don't get in too deep, eh?"

★ ★ ★

They walked home, refusing the ride Lars offered, because even though it was cold, the stars were out, shining brilliantly, and he felt it would be good to walk off the big meal. Lars had given him a flashlight, which he turned on now and then to see the road ahead of them. A quarter-moon showed in the sky, a crescent, a cradle, a scythe blade of pearly white. He preferred walking in the dark, checking only occasionally with the flashlight to make sure they hadn't passed the lane.

"I think you should tell me more about your stepfather and mother," he said.

"Oh, not now, Phil. Please, not now. I feel so good. I'm so happy, just walking tonight. It was such a nice dinner. I like Erika. She's so . . . so real, and good, so kind. I wish I could be like her. Did you hear her say how she just started over, in a new country, not knowing anyone?"

"Yes, I know," he said.

"Lars I don't know about. He grabbed my ass in the chicken coop."

"What?" Phil said, stopping in his tracks.

She tugged at his arm, and he began walking again. "Oh, come on, it wasn't that bad. I probably shouldn't have told you. Actually, he just came up behind me when I was bent

360

over, looking for eggs, and laid his hand on my butt, very casually, you know, like you'd touch somebody on the shoulder, and asked me if I could see any eggs. No big deal. It didn't surprise me."

"Why didn't it surprise you?"

"Like Erika said, Lars is big talk. He's got sex on his mind. You'd think he'd give it up, as old as he is."

Phil cleared his throat. "Yeah, you'd think so," he said.

The house was cold and dark when they came in. "What about the boat?" she said. "I'd forgotten about it. We left it there."

"I'll get it tomorrow," he said.

She yawned, and standing on her tiptoes, kissed him on the cheek. Her breath smelled winy and sweet.

"Good night, Phil," she mumbled. "I'm going to bed. I'm so tired. See you in the morning."

He watched her climb the stairs, her small hips moving from side to side. When he thought of Lars putting his hand there, he felt anger. Or was it jealousy?

10

Her hair was falling out.

Joyce stood at the bathroom sink, gazing down at the little nest of hair lying in the basin. How could this be happening?

In the beginning, the loss was hardly noticeable. It seemed as if she was shedding slightly, like a dog ridding itself of unneeded winter hair. But then, as the summer progressed, a bald patch appeared, and then another. Whole clumps began falling out. Hair clung to the pillowcase in the morning, drifted onto the floor, appeared on her clothes, and clogged up drains. A rash emerged on her scalp, and small irksome sores.

By the end of the summer she had felt worried enough to consult a specialist in Pocatello. The doctor had taken tests and prescribed vitamins and a special shampoo, but nothing seemed to help. In the end, he didn't have an answer to what was causing the problem. His guess was some nervous disorder. The loss of your son, the doctor said, could have caused emotional stress, created chemical imbalances. Since the tests hadn't shown anything conclusive, he was uncertain what to do, although he thought a tranquilizer might help. He prescribed Valium, which he said would calm her nerves.

When she felt nervous she took a Valium, at first irregularly, and then, when she discovered their great tranquilizing effects, two each day — one to relax her for the morning hours, and one to do the same for the evening. She cut her hair short to keep from having to brush it, but the short hair only made her bald patches more noticeable and caused her to feel more self-conscious. The hair continued to fall out anyway. What was left turned from auburn to a mousy gray and had the oddest texture, rather like fake fur. It tufted in patchy clumps and stood out in little ruffs around her ears. It was clear she would soon be completely bald.

During the last visit to the doctor, she had told him about her mother's baldness. It wasn't a good sign, he said. It indicated hereditary predisposition toward hair loss in the menopausal cycle caused by hormonal withdrawal in a reproductively inactive woman.

"*What?*" she had said.

"Hormonal problem," he had answered, and shook his head gravely. "We'll try estrogen treatments."

"Can I still take the Valium?"

"If you think it might be helping."

"Oh, I think so," she had said, and he'd renewed her prescription.

Was this justice? she wondered, looking at herself in the mirror. What was happening to her now must be very much like what had happened to her mother. Her mother had always claimed her baldness came with the pregnancy that had resulted in her own birth. Could losing as well as birthing a child take your hair from you? In any case, it had come to this: she was getting a wig. She had an appointment at the hairdresser's at noon.

She cleaned the hair out of the sink, wet her face and dried it, tied a bandana around her head, and went out to feed the dogs before she left.

She didn't have much feeling for the dogs. The kennel was supposed to have been Luke's money-making venture. He and his father had built the pens last spring, although she had thought of the clever name and encouraged him to undertake the project. Everything had gone wrong, however. The kennels had hardly been completed before the accident took Luke's life. Now they served as a sad reminder of her lost son. Simply taking care of Beanie and Red had begun to feel like a burden. She wished to be rid of the dogs.

They stood at the end of their runs, watching her approach. As she opened the door to their pens, Red bolted past her, ran across the lawn, and disappeared down the lane.

Damned dog, she said to herself. It was too late to worry about it. He was gone. She didn't have time to go after him now.

She took a Valium on the way to the beauty parlor. By the time she pulled up in front of Helen's Hairport the pill had taken hold and she felt the usual gauzy detachment surrounding her every move. As she freshened up her lipstick before getting out of the car, she wondered what kind of wig she would end up with. They made beautiful wigs these days, out of real hair, cut to the latest style. Imagine, she thought, I can have any kind of hair I want. She pictured herself as a blonde, then a redhead. How would it be to have the kind of bouncy, curly hair she'd always wanted?

The shop smelled of hair spray and permanent-wave solution. Bright lights bounced off mirrors and gave the place a festive feeling. Pictures of women with exotic hairstyles lined the walls. At the far end of the room, Helen Dopp looked up from her customer and said, "Lookie what the cat dragged in." She recognized Helen's customer, Marge Wells, the druggist from over in Paris.

"Hello," she called to them.

"I'll be through with Marge in just a second," Helen said. "Make yourself comfortable. Take that first chair."

Joyce settled in the chair and looked at herself in the mirror. Her face appeared rather plump and plain, she thought, with the ugly bandanna on her head.

"Do you want a magazine, honey?" Helen asked. "Here, look at this for a minute."

Helen handed her a magazine, and she opened it and thumbed through the pages. She felt relaxed, as always, after the Valium, and she also had the lovely sense that she was about to be fitted with a beautiful head of hair. A pleasant thought occurred to her: I'll never have to sleep on rollers again. Of course, I'll be bald, won't I? For a brief moment, she considered what it would be like to go around bald, like a concentration-camp inmate or a cancer victim. Wouldn't it suit a mourning mother as well, distinguish her from all the women whose sons were alive and well and still turning up at the dinner table each evening? The thing that happened when she took a Valium was, she saw all the nice possibilities that existed because the good wasn't blocked by the bad.

Even baldness became acceptable.

Radio music wafted on the air, floating around her softly. Nice music. "Moon River." Andy Williams, the Osmond children. What had happened to them? Marie divorced. Andy divorced. Hadn't his wife shot someone?

She turned the pages of the magazine until she came to an ad for shoes, beautiful shoes, the kind of shoes no one she knew ever wore. Then Helen was there, hovering over her, immense and noisy and odorous, standing so near that her ample breasts lightly poked the back of her head. They felt like sofa bolsters, both soft and firm at once. What was Helen saying? The bandanna? Oh, yes. She undid the bandanna. Tiny sprigs of hair, loosened from their covering, stirred on her scalp as if moved by some unseen wind. In the mirror, she appeared wide-eyed, as if a little frightened by her own baldness. She felt Helen's hands on her scalp, warm and calming, like those of a matriarch bestowing a blessing, and then she simply began explaining everything, all the intimate, horrible details about her hair loss, murmuring softly, as if confessing.

"How terrible," Helen said at last. "But it could grow back. Those hormone treatments might work. Until then, you can just wear a wig. Let me get one or two and we'll try them on."

As Helen stepped into the back room, Marge Wells turned to her and said, "How's your father, Joyce?"

At the sound of the word "father," she felt a slight buzz run through her body. She hadn't spoken to him since Sunday, when he had managed to ruin Dan's birthday and embarrass her in front of everyone. What was happening to them? They were supposed to be coming together as a family, growing closer because of their tragedy, but each day that passed seemed to bring new distance.

"Is he getting along okay these days?" Marge asked.

"He's doing fine."

"I saw him the other night at the drive-in."

"The drive-in?"

"He looked wonderful," Marge said. "You wouldn't ever think he's been through what he has. He's lost weight, hasn't he? He looks so much younger, though your dad always was a handsome man — "

"The drive-in?" she repeated. "You mean the Arctic Circle?"

"No, the drive-in movie."

"I don't think it could've been Dad you saw. He wouldn't go to a drive-in."

"No, it was him, I'm certain about that. He was with a young woman."

"A young woman? Who?"

"I thought maybe she was a relative."

"What did she look like?"

"Well, she had blond hair, kind of ratted up the way kids do, you know, she was about sixteen or seventeen, very pretty — "

"Here we go," Helen said, striding toward her, bearing wigs aloft on each hand. One was brown, the other an alarming color of red.

"Let's try the red first."

Sixteen or seventeen? Blond hair? Who could Marge have seen him with?

The red was all wrong. She looked like a human Beanie. The brown was better, but not exactly right either. The wigs weren't made out of human hair; they were synthetic and looked cheap, the sort of wigs old women in rest homes wore. Her good mood evaporated. Panic set in. She simply wanted to escape the harsh lights, which made her face look so pasty, get away from Marge Wells and her nosy presence. What could it mean, her father at the drive-in with a young woman? A *girl?*

Helen wanted to try a short blond wig and she didn't refuse her, although when she saw herself in it, she felt even worse. "No, no," she said, "that's not right." Helen tried a black one. Each wig looked worse than the one before. The news that her father had been out with a young woman confused her completely, and she simply wanted to be home, alone, where she might think about things.

In order to escape, she said, "I'll take the brown one, it's fine," though she didn't really like it at all. She paid for it quickly, and left the shop wearing it.

The wig was driving her crazy by the time she arrived home. Her scalp itched and felt hot, as if she'd been wearing a prickly wool cap. When she glanced into the hall mirror, she realized with a certain horror whom she resembled: Her mother!

Quickly, she pulled the wig off and put it on the Styrofoam head. It was the wrong day to buy a wig. She'd take it back first chance she got. There were other places she could look besides Helen's. She could drive to Pocatello, if necessary, or even Idaho Falls, one of the bigger cities. It angered her that she'd settled for something that she didn't really like. Anxiety began to fill her again. She had to do something. She couldn't allow her father to distance himself this way. Not after what she'd been through. Not after what she'd done.

She covered her head with the bandanna again and took another Valium. She went to the phone and dialed her father's number.

After ten rings, she hung up, put on her coat, and prepared to leave the house. On impulse, at the last minute before going out the door, she pulled off the bandanna and put the wig on again.

At her father's house, she didn't knock, but instead opened the front door and called out, "Dad?"

A girl sat on the floor in front of the fireplace. She looked up at her with a startled expression.

"Oh!" Joyce said, shocked to see her. "Who are you?"

The girl said nothing, just stared at her frowning. Joyce stepped forward, closing the door behind her. She looked around the room for her father, who did not appear to be there.

"I'm looking for my dad."

"Phil's gone out. I'm . . . a friend of his."

"Where is he?"

"He went to the bank."

"The bank? The bank closes at three."

"It's Friday. They stay open till six today."

She edged forward, removing her coat. "I'm Joyce, Phil's daughter. What's your name?"

"Louise."

Joyce sat down on the couch and stared

at the girl. She was very pale and thin. Her skin appeared almost translucent. She had a very odd look, sullen, not the least bit friendly. Her blond hair was a mass of tangles, and she wore a bracelet made of heavy metal links that looked like Beanie's collar. Her eyes were outlined in black. The most startling part of her appearance was the red lipstick covering her mouth. Her mouth looked like a wound, a gash, opening onto a little pink portal of tongue and teeth, which was visible, because she was rather slack-jawed. A Spiegel catalogue lay open on the floor in front of her.

"How do you know my dad?"

The girl was slow to answer. "I just met him."

"Where?"

"He was up in the mountains, having a picnic."

"A picnic? You met him on a picnic? Where was that?"

"Up near Lava Hot Springs."

"Were you with the church group?"

The girl laughed. "No."

"I don't know why I said that. I guess I thought you might have been staying up at one of the church camps. We have a church camp up there," she said. "A lovely place for girls."

"No, I wasn't with any church group." She began laughing again as if she'd said something very humorous.

What was so funny? The conversation seemed to hit a wall, and an awkward silence hung between them. Louise went back to looking at the catalogue. Joyce studied her every movement.

Louise said, "He should be back pretty soon. You can wait if you want."

"Yes, I think I will, thanks." My house, she was thinking, the house I grew up in, and she tells me I can wait if I want?

Louise stood up abruptly. "I'm going to make something to eat," she said, and left the room.

Joyce heard her in the kitchen, rattling pots and pans. What was going on here? It appeared the girl wasn't visiting, but actually staying here. A car entered the driveway. A few moments later, her father walked in. He hesitated when he saw her. She thought he looked as if he wanted to leave, as if he were considering the possibility of turning around and walking right back out the door. His eyes quickly scanned the room.

"Hi, Dad," she said to him.

"Hello, Joyce. I didn't see your car outside."

"I parked behind the garage. I thought

I'd just stop by."

He removed his coat and hung it on the rack near the door, moving rather deliberately.

"I don't want us to have bad feelings," she said.

Slowly, he crossed the room, added another log to the fire, and stirred the coals. The flames caught and flared brightly, illuminating his face. "It's getting cold," he said, "isn't it? I think it could snow tonight."

"Did you hear what I said, Dad?"

"Yes, I heard," he said. "If it was important to you to tell your little white lie because you thought it was going to make Ralph feel better, well . . . I guess I can live with that."

"I want to forget about it."

"I'd like to forget it, too."

"I came to make up. Everybody knows the truth now anyway."

"I'm not holding any bad feelings."

Louise came to the doorway. "Hi," she said to Phil.

"Hello. Did you meet my daughter?"

Louise nodded, and twisted her mouth to one side. "Yes, we met."

"We talked a little before you came," Joyce said.

"Did you get my Coke?" Louise asked him.

"I'm afraid I forgot."

"Oh, hell," she said, and laughed. He laughed, too. "I've been thinking about having that Coke."

"It slipped my mind," he said. "I'm sorry."

"It's okay. I'll live." She turned and disappeared into the kitchen again.

As soon as she was gone, Joyce said, "Dad, who is that girl?"

Phil sat down in the rocker opposite her. He glanced in the direction of the kitchen and shook his head, placing a finger to his lips.

"What's she doing here?"

He shrugged and patted the air in front of him, indicating she should talk lower.

"Is she staying with you?"

"For a few days," he said softly. "Just a few days."

"But — "

"Shhhh," he said.

"How old is she? She looks terribly young. What — "

"She's had a little trouble," he whispered.

"Trouble? What kind of trouble?" Her voice had risen again.

"Quiet," he said.

"How did you meet her? She said you were on a picnic. But how did you get . . . how did she get here?"

"Leora and I were up in the mountains near Lava Hot Springs," he said softly. He glanced again toward the kitchen door. "She was hitchhiking. We gave her a ride. She needed a place to stay for a night or two. She likes it here and she's decided to spend a few more nights — "

"But Dad," Joyce said. "This isn't like you! To just take a stranger in — it sounds so weird to me. It doesn't seem right."

"Nevertheless," he said, interrupting her. "I don't think there's anything wrong with it, either. It's certainly nothing you need to worry about."

Her father took out a white handkerchief and wiped the corners of his mouth, folded it neatly, and put it away again.

"How long are you going to let her stay?" she said, quite loudly.

"Let's drop this now," he whispered. He jerked his head in the direction of the kitchen, and frowned.

"Okay." A bitter feeling arose in her. After all that had happened, she felt displaced by a stranger, whose feelings he seemed more concerned about than her own. She pressed her lips together to avoid saying what she was thinking, which was: How can you be so insensitive to me?

"How's Dan? Is he feeling any better?"

"Not really. His stomach's still bothering him."

"That's too bad."

"And Red ran away again this morning."

"Have you looked for him?"

"I haven't had time."

"I don't think those dogs get enough exercisc. They need more attention. I noticed their pens were awfully dirty." As he spoke, an idea came to him. He didn't really understand why he hadn't thought of it before.

"We do the best we can with them," she said rather defensively. "It's been awfully hard. We've been so busy with the orchard."

"Perhaps I should take the dogs."

"Take them? You mean, you want them to come stay here with you?"

"I don't see why not," he said. "I've certainly got the room, and plenty of time to give them."

"I don't think you know how much trouble they can be. But if you want them, I guess you can give it a try. I'll talk to Dan about it. I'm sure he won't mind. He's always saying what a nuisance they are, how he doesn't have time for them."

"What have you done to your hair?" he asked.

"It's a wig."

"Phil?" Louise called from the kitchen.

"Where's the fry pan?"

"It's under the sink," he said.

"I guess I'll go," Joyce said. "Dan will start wondering where his dinner is."

"All right, Joyce. Thanks for stopping by."

"Helen is coming down on Sunday. Maybe we can all go to Swenborg's for lunch. Even her, I mean Louise, if she's still here."

"We'll see, Joyce," he said.

"If we don't make an effort to be a family — "

"Yes, Joyce," he said. "Don't worry. It shouldn't be that much of an effort. We *are* a family."

She kissed him, a kiss that felt moist and hard to her, as if she'd touched a wad of raisins to her lips, and then walked to the kitchen door and said, "Goodbye, Louise. Nice to meet you."

Louise was bent over, peering into the oven. She turned and regarded her coldly. "Goodbye," she said, her mouth curling to one side in a severe little smile.

That night Joyce slept badly. It began snowing during the night, the first hard winter storm, driving down from the mountains on fierce winds. The screens rattled, and branches broke in the orchard. Once she awoke with a start and saw someone standing at the end of the room, staring at her. But it was only the wig, perched on its white Styrofoam head, sitting on top of the dresser. She curled against her husband's back and held on to him, clasping him around his soft belly. Once she whispered, "Dan," because she wanted him to wake up and talk to her. But he didn't wake, and she was afraid to say his name again and rob him of his sleep.

God was synonymous with peace, she thought, but she wasn't peaceful, she was dancing on one foot, a delirium dance, off-balance, a dance of cheap Valium cheer. Where was God now? Some new terror gripped her heart, undefinable and black. She felt panicked, afraid of the future, and the fear wouldn't leave her but grew worse, curling around her heart like a snake, squeezing harder and harder, causing her to burrow in closer against her husband's back.

The promise of heaven was a guarantee of reunion. She had seen her mother after she died. It was her, and yet it wasn't. She had seen her son alive, and yet dead. The dead were there, quite near: they answered everything with muteness. They hovered around you, insinuating themselves in the vaporous air, taking shape as thought or memory, messengers without substantive shape, palpable and sentient and close. She missed her son deeply. She wanted to talk to him, to see him again, and instead, there was only this abyss of silence. Her faith now seemed small against this silence, but if she were to receive a sign, some indication from God, perhaps her faith would be strengthened.

Quietly, she slipped out of bed and went to Luke's room. In the stillness she stood before his dresser and looked at the objects lying in the moonlight — his picture and watch, a piece of petrified wood and a small arrowhead. As she gazed at these things, she felt tremendous grief. She bowed her head and whispered, "Dear God . . ." She prayed for a sign.

For a long time she stood before the dresser, her eyes closed, waiting. Nothing came to her that could be called a sign. She felt only fatigue. She groped her way to the bed nearby, full of a tiredness born of insomnia, plaguing her night after night. Lying down, she fell asleep in his bed, and began dreaming of faint beeping signals.

When it came, it awoke her from sleep. The sign arrived in the form of a ringing bell — not the brash clang of an Easter peal, but rather the soft reverberation of delicate tinklings, a noise light and beckoning, eerily soft and and melodic, like a monk's finger bells. The sound was sweet and calming. She raised herself on her elbows, straining to hear the noise. Where was it coming from?

She peered out the window. The faint, jingling sound seemed to come from outside. It moved across the front lawn, grew louder, and then louder. She went to the window and parted the curtains and peered out. The storm had abated, and there, in the moonlight, she saw the shadowy form of the dog, slinking across the whitened lawn toward the orchard, the little metal tags swinging melodiously from the chain encircling his neck as his paws struck the ground, breaking through the beautiful whiteness of freshly fallen snow.

11

At Fashion Crossroads, the clothes were hung on racks according to color. The sections were marked "Juniors" and "Misses," but all the clothes looked the same size, except those on the rack marked "Large Ladies." The store was pink inside with gravy-colored pillars, paint that wore the grime of years and gave the place a drab feeling, as if the walls were slightly greasy. A curling cardboard sign affixed to a metal stand read, "Sale! Sale! Sale!"

Louise could see the Fluff 'n Floral shop across the street, and the Big E Store; pigeons had perched on the letter E. Phil sat on a chair near the store's entrance, staring out the window in the direction of the Fluff 'n Floral. His profile was calm and thoughtful, and she wondered if he was watching the pigeons. She fingered a skirt, recoiling from the feel of the cheap material, and thought, I have to get out of here.

She walked over to him. "Nothing's right," she said. "Let's get out of here."

"Did you look at the coats?"

"Yeah. They're terrible. Let's go." She

couldn't wait to get out of the store. All those flowered dresses, lace and ruffles, aqua and pink. Hadn't they ever heard of red or black? She should have listened to her instincts and not let him bring her in here in the first place.

They walked down the street toward Wally's Jewelry Store and the sign that read, "Bulova for Quality Time."

"You've got to get a coat," he said. "Look how you're shivering."

"Yeah, but that wasn't the place to buy it, believe me." She wrapped her arms around her chest, hugging the folds of the big brown sweater against her. She walked fast against the wind, which stung her ears and blew her hair straight back from her face. The town was one long main street. From one end to the other she could see all the business signs jutting out above the traffic: Elmo's Imports, Shoe World, Milmo's Hotel, Sears, Transmission City. Some of the signs on the buildings were so old they didn't match the businesses inside anymore. Milmo's Hotel wasn't a hotel at all now — it was Thelma's Yarn 'n Darn. She remembered a thrift store way down at the other end of the street, where the road divided and rose up to a viaduct, passed a row of seedy bars.

"What you need is something like a car coat," he said.

"Yeah, right. A car coat."

"Or a parka. Something good and warm."

"I'll just look until I find something."

"Do you want to go somewhere else? Maybe Sears?"

"Look, why don't you just go have a cup of coffee or something and I'll meet you in about half an hour. I want to check out a thrift store."

"Okay," he said. "I'll be at the Busy Bee. Do you know where that is?"

"I know. One block over."

He turned and started to walk away from her.

"Phil?" she called.

"What?"

"Well, what about money?"

"I'm sorry," he said. "I forgot."

She watched him take out his wallet. He'd offered to buy her the coat. She hadn't begged. Nevertheless, when it came down to it, that's what it felt like she was doing. He gave her three twenty-dollar bills.

"Thanks," she said. "I won't be long."

She passed Rudy D's Cuisine, food to go, and the Ex-Lax thermometer sign, Keep Regular with Ex-Lax. She was freezing. Maybe there'd be a good coat at the thrift store, something warm that wouldn't cost too much, and she could keep what was left of the money. Would that be wrong? She'd have to think about it.

In the thrift store, the lights were so low she could barely make out a man behind a desk at the back of the room. He was listening to Elvis Presley's "Love Me Tender." In the dim light, she saw the dusty objects lining the shelves and sitting on the bare concrete floor. There was a pack saddle, bridles, a halter, and some stirrups, along with oil cans, hoses, and sets of tools. On other shelves there were batteries and encyclopedias, a chain saw, chipped dishes, and figurines. It didn't look too promising.

She picked up a bridle, the leather old and stiff. The bit was stained with flecks of mossy green. She wanted the bridle, wanted to own it against the day when she might have a horse again. She could clean it and oil it. She imagined bringing it back to life, restoring a richness to the leather. Then she dropped it, tossing it carelessly aside. It was a dream. There wasn't any use in dreaming. She scanned the store, wondering if it was worth looking any further. Her eye picked out racks of clothing at the back of the room.

"Can I help you?" the man sitting behind the desk called out.

"Just looking." As she walked toward him, she could see he was small, with black hair neatly parted, sitting perfectly still, holding a small stub of a cigarette in front of his lips so that to look at her he had to peer through smoke wafting past his eyes. He had squinty eyes, and he looked stupid or crafty — one or the other, she couldn't tell.

"If you're looking for anything special, maybe I could help you find it." He wiped the corners of his mouth with the side of his little finger. His lips were liver-colored and shiny, and his face had the lined gray pallor of a chain-smoker.

"I'm looking for a coat," she said.

"Over there." He pointed to clothes packed tightly on a rack against the wall. They were all women's coats, wool three-quarter-length things with collars made out of fake fur, knotted and gray, dressy coats with big buttons in bad plaids and dreary golds and browns. But there were men's coats hanging next to them, and they were more interesting.

"Finding anything?"

"Yeah," she said, "a couple of things."

There was a long overcoat made of dark green wool, which looked very military, and a couple of shorter, padded jackets. She slipped the overcoat off the hanger and put it on. It felt heavy, almost oppressively so.

The sleeves covered her hands. It was cut for a big man.

"You got a mirror anywhere?"

"Over in the corner."

"Where?"

"By the skis over there."

The coat flapped against her legs as she walked. Without the sweater it would feel better. The sweater and the coat were too much — their bulkiness weighed her down.

"Isn't it a little big for you?"

"I like it big." She stood in front of the mirror and rolled up the sleeves. It was definitely a good coat. But she needed some boots. The coat didn't look right with her shoes. She buckled the belt that came with the coat. It looked even better.

"How much for this?"

"Fifteen dollars."

She tried on another jacket made of plaid wool. It smelled bad and she felt the grimy collar against her neck. She pulled it off and shoved it back on the hanger, holding her breath against its odor.

"Do you have any work boots?"

"I think there are a couple of pair up front, by the tools."

She found a pair of boy's black high-top boots, close to her size, and tried them on. They were a little large. What she needed was some thick socks. There was a box of socks near the shoes.

"Find any boots?" he called.

"Yeah."

It was hard finding two socks that weren't stained or yellow, or thin at the heels, but finally she found two good gray ones that matched, and bending lower, she stuffed the socks inside her sweater, jamming them into her bra.

"I'll take these," she said, setting the coat and the boots on the counter in front of him.

"That's fifteen for the coat, and seven-fifty for the boots."

"How about five for the boots?" she said.

"Well . . ." He hefted one boot, using both hands, leaving the cigarette burning in his mouth and squinting against the smoke. He turned it over and examined the heels.

"Twenty for everything," she said.

He seemed put out by her bargaining, but finally said, "All right." He took her money without moving the muscles in his face.

She left the shop, wearing the overcoat and carrying the boots in a paper bag. When she came to the corner, where the road dipped down past the bars, she reached inside her sweater and took out the socks and stuffed them into the paper bag with the boots. She also took a pair of earrings out of her pocket. She had stolen them on the way out of the store. They were thick hoops, circles formed by ram's heads meeting in the middle. Fake rubies had been set into the eyes of the rams. The earrings were tarnished and cheap. Looking at them, she felt a wave of regret run through her. Why had she bothered to steal them? And the socks? There were socks in the boxes downstairs at Phil's. The earrings were so tinny. Bad judgment again.

She looked around, wondering where there was a bathroom she could use. There was a VFW bar across the street, and next to it the bus station. She crossed the street and went into the bathroom in the bus station, a small tiled room with high windows leaking gray light through clouded panes. It was cold and smelled of smoke and disinfectant. The toilets required dimes. She sat down on the floor and took out the socks and boots. As soon as she'd put them on, she felt better, much warmer.

She stood up and went to the sink, looking at herself in the mirror. She put the earrings on. They felt heavy, and yet when she turned her head, she liked the way they banged against her neck. Opening her small purse, she took out the lipstick and made her lips very red. She relined her eyes with black pencil, then ratted her hair and stuck bobby pins in it so that it erupted from the top of her head in a fountain of snarls. She took off the brown sweater and put it in the paper bag. Underneath, she wore only a T-shirt and a pair of black tights. When she slipped the coat on, she could feel its silken lining against her bare arms. She wanted it to feel better than it did. As she bent over to pick up the bag, her body felt weighted, drawn down by the overcoat.

Outside, she put on her dark glasses and began walking down the street, toward the viaduct. The boots struck the pavement firmly, making her feel taller and more solid. She stopped in front of the VFW bar and stood next to the wall, waiting. She was looking for the right person. A couple of guys came out, but they were older, men who would probably end up lecturing her. Someone younger came out. He stood in front of the bar, twirling a toothpick in his mouth. He had a ponytail and wore work jeans that were covered with white dust. His hands were cut, the skin broken in places over his knuckles.

"Hi," she said.

He turned abruptly and looked at her. A

smile broke out across his face. "Hi," he answered gruffly, but it was the mock gruffness some men affect in order to appear cool in the presence of a woman they might want to impress.

"I wonder if you'd do me a favor?"

"What's that?" he said.

"If I give you the money, will you go back in there and buy me a beer?"

"Buy you a beer?"

"Yeah." She smiled.

"You want me to go back in there and buy you a beer?"

She held out the twenty to him. "Yeah."

"What's in it for me?" He looked at the money.

"Grandeur," she said. *You know what you get from pistachios? I'll tell you. . . .*

"Grandeur?"

"Come on," she said. "Please."

He took the bill between his first and second fingers, as if they were the two parts of a pair of scissors, and drew it away from her.

"I don't know. I could get arrested for contributing to the delinquency of a minor by doing this."

He wanted to be cute, to be funny, to draw this out, she thought, so let him.

"Hey, thanks," she said.

"What kind you want?"

"Any kind."

She watched him go back into the bar. Beneath the viaduct she could see layers of garbage, old batteries, discarded tires. In no time, he came back out with the beer.

"Technically, you're not supposed to take any liquor out of the bar." He had the beer hidden inside his coat. When he handed it to her, he moved close to pass it between their bodies, and his knuckles brushed her breasts.

"Thanks," she said.

"Where are you from?" he asked.

"Nowhere."

"That's an interesting place to be from."

"It keeps things simple. That way it's not hard to be nobody."

"So you're nobody from nowhere?" he said, looking down at her and grinning. "You look about fifteen to me."

"I'm also ageless."

"Where are you going to drink that? Not anywhere you'll be seen, I hope. They'll bust you around here if they see you with a beer on the street. Especially you. You're underage."

"I'll watch it."

He started to walk away.

"Hey!" she called. "What about my change?"

"Oh." He came back, and extended his hand, fist closed. "I thought the change was my commission."

"That's a little more than I can afford right now."

He laughed, and dumped the money into her outstretched palm.

She walked up a side street into a neighborhood of old houses with fenced yards and big trees. Tricycles stood abandoned on broken concrete walks, and dogs were tied up on yellowed patches of grass. The trees lining the sidewalk had lost their leaves, and here and there someone had made an effort to sweep them up, leaving piles that had begun to rot. She kicked through one pile, scattering the moldy, golden leaves. Two women drove by in a car, staring at her, and began laughing.

At the end of the street she came to a small stream, which ran through a little gully. Beyond it, separated by a field of weeds, was a fenced pasture where a few sheep grazed. She climbed down the embankment and sat down against a tree. Taking the beer out of her coat, she popped it open. The coat created a warm shield against the wind coming up the draw. Below her, the stream ran past in a silver trickle. Leaves clogged its path, and here and there it disappeared and then emerged farther on as a pale twisting ribbon. Bottles and fast-food containers and an old sock were strewn near the streambed, matted in mud and leaves. But where she sat there was no garbage, and it looked beautiful the way the weeds had been swept flat by the wind.

She leaned back against the tree and sipped her beer slowly. The last few days she had felt restless and moody, just as she had with Wendall. How was Wendall? She wondered. Was he sorry now for the things he'd said?

Sometimes she felt so depressed it was hard to keep it from spilling out on Phil. She'd felt good, just being away from Wendall, staying in a place that was so nice. But her mood had begun to change the day Phil's daughter had come to the house. She overheard them talking about her in the next room, heard the disapproval in his daughter's voice, listened as Phil tried to explain her presence, and she had felt small and worthless again, no better than a beggar. Where was her place in the world? As far as she could tell, she didn't have one.

Sometimes she dreamed of being like Erika, capable of starting over in a new world, but what worried her, and what depressed her, was that she seemed to lack the strength it would take to discover such a place. There was no new world she could see. She didn't know where to go. She felt lost.

She finished the beer and stood up and looked around her. The neighborhood was quiet, the streets empty, except for a child who rode a tricycle down a driveway. The beer had made her light-headed, but no happier. All these neighborhoods are the same, she thought. I could be in Coeur d'Alene, or Pocatello, or Casper. Nothing changes. Yet something had to change.

"Sorry I took so long," she said. He glanced up from the newspaper he was reading, startled by her voice. There were no tables at the Busy Bee, only one long counter. She took an empty stool next to him.

"What did you do?" he said, looking at her with his eyebrows furrowed.

"What do you mean, what did I do?"

"Your hair . . . that coat . . ."

"What's wrong?"

"You look . . . so different. Did you buy that coat?"

"Yeah. It's a good one. It's warm. I could use a cup of coffee."

"That coat would fit me."

"Well, I'll let you borrow it anytime."

"I didn't mean — "

"I know what you meant. What's wrong

with that waitress? Hey!" she shouted. "I'd like a cup of coffee, please!"

Phil said, "Don't shout, Louise. Where have you been? Your breath smells like beer."

"I don't know," she mumbled. The way he was looking at her, his scrutiny of every little detail, annoyed her. Why didn't he just let her be? She could feel him becoming the dog with the vacuum cleaner. He was edging away now. He stood up.

"I'm going to walk over to the drugstore for a moment. Go ahead and have your coffee." He took the check and left a dollar on the counter. As soon as he turned his back, she took the dollar from the counter and put it in her pocket.

She picked up the newspaper and scanned the pages. There were a couple of articles that interested her, and she read them carefully. Three men had had a conviction of rape overturned on appeal because it took too long to bring them to trial. The rape had occurred in Rock Springs in 1981. The men had forced a woman into their car and driven her around town for several hours, repeatedly raping her. There had been witnesses. There was no question the men were guilty, and yet now they were free.

She went on to another story. A woman had been murdered in Cheyenne, her body found in a gravel dump several years ago, but the victim had never been identified, and now police were reopening the case and asking for help in solving the murder. The woman was described as weighing 115 pounds, with layered brunette hair. She had been wearing Western clothes when she was found, with a pack of Kool Lights in the shirt pocket. Her age was guessed to be twenty-five or thirty years old.

She closed the paper and stared down at her coffee. It made her crazy, these stories. It was always the same. Men always got off did things and didn't have to pay for them. It wasn't a woman, was it, who'd left a brunette with layered hair lying dead in a gravel dump, or ridden around on a raping spree for hours? It wasn't a woman because it couldn't be! Who organized the yearly nigger shoot? Not a woman, but men, who attached cardboard cutouts of running blacks to trees and gave prizes for heel shots.

"Hey." She lifted her cup and got the waitress's attention. "I'd like more coffee." Her voice was loud, and she didn't care. She knew Phil thought she looked foolish, and now the coat even felt stupid to her. She didn't have any judgment. That was the problem. And if you didn't have any judgment, how could you ever go to a new world and start over?

"This coffee's bitter," she said sullenly as the waitress poured her another cup. "Maybe you should make another pot."

She knew the waitress was disgusted with her. She wouldn't respond to her suggestion. She turned her back on her and walked away.

She looked around to see if anybody smoked and noticed a man with a pack of cigarettes sitting a few stools away. She walked over to him. He turned his face in her direction as she approached, and what she saw startled her. His eyes stared off in different directions. The whites were mottled with yellowed knots of flesh. The irises were cloudy blue marbles, filmed with white. He was blind.

"Can I bum a cigarette from you?"

His lips curled back to reveal stained teeth.

"So you want a cigarette, do you?" he said softly. Hair grew out of his nose and ears, and his breath made a little whistling sound. He smelled like mothballs and wool.

"Yeah . . . if you can spare one."

"You're a loudmouthed little thing, aren't you?"

She didn't say anything. His words surprised her.

"You should learn to be nicer," he rasped.

"I didn't ask for a lecture, only a cigarette."

"I wouldn't give you the time of day."

"I don't need time, just a smoke."

"You're wrong," he said. "You need a lot of time . . . time to understand a few things."

"Really?" she said, her heart starting to pound a little. *I feel everything in my heart. . . . Everything? All of it. . . .*

"Like what?" she added.

"The Golden Rule," he said.

"What about the cigarette?"

"Are you beyond redemption?" he asked breathily.

"I'm not looking for religion, only a cigarette."

He laughed and shook a cigarette out of the pack he held in his trembling hand.

"Thanks," she mumbled, and reached for the cigarette, but before she could take it from him, he grabbed her wrist with his free hand and held her tightly. "Do unto others," he said, "as you would have them do unto you."

She tried to pull away from him, but he held on to her, squeezing her wrist. He was stronger than she was, and he frightened her with his wild, unseeing eyes. He held her quietly, firmly, in his grasp, and she realized no one else around them knew what was going on.

"Let go of me," she said.

He tightened his grip and drew her a little

closer. "I know things," he said. "I feel them. You'll come to a bad end unless you learn the Golden Rule. That's not religion, dearie, that's the secret of life."

"You're hurting me."

He released her arm and held the cigarette up in front of her. "Go ahead," he said. "Now you can have it."

She snatched the cigarette and backed away from him. He reached beneath the counter, fumbling with his hand until he found his white stick, then stood up slowly and began tapping his way to the front door. He left the restaurant, exiting to the sound of a little tinkling bell attached to the door.

No matter how much she tried to tell herself he was a crazy old man, she couldn't get over the anxious feeling his words had left her with. She felt gloomy, as if she'd been jinxed by someone who could actually make bad things come true. By the time Phil showed up, she was beginning to feel ill.

During the drive home, she rested her head against the window and fought down the feeling of sickness. She couldn't stop thinking about the blind man, the dead woman in the dump, and the carload of men raping a single, defenseless woman. What kind of horrible world was it? And her step-father was still out there, preaching the gospel of racial purity. She pulled the coat around her. She looked stupid, she knew she looked stupid, but the world was more stupid. How could you ever get out of it? My God. No new world, only the old one. What had he said? "You'll come to a bad end. . . ."

"Phil," she said, "I . . . I think . . ."

"What is it?"

"Pull over."

She huddled at the edge of the road, holding her stomach, and retched so violently she broke out in a sweat. She felt as if she were vomiting up all the bile in her life, the bitter blackness of hatred and loss. Even as she knew herself to be empty and dry, she continued convulsing, just as she had done in the spring. She felt the opposite of pregnant: she felt barren. What waste, what loss. She would be having a baby right now if she hadn't done what she'd done, and then where would she be? How could she ever have managed yet another life?

Tears filled her eyes, and she spit. She felt his hands on her ribs, and he was lifting her, wiping her mouth with a soft white handkerchief that smelled of him, male and yet clean and pure, and she straightened up, leaning on him, and looked up into his face, which was so worried, so full of concern.

"It's nothing," she said wearily. "Let's go."

12

"It's not a good idea," Dan said. He leaned on his shovel and stared over Phil's shoulder, his eyes fixed on something in the distance. "I don't think you know what you're getting into."

"I thought you'd be happy for me to take the dogs."

"You want them, you can have them," Dan said. "I just don't think you've thought this through."

"What's there to think through?" Phil gazed at Beanie and Red, standing perfectly motionless behind the chain-link fencing.

"Phil, you've never had dogs — "

"That's only because of May's allergies," he said. "It isn't that I wouldn't have liked to have a dog."

Dan sighed and looked over at the dogs and shook his head. "They're trouble," he said. "You take these dogs and where are you going to put them? You don't have a kennel. They're a lot of responsibility. If you want to take a trip, go somewhere for a few days, you'll have to worry about them."

Take a trip? Where did Dan imagine he

might be going? He stared at Dan's head, bald except for the swaths of graying yellowish hair swept behind his ears. I ought to say something to him, he thought. I should apologize for ruining his birthday. But he sensed an apology wouldn't make any difference. There was deeper trouble between them. Maybe what it came down to was Dan couldn't part with one more thing, his son's dogs, even though he didn't want them.

"You really want to do this?" Dan said, raising his eyes to look at him. His face looked hard, unreadable.

"Yes," he said. "I'd like to try it, anyway."

"Go ahead and take them, then. Good luck. You'll need it." He strode off in the direction of the orchard.

He opened the gates to the kennels and the dogs shot out. They circled him, sniffing, trotting like circus animals moving in unison. They were a matched pair, racing and biting at each other, mother and son. They acted as if it had been a long time since they'd known freedom. For a moment, he had the feeling he might lose them. They ran to the edge of the driveway and looked down the road, poised for flight, ready to bolt. He imagined the boy's voice, calling to them, and they turned and looked at him, as if they, too, heard something ghostly.

"Red," he called sharply. "Beanie! Come over here." They turned and ran back to him, matching strides, bumping into each other and wagging their tails happily. As he walked toward the car, he felt them close at his heels, an exuberant, panting duo bumping against his legs. When he opened the back door, they bounded inside as if they had been expecting this moment, just waiting for their liberator to arrive like this, in an aging Buick with a big backseat.

Behind the wheel, the heater blew cool air toward him — broken again. He had to get it fixed. The dogs perched on the edge of the backseat, looking ahead, their heads so close to his he could smell their breath. "Now we're going somewhere," he said, swinging wide to miss the pothole at the end of the drive.

He talked to the dogs intermittently all the way over the pass. "Plover," he said to Red, who had perked up and rushed to the side window at the sight of a bird lifting off the shoulder of the road. "Which one of you is the best bird dog? Who knows. Maybe you'll get a chance at a real bird when Lars gets that new duck blind built." Red began licking him behind the ear, his big tongue lapping roughly against his skin. Phil laughed, and pushed the dog away.

Coming down the switchbacks, he turned on the radio, picking up the Boise station and classical music. Below him, the lake filled the basin with blue. He ran into construction on the highway outside Paris and had to wait awhile in a line of cars. He didn't care about waiting. The day stretched before him, empty and undemanding.

He wondered if Louise was awake yet. He'd left early, with the first light, and stopped in the cemetery at dawn. Sitting among the tombstones, he'd watched the light come over the valley. He'd been struck this time by all the children's markers. Most of them died in winter. He sat at the foot of May's grave and felt the cold wind blow up the sleeves of his jacket.

You had to work hard to live in a land like this. You couldn't take anything for granted. The graves were the testament to hardship. Four small tombstones and two larger ones stood near May's grave. Four babies lost to one couple, John and Lucy Lewis: Elsie, Thelma, Alvin, and Jacob. *In heaven there are four angels more.* There were no other graves near the Lewises. He assumed that the Lewises lost every child born to them and went on to spend their days childless. Not far from Luke's tombstone was a grave for Effie Wallantine, born May 21,

1898, died October 12, 1909. Eleven years old. *We loved her yes, no tongue could tell how much we loved her and how well, God loved her too and he thought best, to take her home to be at rest.*

In town, he stopped at Stinson's and bought eggs and bacon and a fresh loaf of bread. He came home the back way, past Dingle and the old water tower with its sign that had been there for years: "If you think this world is bad, hell is forever. Jesus Saves." For some reason, the sign made him think of the name his daughter had thought up for the kennel business. Ark Animal Care. Leave it to Joyce to come up with a biblical reference, even for a dog-sitting business. He looked in the rearview mirror at the dogs, who were being very well-behaved, sitting quietly next to each other. They could have been a pair off the ark. "The boat finally landed, didn't it?" he said. "Now you get to try land for a while."

Louise was sitting out on the porch when he returned, her big coat thrown over her like a blanket. When she first walked into the Busy Bee the day before wearing that coat, he had thought it was a joke. He'd hardly recognized her. The coat, the boots, the heavy makeup. He still didn't understand it. She seemed bent on making herself look foolish.

The dogs bounded out of the car as soon as he opened the door and ran up onto the porch. He followed them at a slower pace.

"Do you feel any better?" he asked, stepping up onto the porch.

"I'm still a little sick."

"What is it?"

"Stomach flu." Her mouth was faintly pinked, and her cheeks flushed. There were dark circles beneath her eyes.

"You shouldn't be out here in the cold," he said.

"Where did the dogs come from?" she asked.

She patted her chest, and Red rose up on his hind legs, his front paws landing lightly against her coat. She smiled. "He's really nice." She reached out and cupped Beanie's muzzle in her hand. "So are you," she said to Beanie. "Whose dogs are they?"

"Mine now, I guess. They belonged to Luke."

"Your grandson?"

He nodded. "Joyce doesn't want them anymore."

"Joyce?"

"My daughter."

"Oh, yeah. The one with the bad wig."

She stood up, and the coat dropped away from her. She caught it before it fell. She wore nothing but a big old T-shirt. He saw her pale legs, bare and white.

"What's his name?"

"Red."

"Red? And who's this?"

"Beanie. Beanie's Red's mother."

"Ah," she said. "Mother and son. How touching." There was some new quality to her voice. It disturbed him.

"Have you had anything to eat?" he asked. "I brought something, bacon and eggs."

"I can't eat anything. I don't feel like it. In fact, I think I'll just go back to bed. I just don't feel very good. I couldn't sleep last night." She started for the front door, and hesitated, her hand on the doorknob. "Can the dogs come inside?"

"They'd better," he said. "They have to get used to this place. They've got bad reputations for running away from home."

"Oh, bad dogs," she said. "Who would ever think you were runaways? Just like me. I understand. You're beautiful," she murmured, bending over the dogs, letting them lick her chin. Red wagged his tail happily and tried to jump up on her again.

"I think they like me. Can I take them up to bed with me?"

"I suppose," he said. He followed her into the house. "Louise, listen, I think we should talk."

"Talk? About what?"

"What you said. About being a runaway. If you've run away, somebody must be looking for you. You're going to have to do something. We can't just pretend — "

"Do we have to talk about it now? I feel so tired."

"But that's what you always say when I try to talk to you. You've always got some excuse, some reason for not facing things. I think you have to let your parents know you're safe — "

"Are you crazy?" she said. "Do you know what will happen if they find out where I am? I'll get sent back to them. No way am I going back." She folded the coat around her and glared at him.

"No. Way." She spoke the words separately, loading them with emphasis. The dogs moved excitedly around the room, sniffing the rug, the furniture, their tails waving like plumed dusters. Their exuberance contrasted oddly with Louise's rigid posture. "I know you want to get rid of me, and I'll go, anytime you say, but I won't call my parents. You can forget about that."

"Get rid of you," he said, pulling off his

coat and turning his back on her. "That's all you can think about, how I want to get rid of you."

"Well, you do, don't you?"

"I don't know, it's not so — "

"Yes or no? Do you want me to stay or do you want me to leave?

"Never mind," she said. "You don't have to answer." She turned and started up the stairs, and the dogs followed, bounding past her.

"Louise . . ."

"Later, Phil," she said.

The dogs nestled beside her in bed, lying on top on the covers, one on each side. "Bad dogs," she whispered. "Bad runaways." She patted their heads. Red was the dopey one. She could tell that. Sweet, but a little dopey. Beanie was the one who got to her. She had very soft eyes that communicated something. Sadness. Longing. Resignation. What was it? She could only look at you briefly, then her eyes flicked away, only to return moments later, seeking you out again. Beanie's muzzle rested on her thigh. She could feel a knot of fur behind her ear. Later she would brush her. Red too. She looked out the window. The light was falling fast. It was almost dark. She'd spent all afternoon in bed. Turning on the bedside lamp, she picked up her diary and opened it to a clean page.

It's October, I don't know the day, but it hasn't been a good one. I can't get past the feeling that something bad is going to happen, just like the blind man said yesterday. I feel sick inside. I don't belong anywhere. I can't go back, and I don't know how to go forward. Phil has been downstairs all afternoon. I can hear him once in a while, tapping away. Working on the tombstone. He couldn't say he wants me here when I asked him earlier because I know he doesn't.

I didn't tell Phil that I went to see Erika this morning. I wanted to ask her if I could get a job working where she does, in the greenhouse, but she says they won't hire me. I'm too young. Erika tried to tell me I should finish school, stand up and fight, not run anymore and try to hide from my problems, but how can I fight? She says she would help me contact some agency and explain my situation and maybe the state would find me a foster home. I don't want a foster home. I can't live with strangers telling me what I can and can't do.

When I told Erika this morning that I only want to start over, just like she had, she said that I didn't understand that she was a lot older than me when she left home, and she had experienced things that made her strong and ready to be on her own.

I told her about the abortion. I don't know why, I guess I just wanted somebody to know. I told her about the dream I keep having, the one where I have a baby and I'm not taking care of it. I forget to do things for it, and then I wake up. Usually in the dream the baby isn't crying or complaining. I just walk into a room, and there's the baby, and I realize it's my baby but I've forgotten about it and I'm so unhappy when I see it and realize I've ignored it for so long. Erika said I should try not to be too troubled by the dream, that it will go away one day.

Erika said something else that surprised me. It was about Phil. She said she had known him a long time. She said, "Be careful, Louise, you could hurt him." When I asked her what she meant, she wouldn't say more. She did say she thought he cared for me and I shouldn't take advantage of that. I can't imagine she means what it sounded like, but I

412

think she was telling me it wasn't good for me to stay here with him any longer. All the way home from her house I could only think, I don't want to leave, I want to stay here. Why can't I stay? Why?

Downstairs, beneath the single bulb dangling from the ceiling in the basement room, Phil wiped the stone clean, removing the dust from his work. He felt tired, and he knew it was time to quit. He looked with satisfaction at his work. The marble had a warm luster that seemed to come from deep within. The finished letters were perfectly even. He touched the name with his fingertips: Luke Beery 1970-1986. A little dust lay in the grooves. He moistened his fingertip on his tongue and traced each letter, repeating the motion, using his fingernail to remove the fine dust, his hand moving from his mouth to the name as if his fingers carried kisses from his lips to the writing on the stone. 1970-1986. It hardly seemed enough time to make any kind of life. But it had been a life — a very short one, but very real. He stood up and went to the stairs. Grasping the banister, he made his way up to the landing, flipped off the light to the basement, and closed the door to the chilled and darkened rooms.

13

He watched her soak up syrup with a piece of French toast, stirring it with a fork around the edges of her plate before popping it into her mouth. She had eaten very little over the past few days, spending most of her time in her room, but now she seemed hungry and ate quickly. Syrup puddled in the little cleft of her chin. She seemed unaware of it, and he had a great urge to wipe it away for her with a napkin.

"Helen is coming today," he said.

"Who?"

"My daughter Helen and her family. We're going to lunch at Swenborg's. Joyce arranged it. She's invited you, too, if you feel like going."

She shrugged. "I don't know if I feel like it."

As he turned a piece of French toast out onto a plate for himself, she went on, "I didn't think your daughter liked me. I don't know why she'd invite me to lunch unless she just wants to check me out some more. You know, look at the freak." She rattled her knife nervously against her plate.

"What are you talking about?"

She dropped the knife, and it clattered against the plate. For a moment he wondered if she hadn't broken it. It was a rude thing to do, and it shocked him.

"Why are you acting like this?"

"I heard you talking about me with your daughter. Yeah, I heard you two, don't think I didn't."

"So?"

"She didn't approve of me," she said, her voice flat.

"I don't think she disliked you."

"Well, that's great. I feel great about that."

"I think she was surprised to find you here. That's all."

She looked away and shook her head. "She thought I was weird. She didn't think I had any right to be here. She's uptight."

"Now who's uptight?"

"She didn't like me!" she shouted.

"I don't know why you'd care one way or the other whether she liked you or not." He didn't know why, but he felt like laughing. He remembered feeling this way a good deal with his own children. Things they thought were so important often looked ridiculous. You wanted to laugh and say, "You can't really mean to make so much out of this." Sometimes she liked to act the tough part, but how tough could you really be if you worried so much about whether somebody liked you or not?

"You're laughing at me."

"I'm not laughing."

"You're smiling!"

"Yes, I'm smiling."

"I don't think what I'm saying is funny."

"Would you like to drop your knife again, slam it down on the plate, to show me just how serious this is and how rude you can be?" His voice had changed. He was slowly becoming angry with her.

"Why should I have lunch with somebody who judges me?"

"Look here, Louise." He sighed and began speaking slowly. "If you don't want to have lunch with us, don't. Joyce invited you. But you're welcome to stay here by yourself. Don't feel I'm forcing you. I don't mind if you don't go. But I don't see why you act like this. Why you get so hostile so suddenly. What's gotten into you these last few days?"

"Just don't tell me that what I hear with my own ears and see with my own eyes doesn't matter!"

He felt exasperated. "I don't know whether I've ever met anyone with such — "

"There's a car pulling up out front."

" — a chip on her shoulder."

"I said, somebody's here."

"It's probably Helen."

"Oh, great."

He stood up so he could see out the window. Helen was just getting out of the car. She wore a pink pantsuit that looked unnaturally bright against the grayness of the day. Col and Philly climbed out and went around to the front of the car. Col lifted the hood and peered worriedly at the engine.

At the sound of the car, the dogs had risen from the floor where they had been sleeping and begun barking loudly. Their claws skittered across the floor as they raced to the couch and jumped up on the cushions, barking even louder, agitated by the sight of Helen coming up the porch steps.

"I wish they wouldn't bark," Phil said, heading for the door. "I didn't know they had this bad habit."

"Shut up!" Louise yelled at the dogs. "Get over here, you two."

The dogs jumped down off the couch, quietly obeying her. He smoothed his hair back, unsettled by the commotion, and opened the door.

"Hi, Dad!" Helen said, encircling him with her arms. She smelled like cigarette smoke and perfume.

"Hi," she said to Louise, turning her head

briefly in her direction, and then she saw the dogs. "Oh, look!" she cried. "Beanie and Red!"

They came to her, and she rubbed their heads. She seemed happy to see the dogs and turned all her attention on them, and Phil and Louise watched her playing with them for a few moments. She made woofing noises for them and kept saying, "Hey! Hey! Hey! You guys settle down, you're too excited!" But the more she talked to them, the more excited they became.

"You took them," she said. "I can't believe it." She smiled. Her flesh looked rosy and bright. She fairly glowed with health. "You must be a glutton for punishment." Her shoulders shook slightly as she laughed. He felt one of the dogs come to his side and take his hand lightly in its mouth, trying to get him to play.

She turned to Louise. "This man wouldn't let me have a dog when I was growing up, and now he has two of them. It hardly seems fair, does it?"

Louise allowed one side of her mouth to twist into a half-smile, but she didn't say anything.

"All I ever wanted was a dog. I got to have a turtle instead. The turtle lasted about three months. Slow death. Never, ever, buy a child a turtle."

She walked around the living room, looking at the place. "Nothing's changed," she said. Turning to Louise, she added, "That's the thing about Dad. You can count on everything being in exactly the same place as the last time you were here."

Phil said, "Would you care for anything?" He realized he hadn't introduced Louise yet, but Helen was acting strange, as if she already knew her.

"Feed me — I look like I need it, don't I?" She stood with her arms lifted to her sides, palms out, like an opera singer. She was large, it was true, quite overweight but graceful. Unlike many heavy women, she seemed buoyant, like some sea animal suspended in ocean lightness.

"Well, caution to the wind, I will take a Coke if you don't have chocolate cake. I'll take anything to drink." She wandered into the kitchen. She walked with her feet spayed slightly out and led with her stomach.

"I'm Helen," she said, "and you're Louise."

Louise tilted her head back and regarded her with a little suspicion. "Yeah."

"My sister told me you were staying with Dad for a while. It's a good thing. He's stuck out here all by himself, and he's gotten to be a hermit. Haven't you, Dad? Has he taught you to play cribbage yet?"

"Yeah. Sort of."

"I figured. Watch him. He takes his cards seriously. He's crafty. That's the only word I can use to describe his card-playing mentality. Very crafty. Where's Col and Philly? Can you see them, Dad? How come they don't come in?"

"They're looking under the hood."

"That car. It started making a noise — you know, one of those mysterious noises that only one person can hear? Col kept saying to me, 'Can you hear that?' I couldn't hear anything. I should take the dogs outside and show Philly. He'd get a kick out of the dogs." She took a Coke from the refrigerator. "It wasn't that he really wouldn't let me have a dog," she said to Louise. "He wasn't that mean. Mom had allergies, didn't she, Dad?"

"Yes," Phil confirmed. The dog wouldn't stop trying to get him to play. Now it had hold of his shirt cuff and was tugging on it gently.

"Boy, it's cold, I can't believe how cold it's gotten all of a sudden. The heater's broken on the car — well, not completely broken, but only the defrost works, so your feet end up freezing. I don't know why those guys don't want to come in and get warm." She looked out the kitchen window. "Philly's gained weight, did you notice? I can't believe Joyce made reservations at Swenborg's. She loves to eat where there's organ music." She sat down at the table opposite Louise. "So, where are you from?" she asked.

"Nowhere."

Helen hesitated, looking straight at Louise, and then she turned and looked at her father, who was still standing near the door, his arms limp and awkward at his sides, as if they'd suddenly grown a little heavier and longer. Her face went blank. To him, she appeared confused, as if appealing to him for an explanation. He wanted to say something, but he couldn't think what.

"Excuse me," Helen said. "I'll take the dogs outside for a minute." She left the house, coaxing Beanie and Red to follow her. Once she'd gone, the rooms seemed unnaturally still.

"If you're going to act like this," he said quietly, "I won't be able to take it. I shouldn't have to take it."

"I just feel rotten," she said. "I've got a sore throat and my head is all stuffed up." She sniffed loudly, as if to demonstrate how congested her nose was.

"You may feel rotten, but you don't have

to act that way."

"I have a cold. I don't feel like being sociable."

He looked at her. She wore a pouty expression.

"I'm sick," she moaned.

"All right. I'd go to bed then if I were you."

He went outside and walked slowly toward the parked cars, where he could see Helen and Philly playing with the dogs. Col was bent far over the fender of the car, standing on one leg. His other leg was lifted behind him, sticking straight out.

He thought, I won't take this from her, I shouldn't have to. Sick or not sick. I won't take her to lunch now even if she wants to go. Why subject people to her? I'm ashamed of her, he thought. What makes a person think she can act like that?

And just when he'd begun to feel a closeness to her, when he'd begun to think maybe . . .

"Grandpa!" Philly came skipping toward him across the lawn. He tried to greet the boy with affection, but he found himself still thinking about Louise. He patted his grandson on his shoulder absentmindedly. Philly hung on to his coat as he walked over to the car.

"How are you, Col? Got problems there?"

Col rocked back and straightened up. Phil tried to force his facial muscles to relax so he wouldn't show how upset he was. It felt as if elves had hold of his cheeks and were pinching them from the inside.

Col said, "I think it's time to get a new car." He wiped his hands on a pink rag.

When he'd met Col for the first time, Helen had introduced him by saying, "Dad, call louder," and he'd thought, Call who louder? But then he'd realized that was the man's name — Col Lauder, Jr., short for Colin. He was a thin man with a patchy beard who spoke so softly Phil often had to ask him to repeat what he'd said. He wasn't shy, simply quiet, although he could be quite funny when he chose to be, usually after a few drinks. He wore glasses held together with tape. Behind the glasses, his eyes had a certain glint. Wildness, May used to say. He's got a wild look in those eyes. But he wasn't wild at all, just a little eccentric. Phil thought the look in his eyes had more to do with his profession. An astronomer. Always thinking of stars, the distant spaces in the universe.

"Do these dogs live here now?" Philly asked.

"I reckon," Phil said.

The boy was full of questions about the

dogs. Why had they come there to live? What did he do with them at night? Did they bite? Had they ever had puppies? They stood in the lane awhile, talking. Phil could feel the gravel beneath the soles of his house slippers, and the cold rising from the ground. It began to snow, very lightly, hard grains driven by a strong wind. Phil looked back at the house, wondering what she was doing in there. He hoped she had gone up to bed.

"Come on," he said. "Let's get out of this weather."

She had not gone to bed. She was sitting on the couch, reading *Reflexology,* the very book he'd asked her not to touch. She looked up and smiled at him, a smile that did little to mask the sourness beneath it.

"Is it snowing out there?" she asked.

"Yes," he said.

"Louise, this is Col and Philly."

"Nice to meet you," Col mumbled. Philly held up his hand, like a wooden Indian, in a wave.

"Can I build a fire, Dad?" Helen asked.

"I don't mind."

Helen sat at the hearth and opened the fire screen. Philly knelt at the wood basket next to her and began handing his mother sticks, then logs.

"Slow down," she said to him. "We've

got to get the thing going first."

Col settled down in the rocking chair and picked up the newspaper. Phil felt awkward. It seemed to him that he was the only one who didn't know what to do in his own house. He noticed the dogs were tracking mud, and he made them go back out on the porch so he could wipe their feet with an old towel.

Standing in the swirling cold on the porch, the fields beyond him obscured by the storm, he took his time cleaning the dogs' feet, straddling them and lifting their paws. They bit at him playfully, thinking they were wrestling. The snow, falling harder now, eddied at the edge of the porch. He felt slightly excited by the snow, as he always did at the beginning of winter. Later in the season the snow would imprison him, making life hard, but now it was stimulating to feel the hushed and billowy onset of winter descending with force. When he came back inside, Helen was sitting next to Louise on the couch, talking to her.

"It really does work," Helen said. "Would you like me to try it on you?"

"Oh, I don't know." Louise turned her head to the side and laughed in a breathy way, tucking a strand of hair behind one ear.

"It works, I'm telling you. You kind of twist the toes, you know, pull on them, and that clears the sinus area. My mother used to do this for me all the time. Didn't you say that was your problem, your sinuses?"

"Well, I don't know," she said. "How are my toes connected to my sinuses?"

"Everything's connected. It's the first law of physics."

Col snorted, suppressing a laugh. "What kind of physics are you talking about?"

"Human physics," Helen said. "I'm making it up as I go along. Don't pay any attention to him," she said to Louise. She lifted Louise's foot and began unlacing her boot. "Sit back and relax. You're too stiff. You've got to try and relax or it doesn't work."

Phil felt tired and wished to be alone. He climbed the stairs to his bedroom and closed the door. For a while, he sat on the edge of the bed, looking at the way the sky was completely featureless, engulfed in the whiteness of the storm. Then he lay down and tried to sleep. But he couldn't. He kept thinking someone was going to knock on the door to ask why he didn't come downstairs and join them. Why didn't he? Because he felt unhappy and he didn't want his unhappiness to show.

He gave up trying to nap and opened the

door, straining to listen, wondering what was happening downstairs. He heard Helen say, "Tell me if it hurts," and a moment later, Louise yelled, "Ouch!" The fire crackled and popped. Philly said, "This is Ninja! Ninja is looking for the evil monster!" They were fine. He felt relieved, as if he wasn't responsible for all the things it sometimes seemed he was.

He wandered into May's study and sat down at her desk. Opening the atlas, he looked up the Maldives. They were a tiny cluster of islands, floating like mold spore on a liquid sea. He tried to read about the Maldives, but it was difficult to concentrate. He kept scanning the paragraph on the page, waiting to hit on something that would interest him. He didn't care about gross national product or total population figures. He wanted to know something about the Maldivians themselves, something about what the landscape looked like there, what the people ate, how they dressed and made their livings.

Perhaps the encyclopedia could tell him these things. He went to the bookshelves and took down the volume marked "M," but where the Maldives should have been there was nothing; it went straight from "Malaysia" to "Malformation, biological," an entry that began: "The processes of development are regulated in such a way that few malformed organisms are found. Those that do appear may, when properly studied, shed light on normal development." It seemed compelling, this information, and he went on, only the next sentence wasn't so interesting: "The science of teratology — a branch of morphology or embryology — is concerned with the study of these structural deviations from the normal, whether in animals or plants." What did he care about ologies? On the next page, the defects of the brain and head of man were detailed — absence of brain, abnormally large or small brains.

He saw the morbidity of it all, how he had been taken from the Maldives to the subject of people born without brains. What was he doing, hiding up here when his daughter had driven so many miles to visit? He felt trapped in his own house.

At the end of life, the question asked of everyone was: Have you had enough? And nobody ever said yes. He hadn't been able to say yes. He'd said, No! I want more life. And now he had it, an abundance of time.

"Dad?" Helen yelled. "Are you up there?"

"Yes."

"I'm meeting resistance down here. Tell

her to sit still. She doesn't think it's going to work."

Everyone wants more time, he thought. For years, we muddle through, and then we find ourselves old and frightened, and we'll do anything — take someone's heart, kidneys, swap dollars for organs, and pray to gods we've ignored for decades — all for a few more years.

"Tell her it really works!" Helen cried. He heard laughter, then Louise saying, "No! Don't! It hurts!"

"Dad?"

"It really works," he called out loudly.

"She'll find herself enormously relieved, won't she?"

"Enormously."

"Ouch! Ooohh!"

"Dad? What are you doing up there?"

"Reading," he called out. "Just reading."

He remembered a woman they had lived next to in the neighborhood where they moved just after they were first married. She had come to May for treatment not long after May returned from taking her first course with Dr. Maybelle Segal. Later May had told him that the neighbor came to her saying she was having pain in her right breast. There were no lumps or swelling, just pain. She had seen her physician, who gave her a complete physical examination and said there was nothing to worry about, that it was simply muscular pain. This was great news for her, but it didn't relieve the pain. May went to work on her feet, but the woman became so nauseated that May had to proceed with caution. The next day, a rash broke out over the woman's breast. But the pain and the rash went away, and neither ever came back.

She could do that to anyone, take the pain away, or at least ease it, though he never fully understood how. She had the gift of healing. She could cure everyone, except herself. The hands could not turn back on themselves, on the source, and so he had watched her wither and die, her beautiful gifted hands useless to her.

Helen's voice came from downstairs again: "Aren't we supposed to meet Joyce at the restaurant soon?"

"What time is it?"

"Almost noon."

"Yes. We should leave." He arose wearily and went downstairs. Louise looked up at him. She watched him cross the room to where his coat was hanging on a peg by the door. He felt she was trying to catch his eye, but he avoided looking at her.

"I hate eating at Swenborg's," Helen said,

giving Louise's toes a final crack. "If I want to eat surrounded by cows, I go on a picnic."

Swenborg's, one of the oldest restaurants in the valley, raised its own beef. The windows of the dining room looked out over the corrals where steers were fattened.

"Who can eat with your food standing outside staring at you, waiting for the ax to fall?" Helen said, addressing the question to no one in particular.

She turned to Louise and said, "Wait until you hear Mrs. Kleinhoffer on the organ. The Swenborgs only butcher cows. Mrs. Kleinhoffer does in Ravel and Debussy. 'Clair de Lune' never sounded so bad."

Everyone began preparing to leave, except Louise, who sat quietly on the couch, her feet still bare. She's not going, he thought to himself.

"Phil?" she said.

"Yes?"

"I think I will go to lunch with you. Is that all right?" There was something pleading in her voice, an unusual meekness.

"Fine," he said.

Helen, Col, and Philly were the first out of the house. Col wanted to start the car and let it warm up. Louise put her boots on and wrapped herself up in her heavy coat. He didn't look directly at her, but was aware nonetheless of her every movement, glimpsed out of the corner of his eye as he checked the fire, then the coffee machine in the kitchen to make sure it was off. She stood by the door, waiting for him. He remembered something. He'd left the light on upstairs in May's study.

"Did you forget something?" she asked, standing quietly, watching him start up the stairs.

"Just a light. Go on out to the car," he said. "I'll be right out."

"What about the dogs?"

"We'll leave them inside." He finally looked at her, gazing down from the stairs. She seemed pathetically small, a pale figure huddled in the folds of her ridiculously large coat, and yet the seriousness of her look imparted a womanly quality to her face, which in spite of the hideous makeup was undeniably strong and attractive. When would it all end with her, and where? Her eyes looked sad and remorseful, but he didn't trust the look. She was as mutable as the lake, changing moods quickly, as the water changed its color. The worst part was, he had grown fond of her. He'd opened his heart a little, and now he felt it was a mistake.

"Go on," he said. "I'll be along soon."

★ ★ ★

His breath came a little short as he climbed the stairs. It was the sight of her, gazing at him with such a look of . . . of what? She had an uncanny power to disturb him, at one moment drawing him near and the next repelling him. He wished he could go to his room and lie down, sleep, get up later in a quiet house, make some soup, and settle in for the evening with the dogs close by. But no, he had to go to Swenborg's and make conversation, order food, eat it, appear calm and happy to be with his family, while Louise would be there at the table, the odd foundling cast amid relations whose ties had stretched thin.

When he reached the study at the end of the hall, he went to the desk and turned out the light. The room fell into shadow. He examined the bleak scene outside the window, the gloomy fields, partly dug up, still partially covered with rows of dried corn, the stalks flailing in the wind. He gazed down at her picture. May in the dress covered in little purple violets. "Forgive me," he whispered. "I've let things go. You should never have left me. I haven't managed so well without you."

"Are you mad at me?"

He turned to see Louise standing in the

doorway, her head tilted slightly back, so that she looked at him with hooded eyes.

"No," he lied.

"I'm sorry. I try, but it's never good enough."

"Why are you so hostile to people? Why couldn't you answer my daughter when she asked where you're from?"

She pursed her lips, so perfectly outlined in red, as if considering how to answer, then she said, speaking slowly, "When anyone asks about my past, I want to hide it. I didn't know she was going to be . . . so nice to me."

"Why must you act so rude — "

"Why am I the way I am, right?" She turned her head to one side and shook it slowly. When she looked back at him, she had tears in her eyes.

"I'm me. That's all. I just am what I am."

It stirred a memory in him, a biblical saying, *I am that I am*. The words rang inside him softly, a tiny tinkling of truth, an undeniable statement of existence on the most primal plane. But couldn't she be different if she wanted to be? Or was she like that malformed organism described in the encyclopedia, a creation that had slipped through the processes of normal development, unalterable now, a fixed aberration?

"You could try harder," he said.

She looked at him, pain shining in her eyes like fever. "There's the chance," she said. She turned and left the room.

The quiet in the shadowy den enfolded him. Pale winter light fell on the pictures of May, his children, and his grandchildren before him on the desk, a family that had once been whole.

He heard a sound just beyond the doorway. She was still there. He stepped out into the hallway. She stood facing the wall, her forehead leaning against it. There was very little light, and yet he could see her features in profile and observed how she had calmed herself. He couldn't bear this hard and bitter refusal he felt in his heart. What misery lay beneath the surface of every life, and what longing. How did a person survive without intimacy? Didn't you need at least one person in the world to know who you really were? His heart went out to her, although at that moment, he felt very clearly how it wasn't his heart, he was aware of its source, and he could hear the boy's voice inside him, whispering, *There you have it,* the phrase he had used so often.

He stepped to her side and put his arm around her shoulders.

Come on, the voice cooed, soft and full of

longing. *It's okay. It'll be all right.* The boy was soft-spoken, his voice deep, full of his husky change to manhood.

He believed, because he heard the voice, that somehow it wasn't himself who was holding her, rubbing her shoulders, gathering up the swaddled form and pressing it against him. It was the youth of the world he held, the boy he had lost, the life he'd once known that had disappeared forever. He was obeying the exhortation *Take a child! Any child!* He was taking her firmly, whispering words low and loving, in a father's anguished voice, and a lover's murmur, words of encouragement. "Don't feel bad," he said. "It's going to be okay. Everything will work out."

She held on to the front of his coat. He felt her knuckles grasping the lapels beneath his chin; a small fist pressing against his jaw held him fast.

"I'm not so bad," she whispered. They stood with their heads bowed toward each other, as if praying. He felt the woolly tickle of her hair against his face. He tried to step back from her, but she held on to him. Her hands were like hooks, caught in his coat. She awakened in him all his passion. He was a boy again, longing to feel these things, the wholeness of life, and of the body, and he gave in, surrendering himself to feelings so overpowering they formed one great affirmation, *Yes, yes, yes!*

Suddenly he heard a noise at the end of the hallway and drew back from her quickly. He turned to see Helen standing in the shadows, watching them.

"Oh . . . I'm sorry," Helen said. "I . . . just came to tell you something. Dad, you'd better come downstairs. There are some people here who want to see you."

He grabbed Louise's wrists and made her let go of him.

"People? What people?"

"The sheriff," she said, "and a couple." She hesitated, and looked directly at Louise. "I . . . I believe they're your parents," she said.

Louise stiffened. "My *parents?*"

"I think they're looking for you."

Louise turned on Phil. "You!" she hissed. "You told them where I was!"

He shook his head. "No," he said. "I didn't. I wouldn't know how . . . who to tell." He shook his head again. "I swear to you. Listen, don't look at me like that."

She stepped back from him, her eyes full of fear.

"I won't see them! I don't want to ever see them again. I'd rather die!" She ran down

437

the hallway, pushing past Helen, and disappeared inside her room, shutting the door behind her. He heard the lock click.

14

He descended the stairs slowly, moving, as it were, against the current of his desire, which was to act as she had done and close himself up in his room. He felt the burden of shame and guilt, mixed with confusion. Her parents? How could her parents be *here?*

In the living room, he found three people waiting for him, a man whose badge read, "Bannock County Sheriff's Department" and a couple in their fifties who were introduced as Mr. and Mrs. Blanchard from Coeur d'Alene. The woman was short and rather overweight. The man was ruddy and big.

The sheriff said, "You're Mr. Doucet?"

"Yes," he said, "I am."

"We've got a problem here. Mr. and Mrs. Blanchard are looking for their daughter, Louise, who disappeared last March. We've managed to trace her to a man named Wendall Larsen over in Pocatello. Apparently she stayed with him for a while. He gave us a license plate number that led us to you. He said you were in the area where he last saw the missing girl, up in the mountains near Soda Springs, about two weeks ago. She's a young woman of sixteen, blond hair, gray eyes. She was wearing a red dress that day. Do you remember seeing her?"

"Yes, I do." How should he begin?

"Do you know where she is?"

"She's upstairs," he said rather flatly, and then wondered why he hadn't explained certain things first. Of course, he would have to explain everything, all of it, right from the beginning.

"Upstairs?" the sheriff said, as if he'd heard him wrong. Phil could not help noticing how the sheriff was looking at him, as if he suspected him of doing something wrong.

"Oh my God!" Mrs. Blanchard cried. "You mean she's here? We've found her?" Her cheeks were a mass of broken veins, which gave her a rather cheery look, belied by the small, tight mouth and nervous eyes.

He nodded.

Mr. Blanchard stepped forward. He was a large, thick-set man, with broad shoulders, wide as an ox. "Are you certain it's Louise?" he said gruffly.

"I gave her a ride," Phil said weakly. "I could see she was in some kind of . . . trouble."

"Could we see the girl?" the sheriff asked. The flicker of suspicion wavered in his eyes, and his voice had grown more serious.

"I could ask her to come down," he said slowly, "but I think we should wait a few minutes. She's rather upset."

Mr. Blanchard's ruddy face darkened, and his eyes narrowed. "Upset? What do you mean, she's upset?"

"Perhaps we should sit down," Phil said. He ought to offer them something — some preliminary nicety was missing, an element of hospitality that might soften the tension in the room. They mustn't get the wrong idea.

Mr. Blanchard shook his head and scowled at him. "What's going on here?" he said. "Who are you? I'd like to see my daughter." He raised his hairy hand to his chin and rubbed the stubble of his beard. Something flashed and caught Phil's eye. A large ring. A golden swastika blazed within a circle of stones. Everything she had told him was true. He stared at the ring, and then lifted his eyes to the man's face, which was cold and mean.

"I . . . I think it might be better if we gave her a little time." He looked over at Mrs. Blanchard, at her sunken mouth and her small eyes, glaring at him. A slight feeling of dizziness came over him, a sense of weightlessness, and he felt himself backing away from Mr. Blanchard, who took

441

a step toward him.

"Listen here!" Mr. Blanchard yelled at him. "We've been looking for our daughter for months. If she's here, we want to see her. Right now! If you won't ask her to come down here, I will. What the hell's going on here, anyway?" He started for the stairs, but Phil stepped in front of him, blocking his way.

"I don't think you should do that just yet. She . . . she doesn't want to see you."

"What the hell are you saying?"

"Is my daughter all right?" Mrs. Blanchard said. "Is there something — "

"She's fine," Phil said. "She's just upset — "

"*She's* upset?" Mr. Blanchard shouted.

"What do you think she's put us through these last few months?" Mrs. Blanchard hissed, her mouth twisting with scorn into a frown. "Pure hell, that's what! Pure absolute hell — "

"Hold on, Hilda, I'll handle this," Mr. Blanchard said. He glared at Phil. "Get out of my way."

"No," Phil said.

The blow, delivered so swiftly by Mr. Blanchard that Phil had no premonition it was coming, landed on his chest, and something instantly felt dislodged beneath his sternum, as if the wires that held it together

442

had snapped, and now the bones ground freely against one another, shifting, as he breathed rapidly, like overriding tectonic plates.

Helen gasped and grabbed her father by the arm. "Are you all right?"

The sheriff quickly stepped forward, standing in front of Mr. Blanchard, his hands raised in the air. "Both of you, settle down," he said.

"Get that goon away from my father," Helen snapped. She glared at Mr. Blanchard. "You don't know what you've just done. You don't know what he's been through — "

"I'm fine, Helen," he said, though in fact he did not feel fine. He felt rather weak, and there was an odd, sharp pain in his chest each time he drew a breath.

"I think it would be a good idea if we could see the girl," the sheriff said.

Little Philly burst into the room. The boy was wide-eyed and breathless. He looked quickly at the sheriff, then at his mother and grandfather, standing together at the foot of the stairs.

"Mom!"

"What is it, Philly?" Helen asked.

"D-d-d-ad said . . . he said . . ." In his agitated state he seemed unable to speak.

"Philly? What is it? Tell me!"

"Dad said to come tell you . . . she's . . . she's up on the roof and she's going to jump!"

The sheriff rushed out the front door, followed by the Blanchards. Phil hesitated, leaning on the banister, feeling quite unable to move. A leaden feeling had overtaken him. He stood rooted to the spot near the stairs. He heard the sheriff's voice, very distant and faint: "Young lady! Stay there! Don't move!"

A cold wind came in through the open door, sending a small flurry of snow scudding across the floor. A bright spot of warmth radiated outward from the center of his chest where he had been struck. Somebody was shaking his arm, and he felt his head wiggle uncontrollably on his neck.

"Dad!" Helen said. "Dad, come on. We've got to try and do something. Are you okay? Come on! Please!"

He was moving then, not of his own volition, but being guided toward the waiting doorway, forcibly thrust and steered toward the bright portal where everything was gray and soft.

Outside, they stood in a cluster in the garden, where withered tomato plants, the stubs of butchered rhubarb, and wind-flattened parsley had taken on new and softer shapes under a thin blanket of snow. He looked up to see Louise crouched on the crest of the roof next to one of the chimneys. When she saw him, she stood up. She wore her huge overcoat, which billowed in the wind, threatening to fill with air like a parachute and send her drifting off into the whiteness. Snow eddied around her, causing her to appear indistinct and rather unearthly, like a tiny gargoyle ornamenting his roof. Her small, thin voice came drifting down from the rooftop.

"*Phil!*" she cried.

Hearing her voice, he came to his senses. She was calling him! Stepping forward, he cupped his hands to his mouth and shouted, "Louise! Don't move!"

"Tell them to leave or I'll jump!" she cried. Her yellow hair blew wildly around her head, so full of air it became a shifting halo of light, a golden, crowning aura. A sudden gust of wind came up and caught her coat. She lost her balance and slipped. Now she lay spread across the roof, clinging to its cornice.

Mrs. Blanchard screamed and lifted her hands into the air. "My God!" she cried. "Do something! Somebody do something!"

Up on the roof, the tiny, clinging form scrambled against the shingles, while down below, they huddled together like spectators at an air show.

"The chimney!" he called. "Put your foot against the chimney."

She swung one foot to the side and wedged it against the rock chimney, then thrust herself upward until her body leaned against the surface of the stones.

The sheriff came to his side quickly. "How did she get up there?"

"I don't know. The bedroom window, probably. There's a ledge."

"Do you have a ladder?"

"Yes."

"Where is it?"

"Behind the house," he said.

"Let's get it." The sheriff turned to Helen. "Keep everyone here," he said to her.

The ladder had lain on the ground for so long that weeds had grown up and entwined themselves around the rungs. As he struggled to lift it, roots tore loose and hung down in dark tendrils. "Help me," he said to the sheriff. He couldn't raise his end of the ladder. He felt weak, unable to use the muscles across his chest. The sheriff pulled the ladder away from the weeds. The wind worked against them as they tried to raise the ladder and stand it on end against the eaves of the house. Grunting and swaying, Phil struggled to hang on to the ladder. The dogs had followed them to the rear of the house. They bumped into him, moving against his legs, threatening to knock him off balance. "Get away," he said, kicking out to the side. They extended the ladder to its full length. It clattered as the sheriff shook it, making sure it rested solidly against the roof.

"Let me go up and talk to her," Phil said.

"I think I'd better go," the sheriff shouted.

"She'll listen to me! I know she will!"

The sheriff shook his head. "I don't know — "

"You're stronger," Phil said. "It's better you're down here on the ground where you can hold the ladder and help me bring her down." Without waiting for a reply, he began ascending the rungs. The ladder shook beneath him, trembling as he climbed past the kitchen window. He had to lean away from the ladder to fit his feet in the rungs, and each time he did so, he could feel it lift slightly away from the house. He moved awkwardly. He stopped for a moment to still the palsied shaking in his legs. It was so tiring, very difficult, gaining each new rung, and he had to go slower, making each move more deliberately. He squinted against the wind driving snow as fine as sand against his cheeks and ears. He could think of nothing except the sight of her, wedged against the chimney.

When he reached the edge of the roof, he hoisted himself past the rain gutter, stepping off the ladder cautiously, until he was crouched low against the shingles. He had nailed these shingles down himself. He knew every contour, every inch of this roof. It had a gradual pitch, and for this he felt grateful, for it enabled him to crawl steadily toward the apex, where he could see her holding on to the rocks of the chimney. She didn't see him until he was a few feet away from her. She turned abruptly, her eyes blazing at him.

"Go away!" she said. He moved the last few feet, and reached out and took hold of her arm.

"If you move," he said softly, "we'll both fall. Please don't move."

She allowed him to edge forward until he had wedged himself next to her. He turned his back on the driving snow and nestled closer to her. "Listen to me," he said. "Just listen."

She was crying. The black around her eyes had run into little charcoal streaks, which puddled at the corners of her mouth. He reached inside his pocket and took out a handkerchief. He wiped her cheeks, the folds of her mouth. The snow had melted in her hair and turned it a darker color of amber gold.

Far below them, he could see the Blanchards looking up at them. Philly and Col and Helen stood a little distance away, near the stumps of raspberry canes. The land spread out beyond them, white and brown, a mottled pattern of earth and snow.

"I don't want to go back," she said. "I can't."

"Please," he said, "please — "

"Dad!" Helen called. "Do you need some help?"

"It's all right, Helen," he yelled. It became brighter around him, and he looked up to see a hole in the clouds had opened, through which a faint patch of blue was visible. The snow let up, now falling very lightly in drifting, whispery flecks.

"Please come down with me," he said.

"Louise!" The deep, booming voice of Mr. Blanchard disturbed the silence, echoing through the woods behind them. "Louise! Come down from there!" His voice had the sound of a man used to addressing crowds and carried effortlessly across the distance separating them.

"Go home!" she yelled.

449

"Honey," Mrs. Blanchard cried. "Please come down!"

Again Mr. Blanchard's voice reverberated, as if magnified by a megaphone: "Give us a chance to help you! I think you owe it to us!"

She lifted her head and screamed out, "Leave me alone!"

There was a short silence, then Mr. Blanchard's voice rose again.

"You're being unfair to us!"

The sheriff appeared at the top of the ladder. He stared up at them, huddled together against the base of the chimney.

"Do you need help?" he called.

"No," Phil said. "Not just yet. I . . . we need to talk a little longer."

"You want more time?"

"Yes. A few more minutes."

"I'll stay here — "

"No," Phil said. "Go back down."

The sheriff hesitated, as if considering what to do, and then he nodded and backed down the ladder. Phil waited until he had disappeared, and then he turned toward her, taking hold of her arm. "We're going to climb down now," he said. "You're going to hold on to me and we'll move very slowly."

He studied her face closely for her reaction, but her eyes showed no trace of emotion.

They were side by side, their faces almost touching. Nothing disturbed the connection they established with their eyes, not even the shouting voice of Mr. Blanchard, which had risen again, pleading with her to come down.

It stopped snowing altogether. Several patches of blue now appeared in the clouds above them. She began speaking, uttering broken words through her sobs, telling him she was sorry, she didn't want to live.

He raised his hand to her lips and said, "Shhh. Listen to me. You mustn't hurt yourself."

"It doesn't matter," she cried.

"It matters very much," he said. "It matters to me."

He put his hand on his chest, hoping to still his pounding heart and the pain that shot through him. "If anything happened to you, I would feel I'd failed. It would be like losing Luke all over again." He'd finally said it, and he knew it was true. He couldn't let anything happen to her. She was so young, just like Luke, with no idea of how good life could be.

"You have everything to live for," he said. "Don't you see that? Louise, you aren't bad, dear, you're good, and you can leave them and all they represent behind you."

She stopped sobbing and looked at him.

"What you've done . . . I mean the decision you made to leave them — that was a good decision." He turned away from her and gazed down at the Blanchards, the wind-blown figures standing in his yard.

"But what if they make me go back?" she whimpered.

"Don't worry, I'll help you. You can trust me."

She stared at him, as if trying to come to some decision. He struggled with his own emotions. It seemed to him that he'd finally understood the power of love, how it would not be held back. He nodded to her, and said, "We've got to reach the ladder now, okay?"

Her head jerked, ever so slightly. An answering nod. "Okay," she said.

He moved first, inching down the roof. The shingles were wet and slick. It was much more difficult going down than coming up. He felt the slightest rise with his toe, the edge of a shingle, and wedging his shoe against it, tested his weight. He extended his hand and she grasped it, moving slowly toward him. Tremulous, uncertain, he moved his foot again, and found another tiny ridge. She followed him, moving just above him, letting him guide her every move. Little by little, he worked his way toward the ladder. Murmuring words of encouragement, he drew her toward him until finally, he could reach out and touch the top of the ladder. He shook it slightly.

"We're coming down," he called to the sheriff. "Hold it steady."

The first thing the sheriff did, once they were safely on the ground, was to ask if they were both okay, a question to which they each replied, Yes. The sheriff then seemed a little confused about what to do next. He stood looking at them, with a rather grim look on his face.

Phil said, "Why don't you take Louise into the house and talk to her?"

"I'd like to talk to you, too," the sheriff said.

"I think it would be a better idea if she told you everything herself, first."

The sheriff pushed his hat back on his head and looked at Phil. "She's going to have to come with us — "

"I want you to understand something," Phil said. He drew a breath and turned to Louise and took her by the arm. "Her parents aren't fit to care for her."

"I don't understand what you're saying," the sheriff said. "Aren't fit . . . ?"

"Oh, God," Louise moaned. Her parents

were coming around the corner of the house, striding toward them, followed by Helen.

Phil held her arm a little tighter. "It's all right," he said. "Go on inside with the sheriff now."

"I can understand there might be a problem," the sheriff said, "I mean there usually is in these cases, but until we figure things out there isn't much I can do except take her into custody."

The Blanchards were advancing on them rapidly.

"You saw that man hit me," Phil said to the sheriff. "I can press charges against him for assault. Just take her inside, please, and speak to her alone. I think you can see she's upset and shouldn't have to confront them right now if she doesn't want to. I'll tell them to wait in the car for you."

The sheriff hesitated.

"Go on," Phil said. "Use the back door." He pointed out the door to the sheriff and gave Louise a little push toward it, just as the Blanchards and Helen reached the place where he stood.

"Thank God you're all right," Mrs. Blanchard said, reaching out to her daughter, who was walking away from her. She started to follow her. The sheriff turned, and glancing at Phil briefly, turned his face toward Mrs.

Blanchard and held out his hand to indicate she shouldn't come any further. "I'd like to talk to your daughter alone for a few moments," the sheriff said. "Would you wait in my car?"

While the sheriff spoke, Phil caught Louise's eye, and smiled at her, just slightly, and nodded.

"In the car?" Mrs. Blanchard said, and looked at Phil, with confusion on her face.

Helen hurried up to him. "Oh, God, Dad, are you okay?"

"I'm fine," he said quietly.

Mr. Blanchard began speaking: "Well, I'm glad you talked some sense into her and got her to come down — "

"Helen," Phil said, turning his back on the Blanchards, "would you please go on inside, and see that Col and Philly come in, too?"

He waited until Helen had walked away, heading for the front yard, and then he faced the Blanchards. He pointed to the lane and the sheriff's waiting car.

"Get off my place," he said. "You heard the sheriff. You can wait for him in his car."

15

The road ran south, through farm country, dropping into a wide valley. Scrawny wind-beaten weeds poked up through a thin crust of snow. He turned his head occasionally to look out the side window toward the river, a wide, silvery band on the horizon.

He'd had to see her, and he'd done that, spent a brief hour with her. Now he was driving home, traveling at dusk along a narrow road. He drove cautiously, keeping both hands on the steering wheel, watching for patches of ice.

She had changed. She'd cut her hair. Was that what made her look so remarkably different? She looked younger, yet more peaceful and natural. The place seemed to suit her.

A few billboards and scattered houses came in sight. He passed a sign reading "St. Anthony" and cruised slowly through the little town. Christmas lights had been strung across the street. At the main intersection, the tattered face of Santa Claus hung down from a traffic signal. So much time had passed. It was almost Christmas, the end of another year.

Was it worth it, what he'd gone through in these last few weeks? What had her social worker said to him? "It's unfortunate, but there's a witch-hunt mentality in the Child Welfare Department these days. Everyone is suspect. Sometimes innocent people are scrutinized unfairly. I'm sorry if this is the case with you." She seemed so young to him. It was remarkable to find himself questioned the way he'd been. Asked such embarrassing questions. At his age. After a long life when he'd thought almost everything that was going to happen to him had already happened.

He felt some question of his guilt remained, though perhaps only in his own mind. Was he truly blameless? He had said to the social worker, when she apologized for having to ask certain questions, "Yes, of course, I do understand," assuming the posture of a purely innocent man.

The investigation hadn't really been so bad. He'd survived the interrogation. (Did you ever have any physical contact with the minor in question? Why did you take her into your home in the first place? Didn't you see any impropriety in allowing a young girl to stay with you alone in your house?)

The thing about the unaccompanied life was, you had to rely heavily on the kindness of your own heart. Daily, hour by hour, you had to release yourself from too much blame, just to exist in the world, where the innocent were mingling so freely with the guilty, and the power to differentiate between the two was so often uncertain.

Somehow, he'd managed to forgive himself. But what about his daughters? Would they ever understand what had happened? Particularly Helen, who had witnessed the scene in the hallway? His explanation must have sounded feeble to her. Yet he felt she would go on loving him unconditionally, keeping private what perhaps were her real feelings that he was becoming a little foolish and unreliable in his old age.

And Joyce? What about Joyce? A suspicion lingered. He thought he'd loved his daughters well enough, tried to show them equal affection. But he hadn't. He'd always favored Helen, and not until the accident had he seen this so clearly. Did Joyce see this too? Had she known all along that in some subtle way he preferred Helen's company to her own? After everything that had happened, would Joyce go on loving him as she had before?

He came up on a tractor, moving very slowly along the shoulder of the road. The farmer behind the wheel was swaddled in layers of thick clothing, and as he swung wide to pass, he saw the miserable look on the man's face, as if the cold was unbearable and life irreversibly harsh.

So much had been restored to him, not least of all his faith. Driving toward the Youth Ranch earlier in the day, he wondered, What would become of her? What would happen to Louise Matthews? Was she going to be all right? Had it made a difference, really, that he had helped her, that he had taken a child? She wasn't even a child anymore. She had zigzagged out of childhood, run a brief and crazy pattern though an adult world, and now she would spend time finishing up her teenage years in a more ordinary fashion. He wondered if she could go back to that world. She seemed resigned to it. After the first of the year, she would leave the Youth Ranch and be placed with a foster family where she could resume her schooling. Of course they would stay in touch. That was his bargain.

He had great faith in her. He believed that she would have the chance to live a different sort of life. For now, she was safe, and best of all, she could spend time doing the thing she seemed to love best, riding and caring for the horses at the Youth Ranch.

He had brought her Christmas presents,

a hand-knit sweater from Erika, a book, *Know Your Stars,* from Helen, and from himself, a pair of binoculars, all of which seemed to please her very much.

She had given him a present, too, a leather wallet she had made in the shop at the Youth Ranch, stencilled with his name. Inside she had put a picture of herself sitting astride a horse, with white hills and a primary blue sky in the background.

Standing at the corrals, watching her move among the horses, he had thought of Luke. One life had been lost and one gained. It had seemed clear to him what the true, the *infinite* task of the human heart really was, not simply to endure the grief and mourning, to beat on in spite of pain so deep it chilled the spirit, but to rest in peace. Those were the words he had finally carved on the tombstone: *Rest in Peace, Dear Heart.* It was a message for the living and the dead.

He turned his head and looked out over the cold, frozen landscape. He felt the abundance in the world, an abundance of time, and love, and all of it, all of it was his.

At the corrals, she had turned to him, standing with her arms around the neck of a big brown horse, and smiled. Then, with such lightness and speed, she had gathered up two fistfuls of mane and swung easily up onto the horse's back. The horse had looked startled, lifting its head abruptly and flattening its ears. Without saddle or bridle, nothing to control the horse, it might have bolted with her on its back. But it hadn't. She had lain forward along the horse's neck and murmured to it, and the horse had relaxed, dropped its head, and begun quietly eating again, while she buried her face in its mane and stroked its shoulder.

He passed a little frozen lake, hardly distinguishable from the white fields surrounding it. Snow fences held back sculpted drifts. He thought of her parents, and of others like them, their hearts enshrouded in hatred. At her hearing, which he had attended with Erika, the judge had questioned her parents about their beliefs, and her stepfather had turned belligerent. "It's a free country," he said. "I'm protected by the First Amendment."

They would go on, her parents, preaching their hatred in a free country, but they would never again have power over her. Maybe that was the best you could hope for, not that the evil could ever be eradicated, but that the equally apparent good would rise up and create access to hope, providing a passage through which the strong of heart might escape.

He began to hum, the sound vibrating in his throat. A little tickle interrupted his humming. He laid his fingers lightly on the spot where his scar ended in the hollow between his collar bones and cleared his throat. The light had fallen. It didn't seem to take but a minute for the day to end in winter.

He drove toward home in the deepening dusk, which lent a blue cast to the land, trying not to think about the empty house that awaited him. Instead, he thought of the dogs and how happy they'd be to see him.

He stopped at Millie's Cafe to see Leora but she'd already gone home. He ordered a bowl of soup. A new girl was working behind the counter. She wore a narrow black skirt and a pretty white blouse. He thought he had never seen a more beautiful girl. Her blond hair had been gathered into a smooth ponytail, a silken switch that flicked from side to side as she moved. Everything about her was so graceful, so youthful and unblemished. She dusted cabinets and straightened the display of chocolates on the counter.

At the table directly in front of him, a woman sat alone reading a paper, furtively glancing up from time to time in his direction. At other tables, there were families and couples. Only the woman reading the paper and he were alone, two solitary diners. Soft voices came from the table behind him.

"Retire and enjoy these last ten years," someone said.

To his left, a family waited for their dinners — grandparents, children, grandchildren. A teenage girl sat next to the wall, looking bored and dispirited. The grandfather tapped a silver creamer with his finger and stared down at the tablecloth, looking very lost in thought. From the fountain came the sound of a machine mixing a malt. The girl at the counter had put on a pair of translucent plastic gloves in order to handle the chocolates. She picked them daintily off the tray and placed them on a shelf behind the glass. In his solitude, he was an observer, watching the world.

He stood up abruptly, without finishing his soup, and left the restaurant. Outside, the stars were emerging, a night full of stars, distant and beckoning in their brilliance, stars shining down on the marshes of Paris and the dead orchards of Ovid, stars by the thousands, filling the heavens like the lights of dead souls who dwelt on a plane of peace, and his own soul was lulled by the sight.

His heart was touched by those above, the feeling that the dead were never really far away, that their tranquillity surpassed human understanding, and yet, through careful listening, and feeling, and seeing, one's own soul could be transported to a place of refuge.

He felt himself being drawn upward, imperceptibly rising toward the pinpoints of light, ascending in universal feeling, the lost and the dead beckoning, and he seemed to lay an ear against the muscle of his own heart, feeling it open and close. His soul swooned into some new world, delivered of grief, purified, by the sight of pulsing stars, wave of light by wave of light, renewed in radiance. From somewhere came the sound of a tiny, tinkling bell, crisp and clean on the icy air. He looked up at the stars as if his soul had just been born, and in its newness contained a memory of those left behind. He felt the enchantment of life, and knew its richness. With a fullness of heart, he began walking toward his car, the snow squeaking beneath his feet.